FEEL THE CHILL!!

ICE TOMB

By

DEBORAH JACKSON

Deborah Jackson

Publisher's Note:
This is a work of fiction. Names, characters, places, and incidents are either the product of the author's imagination or are used fictitiously, and any resemblance to actual persons living or dead, events, glaciers, or locales is entirely coincidental.

ISBN: 1-931468-19-2

Cover Design by Jeff Carns
First Printing

The Invisible College Press, LLC
P.O. Box 209
Woodbridge VA 22194-0209
http://www.invispress.com

Please send question and comments to:
editor@invispress.com

For Brian

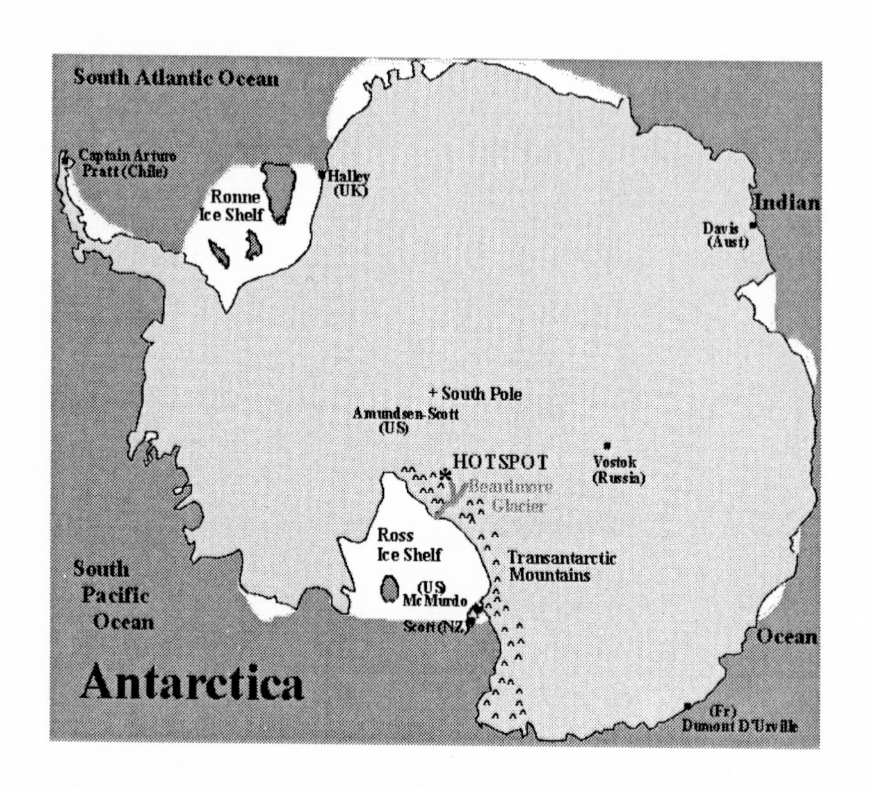
South Atlantic Ocean
Captain Arturo Pratt (Chile)
Ronne Ice Shelf
Halley (UK)
Indian
Davis (Aust)
+ South Pole
Amundsen-Scott (US)
HOTSPOT
Beardmore Glacier
Vostok (Russia)
Ross Ice Shelf
Transantarctic Mountains
South Pacific Ocean
(US) McMurdo
Scott (NZ)
Ocean
Antarctica
(Fr) Dumont D'Urville

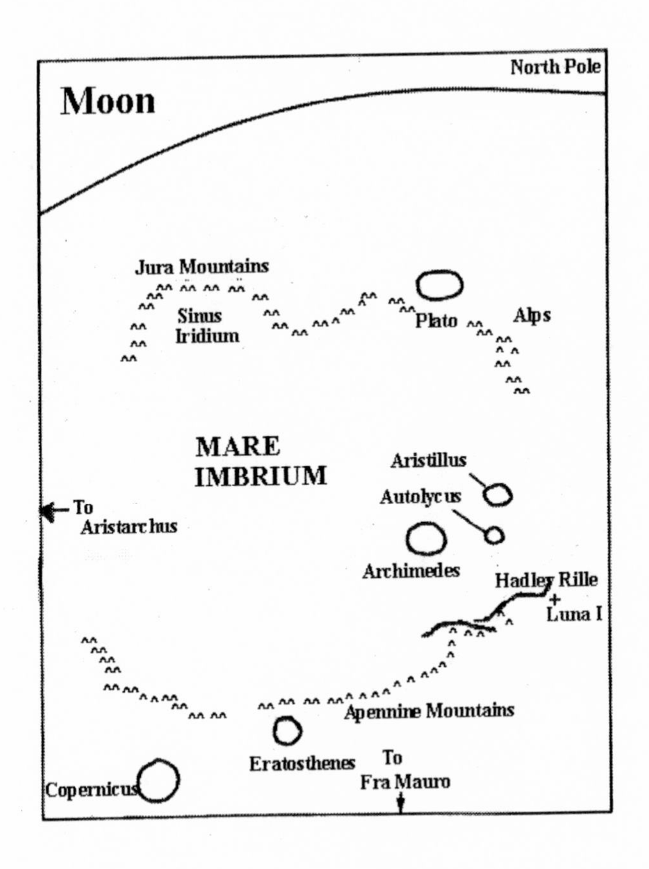
North Pole
Moon
Jura Mountains
Sinus
Iridium
Plato
Alps
MARE
IMBRIUM
Aristillus
Autolycus
To
Aristarchus
Archimedes
Hadley Rille
Luna I
Apennine Mountains
Eratosthenes
To
Fra Mauro
Copernicus

One

It was balmy in Antarctica the day the science team disappeared. The wind had dipped the thermometer from a pleasant -20°F to a more refreshing –35°F, but the temperature made no difference to the stalwart beakers of the south. It was October 14 in the year 2015 – the same year that China became a democratic nation, an 8.0 earthquake struck the heart of Los Angeles and the first lunar residents were settling on the moon. All these world events meant nothing to the people clustered around the radio in the communications center of McMurdo Station – the American science outpost in the southern continent. They were intent on the crackling static.

Cathy Jones, one of the National Science Foundation's guides to the 'Deep South,' was hunkered down amidst the penguins and the beakers, twisting her fingers around her short coils of copper hair and chewing on her lower lip. She was monitoring radio communications with *the team* along with about ten other people crammed into the tiny room. One entire wall of the room was filled from top to bottom with electronics within silver boxes, black dials and knobs projecting from the metal sheaths. The equipment was devoted not only to picking up radio signals throughout the continent but to patching into satellite communications as well. A bank of computer screens flashing for prompts lined a counter below and a mishmash of wires was connected to the hazard of equipment. On a desk in front of Cathy rested a couple of microphones and headsets. As they sat in tense silence, a blast of wind rattled the Chalet building on its foundation, but it was the crisp voice on the radio that rattled her even more.

"Holy cow! Did you get a load of that?"

"Jimmy?" Cathy squeaked as the impact of his voice hit her. There'd been silence from his end for far too long.

"Still here, Cath," he responded in a rich baritone clip. "Bet you were worried."

"I'll say," she breathed. The group of men and women around her let out a collective sigh. There were five scientists and three senior managers for the NSF along with the two communications experts. They'd been jammed in this room ever since Jimmy's plane had touched down in the Transantarctic Mountains about four hundred miles south-east of McMurdo Station. The last ten minutes, much to the chagrin of the white-knuckled lip-chewing group, his signal had been lost.

Gottlieb, the Antarctic Sciences Section Head, nodded vigorously, his silver-streaked hair flipping into his eyes. "We're not about to lose you, Albright," he intoned. "It's enough that our geologists from the Beardmore Camp have gone missing."

"We're all still here, Arnold, although Jeanna and Tom look a little pale."

Cathy blinked. It would make sense that Tom Debow, the slight astrophysicist with the slicked-back hair and nervous tic to his left eye, would be a little chalked from a hardy expedition, or rescue mission - however they were going to coin this in the history books. But Jeanna Sawyer was a glaciologist. They didn't come more weathered or tough than she did. Despite the body of a beanpole, and a sweet, apple-cheeked face, she could set you straight in a minute if you thought she was a pushover with a left hook that had even laid Sal on his butt more than once. Jimmy hadn't even mentioned Sal. Of course Sal Vitrioni, the helicopter pilot, wasn't worth mentioning. He was ex-Navy, bulky with muscle and his eyes were hard enough to turn you to stone. A bloody earthquake wouldn't shake him up.

"W...what's the problem?" Cathy sputtered out, grinding her fingernails into her palms.

There was a pause after the slight chirp of the radio. "It seems we've found some bodies," Jimmy finally said.

Andy and Jamal gasped behind her. "Dave? Mike?" She could hear their hearts in their throats as they choked on the names of their fellow geologists.

"No, guys. Not ours. But they're definitely dead."

A chill ran through Cathy's body, as much from Jimmy's tone as his words. There was an edge to his voice that told her the tall, cool volcanologist had somehow lost his metal. He was spooked.

"It's like the killing fields here," cried Jeanna. "Only in ice."

"Let me get this straight, Jim," said Gottlieb. "Are we talking volcano?"

"No, Arnold. This isn't Vesuvius. These people froze to death, rather abruptly. I'd say they've been here for a while."

Cathy frowned and squeezed her broad shoulders through the mesh of bodies to get even closer to the radio. It was hard to imagine confronting all those corpses in the ice, but at least they weren't their friends and colleagues. 'A long time' meant there was still hope.

"How long do you suppose?" asked Gottlieb.

"Hard to say, since they're frozen. They're sort of deep in the ice though. Could be a few hundred years."

This time everyone frowned. "Um, I thought this continent was uninhabited until the last fifty years," said Jamal, shaking the dreadlocks on his head.

"Well, everyone thought that Christopher Columbus was the first European to reach the New World," said Jimmy with a slight lilt to his voice. "When it was actually the Vikings that beat him by about four hundred years."

"So you're saying these are bloody Vikings?" snorted Andy through his bristly mustache.

Jimmy chortled, although a little nervously. "You're a piece of work, Andy. Think for a minute. You're all scientists – except for a few bureaucrats and that wicked beauty nestled in between you." Cathy felt her face grow warm. Gottlieb and his entourage scowled, although the NSF manager had a quirk to his lips.

"We've learned through extensive study that everything we know, or believe we know, is relative. Einstein taught us that. From our position, it looked like we were the first, given our own little slice of history. But we should never be so arrogant as to believe that we are like Christopher Columbus, that we're one step ahead of the other guy. Usually we find out, to our extreme embarrassment, that we're one step behind."

"Is this a philosophy lesson, or a science expedition?" asked Gottlieb.

"I thought it was a rescue mission," said Jeanna tremulously. "But there's nothing left to rescue here."

Cathy grimaced. It was hard enough to hear Jimmy a little off the mark, but Jeanna… It was unnerving.

"So you turn around and come back," said Gottlieb.

"No," said Jimmy firmly. "This tunnel leads to something. This is where all that roiling heat is coming from. Maybe we can still find Dave, Mike and the others."

"Jim," Cathy broke in. The way she clipped his name from affectionate to imploring made him pause.

"It'll be okay, Cath."

"Dave and Mike disappeared. These people are dead. How can you say 'it'll be okay?'?"

"Because we're being cautious," said Jimmy.

"By plunging through an icy graveyard…"

"Cathy," said Gottlieb sternly. "It's Jim's call. He's a big boy."

Cathy glared at him, but fell silent. What more could she do? They only let her be here out of courtesy to Jim since he was McMurdo's chief volcanologist. She had no business in the communications room unless she was on the other side of the mike, guiding an expedition. Which is where she should be, but Jimmy wouldn't hear of it. He was well aware of the danger. And they were all aware of the danger too. That's why there were ten people here instead of two.

When one or two people disappear in Antarctica, it's a tragedy, but not uncommon. When five or six, it's time to investigate. When ten…

Oh, she couldn't go there. Not with Jimmy in that hollow tube of ice plunging into perilous ground.

"Well, this is interesting," Jimmy's voice crackled over the radio again. "Seems to be some sort of structure. It's so deep under the ice you'd have to crack it with dynamite to build anything here. Or maybe melt the ice with a thermodynamic event."

"Such as a fissure in the earth's crust?" Jamal suggested.

"Possible. But then you'd have a heck of a lot of water to pump out in order to build something this big."

"Define 'this big,'" said Gottlieb, stroking his chin.

"About fifty stories." The room was filled with blinking eyes. "Oh, here. There's a nice little access tunnel, ten by twenty."

"Sounds really damn little," rasped Andy.

"We're going up now. Some sort of ramp. Now this you've got to see."

"Try describing it instead," said Gottlieb in his calm, placating manner.

"We've come to a round, hollow metal tube. Like a huge barrel they use to store hazardous material in. All that's missing is the skull and cross-bones."

"Get out of there!" shouted Cathy furiously.

"Cath, darling. You have no sense of humor. You know how I like to exaggerate."

"Sure," she snapped. "Like the foaming boils of lava on Mount Erebus. They burned right through your suit."

"And I returned, still kicking and driving you crazy."

"You'd darn well better this time too."

"Are you finished?" asked Gottlieb sternly, raising his eyebrows. It would appear that his patience was wearing thin with the lovers' banter and Cathy's frazzled nerves. She nodded petulantly.

"Tell me about this tube," said Gottlieb. "Are you standing in front of it?"

"I'm standing in it, Arnold. It has a diameter of about eight feet…feet…feet. Oh, look at that. It echoes too. You know I've seen something like this before. It was…"

His voice cut out as a loud gong sounded over the radio. Cathy jumped to her feet. "Jim?" A repetitive hammering noise crackled in and out through the receiver. "Jim!" she screamed in abject terror. Then she heard them over the bounding noise. Voices. Some high-pitched, some low-toned, one unmistakably baritone. Screaming.

She was tugging at her hair, ready to rip it from her head. She wanted to jump through the mike and somehow haul him out. Before she could do anything, the gongs stopped, but the screaming went on for another minute. "Jim?" she said faintly, her chest as tight as a drum.

"Oh hell!"

He was still alive. "Jim, are you all right?"

"Right as rain. Just had my head pounded out. I don't know what the heck this is, but it sure is loud. I could feel the vibrations right through my body. Ears are still throbbing."

"Turn around," said Cathy. "Get out of there now."

"We're all okay," he said, ignoring her as usual when she tried to talk sense into him. "This thing is amazing. Somebody build a giant MRI machine."

"Did you hear me!" she shouted.

"Calm down," said Gottlieb severely. "I don't want to make you leave."

Cathy bit down on her tongue.

"What did you say, Jim?" he prompted.

"You know, Nuclear Magnetic Resonance Imaging. Uses sound waves to check out the atoms in your body. How does it work again, Tom?"

"Oh," said Tom a little vaguely. "Yes, well, atoms tend to spin slightly off the vertical axis. What the MRI does is use a giant magnet to make the protons from the nucleuses in the atoms line up at the same time as radio waves pulse energy through the scanner. The protons absorb the energy required to make them spin in a different direction."

"Like stopping and spinning a top in the opposite direction," said Jimmy helpfully.

"Right," said Tom. "Are you going to let me do this?"

"Sorry," said Jimmy sheepishly. "Go on."

"Anyway, by turning the magnets on and off very rapidly, they can take slices of the human body down to the atoms by altering their spin when they're on, then, when they're turned off, the atoms release the excess energy they absorbed from the radio waves, giving us an image."

"I was in one once," interrupted Jim. "Checking out my liver for a tumor. That was when I was on the sauce after my wife died. Bad time." He chuckled mirthlessly.

No one else did.

"It was like this, only smaller. Drum rolls of sound. Very claustrophobic. Very loud. I wonder who's looking for tumors here."

"Jim, I think you... should turn back," said Gottlieb slowly.

"Are you kidding?" said Jim. "This is better than a volcano. Somebody built a giant lab down here. And I'm going to find out what for."

"Dammit, Jimmy..." Cathy tried to blink away the tears, but they crept out anyway.

"But I'll send Jeanna, Tom and Sal back to the helo."

"Not on your life," growled Sal. He'd been unusually silent up until this point, but his military background came into play now. He'd stayed down in Antarctica because he craved this kind of death-defying experience, the more extreme the better. "I never leave a man behind."

"I don't want to go either," said Jeanna in a stronger voice than Cathy had heard earlier. This was the Jeanna she knew. "This place is so strange and miraculous, like science on steroids. I want to find out who made it."

"I'm staying too," said Tom, surprising everyone. "There's something almost celestial about this place."

"Are you feeling the neutrinos?" grunted Andy.

"Maybe," said Tom.

Andy shrugged and rolled his eyes. "Nutcase," he whispered.

"You have to be, to be a physicist," said Jamal. "A lot of genius and a little bit of insanity. That way you can swing your mind around anything."

"Are you insulting me?" said Tom in his high-pitched whiny voice.

"Never," said Jamal. "You the man, Tom."

"And don't you forget it, rock-splitter."

"Hey," said Jamal.

"Well, if you're all in agreement," said Gottlieb, "you have my permission to go forward."

"Thanks for the go ahead," Jimmy said snidely.

Everyone in the tiny room laughed, except Cathy. They all knew that, despite Gottlieb's title as the head of the National Science Foundation in Antarctica, his authority meant nothing to these bull-headed scientists. Cathy clenched her sweaty palms together, infuriated and frustrated by their cool disregard for danger.

There was near-total silence now over the radio - nothing but the clip-clop of their boots on the metal tunnel. Finally Jimmy broke through again with a gasp.

"What is it, Jim?" asked Gottlieb.

"We have a chamber, maybe fourteen feet high. Red granite blocks on top. Small tunnels running out the sides at oblique angles. There's a layer of dust on the floor. No exit. Looks like a dead end."

"Smells funny in here," said Jeanna.

"Ya," said Sal. "Something like a burnt Christmas dinner."

"Burnt a few turkeys in your day, have you Sal?" asked Andy, winking at the others.

"More than a few..."

"I don't see anything funny about this," said Cathy furiously. "You've reached a dead end. There are no people except dead ones outside. It smells like burnt flesh. DOES THAT TELL YOU ANYTHING!" she screamed.

"Cathy!" Gottlieb swung around, his teeth grinding into each other.

"Maybe you're right, love," said Jimmy quietly. "This does look like ash. Let's get the hell out of here."

"What's that!" yelled Jeanna, her calm voice pitched to a soprano shriek.

"There's a door rolling shut. Run, dammit, run."

Cathy's fingers bit into Andy's shoulder beside her. He didn't even flinch. His usually comical face was ashen.

"Oh God, we're trapped!"

"What's that?"

"Light of some sort."

"Fire," said Jimmy in an oddly monotone voice. "Love you, Cath."

There were ear-splitting shrieks followed by a deafening roar, then silence.

Cathy felt her knees buckle and the world blacken around her.

Two

Near the opposite pole on the tongue of the Alaska Peninsula, Erica Daniels was shinnying up a rope over teardrops of glacier ice and sheer charcoal basalt. It was near noon, when the sun shed a few pitiful rays before the gloom of twilight chased away the light for the remainder of the day. She could make out each notch in the rock where she stabbed a hand or a foothold, but just as she placed her fingers in the next tiny groove above her, the mountain began to shudder and shake. The convulsions pummeled her tiny frame against the rock face, jarring her hands and feet, and she felt her precarious grip slip away. Erica dropped a few sickening feet before the line snapped her back. Shocked and a little winded, she hung suspended from the rope that was sawing back and forth over the sharp edges of the cliff like a pendulum. At the same time Veniaminof coughed and spewed a spray of steam from her cone.

That woke her up in a hurry. *Not dead yet* – the thought hooked a smile from her lips. With renewed determination she dug back into the crags of the mountain and scrambled up to the narrow ledge where her grappling hook was lodged. With a sigh, she rolled over onto the icy ground.

"Can you give me a hand?" yelled Murdock from below.

Erica leaned over the edge and grasped the guide's huge hand as he tried to clamber up the side of the volcano. His rope was swaying ominously in the continuous seismic shivers. She hauled at him, feeling the convulsions try to jimmy his hand from her grasp. "No, you don't," she addressed the mountain firmly. With her muscles pumped to the limit, she pulled him the last few feet and flipped him onto the plateau. Murdock lay there, catching his breath.

"Damn crazy woman," he muttered.

"Oh, come on, now. Isn't this fun?" said Erica, winking a cobalt eye. "We get to see the young lass foaming at the mouth."

The 'young lass' was Mount Veniaminof, an 8,225-foot volcano that projected from the middle of the Alaska Peninsula – the northern belt of the 'Ring of Fire' in the Pacific. She was actually not so young – 3,700 years old - with a spectacular steep-walled summit caldera, 4.8 x 6.6 miles in diameter. The caldera was filled by an ice field, except for a protruding cone in the middle. An electric-blue alpine glacier spilled from the crater through gaps on the west and north sides of the rim.

Murdock eyed her from beneath his frost-fringed lashes. "You call this fun? Crawling up a mountain while she's vibrating like one of those beds in a cheap motel? Not to forget the fact that she's letting off steam. Next will be the bloody lava bombs raining down on our heads. I hate Alaska."

Erica smiled. "Liar. It's the most pristine country around. You haven't left it in fifteen years. And it's got volcanoes," she said with that special glee reserved only for madmen and volcanologists.

Jason Murdock slowly sat up and scraped the frost from his bristly bronze goatee. He studied her chafed face with a sideways slant to his lips. "Okay, I don't hate the state," he said. "But I do hate volcanoes."

Erica rolled her eyes and stood up. "You can fool some of the people some of time," she said, tucking wisps of honey-toned hair back up into the bright red toque from which they'd escaped.

"I'm just here for the money."

"Right."

"Well, really, Daniels. This is a little insane. There's lava bubbling out of her cone. Steam being ejected into the air. And that lovely aroma of sulfur. How do you propose we get near the cone anyway?"

"I think of everything." Erica grinned. "Moon suits." She dug into her bulging pack and removed two Nomex flight suits for heat protection, a couple of heat-reflective jackets and some gas masks.

"No, not the moon suit," said Murdock in disgust. "I can hardly walk in that thing."

"But you'll be able to breath," said Erica. "And you won't get cooked by the heat, unless a lava bomb drops on your head."

"I feel so much better."

Erica sighed and shook her head. She knew he loved these caldera walks – living on the edge – almost as much as she did. They divested themselves of their thinsulate Skidoo suits and donned stiff flight suits and silver jackets that did make them look rather rotund and alien, Murdock even more so draped around his large muscular frame. It had been heavy hauling them up the mountain, but at least it had only been a short climb. The helicopter had dropped them off on a plateau about 800 feet below. They had only to rappel the last few hundred feet where the angle of the cone had become too steep to walk. Now came the fun part.

Erica scrambled over the rim of the caldera, taking her first steps into the pristine white snow peppered with slush where steam was hissing out. As she drew closer to the cone that projected from the middle of the caldera like a nipple on a concave breast, the snow became speckled with cinders until they were so numerous they rolled under her boots and sifted here and there where she trod. It was like walking over a huge sea of corn kernels.

Murdock came up behind her, breathing noisily in his mask.

"Isn't it beautiful?" said Erica.

"Sure. I especially like the piss-colored gas rising out of the center."

Erica smiled. She couldn't help herself. It had to be the most thrilling experience in the world, investigating a live volcano, and most people would miss it. For what? Sitting on their couch in front of the idiot box? She chuckled to herself. "Oh look, there's some lava."

Murdock turned his head to where she was pointing. There seemed to be a pulsing pit at the base of the intracaldera cone, bubbling up glowing red and orange globules of molten rock. "Oh goody," he said.

"Let's have a look."

"Daniels, wait." She ignored him and traipsed halfway down the slope. "You really want to be fried to a crisp, don't you?"

"The only way to go," she replied.

Murdock grumbled and groaned, but he followed obediently. "Dante must have been inspired here."

Erica giggled like a schoolgirl as she approached the lava pit. There were pockmarks all through the caldera surface where old lava bombs had hit. Some were living room-sized craters. "It's gorgeous. You think of hell, but I think of life. This is what our planet's made of. And these craters are just like impact craters from asteroids and comets. It's almost like we're walking on the moon, only there hasn't been any volcanic activity there in millions of years."

"As far as we know," he said, coming up beside her.

"Yes," she said, bending down in front of a hissing vent. "But that's going to change soon."

"No doubt," he said. "The great 2015 moon mission. Do you have to get so damn close?"

Erica extracted a sample bottle from her pack and inserted the tube into the fumaroles. It was attached to a glass bottle with two stopcocks. She grasped the pump at the other end and started to evacuate the air from the bottle drawing in the sulfur gases. "It's the only quick way to test it. I'm going to take it's temp too." She withdrew a thermocouple probe from her bag and jabbed it into a globule of lava.

"Can you make it quick?" said Murdock. "This mountain makes me jittery."

There was another large tremor, topping off the continuous small tremors, to punctuate his remark. "One could say that you make Veniaminof jittery."

"No, I don't think it's me. I think it's the tons of magma percolating just below our feet." Murdock pointed deliberately at his boots and grimaced.

"Really?" said Erica. "That's an interesting idea. Oh, dear." She removed the temperature probe from the lava.

"What?" he asked, his voice an octave higher.

"One thousand one hundred and eighty degrees Celsius. She's a hot one."

Murdock blinked. "As much as I like a hot date, I don't like to be incinerated by her. Let's get out of here."

"I think this time you're right," said Erica, "though I hate to leave her. I think she's ready to blow."

As if the volcano were listening to her, it ejected another loud belch of steam and the cone itself seemed to lift upward. Erica gathered her equipment, thrust it into her bag and started to run just as she felt the pressure ripple the ground under her feet. Murdock was right beside her, scrambling over the dimpled caldera toward the rim.

A loud 'pop' came from behind them. Erica stopped and looked back.

"Are you mad?" screamed Murdock. He grabbed her hand and tried to propel her forward, but she held fast. A ball of lava had ejected into the air and was soaring above their heads.

Murdock kept tugging.

"You can't just run blindly," she said. "They're erratic. You have to see in which direction its going to fall, then run."

Murdock stopped pulling Erica and gazed up at the ball of fire. It spiked high, then arced and began to fall toward them.

"Now," said Erica. "Go!"

They raced like the hounds of hell pursued them, which to Murdock would have seemed appropriate, although Erica still had a grin on her face as she leapt out of the way of the incoming impact. It smashed to the ground a few feet away, splattering red-hot lava on the leg of Erica's flight suit. She felt it smolder its way in, singing the skin underneath, but she didn't care. It was just another part of the extravaganza.

Another 'pop' sounded and then another. She stopped at the edge of the cliff and turned back.

"For Pete's sake, Daniels."

The lava bombs were shooting out of the ground like tennis balls from a practice machine. Ash and cinders were pluming in the air. "What a show!" Every time she saw it, it seemed to mesmerize her. She could stay right here and watch as the bombs exploded around her.

Murdock growled at her and broke the spell. She turned to join him, but he wasn't waiting any longer. He bent down and grasped her around the legs, throwing her bodily over his shoulder.

"You are the craziest woman I've ever met. Why the hell do I like you so much?"

"Put me down, you big bully. I was coming."

He ignored her and jumped over the rim with her head bouncing against his broad back. A lava bomb exploded just behind them as they landed on the plateau. Luckily the rim of the crater stopped the bomb from splattering over Erica's head. Murdock dropped her on the ground, grabbed the rope and attached her line.

"Get going," he snarled.

"Yes sir!" she barked, saluting briskly.

She ripped off the gas mask and leaped over the edge, rappelling smoothly down the cliff face. Murdock wasn't behind her. Erica frowned. Maybe she'd been playing chicken just a little too closely. She wouldn't mind if it had been her – she couldn't think of a better way to go – but not her friend.

"Murdock," she yelled.

There was no reply.

"Jason!" she screamed.

She was just about to head back up the cliff when his face peered over the brim. "I'm coming, *Erica*." He smiled. "Just had to radio the helicopter."

He vaulted over the edge and descended the rope, hand over hand. Erica sighed in relief, although she didn't like the way he had said her name. Or the way he'd looked at her. Maybe it was time she left Alaska for a while. She shook her head, bringing her thoughts back to the task at hand. She had to focus on getting down the mountain and out of the hail of lava bombs and cinders. She rappelled as quickly as she could, boots slipping and sliding on the black basalt. Finally she reached the gentler slope where she detached her clip from the rope and waited for Murdock to join her. A couple of seconds later he leapt to the icy ground beside Erica, unbuckled, and grabbed her hand. They raced down the mountain amidst a haze of ash and steam until they came to the level platform of the plateau where the helicopter had dropped them off only a couple of hours ago.

"I think we're out of range now," said Erica, although there were still fluffy flakes of ash falling on her lashes. "Plus I think she's settling down. That was only a little hiccup."

"I'd hate to be caught in a full-scale vomit then,' said Murdock.

"Veniaminof doesn't blow her top. She just lets off steam every once and a while. She's not dangerous."

"Could have fooled me."

Erica smiled. "I know what I'm doing," she said. "Maybe I called it a little close today, but I'm the best in my field. This mountain only ever has Strombolian eruptions. That's just a few burps and hiccups with some lava bombs and ash plumes, but never a full-scale pyroclastic event. She's no real threat."

"Right," said Murdock. "Lava bombs are no real threat. We'd better move further out on the plateau. This ash could mess with the helicopter's intake. But it's no real threat, right?"

Erica shrugged. Her perception of threat might be a little less elevated than the average guy's, considering her profession. As long as you were aware of the risks, what was the problem? They moved further out in the open, as Murdock suggested, but the plume was already drifting to the east.

"I wouldn't want to see you get hurt," she continued. "I wouldn't do that to a friend."

Murdock grinned. "Glad to hear it." He moved closer.

Erica inched away. "That is all..." Her words were drowned out by the rising crescendo of helicopter rotors. "We are," she tried to yell, "just friends."

He tilted his head toward her and cupped his ear, but it was obvious he hadn't heard her.

The brilliant blue and white Bell helicopter dove in out of the sky and drifted down towards them, dusting the snow with its thumping rotors. Erica and Murdock ducked and dashed for their transport as it touched down on the icy surface. Murdock reached it first, opened the door and jumped in, his thick brown hair being flattened by the downdraft. He leaned over and hauled Erica after him, her head smacking firmly into his chest. His arms tightened around her for a second before he let her go. Erica clenched her jaw as she hastened to her seat and buckled in. This was getting too complicated. There was another throaty belch from the volcano as the helicopter lifted off. Soon they were well out of reach of the smoky plume that blanketed the top of Veniaminof.

Erica watched it out of sight, trying to avoid eye contact with Murdock. The sound of the rotors had deadened any chance of normal conversation, for which she was grateful. However, within minutes of take-off, he touched her arm, making her jump. With a deliberate flick of his hand, he motioned for her to put on her headset so she could talk to him. Reluctantly, she scooped up the headset beside the seat and slipped it over her ears, adjusting the mike in front of her lips. The movement, when she shifted in her seat, sent a jolt of pain through her leg and she winced.

"What's wrong?" asked Murdock, loud and clear over the headphones. "Are you hurt?"

Erica shook her head. "It's nothing." She gritted her teeth.

"Oh really? Let me see."

"Don't be ridiculous."

"It's your leg, isn't it? I can already see the burn marks in the flight suit." He bent down and, before she could protest any further, he yanked her pants up over her calf.

There was an angry burn etched in her fair skin peppered with blisters. "Ouch," said Murdock. "That looks nasty." He grasped the First Aid kit from the wall, flicked open the catches and pulled out some smooth gauze and antibiotic cream.

"I can do that myself," said Erica.

Murdock just frowned at her and began to bind her leg. "Best there is," he mumbled.

"Every volcanologist gets burned once and a while. It comes with the territory."

Murdock looked up at her as he wound some Kling around her wound and taped it securely. "I guess it does," he said. "Traipsing around lava and scalding steam vents does seem like a hazardous profession."

"So does guiding people up mountains and over glaciers."

He grinned. "So we're made for each other." He sat up and gazed into her eyes.

Erica opened her mouth, but she didn't know what to say.

Murdock grasped her hand and gave it a squeeze.

She froze. It was happening again. There was no way she could *let it* happen again. She forcefully extracted her hand from his clasp. "Murdock."

"You called me Jason back there."

"That was when I thought you were dead or dying."

Murdock frowned. "That makes me feel so much better."

"You know how I feel about colleagues getting in bed together."

"And I know why."

It was Erica's turn to frown. "How do you know...?"

"I don't know who," said Murdock, "but I know why. You had a relationship with someone you worked with, and you got burned, excuse the pun. But I'm not that guy, and I'd never hurt you."

"You couldn't," said Erica. "Not the way he did." She took a deep breath. "I like you... Jason. You're attractive, strong and tough as nails. But I like you only as a friend."

Murdock looked at her a moment or two longer, then he looked away.

Erica closed her eyes. It had been harder than she thought, but it had to be done. She wasn't about to get into that sort of emotional pain again. It hurt a lot more than the physical pain she felt from any encounter with lava.

Her eyes flew open when Sanders, the slim black-bearded pilot, announced over the internal mike that they were over Katmai National Monument. Erica stared out the window at the spectacular scenery – sinewy rivers and ice-crusted lakes, the mighty mountains whose ebony peaks thrust above the slow-flowing glaciers and of course the rugged cinder cones of the park's plentiful volcanoes.

She gazed down in wonder at the famous Valley of Ten Thousand Smokes – forty square miles of a pyroclastic ash flow deposited by Novarupta Volcano in 1912. The entire area was a bleak gray-black desert. Erica could replay the eruption in her mind – hot, glowing pumice and ash ejected from the volcano and flowing down the mountainside, snapping off trees like matchsticks and carbonizing all life in its path by the blasts of hot wind and gas. Destructive, but so beautiful.

"Hey." Sanders leaned over from the front and broke into her thoughts. "I didn't want to interrupt before, but..."

Erica blinked and met his gaze.

"Well, you're the impact specialist, right?"

She raised an eyebrow.

"You study meteorite craters as well as volcanoes?"

She nodded.

"Well, I've always wondered. Is Savonoski crater, you know, a meteorite crater?"

Erica smiled. She glanced out her window again as the helicopter edged over the water-filled bowl in the middle of the park. "Some people think it's a maar," she replied. "That's when a magma pipe – magma's just another word for lava that's under the earth – well, it strikes the water table before it reaches the earth's surface and the steam blows away the overlying rock to form a circular pit. It's sort of like a sneeze compared to Veniaminof or Novarupta. But I don't think it is. You see, this bowl occurs in sandstone, not basalt like any other volcano. Basalt is basically hardened lava. I couldn't find any shock features, like quartz crystals that have been altered, their grains crisscrossed – that's an elemental signature of a meteorite or asteroid impact - but everything around here has been carved up and carried away for thousands of years by the glaciers. It's very hard to prove it's an impact crater without those features. I just look at it, though. It's a big round gouge in the earth's crust. I would put money on its extraterrestrial origin."

The pilot was listening patiently to her rather lengthy analysis, nodding and smiling. Murdock hadn't turned his head back to her the entire time. He must hate her now. Why was it that men could never accept an offer of friendship? It always had to be more, or else it had to be nothing.

"Oh, I almost forgot," said Sanders. "Somebody's been trying like hell to reach you. Is your satellite phone busted or something."

Erica zipped open her pack and stared at the dainty black portable. "I don't think the signal works very well during an eruption." She slid her hand surreptitiously into the pack and flicked the power back on.

Sanders nodded, but there was dark cast of doubt on his face. "I guess. Anyway, some hotshot in NASA wants you to contact him right away. Name of Dellows."

"NASA?" Erica's mouth dropped open.

Sanders shrugged. "Maybe they want to send you to the moon or something."

Erica's eyes grew larger. She turned and found Murdock was finally looking at her again, his eyebrows raised. "You are the best," he said.

Three

Despite the warm turbulence buffeting the plane, Erica felt a chill slice through her body like a cold Alaska wind. The 747 yawed through the storm much like the bush planes of the arctic. Erica's stomach threatened to claw its way out of her mouth.

"Quite the storm," yelled the man beside her in a clipped British accent. He had all but hid behind his paper when she'd boarded in Toronto after the long flight from Anchorage. Now his tan, angular face refused to come clear in the midst of the moguls.

Erica put her hand to her mouth and nodded. She gripped the plastic bag.

"They say there's a run of tornadoes west of Talahassee."

Erica's eyes widened. "We can't fly through…"

"No, they've rerouted our flight. We'll never make Houston."

"Where?" she managed to mutter.

"Orlando, if we're lucky."

Another hard hit and Erica's body strained against the seat belt. She tried to focus on his face and breathe deeply. "This can't be happening."

"Something big up in Houston?" he asked. His eyebrows were raised over sea-green eyes. She could see them more clearly now, which meant that the turbulence had subsided, at least for the time being.

"Depends on your definition of 'big.'"

His lips twitched. They were firm masculine lips with a thin rust of five-o'clock shadow tracing the crescent of his mouth. "Sky's the limit."

"Quite possibly." She licked her own thick lips and threw back a tangle of flaxen hair.

"The moon mission?" he said.

Her lips parted in shock. "How did you know about that?"

"I read about it." He tapped a copy of Newsweek in his lap. "Quite the competition for a science team up there. First time living on the moon. Everyone's scrambling for a spot, aren't they?" He smiled shrewdly.

Erica's brow furrowed. "How did you know I was a scientist?"

"You've got the look."

"Which is?"

"Preoccupied. A little rumpled." His hand swept over her wrinkled polyester jacket and her battered leather briefcase. "And weathered."

"Excuse me?"

"In a nice way, but definitely outdoors. A field scientist, but a scientist nonetheless."

"Why I could say that you have the same traits." Her eyes crawled over his tan face, his grizzled jaw and the skin cracks in his hands.

"You see. We're easy to identify."

She stared at him. "You're a scientist?"

He nodded.

"Then you are…"

"Not a volcanologist, like yourself."

She shook her head again. Another round of boxing from the wind sent her careening into the window of the plane.

"Don't look so surprised." He tapped the magazine again. "If you spent less time crawling in volcanic craters or picking up rocks from meteorite sites and more time reading some journals, you might see yourself sometime."

She grabbed the bag and held it close as another giant gust of wind threw the plane back. "I'm not that famous."

"So modest. You wrote the book on impact craters."

Erica looked away. "I do know my craters." She didn't just know them, she loved them. The mere thought of those crisp gouges in the earth - from the bubbling vents of volcanoes to the mysterious pockmarks of asteroids and meteorites – swept away some of the nausea she was feeling right now. Craters were her life, maybe because she'd grown up in one. Sudbury wasn't a well-known city, even in Canada, but its mines were renown. The nickel and copper deposits were the result of a giant impact with an asteroid – twelve miles in diameter – that had gouged out a kidney-shaped basin in Northern Ontario forty miles long by sixteen miles wide almost two billion years ago. Sudbury was located right in the middle of the basin. So to Erica, craters were as fascinating as they were second nature. She'd been building miniature volcanoes when she was eight and erupting them all over the kitchen table, much her mother's dismay. Nothing excited her more than to view the old footage from the Apollo missions where the astronauts actually set foot on a world of impact craters. That had been her goal through university in Toronto and on through graduate school in California where she'd met *him. Damn him!*

The nausea swallowed her again, although it had less to do with the turbulence and more to do with the thought of *that man.* The voice from the seat next to her broke into her thoughts, thankfully, and she could thrust him aside again.

"Which should make you a shoo-in for this moon project since craters are about all that's up there."

"You would think," said Erica. "But I still have to bid for the position and if I don't make this conference at NASA in time..." Erica looked at her watch. 11:45 A.M. The conference started at one.

"Out of the running, Dr. Daniels, unless..."

"Unless?"

"You boot it for Kennedy Space Center and link up with the video conference."

Erica smiled. "Yes, that could be the answer." She studied him closely, suddenly impressed with his dusky face. She held out her hand. "*Erica* Daniels," she stressed. "But you have me at a loss, Mr. Scientist."

He grasped her hand solidly and squeezed ever so slightly. "Allan Rocheford."

Erica whipped her hand back. "*The* Allan Rocheford?"

He nodded.

"The burial chamber beneath the Sphinx?"

"Exactly the one."

"I wouldn't *exactly* call myself a scientist, if I were you," she snarled.

"Archaeologist."

"You plundered that tomb." Erica's face flushed. Suddenly all the nauseating motion was washed away in a sea of red.

"I studied it, scientifically. But of course I had sponsors that had to be reimbursed. Everything is on display in the appropriate museums."

Erica shook her head. "Everything should have stayed in Egypt, exactly where you found it. You're no different than the treasure-hunters of the Caribbean. At least they admit that they're greedy pirates and don't hide behind science."

Allan shrugged. "Most people don't look at it that way. We learned a great deal about the origins of the pyramids."

"Oh, don't spout that Atlantis crap at me. I'm not interested in myths that you perpetuate in the name of science."

He smiled malevolently.

The pilot muttered something over the loud speaker. It wasn't very loud considering the jolts they were still receiving. None of that seemed to matter now. There were only herself and this miserable excuse for a scientist in front of her.

"How rich did this *science* expedition make you?"

"I don't suffer," Allan shouted as the engines screamed. "But I think you're rather well financed yourself."

"To study volcanoes and impact craters, not plunder gems."

The plane banked to the right. Erica was thrown against her seatmate, her head thumping his solid chest. She could feel the bulge of his pectorals under her cheek. His breath fell on her hair, hot and moist. She gasped as his lips brushed her nape.

Fighting gravity and the torque of the plane, she pulled herself off him.

"How dare you!" she screamed.

"What?" He shrugged, all innocence. "I think we're landing."

"Thank God. I hope this is the last I see of you, pirate!"

He leaned toward her as the wheels touched down with a thud. His lips were a hair's breadth from her ear. "I doubt it, prude."

She turned to give him a slap, but he was already out of reach – whistling, with his carry-on flung over his shoulder and sauntering arrogantly down the aisle.

"Well, that certainly was an intense flight," said a woman behind her.

"You're telling me," Erica muttered. She grabbed her duffel bag from the overhead bin and headed toward the front of the plane. "Prude, indeed."

Four

Balmy air enveloped Erica as she lighted from Orlando International Airport. It had seemed an intolerably long haul, wading through the endless stream of passengers and ferrying over to the main terminal on the shuttle. Then it had been an interminable time waiting for her luggage, but she'd finally managed to claim her bags from the belt. She looked everywhere for the sandy hair of the pirate, but he'd been swallowed by a hungry wave of tourists, thank goodness.

Erica headed determinedly for the taxi plateau, scrambling, like everyone else, to escape the hustle of the airport. She stripped off her jacket as she walked, sweating despite the cool temperatures for a mid-October Florida day. The storms that tracked the southwest had chilled upper Florida to the low 60s, but it was tropical compared to Anchorage.

Erica spotted a taxi idling on the tarmac. Her feet flew over the sidewalk as she brushed stray tourists out of her path. She flung her bags into the trunk and caught the door handle at the same time as a man's hand grasped it as well.

"Well, fancy that," he quipped in his stilted British accent. "We meet again, *Erica.*"

Erica leaped into the taxi and tried to slam the door. He held it back, jerking the door open and leaping in beside her, almost on top of her.

"Despite your feelings about my work, there's no need to be impolite." The grin on his face was definitely mocking.

Erica scowled. "It's hard to be polite to someone you don't respect. Besides, you know how urgently I have to get to Kennedy Space Center."

"Kennedy?" the taxi driver said, turning troubled mahogany eyes toward her, a line of furrows tracking his baldpate. "That's a little out of my area."

Erica turned to him and smiled sweetly. "But this is an emergency."

"Sorry." The cabbie shook his head with a determined set to his jaw.

"I'll make it worth your while," Allan said, peeling off some hundred-dollar bills from his black leather billfold.

"Sure thing, buddy," said the cabbie as he laid his hands on the cash. He tucked them neatly into the pocket of his rumpled green and tangerine Hawaiian shirt and gunned the engine, nearly sideswiping a shuttle bus.

"Don't do me any favors," Erica growled.

"No favor," said Allan. "I happen to be heading in the same direction."

Erica glared at him suspiciously as the cab squealed around the corner.

Allan shrugged. "Enjoy the ride."

"How can I?"

"Well, at least enjoy the scenery." His eyes swept over the luscious growth of palm trees and Florida pine. "A far cry from the dark, icy Arctic."

Erica thankfully broke her gaze with the irritating Briton and looked out her window. The palms bent low in the wind over scattered ponds and swamps frothed with algae; a carpet of emerald grass and ferns were thrusting through every murky bit of land. Alongside the road, a blaze of tropical flowers wreathed carefully coifed gardens in hues of red and orange, yellow and lavender. The peninsula was so lush and verdant, not tempered by crystal snowscapes or ivory-encased aquamarine glaciers. It was so dense, so crowded. Even the air seemed heavy. "You've never been there. How would you know?"

"You're right," he said, amusement plain in his voice. "I have no concept of the cold north. The desert sand is what I'm most familiar with. Equally barren and maybe just as exciting for its challenge."

Erica's eyes trickled reluctantly back toward the archaeologist. He was thick-lashed with mossy eyes, a narrow nose and wavy sand-colored hair. His skin was toasted and overcooked in some dried out patches, but overall he would have looked good on a beach, or in a desert. She could tell he had that rugged burn for nature. Why did he have to be who he was?

He caught her glance and returned the look. It was appreciation, she knew, for more than the scenery.

Erica flushed and crossed her arms over her firm high-tipped breasts. "What business do you have at the Space Center?" she croaked.

"Oh, it has to do with a new dig. NASA may be financing it."

Erica snorted. "Why would NASA finance an archaeological dig? They're interested in new frontiers, not old ones."

"You'd be surprised what they're interested in," Allan said.

"Are you going to fill me in?"

"No."

She raised her brows. "Is it a state secret or something?"

"Maybe."

Erica shrugged. "Suit yourself. Just making conversation, since we're stuck with each other."

"Obviously."

She frowned and turned away.

The drive took about forty-five minutes along the Beeline Expressway, a toll highway from Orlando to the Cape. They crossed the long NASA causeway over to Merritt Island, bordered by an ocean inlet that gradually gave way to tangled mangroves and ditches of swamp water. A few cruising alligators lurked in the shallows, or watched them from the long grass with a measuring gaze. A couple of snowy egrets were spearing fish with their long sharp bills and roseate spoonbills clustered in a brilliant pink and white mosaic that spread over the water. Erica saw the large bowl of an eagle's nest in one of the trees as they passed by. It was amazing how the latest in space technology made its bed within the cradle of nature. As they passed the Visitor Complex, the irony of it hit her full in the face. Alligators cruised in the pond next to towering commemorative rockets and a space shuttle mockup. Tour buses shuttled in and out of the complex, ferrying people through the unrestricted areas of the Space Center past launch pads and the crawlerway - where rockets and the space shuttles were hauled to the pads - across which tortoises crept and diamondback rattlers slithered. This hub of civilization's advancement – and popular tourist attraction - truly lived a symbiotic relationship with the wildlife of the Merritt Island Nature Preserve. It drew a smile from Erica despite her traveling companion.

The grin was soon wiped from her face as she drew level with the scowling NASA security officer. He had short spiked hair and beady eyes above a hooked nose that he seemed to look down at her through. It took her a good fifteen minutes to get through the barrier to the restricted area that housed the Headquarters building, the Operations and Checkout and the International Space Station Center. They had to abandon the taxi. Despite all her credentials, the guard still seemed leery of her even with the most reassuring smile she could coax from her lips. Allan, however, he instantly recognized from his stint on Fox where the entire world watched as he unearthed the treasures beneath the Sphinx. The guard bantered animatedly with him and passed him through without a challenge. He even commandeered a ride for him. If it weren't for Allan, she probably would have been walking to the administration building – the Space Center Headquarters. It grated against her pride that she had to feel grateful to the scoundrel.

Headquarters was the first building past the barrier, basically two rectangular sections attached to a taller slab in the middle. She had a clear view from here of one of the largest buildings in America – the Vehicle Assembly Building with its overpowering Stars and Stripes flag painted down the front. This was where the massive Saturn V rockets had been constructed for the Apollo missions to the moon. It sent chills through her body just being close to it again. How close would she get to the moon?

"Dr. Daniels?" said a tall security guard with a round pleasant face. He held the door open for her at the front of the administration building. "I'm Stewart James. The video conference room is this way."

He showed her down a labyrinth of stark white passageways to a boardroom with a burnished mahogany conference table and plush brown leather chairs. A large video screen dominated the far wall beside which sat a couple of computers with the superfine plasma monitors. Three men were already in the room – average height and build, close-cropped hair and bland poker faces. The only way she could distinguish one from the other was by the color of their ties. They were red, white and blue. They nodded silently at her as she took her seat facing the screen.

The conference was well under way. On the screen she saw an array of men and women from the science community with intense eyes and very smooth skin passing out materials over another boardroom table of rich mahogany. A man at the head of the table was standing and discussing the hazards of space habitation.

"As you can see, from a geological standpoint, Mr. Marsh has made an excellent point regarding safeguards and backups for oxygen production."

Erica froze.

A tall broad-shouldered man of about thirty-five was seated to the right of the screen. A lock of russet hair fell over his face and he swept it back with a flip of his head. The idiosyncrasy was unmistakable. David Marsh. Erica took a deep breath as she took him in. His crisp navy suit was impeccable; his hazel eyes were focused on the speaker with the intensity of a ray of light; his manner was self-assured and brimming with smug satisfaction. Volcanic lava foamed beneath her gritted teeth.

"Excuse me," Erica interrupted. "I'm sorry I'm late, but my plane got rerouted because of the storms on the Gulf."

The man at the head of the table looked up. He scratched his smoke-gray hair and examined her with slate-gray eyes. She recognized him immediately. Matthew Dellows, Science Team Coordinator of the moon station – LUNA I. "You are?" he asked.

The door to the conference room opened abruptly. Allan Rocheford slid into the seat beside her with a sly sideways glance. She cast him a stern look and replied to the screen.

"Erica Daniels, volcanologist and impact specialist."

"Oh, yes, Dr. Daniels. I've read about you. Some interesting work on impact craters in North America."

She smiled nervously. "Thank you."

Allan shuffled some papers and winked.

"Yes, well." Dellows frowned. "We've already considered your credentials, despite your absence. However a choice for team geologist has already been made."

Erica blinked.

"David Marsh has presented an excellent dossier, along with his work producing oxygen from lunar rocks. He will be a great asset to our team."

"But..."

"There may be other opportunities in the future when the colony is well established."

"My work with impact craters. Surely my expertise in this area..."

"Yes. Well, Dr. Marsh may need to consult you from time to time. I'm sure you wouldn't mind the bonus work, would you Dr. Daniels?"

"Was it because I was late?"

Marsh smirked. She wanted to slap him.

"No, Doctor." Dellows was as poker-faced as ever. "You simply weren't sufficiently qualified."

Erica squinted. "Not qualified. I'm every bit as educated as any one of you NASA beakers."

Allan winced.

"My research is known and respected worldwide. I've braved the harshest conditions while Dr. Marsh, there, melted rocks in a laboratory."

"Dr. Marsh," said Dellows, his gray eyes as cold as an arctic sky, "is well known to NASA. He also comes with the highest credentials and the highest recommendations."

"It's because I'm a woman, isn't it?"

Rocheford coughed.

"You think I can't hack it in space."

"We have other women on this project."

Erica looked around the boardroom in Houston, counting the women. There was only one. "Do you mean the astronaut to the right of Dr. Marsh? Is that your idea of 'other women?'?"

The small black-haired woman with Asian features stared back at her. She frowned as she turned and surveyed the group around her.

"At the behest of the Chinese government, I suppose," continued Erica, "since this is supposed to be an *international project.*"

Dellows cleared his throat. "I think you've made your point, Dr. Daniels, but you'll have to take it up with the review board."

"I think I'll take it up with the press," said Erica.

Allan shook his head.

Dellows' mouth fell open. His eyebrows pierced his thinning hair. Before he could respond, Erica scraped her chair back, gathered up her portfolio and charged out of the room. There was an eruption of voices behind her.

She marched up the passageway with her guardian shadow, Stewart James, close behind. He was muttering into his walkie-talkie. She was just about to dash out the door when he jumped in front of her.

"Dr. Daniels. You're wanted back at the conference room."

"I am?" Erica smirked. "Well, that was quick."

She spun around and headed back. James swung the door open for her as she entered a rumbling room. Allan looked back at her and grinned.

The rooms fell silent on both sides of the video screen as they noticed her reappearance. Allan leaned into her and whispered, "Quite the shit disturber, aren't you?"

Erica ignored him and sank gracefully into the ridiculously plush chair as if she were the Queen of England. She did feel decidedly regal at the moment, having snapped her fingers and gotten instant gratification.

"You've recalled me?" she asked.

"Yes," said Dellows politely. "There's no need for hard feelings."

"Isn't there?"

"Oh course not. We admire your work a great deal. In fact, Dr. Albert, our expert in satellite imagery, has a proposal for you."

"A proposal?" She was waiting for the gift and she got a proposal. "What kind of proposal?"

"Ahem." A white-haired Goliath stood up at the far end of the table, meeting her gaze with warm eyes and sweeping his hand in front of him as if he were about to bow. "I would like to say what an honor it is to finally meet you, albeit not in person."

"Cut the chit chat. What proposal?"

He looked a little startled. "Yes, well...We have a problem in Antarctica."

"Antarctica?" It was Erica's turn to be shocked.

"It's right up your alley."

"Really?"

He caught her glare and looked down, the warmth seeping from his face. However, David Marsh was fighting hard to keep from laughing out loud. The scum!

"We have some recent photos from our Terra II satellite that you might find interesting. It was captured by our MODIS, our Moderate Resolution Imaging

Spectroradiometer that we use to monitor the earth's surface." He enlarged a photo on a screen behind him.

Erica squinted. "Very interesting blob."

"Ah, maybe if I sent it to your processor. One moment, please."

Erica looked at Allan who had a surprisingly benign expression on his face. She whispered, "Now I'm on hold."

He chuckled behind his hand.

"There, the images should be coming through now."

Erica turned to the computer set to one side of the screen. One of the three totem poles in the room was fidgeting with the keyboard. She should have left the room long ago. This whole proposal deal stank. Antarctica, indeed. Yet she was intrigued. They had caught her and she knew it.

The satellite image cleared and the trough of the Ross Sea in Antarctica became evident. Dellows swung the view around and focused on the sheer black and white peaks of the Transantarctic Mountains. It was difficult to discern anything but blur from the ice and snow at this height.

"What exactly am I seeing here?"

"If you would enhance the image with your zoom apparatus," he said blandly.

Erica focused and zoomed in on a section of the mountains just to the north of the Beardmore Glacier, an area a few hundred miles northwest of the South Pole. Beside a small peak that pierced the ice, the snow had an oddly discontinuous mass. It was as fractured and rippled as the sea ice in the ice pack that surrounded Antarctica. The steady flow of glacier ice from the vast ice sheet through the passes in the mountains to the ice shelf in the sea had been disrupted.

"Your ice sheet seems to be breaking up."

"Yes, it is. Unusually fractured."

"Is that from global warming?" she asked, tracing the chop with her fingers on the screen.

"Possibly, but I don't think so."

She looked up and met his eyes. They appeared troubled and he was shifting from one foot to the other. "Can you elaborate, please?"

"This is an absurd 'hot spot.' It's isolated too far in the continent to be connected with global warming."

"Could it be volcanic then?"

"More likely, although we know of no fracture zones in this particular area." He smiled, inviting her to draw the logical conclusion.

"So you need somebody to check it out."

"Yes." He nodded vigorously. "You would be the ideal candidate."

"Why do I get the idea this is the runner-up prize?"

"We need your expertise here," Dellows said.

"Really, Dr. Dellows. You didn't seem to need it a few minutes ago." He started to reply, but she waved him down. "Don't you have any other scientists down there that could investigate this? I'm sure there are volcanologists at McMurdo Station that are watching Mount Erebus."

"None with your celebrated abilities."

"I find that hard to believe."

A sad smile crept over Dellows' face. "Unfortunately, it's true. We could really use your help."

"So you want me to go to the most bitterly cold place on earth."

"I'm sure that doesn't bother you, considering your work in Alaska."

"The moon would be even colder," Marsh inserted.

Erica's eyes flashed. The SOB was so arrogant. He was enjoying every minute of this. "Yes, it would be," she snarled.

"We train some of our astronauts in Antarctica," said Dellows quickly. "It would be a good experience and be helpful in making our decision for the next science team after Dr. Marsh's year is up."

Erica sighed. She could see right through them. Holding out a bone as they threw the steak to the other dog. This assignment was as remote as they came. Yet she couldn't stem her curiosity. She'd never worked in the 'Deep South,' and she'd always been attracted to it. If she kept busy down there, it might keep her mind off what she'd missed.

"All right," she said. "I'll go."

She looked right at Marsh. He seemed more stunned than anyone, his eyes opened wide. But he also seemed a little relieved as his chest visibly heaved. So there had been a tug-of-war. And he had won, just like he always did.

"Very good," said Dellows. "We'll make preparations."

She nodded.

They signed off and the screen went blank. The three men, who had never introduced themselves, stood to leave. "Wait a minute," she said. Larry, Curly and Moe turned around. "Are you finished with the conference already?"

Larry smiled gently. "Dr. Daniels. We were here for your benefit. All the key players were already in Houston."

Erica frowned. "But I was only informed of the conference yesterday. Surely someone else was delayed as well."

"I don't know, ma'am. I only work here."

"I don't understand," said Erica. She was suddenly profoundly suspicious. "Why was I told so late? Why did they call me at all?"

The men shrugged and left.

Allan came from behind and put a hand on her shoulder. "I don't think they ever wanted you for the moon project, Erica. I think they used it as your draw."

She frowned. "Antarctica?"

He nodded.

"Well, I'll be darned." She turned to him, feeling the pressure of his hand on her arm. "And what's your role in all of this?"

"Me?"

She shook his hand off. "Yes, you? Why were you involved in a specially arranged video conference between me and the NASA elite team?"

"I have connections with the underworld."

"Obviously."

"And there may be something archaeological in this 'hotspot'."

"Really? In Antarctica?" Erica threw her head back and laughed. "It's a barren wilderness, Allan. Nothing lives there, or lived there, but ice and snow."

"Give me a chance," he said. He motioned her over to the computer terminal and called up the sat image again. This time he called the thermal data image as well. "Look at it," he said.

"A mountain peak surrounded by melting ice."

"Okay. Now, look closer."

She leaned toward the screen and studied the image. "It just a sloughing glacier."

"No. Look below the ice."

Erica frowned as she squinted at the image. The red glow had a distinctive signature in the blue heat sink of the frozen continent. "All right. It's a pyramid-shaped 'hotspot.'" He raised his tawny brows. "You're not suggesting…"

"It's hot within. It's not reflective."

"Volcano, Allan." It was hard not to be patronizing.

He smiled. "Okay. I won't ask you to suspend that rigid disbelief. But I'm not the only one who sees this. Why do you think I'm here?"

Her eyes opened wide, but he turned his back to her. He hit the x and the image faded. "I'll see you around," he said as he walked away.

"I doubt it," she said. "I'll be in Antarctica."

"I know." The door slammed shut.

Five

David Marsh sighed audibly when the video screen blanked. It had taken Dellows a good three minutes to alleviate the fear he felt in the room when Erica had announced her threat and vacated. There was nothing that terrified these people more than the press, especially when it became a 'woman's issue.'

The Chinese astronaut had made things worse. Jing-Mei Wong was suddenly, as if she hadn't noticed before, dismayed and shocked that NASA was only admitting one woman on the first team to inhabit the moon. They'd cited 'complications', but she wasn't buying it.

"What complications?" she'd demanded. "You've had women flying missions on the space shuttle for years and living on the space station for three month periods at a time. Why no women but me for this mission?"

"This is a year-long mission, Commander Wong," Dellows had responded, his feathers only slightly ruffled. "We don't need 'relationships' to develop, which inevitably leads to complications. There is very limited space in the habitat, so you will be sleeping next to the men, regardless of what happens."

Jing-Mei had scrunched her crescent-shaped eyes and scowled hideously at the science team leader. "I don't foresee any 'complications' that aren't generated by the 'men' in your team. Please reconsider the Daniels woman's application."

"I've considered it. Dr. Marsh is our geologist for this mission. However, I might have something to alleviate the poor woman's disappointment. Sam?"

He'd nodded to Dr. Albert who rose and smiled. "Antarctica?"

"Yes. It should grip her attention."

David had been taken aback by his smooth launch into this new worm he was dangling for Erica. He'd been surprised and pleased.

"Shouldn't you call Kennedy?" he'd asked.

Dellows had grinned smugly. "That's already been arranged."

David's eyebrows had arched in surprise. None of this had been an accident, but neither would she walk away with his position.

Jing-Mei, however, had maintained stormy silence throughout their exchange with the volcanologist. She scowled at him now as she swept up her dossier from the table.

"What are you looking at me for?" he asked, crossing his thick arms. His newly burgeoning muscles, from the extra fitness training NASA had prescribed, were straining at the thin material of his suit. "I was chosen long before she came into the picture. I didn't take anything away from her that was even hers to begin with."

"You're all the same," she grumbled. "Professional hypocrites."

David frowned and shook his head vigorously. "No, we're not... We played the game fair and square. Credentials and experience."

"Then why in the world did you invite her down here, huh? It had nothing to do with the moon, but you used that to get her here." She slammed her fist on the table. "You'd better be damn good, *misser*. I'll be counting on you up there," she pointed vigorously at the ceiling, "when there'll be nobody else to hold your hand."

The woman flung her hair behind her and stamped out of the room.

"Why do I get the blast?" said David innocently, although he felt a shiver slither down his spine. He turned to Dellows with wide blinking eyes. "It should have been *you* she put through the ringer. *You* chose the team."

Dellows shrugged. "Women are complicated. That's why I'd rather we left them out this time. Unfortunately, the Chinese Space Program didn't see it my way. I'm just glad Daniels took the bait."

"How did you know she would take it?" asked David, his left eyebrow cocked.

"I didn't. It was a chance I had to take."

David frowned. "It sounds almost as if you were planning this all along. What's really going on in Antarctica?"

The gray man shrugged. "No one really knows. But since we have the moon post squared away, we do need another expert to investigate. It might as well be your old friend."

"Friend? I'd hardly call her that."

"You were classmates, weren't you?"

"That was a long time ago. I haven't seen her since. And I really don't care to, either."

Dellow's eyes narrowed as he gazed at David. "It sounds like you might have been more than friends."

"Where did you get that impression?"

"By the way she looked at you. I could see the lava spewing out of her eyes."

David fiddled with his pen. "We have always sparred on a few issues. You've heard of friendly rivalry."

"Didn't look friendly to me."

"Well, it's only friendly if she wins. Too bad that doesn't happen very often." He smirked and his eyes crinkled, although the intensity beneath dispelled the casual tone of his voice.

"Interesting." Dellows swabbed his left eyebrow with his thumb, studying David from beneath hooded lids. "Correct me if I'm wrong, but I think you'd like to pummel her."

David shrugged. "Maybe. But the only way you can pummel a woman is in the field."

Dellows nodded. "I suppose. I still think there was more to it than academic rivalry. She looked like a woman scorned, if you ask me?"

David stood and gathered up his files. "She can't take a joke," he snapped.

Dellows frowned. "I guess this goes a little deeper than I thought."

"Drop it," said David.

"Already bounced away," he said holding up his hand. "I guess we should get on with it then. Are you ready to throw up some more?"

"You bet."

Dellows nodded and walked out of the room with brisk strides, a general in charge of the troops. David headed towards the door, one step behind, then stopped. The room had emptied out and there was only the dark wooden table, vacant chairs and the blank video screen. He walked back and tapped in the link to Kennedy Space Center. At first the screen remained white snow, then the conference room in the Space Center Headquarters materialized. The room looked empty until there was a flash of gold behind the computer console to one side of the screen. He tracked the movement, zeroing in on her wide blue eyes still absorbed in the image on the computer. Beside her was the sandy-haired man he'd glimpsed behind her at the conference table during their video link where he'd been following every exchange with hungry eyes. The man's hand was resting intimately on her shoulder. He was leaning into her and pointing to something on the screen. David felt some old flame of emotion he'd long since buried rise out of the grave. He punched volume, but got nothing through the connection but static. The intensity of her eyes when she looked at this man made him cringe.

What was he doing? He slammed the disconnect key on the console and watched her fade away. He closed his eyes, trying to wipe her from his mind. She was his archrival. She was always trying to outdo him, in everything. Well,

Dellows had taken care of that quite neatly. Now they were going to opposite ends of the spectrum, which would put her permanently out of his way. He would be celebrated as the first geologist to live on the moon. She would hopefully be forgotten in the vast underworld of ice. Maybe he'd never see her again.

A stab of pain lanced his head, making him grunt and stagger against the table. Massaging his scalp, he scowled at his own weakness, turned his back to the screen and walked away.

Six

Erica gritted her teeth as she waited outside the Neutral Buoyancy Lab at Johnson Space Center in Houston. After a briefing by Dr. Albert about all the strange thermal activity in Antarctica, and a meeting with Mr. Jenkins, NASA's Antarctica Programs' Director, a certain Commander Landry of the U.S. Navy had given her an interview, although it had seemed more like an interrogation. He was a short slim fellow of about fifty with piercing blue eyes and bleached blond hair. Despite his small stature, he seemed to tower over her, his lips like hardened clay and his eyes pinning her to her seat, obviously schooled in techniques of intimidation. At first, he'd examined her credentials in some detail, and then he'd asked her pointed questions about her security clearance, at which point she'd laughed.

"I'm a scientist," she said. "I'm not in the military. Anyway, I don't see what this has to do with a volcano."

"McMurdo is a secure site. The Navy is responsible to make sure it stays that way."

Erica had frowned. "I thought the Navy had left Antarctica fifteen years ago. Isn't the Air National Guard flying people down there now?"

Landry's response had been to scowl at her. "We still maintain a presence in the ocean. I just want to make sure that you're capable of surviving the brutal environment so we don't have to come in and rescue you."

Erica had scowled in return. "I've never needed a rescue before and I don't foresee ever needing one in the future. I'm quite strong, capable and professional. Now if this interview is over, I would like to start packing and get on the prearranged flight by noon."

He had let her go then, without a crack in his very severe face, but she hadn't left for her hotel yet. She'd prowled around until she found out where David Marsh was training.

So here she was, despite the voice in her head telling her to get out while she still could. She cracked the heavy metal door open and gazed in at the pool - 100 feet wide, 200 feet long and 40 feet deep. Marsh was cruising through the deep water in his bulky EMU (Extravehicular Mobility Unit) suit beside a mockup of the solar array the team would be putting together on the moon.

Erica closed her eyes. The anger was bubbling to the surface again, and she had to suppress it. Talking to him would be useless if she lost her temper. She closed the door and waited. Fifteen minutes went by before the door cranked open and David walked out in his orange moon suit, dripping wet and weighted down by the bulky material, but still wearing his usual cocky grin. It washed off the second he saw her.

"What are you doing here?" he asked, his fingers tightening on the helmet he cradled in one arm.

"Didn't you hear? I'm your backup." She couldn't help it. "If anything should happen to you... You'd better be careful."

"Don't threaten me," he said with a sneer. "I know you. You're not the violent type."

"You don't know a thing about me anymore," said Erica. "But that's not why I'm here."

"Then why are you here? I thought you'd be halfway to Antarctica by now."

Erica ground her teeth into her lower lip. She tried not to look at those intense green eyes that used to mean so much to her. She wanted to slap him right here and now. Instead she blinked and touched his arm. "I don't want to fight again. I just wanted to ask you something."

"It was an opportunity," he said, tossing his flaming hair out of his face. "You would have done the same."

Erica paused. Was he talking about now, or before? It shouldn't make a difference, but somehow it did. Before he'd been young and insecure, trying desperately to make a name for himself. Now he was well-established in NASA's echelon and shouldn't have to play dirty tricks to get ahead. "What did you do?" she asked.

He blinked and looked away. "Nothing," he mumbled.

"Right. Well, whatever it was, it had the desired effect, didn't it? You're in the most coveted position a geologist could hope for. Exploring extraterrestrial worlds. So I would like you to do me this one favor."

His eyes flashed. "Why should I…"

"For what we once had, before your conniving ego got in the way."

"Don't…"

She held up her hand. Although his chin still jutted out defiantly, she could see the harsh lines in his face melt somewhat. "Aristarchus."

"It's a crater."

"Of course it's a crater. It's the brightest crater on the moon. And it had some strange activity in 1963. Elongated pink streaks changed to ruby red. It could be volcanism. Recent volcanism."

David rolled his eyes. "The moon is a dead rock. There hasn't been any activity there in over a billion years."

"Maybe 800 million that we know of. The Lichtenburg crater?"

"It's pure speculation because of the relative determination of its age by some hotshot volcanologists. There's no physical proof."

Erica smiled. "Yet. That's what you're going there for. To find out."

"I'm going there to test my 'oxygen from moon rocks' scheme and put it into production. I'm going there to set up a functioning base where people can live."

"It's always about you, isn't it? *Your* opportunities. *Your* schemes. Listen, you're going there to further *our* knowledge of the universe. You're going there as a scientist first, an inhabitant second, and an opportunist last. But I don't care about your motives anymore. I just want you to check Aristarchus for me. Please."

David tilted his head. A sly grin spread over his face. "Maybe if you give me kiss."

"Over my dead body!"

"For science' sake." He leaned toward her, his breath teasing tendrils of hair from her nape.

She leaned back. "Why do you always have to turn everything into a sexual overture? I was asking for a favor, one scientist to another."

"You were the one that put the personal spin on it. For old time's sake? Come on. We did have good times."

"We did, until you ruined it. Now will you do this or not?"

David rolled his eyes and straightened his shoulders, crossing his arms over his muscular chest. "Fine. I'll check it out. But if I find anything - which I won't - it'll be a little hard to reach you down under."

"You'll find a way," she said. "You always do."

She was about to swing around and leave when she did something that surprised even herself. She reached out and grasped his hand in her own. "Good luck."

Erica dropped it before he could return a squeeze. She breezed down the hallway as quickly as she could. Escape was essential, before the loss really hit her. Of course she told herself it was the loss of the mission, but she couldn't help but throw over her shoulder, "Be careful."

Seven

The flight to New Zealand was long, boring and thankfully turbulence-free. Erica had queried the extensive flight plan drawn up by the Air National Guard consultant at NASA. Wouldn't it be faster to head down the Atlantic to Chile and cross over to the South Pole?

"You'll need extreme weather training at McMurdo," Major Ellis had said.

"I've been in Alaska for two years now."

"Ain't Antarctica, ma'am. No one gets in without the training. Need to know how to get around on ice, glaciers and such."

Erica had choked at that remark. "What do you think is in Alaska?"

He'd just shrugged. "Freak storms happen all the time. It's dangerous down there."

Sighing, Erica had glanced at the news flitting across the major's television in the corner of the room – car crashes, murders, fires. "It's dangerous here."

"Commander Landry said you might be heading to Vostok. It's pretty high up there, and bloody cold."

"Vostok? Nobody mentioned the Russian science station. It's a little far from my 'hotspot.'"

The major had just shrugged. "That's what I've been told, ma'am. You'll have to take it up with the people down there."

"Why do I get the feeling people aren't telling me everything that they know?"

The major gave her a cold smile at that point and nodded. She was dismissed. This was a relief. She sure hoped that was her last brush with the military. She was New Zealand bound.

Christchurch, lush though it was, reminded her a little bit of Anchorage from its temperate climate to the backdrop of mountains coupled with some down-to-earth folks. From the plane she was ushered to the CDC – Clothing Distribution Center - where they threw packets of extreme weather gear at her. Snow boots, thick and thin socks, thermal underwear, light fleece, moleskin trousers, a windbreaker layer that consisted of a bib and coveralls and a standard red parka with NSF stitched on the sleeve. She was about to turn away when she was hailed back.

"Wait a minute. Don't forget these." The kiwi behind the counter bent down and extracted more outerwear from some hidden shelves. He came up with another armload, silver-blue eyes twinkling. There were hats, a fleece headover, thin and thick pairs of gloves, goggles (dark lenses because it was summer in Antarctica and there was persistent and retinal-searing sun) and sunscreen. She was at the airport with her mountain of gear, gazing up at the Air National Guard's Hercules LC-130 that truly reminded her of a god, only an ancient weather-beaten one, when a flight engineer gave her the bad news.

"Didn't you hear?" The man was short, stout, with rather merry rounded cheeks and a dazzling smile.

She raised her eyebrows. "Hear?"

"The flight's been delayed for another day."

"Bad weather?"

"No. We're taking on some more passengers. NASA had some final debriefing to do with them, I guess. We're flying out at ten hundred hours tomorrow."

Erica nodded. "What do I do with all this?" She pointed at her gear.

"I'll load it for you. No need to cart it around." He was already gathering up her supplies before she could give a halfhearted protest. These kiwis were a friendly sort.

"Thanks," she said. "Now I need to find a hotel."

"We use the 'Church Inn.' It's about five blocks east of here. I'd be happy to show you…"

"No, no. You've done quite enough already." Erica smiled gratefully. "I'm sure I can find it on my own." With that, she thanked him again and left the airport.

Christchurch was a pristine, decidedly British city bordering the ocean and a broad alluvial plain that extended to the Southern Alps in the west. She passed some cleanly coifed golf courses and superbly flowered gardens around neat and tidy terraced housing projects. The particular eye for detail and the obsessively prim and proper maintenance of the vista reminded her of pictures from an English Town and Country magazine. The sweep of the plain beyond the airport shadowed by the looming mountains in the background was not so much like Alaska as the Canadian prairies with the Rocky Mountains as its guardian. Despite the small splash of civilization in the middle of the South Island, New Zealand had a raw rugged beauty that was rapidly disappearing from this overpopulated world.

The weather was definitely crisper than Florida, but she still sweltered a bit under her light jacket - tossed it off and tied it around her waist. She found the inn with little difficulty – the frontage consisted of a two-story stone structure with a peaked roof and neatly trimmed hedges on either side of the path. The rooms were in two separate buildings in the back divided in the middle by a restaurant. Erica's room was immaculate and austere – a simple bed and night table with crisp sheets and a wrinkle-free floral bedspread - but certainly comfortable enough compared to a tent, which she'd used on more than one occasion during her excursions in the field. She soaked in a warm bubble bath, probably the last one for many months. After the bath, her stomach rumbled in near seismic proportions. The bland, overcooked airline food hadn't sustained her for long. She considered room service, but then thought better of it and slipped into her only semi-formal dress - a slinky black silk V-neck that showed off her firm breasts. The restaurant in the inn was too casual for her chic attire, so she sauntered down the street to an Italian haven with a bar and dance floor attached.

The place was dimly lit and classy - tables draped with rust-colored tablecloths and matching napkins stuffed in tall crystal water glasses. There was a long bar down the right side of the establishment, mostly filled with the after-five crowd of men and women wearing that 'thank God, it's Friday' look. The host bowed obsequiously as she floated through the door, his trim dark moustache twitching as he gazed at her from beneath hooded eyelids. It seemed that all the kiwi males at the bar had turned their heads as she entered. One dark-haired businessman was nudging his mate. She tried not to laugh. So she still had it, despite the desolation, the 'weathered scientist look', as Rocheford would say. She reserved a table for two – hopeful, she supposed – then sidled up to the bar and ordered a gin and tonic.

"May I get that for you?" asked a kiwi with jet hair and a cocky little smile.

She shook her head. "Thanks anyway. I'm waiting for someone."

He nodded and turned away. She could have kicked herself. He was attractive and self-possessed. What was her problem? He would certainly take the edge off her loneliness.

The hostess came by and led her to her table. "Shall I look out for your companion?" she asked.

"I'll look out for him, thank you."

She nodded and turned away. A half-hour went by. She finally decided to order. What was she waiting for anyway?

As her soup and salad arrived, so did a drink of champagne.

"I didn't order this."

"The gentleman at the bar did." The perky waitress, with the name Susan printed on her nametag, nodded to the dark recess of the bar.

"He doesn't give up, does he?"

"Shall I ask him to join you?" She winked. She'd seen right through Erica's game.

"All right."

Perky Susan disappeared into the nether regions of the bar. The man she spoke to got up. Only he wasn't the kiwi with the black hair and the sure smile that she'd encountered before. He was sandy-haired and green-eyed and she already knew him, although she wished she didn't.

"Hey, mate," he said cheerfully, as he slid into the seat across from her.

Erica flushed blood red. "W…what are you doing here?" she sputtered.

"Same as you, darling. Adventure down under."

"You're the person they held up the Hercules for?"

"One and the same." He winked and rolled his shoulders.

Erica hid her face in her glass. How could this be happening?

"Like the dress," he said.

She could feel his eyes creep over her. She shivered.

"Little drafty though, isn't it?"

"I'm not taking you with me," she growled.

"I believe it's out of your hands."

"You have absolutely no experience with extreme weather conditions."

"That's why I need a guide." He smirked.

"You bastard."

He smiled and touched her hand. "Prude."

She snatched it away from him. "I am not a prude."

"Really?" He looked at her massaging her hand. "Name calling aside, don't you think it would be a good idea if you got to know me before you made all these raw assumptions? We're going to be spending a lot of time together. It would be nice if we got along."

"I don't intend to spend any time with you."

"Indeed. How do you intend to avoid it, since we're both headed for the same science station?" He cocked his eyebrows in an irritatingly superior fashion.

"We'll see about that." Erica hauled out her cell phone and speed dialed her NASA direct line.

"Mr. Jenkins, please," she asked the receptionist at NASA headquarters.

The woman seemed quite put out by her call. "It's four o'clock in the morning, ma'am."

"I don't care how late it is, you need to get him for me. This is of vital importance." Erica tapped her toes on the smooth tiles. Allan sat back, crossed his arms and grinned. He was such a self-assured SOB.

Finally NASA's Antarctica Programs Director came on the line. "Who is it?" he asked in a sleep-slurred voice.

"Good evening, sir. It's Erica Daniels."

"Dr. Daniels, do you realize what time it is?"

"Yes, I know," said Erica apologetically. "We're not exactly in the same time zone, but this is very important. You've sent along some amateur archaeologist as my sidekick and I don't think it's funny." Her eyes burned right through Allan but he didn't flinch.

Jenkins grumbled something about the archeologist being a consultant. He yawned loudly in her ear.

Erica frowned. "Consultant? I hardly think he can consult on volcanic activity."

"There are other bizarre occurrences concerning this 'hotspot' that he might be able to assist you on."

"Other bizarre occurrences? Why haven't I been apprised…"

He cut her off. "You will get a full briefing when you arrive. Now let me get back to sleep!"

"Sir, I don't think he's capable of scientific…"

"Dr. Daniels!"

"Look, this man isn't even a real scientist." She continued to protest but he rebuffed her at every turn. "No, I haven't checked his credentials. But his reputation… I don't care if NASA's satisfied, I'm not. I can't get along…" There was harsh click. "Sir? Sir? Shit!" She carefully folded the phone and slipped it back into her purse. She didn't look up, couldn't look up.

Allan leaned forward and lifted her chin with his index finger. "I'm really not that bad a chap, once you get to know me."

Erica scowled. "Well, I guess I don't have a choice. But don't expect me to save your ass when you fall down a crevasse or some other stupid thing."

"Wouldn't dream of it." His smile was so smug Erica wanted to punch his lights out.

She couldn't stand it another minute. "I'm going back to my hotel."

"You haven't finished your dinner." He took a bite of her crusty bread and chewed contentedly.

"I seem to have lost my appetite."

"Pity. I wanted to gaze at that lovely angry flush one more minute."

The flames rose again. She just couldn't help herself. The toe of her pump thumped into his calf.

"Humph." He spit out the bread. "Hellcat!"

Erica spun around and ran out of the restaurant.

"See you tomorrow," he called after her. Despite the quip, she thought she heard an edge to his voice. She hoped it was pain.

Eight

Cathy Jones started at the abrupt pounding of fists on her thin dormitory door in McMurdo Station. She swiped tears from her damp face with a sleeve and stood up from the narrow twin bed.

"Who is it?" she asked tentatively. She really didn't want to see anyone right now.

"It's me. Jamal. Open up, Cathy. It's not over 'till it's over."

Cathy shuffled to the locked door. "Go away," she croaked.

"No, sugar. Gottlieb told me to get you. We have news."

"What?" Cathy quickly unbolted the door and flung it open. "What news? Did they hear from Jimmy?"

Jamal shook his thin braids and smiled rather grimly. "Not yet. But they're sending us another team. This one's coming through NASA."

The ray of hope that had lit up her eyes faded just as quickly as it had come. "What good will that do? Another team. And then another. And another. How many more before we just give them all up for dead?"

"We don't know that for sure," said the geologist firmly. His eyes were practically melting with empathy, yet there was a spark of hope in them as well.

Cathy ground her lower lip between her teeth. She wanted to grab that hope and hang on as if it were a life raft. But she couldn't. It was pointless. "Don't you get it? We heard them screaming."

"That doesn't mean they're dead. They may be injured. Their radio might have been damaged. This new team has a crack volcanologist with them. And some other specialists. They're going to find Jimmy and Tom, Jeanna… all of them."

Cathy scowled at him. "Jimmy was a *crack* volcanologist."

Jamal's eyes widened. "Cathy, I didn't mean…"

"And what do you mean by 'other specialists.' We have almost as many scientists down here as they have at NASA."

"I didn't mean scientists."

Cathy blinked. "What did you mean?"

"I can't get into it right now. Let's just say you'll be well protected." He grasped her arm and started to pull her toward the door.

Cathy wrenched her arm away. "Did you just say *I'll* be well protected?"

Jamal looked at his empty hand for a second, then lifted his head to face her. "Oh, didn't I tell you? Gottlieb wants you to be their guide. It's only fair, since Jimmy was your…"

"You can say it, Jamal. Lover. Partner. Companion. Jimmy was everything to me, and I'm going to get him back." Jimmy's face floated in front of her now, an angular face framed by curly salt and pepper hair and a smile that never quit. Despite a wind-chill of -50°F, he could warm her heart just by looking at her.

Jamal had clasped her arm again, more gently this time. "You bet, we are. We don't give up on a 'man down' in this godforsaken continent. We're going to bring him back." He thrust her bulky parka into her hands and tugged her toward the door again. Cathy blinked back tears as she followed him down the long hall. Jimmy had given her something that no one ever had. Hope.

Like everyone else in Antarctica who wasn't a laser-vision scientist, she'd come here to escape the real world. It's what she'd spent her life doing. Climbing the highest peaks, playing survivor in the wilderness – anything to get away from the nine-to-five job. Anything to get away from a mother who loved her to death and clipped her wings to keep her safe. She'd been twenty-two years old when her friends had invited her on her first white-water rafting experience. Her mother would have locked her in her room if she had known, but she'd lived on campus then, in her third year of college. It had been so exhilarating, plunging through teeth-rattling rapids, feeling the spray on her face, and facing danger with the same bravado as her father had. After that experience, there was no turning back. She'd walked away from her mother, from a lucrative teaching position, from everything that had kept her penned. Yet in all the time since she'd broken away, she had never really loved anyone. That was, until Jimmy.

Jim Albright wasn't like the other men she'd met. Where they were determined to take care of her, Jimmy had always given her space. He was wild and carefree; he seemed to love living on the edge and wasn't about to rob her of the same experience. Their first date had been a trek up to the top of Mount Erebus where he'd danced like a crazy man around a boiling cauldron. Maybe he was a little insane, but that was the heart of McMurdo. You were either very dedicated or a little crazy to work in the coldest place on the planet.

Of course, Jimmy hadn't always been so light-hearted and sparkling. He'd told her after one of their uninhibited mind-blowing sexual encounters that he was a coward. She'd laughed at him until finally his very serious face came into focus through the tears spilling down her cheeks.

"How can you say that? You work on the brim of an active volcano. You risk your life every day."

"It's called escapism," he had explained.

"From what?" She'd eyed him uncomfortably.

"From life, Cathy. I used to hide in a bottle. Now I hide on the coldest continent on earth, traipsing around the deadliest mountains to keep my mind off of life."

"Jimmy, life isn't so bad."

"Isn't it?" He'd lifted his salted eyebrows and captured her chin in his hand. "I watched my wife – a vibrant intelligent woman – shrivel up into a husk. A pain-wracked skeleton eaten up with cancer. She begged me to kill her. I was too cowardly even to do that."

Cathy had tried to look away, but his hand held her fast. "That's horrible," she'd muttered.

"I'm not saying it's all bad, but it certainly isn't all good, like I pretend it is. Like you pretend it is, but you're hiding too."

"What do you mean? Nothing that terrible has happened to me."

"Hasn't it?"

It was strange how he could always read her so well. She'd told him then about her father, and her smothering mother and he'd understood. It seemed there was no one on earth that understood as well as Jimmy. He couldn't be lost to her. Life couldn't be that cruel again.

The jarring cold brought her back from the past. Jamal propelled her out into the main thoroughfare of McMurdo leaving the jumble of prefabricated metal buildings of the dorms behind. Cathy hunkered down in her parka; the wind screaming around the structures had made her face numb already. Everything around her was dark – the station, its background hills – composed of porous volcanic rock with only a patchy mantle of snow – and it was etched even darker by the white light of the sun. The sun rarely slept in Antarctica at this time of year – just a few gloomy hours around midnight and then it was streaming through the swirls of snow, blinding anyone without a good pair of sunglasses or goggles. Cathy raised a hand to shield her eyes as they walked down the main street, which was hardly a street but a gray uneven lane with the dust of crushed basalt coating everything and the tripwires of the base underfoot. Water and sewer pipes crisscrossed and electrical wires sent feeder lines to every stalwart structure, making walking a hazard if you weren't looking where you were going. They remained exposed because nothing could be buried in the frozen ground. Normally Cathy would have looked away from the scarred peninsula up to the majestic cone of the volcano, but not today. She couldn't look at it anymore without feeling the ache of loss and an overwhelming emptiness inside.

Jamal led her solemnly toward the Chalet, the administrative headquarters of McMurdo where Gottlieb was assembling personnel in preparation for the arrival of the new team. As they approached, Cathy glanced over at the Helicopter Hangar that was just adjacent to the administrative building. There seemed to be a bustle of activity there, pilots shuffling copters off the pad and into the hangar.

"What's up with the helos?" she asked.

Jamal tossed his head back and glanced up. "Oh, that. They're just making room."

"Room for what? We'll need a Hercules to get us to the site. We don't need more helicopters."

Jamal shrugged. "Boss's orders. I'm just the lackey. Have no idea what up with that."

Cathy squinted at him suspiciously. "You're no lackey, Mr. Washington. You're one of those beakers that thinks he knows everything. And if he doesn't, he finds out, just like Jimmy. Now tell me, why do we need more helicopters?"

Jamal smiled and whispered. "For the military escort."

"Ah, now I'm getting the picture."

"Ya, well, don't let on that I told you. It's supposed to be 'classified' or some such idiocy."

Cathy smiled. Most of these scientists felt the same contempt for 'proper channels' as she did. They drew up to The Chalet – a lodge that boasted a little more style than prefabricated huts – even though it was imitation Swiss. It was situated on a small hill overlooking the helo pads and hangar, which gave Cathy an unobstructed view of the flurry of chopper activity. The military. She shuddered. It should make her feel safer, but it didn't.

The silver letters glittered beneath the A-shaped roof of the Chalet: National Science Foundation. She entered the building with a confused jumble of feelings – hope, fear and the unflagging surety that the almighty quest for science had just uncorked a more deadly volcano than even Jimmy could have imagined.

Nine

David Marsh staggered out of the T-38 training jet at Ellington Airfield - just outside of Houston - still gripping his vomit bag. His face had a teal tinge to it that seemed to match the cactus near the landing strip. The pilot, Carl Edwards, grinned as he jumped down from the needle-nosed supersonic aircraft in that cocky manner that all pilots seemed to have and clapped him on the back.

"Good show, buddy," he said. "You held it in this time."

David grimaced and bit down on his lower lip to subdue the roiling in his gut. "Ya, great," he mumbled.

Edwards winked and swaggered back toward the NASA hangar. David hadn't made it two steps further before Dr. Dellows intercepted him in front of the formation of jets that were looming over his shuddering body like a pack of laughing hyenas.

Dellows eyed David's pallid face. "Nothing like the feel of g's, right Marsh?"

"Sure. Ya," said David. He took a deep breath and his head seemed to clear. "Do you always come out to the field to check on your initiates?"

"Just the green ones." He chuckled. "Actually, there's been a rumble up on the station."

"Rumble? What do you mean by 'rumble?'"

"Moonquake," said Dellows.

David frowned and licked his lips. "Well, it couldn't have registered much. A firecracker would create more seismic activity than a moonquake."

"It was 5.9."

"That's not possible," said David adamantly. "It was probably a solar flare, or a meteor strike."

"Most likely. We didn't track anything with our satellite up there, but it could have hit the far side. Our experts are searching for an anomaly as we speak."

David squinted at him. "Does this mean that we're delaying the launch?"

Dellows shook his head. "There are two people already up there. They'll let us know if we need to abort. Besides, if there is some kind of seismic activity, I want my geologist there to investigate."

"I'll certainly look into it," said David, his eyes straying to the horizon. Seismic activity was not his specialty.

Dellows nodded. "Aren't you a little bit nervous?"

"Are you kidding? I live for danger." David winked, although another swirl of queasiness made him grasp his gut.

"Right," said Dellows, his voice edged with doubt. "Well, I have to get ready for the launch. Good luck." He nodded and walked toward the parking lot.

David headed back to the hangar, the wind buffing his face and washing away the nausea.

The thrill of his approaching mission was rippling through his body. There was just a benign stroke of anxiety regarding the moonquake, but not enough to take away the exhilaration. He would be the first geologist to live outside the earth's atmosphere. He'd beaten them all – all those clamoring classmates who'd foreseen brilliant futures as they pitched their theories at University of California in Berkeley. Erica had revealed all her dreams to him, as she lay curled up in his arms after a raging night of sex in her dorm room. They'd stared up at the moon and stars. She wanted to walk upon another planet's soil and explore the volcanoes and craters. That was Erica. A need for adventure. A life of exploration. He had to settle for 'melting rocks in a laboratory,' as she put it. Well, not now. He would never play second fiddle to her again. No matter how much he had enjoyed the sex – something he couldn't put out of his mind after seeing her nice round butt and her firm breasts thrusting through a molded T-shirt outside the NBL – he had never enjoyed her superiority in every class, on every trip into the field. It had continued afterward too, in her pursuit of the new asteroid impact field of study. Every time he picked up a science journal, or even a 'hard news' magazine, there would be her sun-hardened face, smiling at him as she one-upped him again. Not this time, though. This time *he* would be the one pictured on every newsworthy magazine on the planet. *He* would be the first geologist to experience the minimal gravity of the moon and the weightlessness of space. *He* would walk upon her treasured craters and cradle the rich basaltic rock and impact-melt breccias in his arms. *He* would live the life that she had only dreamed of.

David remembered as a boy how he'd failed his father so many times. How could he miss the puck in that hockey game? How could he strike out in Little League? How could he not win that foot race? He'd get a cuff on the side of the head, or a dressing down as soon as he got home. That was until he found a way to win. When they turned the corner in the track, a little nudge or misplaced foot and his opponent would go down. Wander a little bit onto the base and the ball would hit him – he'd get a walk. If he couldn't quite reach that pass with his hockey stick, then neither could the other guy, with a slight hook or a sly slash. He started to win, but it still wasn't good enough for his father.

"Damn boy will never amount to anything."

It made him more determined than ever to succeed. When his science fair project of rock specimens just wasn't as cool as Bill's oscilloscope tracing the jagged EEG's of various animals, he just had to pull out some wires when the other boy went for a snack. It was easy to win, if you knew the game. When it came to science, ideas were the game, and it was easy to steal ideas. His dad wasn't frowning or yelling at him now. He'd made it to the big leagues. And what had it cost him? A few scruples. One woman whom he hadn't really loved. Not really.

"I hope you enjoy the ice, Erica," he whispered.

A tall slim pilot sauntered past and raised an eyebrow.

Oh, oh. Better stop talking to himself. They'd hold him back for a psychiatric assessment. He grinned. Nothing was going to stop him now. Erica, the one thorn in his side, was off to the remotest destination on the planet. He was heading for the adventure of a lifetime. There was no more need for deals with the devil.

Ten

The morning of October 20th Erica was at the Hercules LC-130 bright and early. The hollow inside the aircraft resembled the hangar of the airport in size as she made her way up the ramp and through the pressurized doors at the rear. Her luggage she cast behind a net in the cargo hold along the side of the aircraft, before she headed toward the front and the tiny canvas seats bolted to aluminum tubing and resting against the raw walls of the plane. The middle of the Hercules was littered with olive and tan seabags loaded with McMurdo-bound equipment and strapped to the floor, which left very little legroom between the seats and the cargo. Two kiwi helicopter pilots, one tall and lanky with frizzled blond hair, the other short and robust with a brush-cut of thin chestnut spikes, and both dressed in khaki pants and leather flying jackets, occupied the rear seats. They were probably on their way to New Zealand's Scott Base just east of McMurdo Station. As she made her way past, they smiled in synchronicity, hopped to their feet and graciously squeezed her hand. Kiwis! They were such friendly folks. She slipped into a seat in front of them, facing the opposite wall and far enough away so she didn't have to strike up a conversation – she wanted to go over the geological maps of the area. She still had an hour before take-off so she flipped up her laptop and pulled up a map of the Ross Ice Shelf and Ross Island. She put her mind to memorizing the topographic relief so she hardly noticed someone slip into the seat beside her.

"Studying the volcano?" he asked, jolting her out of her concentration. Allan grinned, his canines glinting wolfishly.

Erica glared back. "I don't remember you asking if this seat was taken."

"I presumed, since you're traveling alone..."

"You presume too much sometimes."

"You know, some people are beautiful when they're angry. They have this rosy glow about them. You, on the other hand, my dear, have deeper weathering."

"I should have kicked you harder," said Erica.

Allan shrugged and buckled his seat belt.

Erica snapped her laptop closed and stood. "I think I'll take a seat further forward."

"Suit yourself," said Allan.

She made as if to pass by him, but he stubbornly refused to move his legs aside. Erica gritted her teeth, and was about to kick him anyway, when a strange group of new arrivals tramped through the plane. There were twelve men: brush-cut or bald, ranging from Asian or Italian features to muscle-bound Swede with a swagger that labeled them undoubtedly American. They wore white parkas and leggings, carried M16 assault rifles cradled in their hands and their faces were grim and intent as they took seats all around her. Erica blinked twice. The men looked decidedly military, but white Gortex panels concealed their rank insignia and any flags they might have worn on their shoulders. Two men stopped right beside the seats she and Allan were occupying. There was a tall, rigid sort of fellow of African American descent and a muscular lackey with short spiked blond hair.

"Dr. Daniels, I presume."

"Yes?"

"I'm Commander Staten, United States Navy. I've been asked to accompany you on your expedition as a military liaison."

"By whom?" Her face crinkled, etching those fine weathered lines.

"Admiral Johnson."

Erica frowned even more. "Is he Dellows flunky?"

"Excuse me, ma'am." The Commander's face flushed a deeper shade. "The Admiral is nobody's flunky. He deals with all Antarctica operations and he felt that the situation might be too dangerous to proceed without an escort."

"Dangerous? I've dealt with more danger than you can imagine, Commander. There's nothing the earth can hurl at us that could frighten me. Unless there's more to this than just a volcano."

The Commander grinned enigmatically. "There's far more dangers than you can imagine in Antarctica."

Furrows tracked Erica's brow as she stared at the man. What could possibly warrant a group of soldiers accompanying a scientific expedition? The National Science Foundation ran hundreds of these during the summer months. They were certainly equipped to deal with Antarctica's 'dangers.' "I don't understand what the Navy has to do with this expedition. In fact, I was under the impression that the Navy had pulled out of Antarctica in 1999."

Staten's dark face grew even darker. His eyes narrowed. "Although this is no longer a military installation, we still maintain a hand in it for emergency situations. You'll need briefing, and a military liaison should we need to call an emergency EVAC by military personnel."

"I was under the impression we would have an NSF guide for this operation," Allan interjected.

"The National Science Foundation guides do not have my authority, Dr. Rocheford. That is your name, isn't it?"

Allan nodded stiffly.

"I was wondering why you were listed as 'specialist' for this expedition. Perhaps you can enlighten me."

"Oh," said Erica, smiling. "He's the archeologist."

Commander Staten tilted his head.

"You know, in case we find any dinosaur bones, or lost civilizations. That sort of thing." TWO DIFFERENT FIELDS VOLCANO GIRL.

"I thought that Antarctica had no relics to find."

Allan opened his mouth. "My good Commander, you would be amazed…"

The jet engines screamed at that moment, cutting him off. Erica grinned and gave him a thumbs-up. Commander Staten shrugged and settled into the seat alongside them on

Allan's left, his flunky taking the last one open, effectively eliminating her chances of escaping Allan Rocheford. She scowled and plunked back down in her seat.

Allan leaned over as the Hercules lurched forward and screamed in her ear. "You're caustic, lady, but I like you anyway."

Erica leaned toward him, nearly meeting his eyebrows. "I don't like you. In fact, I'd rather sit beside the Commander."

Allan winced. "Low blow." He sat back, curled up in his overheated fleece and parka, and went to sleep.

Eleven

The seven-hour flight was the longest of her life. The scream of the jet engines made conversation impossible - the one blessing – but it couldn't remove the man beside her, who alternated between sleep and perusal of her. She suffocated in her parka, broiling and freezing in the undulating waves of hot and cold that rippled through the inadequately insulated Hercules. There was no view except cloud and sea, and the worst was contemplating weeks, if not months, in the company of these irritatingly chauvinistic men.

The Navy men made her uncomfortable to say the least. They sat rigidly in their seats, looking straight ahead – unfortunately that meant that the two across from her were looking directly at her. Of the others, occasionally the gaze of one or two of them would drift her way as well. The look in their eyes made her shiver. They had focused, icy, ready-for-death or ready-to-deal-death countenances. The odd man would caress the steel carapace of his gun in an obscenely affectionate way. Guns. She shivered. They were outlawed in Antarctica. Then why was a group of men – Navy, so they said, yet covering up their insignias - carrying weapons onto the peaceful continent? What, indeed, weren't they telling her?

It was a relief when she finally drifted off into blessed sleep for a few hours. She was abruptly awoken by a prickling sensation that ran down the left side of her body. She blinked and found the vulture awake again, looking at her like she was a delectable carcass. Finally she typed out a few words on her computer and handed it to him.

"What the hell are you looking at?"

He smiled and typed: "I like a room with a view."

She scowled and wrenched back her laptop when she noticed him pointing at the porthole window behind her.

The clouds were wisping away in delicate threads and she could clearly make out snow-blanketed ranges that rivaled any she had ever seen in the north. Scalloped sea ice, like still-shot waves, had been sculpted by the relentless winds blasting off the coast leaving an undulating landscape of the purest lily-white. Soon, even the curdled mass of the pack ice solidified as the plane drew up on a majestic scene that had hooked her from the time she was a six-year-old child. The volcano. Mount Erebus, a vanilla-capped sundae with dark runnels of chocolate sauce down its slopes, was a twelve-thousand-foot stratovolcano with a persistent convecting lava lake at its summit. It was known for its continuous Strombolian eruptions, consisting of lava bombs and lava flows and occasionally small ash eruptions as well. Right now, the volcano was calm, simply venting steam into the frosty air over its rosy summit.

Mount Erebus rose out of center of Ross Island, essentially drawing an ebony pocket of land out of a wilderness of ice. In fact, the entire make-up of Ross Island was volcanic basalt. Banking over the reaching fingers of ice and crystal slopes as glaciers tumbled slowly into the sea from black cliffs, the Hercules began to descend toward the jutting tongue of the island called Hut Point Peninsula. The plane circled, making a flyby of McMurdo Station before landing. The buildings Erica could glean from the distant view were low rectangular boxes with green and white roofs scattered over the dark basaltic rock of the island. Between each building was a web of crisscrossed pipes and wires connected to each other in a chaotic mix.

Allan yelled in her ear, "Breathtaking, isn't it?"

Erica looked at him queerly. "I take it you mean Erebus."

"What else would I ask a volcanologist about, a frontier town?"

She nodded. "She's a beauty. I wouldn't say that about McMurdo. We humans seem to be so good at marring nature."

Allan shrugged.

The plane nosed down and headed for the compacted snow runway on William's Ice Field – the main airport for the island. When it hit the ground there was hardly a jolt; then it skidded gracefully to a stop on its landing skis. As the engines wound down, Erica could finally hear her own breathing. "Wow," she screamed, putting her hand to her face the instant she'd said it. The Navy men were staring at her openly.

Allan chuckled. "It is good to hear once again. But what you said about marring nature... Not every culture was efficient at it. The Egyptians often enhanced the sublimity of nature. Their predecessors even more so."

Erica looked at him sideways as she started packing up her laptop and personal gear. "The cavemen, you mean? Or was it Adam and Eve?"

"My dear Erica, you dismiss the Atlanteans so easily. I'll make you bite your tongue."

"I'd rather you bit yours." Erica grinned as she tossed her bag over her shoulder. She brushed past him and got in line behind the kiwis to disembark the plane. The aft platform was lowered allowing bluish polar light to flood the interior creating an aura around the passengers. Erica glanced backward and saw Commander Staten standing stiffly, holding his briefcase and nothing else – which seemed ludicrous considering his Michelan Man outfit. He was staring at her, obviously eavesdropping, and made no attempt to join in the conversation. This made her even more uneasy. Albeit he had military training, but his actions smelled of espionage. She had so many suspicious characters on this trip it was a bit like a Ludlum novel. She would have to watch her back.

When she stepped off the plane, the wind hit her like a ten-ton truck. The chill seeped through her so-called impenetrable parka and left her numb already. The pilot had announced it was a balmy –10 degrees Fahrenheit, but had failed to mention the wind-chill that put it at about – 40. It was still welcome to the chill she'd felt inside the aircraft from the icy gazes of the Navy men, and her trips up the glaciers in Alaska had further prepared her for extreme cold. It would only take a few days to adjust. However, she sorely enjoyed watching Allan's face as he stepped off the plane. The wind sucked the color right out of him. His whole body cringed into itself, seeking desperately to conserve warmth.

"You really think the Atlanteans were penguins?" she asked over the whistle of the wind.

Allan shrugged inside his parka. "Maybe there was something here that they couldn't get anywhere else."

Erica frowned and opened her mouth to ask him more, but he was already running to the waiting snow bus that their gear was being loaded onto by some hardy airport handlers in scarlet NSF parkas. Erica stared with an open mouth at the monstrous bus that idled on the ice like a shivering mastodon. It was bright red with enormous wide tires and labeled 'Ivan' the Terra Bus II. It was to be their transport the ten miles from the landing strip at Williams Field to McMurdo Station. One of the handlers, a tall sturdy woman with sprays of copper hair escaping from her turquoise toque, turned and headed toward her.

"Dr. Daniels?"

"Yes?"

"I'm Cathy Jones, your NSF guide."

Erica's jaw dropped down. "What are you doing loading luggage?"

"We're not your typical international airport." She smiled and her enormous brown eyes sparkled. "We run our own show."

Erica regained her composure quickly. "I'm sorry." She shook hands vigorously. "I should be unloading my own gear."

Cathy shook her head. "It's all right. You have to adjust to the weather, so you need to get inside quickly the first time. Next time, however, we expect everyone to pull their own weight."

Erica walked beside the guide toward the bus. "That's fine by me, but you may have trouble with some other tagalongs." She motioned to Rocheford and Commander Staten.

Cathy raised her frost-fringed eyebrows.

"Rocheford," Erica explained, "is a desert flower."

The guide chuckled.

"And the Commander, there, looks like he just stepped off an aircraft carrier in the Persian Gulf." The man's face was almost as pasty as his suit.

"Commander? Is he Air National Guard?" Cathy asked.

"Navy."

Cathy nodded slowly.

"Correct me if I'm wrong, but didn't the Navy leave here in 1999?"

"Yes, they did." She was staring openly at the formation of troops that were exiting the plane. "He appears to have brought a good portion of the Navy with him."

Erica nodded. "They seem to feel I need an escort. Do you have any idea what this is all about?"

Cathy took a deep breath. "I can't get into the details right now. I'll fill you in as soon as you're settled."

"I mean why all the fuss about a volcano?"

Cathy sucked her lower lip between her teeth and looked away.

"If it is a volcano…"

"It's certainly hot," said Cathy. "But I can't say what it is for sure. Although it would appear that a lot of people are interested in it."

"Quite a lot," said Erica. ""NASA, the Navy, NSF, freelance beaker, that's me and Mr. Archeologist/pirate. Everyone wants a piece of the pie. The question is, what's in the pie?"

Erica followed Cathy across the thick ice, taking in the great expanse of hardened seawater. The airport itself consisted of three other Hercules, a few red buildings on wheels with giant hitches at their fronts and some plow trucks and huts. Erebus loomed over them like an open pit oven in the middle of an icehouse, its crest shrouded in steam that crystallized before it rose too high in the frigid temperatures and settled back to the sea in fine feathers of snow. They climbed into 'Ivan', Erica reluctantly turning away from the volcano and settling into a seat with her guide. Thankfully Allan was ensconced in the back, trapped by the Commander's huge body and tiny briefcase. However, the other Navy men were nestled all around her like a tight cord that she had no hope of escaping. The massive bus trundled slowly across the ice toward McMurdo Station, crunching over crisp waves of snow or slippery patches of bare ice.

The short ten-mile trip took them over a snow packed road to a bumpy transition zone where the solid ice of the Ross Ice Shelf met the rock of Ross Island. As they bounced along, they came past some wastewater and power plants, two and three story dorms – one named 'Salmon River Inn' which made Erica grin but didn't bring a twitch of expression from the men with Commander Staten – until they reached their quarters: the Hotel California. It was hardly a hotel and it was hardly in California, but she'd slept in worse. The structure was basically a dilapidated two-story box of prefabricated metal. Cathy helped her unload her luggage through two sets of doors, up a narrow staircase to an upper dorm room. The rooms were tiny and housed four bunks apiece draped with down comforters of stark white, a small refrigerator that seemed to hum and rattle alternately and a stout Formica desk over which a gooseneck lamp perched. There was a bathroom off to one side that was shared with the room adjacent to it, the guide explained.

Once Erica had stowed her gear, Cathy handed her an itinerary on two rumpled sheets of paper. It included a lecture by almost every person with an authoritative title in the station to the actual three-day survival course.

"Do I really need this survival course? I've climbed half the volcanoes in the 'Ring of Fire' to their summit. I've weathered some of the worst storms in the north. I know what frostbite is."

"Standard requirement of the bureaucratic bullies down here. They'll never let you leave until you pass their course. Your itinerary," she pointed to the document, "is basically the same as any science expedition."

Erica glanced down at the pages and read:

Day 1
Housing Assignment
Orientation at Chalet

Day 2,3 and 4
Science Meeting
Pre-field Logistics: Fixed Wing
Operations Arrive in McMurdo Station
Coordinator, Helicopter Radios
Antarctic Driver's License
Field Maintenance Training (MEC)
Liquor Rations
BFC gear check and Sort
Food Planning and Packaging

Day 5
Put-in Load Planning and Packaging
Turn in cargo to Science Cargo (LC-130)

Day 6, 7, 8
Survival Training and/or Shakedown

Day 9
Put-in Load Planning and Packaging
Turn in Hazardous Cargo to appropriate department

Day 10
Package and Turn in Remaining Gear from Shakedown to Science Cargo (if LC-130 supported) Re-adjust, Add, Subtract, etc., any Gear and/or Equipment from Shakedown
Miscellaneous Last Minute Tasks

Day 11
Put-In (may take one or two days depending on weather, aircraft, etc.)
Destination - Anomaly in the Transantarctic Mountains

Day 12
In the Field until Pull-Out

Pull-Out
Back In McMurdo

"Don't sweat it," said Cathy. "It's just a standard science expedition format. Some of it you'll be able to skip. It won't be a month's long field trip. Only an in-and-out sort of thing, to check out the anomaly."

"Anomaly?" Erica eyed Cathy curiously with arched eyebrows.

"That's what they call it around the station." Cathy looked away. "I'll bet you anything those Navy men skip most of this. They looked like 'hotshots'."

"What are you saying?"

"You know. Special Ops, Navy SEALS or something."

Erica frowned. "Where did you get that idea?"

"Let's just say I have insider information. Besides, my father..." She broke off, slanting her cinnamon eyes to the ground. "Anyway, I'm pretty sure that's what they are."

Erica nodded, reading the pain in the taut pull of Cathy's face. Despite the woman's size, she looked like a lost little girl. Erica smiled encouragingly at her, although Cathy's observation had left a hard knot in her gut. "I believe you. I just don't get it. What is so dangerous about this anomaly to call in a crack team of Navy SEALS?"

The guide still refused to meet her gaze, her eyes sweeping the carpet instead. "I'll take you right now to our monitoring station and call up the latest sat photos on the Transantarctic. You'll want to see them."

"Can't wait," said Erica, fighting the urge to lift the woman's chin and pry answers out of her. Instead she let Cathy lead her out of the 'Hotel' and into the deep freeze outside. She followed the tall guide over the snow-rimed pebbles of basalt, having to lift her feet every so often to avoid the trip wires of the base – plumbing and electrical and whatnot. As they walked Erica's gaze drifted toward the small hill that was called Hut Point, the highest spot on the base, which would have an unobstructed view of the station and the sea ice beyond. She anticipated the vista there, of Erebus with crystal glaciers tumbling down bleak black slopes and the endless fields of ice that swept around her. Perhaps she would have time later on to explore. She certainly hoped so. Taking lectures on topics that she was all too familiar with seemed a colossal waste of time. At least if she could examine a little of the continent, she might get a feel for the lay under the land, the percolating mantle and what was causing this new disturbance.

At the moment, Cathy was leading her past a building with a peaked roof just a shade of lighter brown than the sides that she called 'The Chalet' – the administrative headquarters of the NSF in Antarctica. To her left was the helicopter pad, which seemed strangely empty of copters at the moment, although there were men running across the field toward the hangar beyond. The next building past the Chalet was the science lab – also called the Albert P. Crary Science and Engineering Center – named for the geophysicist and geologist Albert P. Crary, the first man to set foot on both the North and South Poles. It was located just a couple of buildings over from the hotel. The science building consisted of three fairly small connecting block-style buildings with a library on top of the highest section. It was probably the most expensive building in the world, Cathy explained. The walls were thirty inches thick to keep out the cold and the entire structure was elevated on stilts to provide access to the insulated, above ground water and sewer pipes and electrical conduit. When they entered the building, Erica noted that there were two sets of doors just as there had been at the hotel, one akin to a refrigerator door and the second a normal exterior door. They all opened inward instead of outward.

"I guess these aren't your standard fire doors," she said.

Cathy shook her head. "There's more danger of being frozen to death in Antarctica than being burned. They're designed so you can get in quick in blizzard conditions."

Erica nodded and followed her into the warm hallway of the science building. The NSF guide drew her past the environmental and microbiological room loaded with microscopes and slides, petri dishes and scientists in white lab coats, then through a special area for geology adorned with all species of rocks where a goggled geologist in dreadlocks was pounding out a section of granite. The geologist looked up as they walked past, grinned and winked conspiratorially at Cathy. What was that all about? Cathy hustled her on with barely a nod of recognition, then drew her through the double doors to a computer lab where they had access to the Internet, telescience and Radarsat images and data. She stepped into a narrow cubicle with a computer and large plasma monitor and logged on to the network.

"You'll have as much access as the scientists here," she explained. "Your code is in your itinerary."

Erica smiled, pleased. At least she wouldn't have to bother someone on staff at McMurdo every time she needed to check some data.

The screen came to life with a satellite image of the 'hotspot.' It was nestled right up against the Transantarctic Mountains, which were only visible as black peaks webbed by blue-white glaciers. The vast ice sheet flowed slowly from the center of the continent between passes in the mountains and, as glaciers, down the western slope to the sea. There was nothing striking about the image except the numerous cracks and crevasses in the ice beside one particular peak. Next Cathy clicked on the screen and called up the thermal image. The first of these encompassed a wider view of Antarctica, white throughout most of the Transantarctic mountain chain, except for the bright red button opposite Vostok science station. Interesting. The anomaly was adjacent to Vostok, although still hundreds of miles away.

"It's getting warmer," said Cathy.

"Have you seen any volcanic flow or ash?"

"None really visible, just a mark of intense heat."

"Strange," said Erica. "It could mark an underground fissure that hasn't broken through to the surface yet."

"Or," said a deep, decidedly unwelcome voice, "it could be an alien spacecraft."

Erica whipped her head up and glared at him.

"But it isn't," he continued.

"Then what is it, *Dr. Rocheford*?" she snapped.

"I won't speculate without proof. Besides, you wouldn't believe me anyway. Not until we get there."

A figure moved in behind him, and Erica saw the rigid Commander Staten listening intently to the conversation.

"Why do I get the feeling I'm being followed?" she muttered.

Cathy smirked.

She returned to the image, but her eyes were drawn back to McMurdo, to the bulging circle of Mount Erebus. She blinked, but there could be no mistake. The volcano was red-hot.

"Hit the deck," she screamed as she flung herself down and crawled quickly under the desk. Allan appeared shocked but he immediately followed suit as well as Cathy. The Commander, however, stood his ground, frowning.

That's when the vibrating started. The station was rattling and shaking. Some computers vibrated off the desks and began to explode. Desk chairs overturned or simply rolled away on their wheels, crashing into the cubicle walls.

Every stack of paper filled with NSF data floated to the ground like gigantic snowflakes.

Commander Staten lost his cool, unruffled military bearing as he stumbled and swayed on the unsteady floor. He screamed as his head smashed into a desk and moaned as he sank slowly to the ground. His eyelids fluttered and his eyes rolled back in his head.

Finally the oscillations stopped. Cathy pawed through her bag and came up with a thick scarf. She scrambled over to Staten and tied the scarf around his bleeding scalp wound. The others began to wobble to their feet looking dazed.

"What was that?" asked Allan.

"I think it was rather obvious," said Erica.

Allan studied her face with a frown.

"It was an earthquake, Allan. Caused by seismic disturbance from Erebus."

"Why is Erebus suddenly waking up?" he asked.

"Because she's a volcano," she explained as if to a small child. "Essentially a pressure cooker and she just blew off some steam."

Allan frowned. "You don't think it has any connection to the 'hotspot?'"

"It's possible," said Erica, " if there's a fault line that connects the two volcanoes, but they're a few hundred miles away from each other. And I don't see any alteration in the thermal image over the Transantarctics. It was probably an isolated incident. Why are you looking at me so strangely? What do you believe, Allan?"

"You're probably right," he said smugly. "One 'hotspot' has nothing to do with the other. Because one is a volcano and the other isn't."

Erica frowned. "I didn't say that."

"No, you didn't, yet."

"And I won't. I don't believe it. Are you trying to suggest that something manmade could radiate that much heat? Something that was made ten thousand years ago?"

Allan blinked and met her gaze. "We'll see, when we get there."

"Um, I hate to interrupt your scientific debate," said Cathy, "but I think this man needs a medic."

Erica tore her eyes from Allan, her teeth grinding into each other. "Of course" she said. "Where do I go?"

Cathy gave her directions. She nodded and turned away from the huddled group, but not before giving Allan a last skeptical glance. What disturbed her wasn't Allan's smug face, however, but the look on Cathy's. The guide was biting her lip and directing furtive flicks of her eyes at Allan. What was going on here? She shook her head in bewilderment as she dashed out of the NSF research lab.

THERE ISN'T A PHONE AVAILABLE? SURELY CATHY GETTING THE MEDIC MAKES MORE SENSE. A CHAPTER WHERE MISS JACKSON DOESN'T MENTION ERICA'S FIGURE? A LET DOWN.

Twelve

David Marsh stood at the elevator doors, his head spinning at the enormity of his next step. He just had to crank his head up and gaze at the towering launch pad cradling the 363-foot Saturn V rocket. It was strange to be using the same booster again, but why mess with a good thing, the proponents had argued. It would reduce the ballooning costs of transporting huge payloads to the moon, rather than the rather expensive space shuttle. Other rockets, such as the Delta Clipper (or DCX), a reusable, remote-controlled launch vehicle was designed for short-range hops, and the design hadn't progressed enough for this long-range mission. There were still serious questions about Russia's Energia – a heavy-lift rocket that had exploded in dramatic footage six years ago that brought to mind the third Vanguard rocket that exploded on the launch pad in 1957.

This had all led to NASA once again adopting Rockwell's F-1 engine that was the heart of the first stage of the original Saturn V. Of course, the rocket had been updated with new materials for the fuel tanks and advanced flight electronics technology in order to put 150-200 tons into Earth orbit for less than a few hundred dollars per pound. This was the third launch in the past five years. The three sections of the Saturn V rocket along with the Lunar Transfer Vehicle (LTV) and the Lunar Lander (LL) had been stacked together in the giant Vehicle Assembly Building, removed through the enormous bay doors to the launch platform and transported to the launch pad by the six-million-pound crawler. The sheer immensity of the crawler/launch platform/rocket combination was enough to blow your mind as it inched along the crawlerway - composed of four layers of river rock, seven feet deep, in order to support its staggering weight. Then it had been racked up against Launch Pad LC-39B, ready for a momentous break from earth's atmosphere and another noteworthy voyage to the moon. David still couldn't quite come to terms with the thought of his small human frame with two other astronauts and one scientist, sitting on top of 7.75 million pounds of thrust.

"Marsh," yelled a voice behind him. David blinked and slung around. Dellows was careening up the walkway toward him, his chill gray eyes for once giving off a semblance of warmth. "Are you ready for this?"

David took a deep breath. "Ya. I think so. Tell me, what are you doing here? I thought you'd be in Houston, watching the 'show' on the big screen."

Dellows grinned. "I booked a seat here. I'll let flight control deal with all the details of the launch. I'm the science coordinator, remember. Besides, I've always wanted a front-row seat when part of my team blasts off into space."

David nodded and grinned. "I've always enjoyed watching a launch, although it feels a lot different from this perspective."

"Savor it, David. It'll never come again. Take in everything and don't forget a bloody detail. Once you're up there, there'll be of a lot of work to do."

"Yes, sir. I'm well aware of that. It'll be good to set up my lab and look for an ideal site for the mining operation."

Dellows waved his hand in a dismissive way. "Don't worry about that right away. You'll have enough to do setting up the HAB and doing some preliminary scouting for me."

David frowned. He wanted to get right to his pet project, but he had to bow to NASA's demands. Everything was up there waiting for them. There had been two previous unmanned voyages to inject the enormous payloads – the original habitat, a crane assembly, the fuel storage tanks that would eventually be used to store oxygen mined from the soil and two Luna Cats. The Luna Cats were an elaborate imitation of the Snow Cats in Antarctica. Their tires were made of strong reinforced balloons designed to bounce easily over rocks and loose soil but to stand up to the jagged edges of the ejecta from the craters – the sharp daggers of rock defined by the massive asteroid impacts on the moon some three billion years ago. They'd been tested in the southern continent as well, where the spears of ice stood up in crests that resembled the ejecta and the climate was nearly as severe. David had spent a couple of months down there during Antarctica's summer, adapting to the EMU suit and the harsh dry conditions he would have to endure on the moon. It hadn't been pleasant, but it was necessary to achieve his goal. He smiled now when he thought of Erica fighting gale-force winds and bone-chilling cold just to investigate a volcano or whatever had caused such a stir in NASA. It had created a bit of a sensation, scientists and bureaucrats whispering behind closed doors. The smile slipped away abruptly. Maybe she had pulled a prime assignment despite his best efforts to exclude her. Oh well. He shrugged. It couldn't beat his mission. The rocket gleamed in the orange cast of the morning sun, three enormous stages of fuel and power ready to blast him into the arc of cobalt sky.

"Time to go, Dr. Marsh," said a dark-haired, dark-skinned technician in orange coveralls, jarring him from his thoughts. The other team members were already ensconced in the wire cage of the elevator that would pull them up the gantry alongside the massive rocket. Leclerk, the slim, blond flight engineer from France brushed a finger over his bristly moustache and looked skyward in cool anticipation. He'd been chosen from a slew of candidates in the European space program for his quick thinking during a malfunction on the International Space Station two years ago. Ejecting a module that had caught on fire saved the rest of the structure including a crew of five other astronauts and scientists. He looked so relaxed now, you'd think he was going on a pleasure cruise in the Caribbean instead of a yearlong mission to the moon. Next to him stood Bosley, the short, balding astrophysicist with overlarge ears, hopping back and forth like a caged bird. His beady blue eyes flicked here and there, unable to contain the adrenaline pulsing through his tiny frame. David rolled his eyes and sighed. It was a shame that the only other scientist on this mission was a hyper little hobbit. Still, he was friendlier than the woman was. Jing-Mei Wong, the astronaut and Commander of this flight, scowled and shot daggers at David with her deep brown eyes. The massive tangerine flight suit bulked out her slender body, making her a little more threatening, but not much. He almost laughed. He'd have her feathers smoothed out soon enough.

Dellows cleared his throat and raised his bushy eyebrows. "I guess this is it."

"Right," said David, backing into the elevator. "I'll see you on my nationwide TV broadcast." He grinned.

Dellows nodded. "Just don't sound as cocky as you are. And don't make the audience feel stupid either, with a lot of scientific jargon."

"I'll be my usual charming self." The elevator jerked and started to rise. Dellows waved, but there was a slight frown on his face. How could he doubt that David would know what to do? He'd made it this far without any major slip-ups. He'd have America and the whole world eating out of his hands.

As the elevator climbed toward the wispy clouds, he felt his heart accelerate, although he tried to brush it off as mere excitement. The cage came to an abrupt halt at the top of the gantry and the door slid open. A narrow catwalk jutted out to the rocket across a sickening drop of over three hundred feet. Dellows was a mere ant below, crawling into the white van that would take him to the bleachers a few miles away where the news crews and other spectators were gathered to watch the lift-off.

"*Bon*, let's do it," said Leclerk confidently.

David nodded stiffly, his suave confidence beginning to slough off as he gazed at the colossal bullet that would fire him into space. Jing-Mei brushed past him and glared one more time before she swept across the catwalk.

Bosley came abreast of him and smiled. "Isn't this the most thrilling experience a man could ever have, barring sex." He winked. "Just think, in an hour's time we'll be heading off into the cosmos, whence it all began. We'll be experiencing Einstein's theories beyond the exclusive domain of earth. This isn't one giant leap for mankind anymore. It's a quantum leap into the future." He chuckled.

David stared at him, his forehead creased into the tight-fitting skin of his flight suit. What a nerd. Thank goodness he hadn't decided to become a physicist. "Ya, right," he mumbled.

Bosley flitted across the catwalk with the same brimming enthusiasm as he'd displayed with his Nobel speech. David sauntered behind, casually throwing a glance downward, which was a mistake - the dizzying drop from the top of the Saturn V choking off his breath. He lurched the last few steps toward the hatch, breathing easy again as he stepped over the threshold into the claustrophobic cabin of the Lunar Module. The technician beckoned him to a seat beside Bosley where he was belted in securely, facing the sky through the portal of the nose cone.

The sky was a soft eggshell blue patched with the ruffled feathers of clouds. It was hard to imagine that this would be the last time he'd look at it from terra firma in a year. In another three days, the earth would be a cream and sapphire semicircle on the horizon, a distant jewel that cradled life in the dead of space. The technician gave a final tug on the belt - making David gasp at the snugness - then he exited the spacecraft, slamming the hatch in place.

They waited. Bosley was silent for once - no more dramatic speeches, although David could sense the pent-up tension in the physicist like a coiled spring. The astronauts rhymed off their pre-flight checks as they waited for the final go-ahead for lift-off. Mission Control came on over the headset, giving David a jolt. This was it.

They started at an hour, testing every microchip for a malfunction. David closed his eyes. He tried to keep his breathing slow and steady, although it still sounded harsh and raucous in his ears confined in the globe of his helmet. He gritted his teeth and tapped his gloved fingers on the armrest. It was the longest sixty minutes of his life.

Finally, with no delays and no detectable malfunctions, thank goodness, they were three minutes from lift-off. It hadn't really hit him until that moment. He could die on this mission, especially in those tiny seconds when the rocket exploded from the ground. He thrust the thought aside. It was too late to back out now, and he could hardly display that sort of cowardice at the time of his greatest victory. This was his shining moment.

The monotone countdown came loud and clear through his headset.

T-minus two minutes.

He licked his lips and glanced over at the astrophysicist. Bosley grinned and gave him the thumbs-up. Yes, the little man was taking that next step for mankind. David was taking the next step to stardom.

T-minus one minute.

Everyone in his seaside hometown in Maine would be glued to his or her TV set.

Forty, thirty-nine, thirty-eight…

He could see his mother's smiling face, so proud of her 'mission specialist' son. Maybe even his father… Well, maybe not.

Seventeen, sixteen, fifteen…

He was on top.

Ten, nine, eight…

Erica was on the bottom.

Seven, six, five…

Why was her face right in front of him? Cold blue eyes jamming right through him. Thick moist lips mocking him. 'It isn't about *you*. It isn't about *you*.'

Three, two, one…

The rumble of ignition began, shaking the cockpit like a force-three hurricane. His brain was bashed against the back of his seat as the Saturn V exploded into the air. Tears streamed down his cheeks that the astronauts would attribute to the severe g's. No one would ever guess that he was haunted by his own ambition.

Thirteen

Erica's eyelashes fluttered as the NSF representative droned on about flight operations and radios – all crucial information for field studies, but something she was more than acquainted with in Alaska. They were in a small auditorium, in the administrative building dubbed 'The Chalet' by McMurdo personnel. Allan seemed to be equally enthralled with the lectures. His tan face was crushed in his fist, supported by his elbow on the squat desk in front of him. Even the men from Staten's unit, usually on constant alert from what she'd seen, were slouched in their chairs and fiddling with their guns probably tempted to shoot the lecturer. Erica was surprised they'd even showed up at all, but she'd heard Cathy give them a stern order to at least acquaint themselves with Antarctica rules, including the prohibition of weapons. One man, lean, dark, with a scar just above his right eyebrow, had laughed at this and walked away. But they had shown up, surprisingly. Maybe because their Commander was still in the infirmary recovering from his concussion.

Now Robert or Roger, whatever his name was - a stocky man with thick black hair and a dimpled face - started talking about liquor rationing. Allan groaned at that one, but the SEALS didn't seem perturbed at all.

Erica leaned over toward Allan. "I thought you'd lived in Cairo the last few years. Isn't liquor forbidden there?"

He cocked his head her way. "You can get anything for a price. It's not run by scientists."

Erica grinned. "This is your lucky day."

She turned back to Roger, rested her head on her hand and sighed. It was a blessing in disguise when Commander Staten wobbled into the room, his head swathed in fresh white bandages that contrasted vividly with his bronze skin. She never thought she'd be happy to see him again, but it certainly took the edge off the monotony. He stumbled toward the back of the room where one of his men, the least restless it appeared, was lounging. He was probably the next in the chain of command, although that was only a guess since they still insisted on hiding their rank insignia and names. This man had a softer face than the others did - not that he wasn't lean and hard, but his mouth was less tight and his eyes had a warmer, almost human, twinkle to them. Staten leaned toward him and whispered something in his ear. Erica strained and caught the name Metzer. The SEAL responded with a terse nod and the twinkle seemed to fade.

"You won't be able to come with us to Vostok, sir?" whispered the soldier.

There it was again. Vostok. Mentioned once in Houston by Major Ellis of the Air National Guard, but there wasn't any indication they were heading there. The itinerary listed the 'anomaly' in the Transantarctic Mountains as their 'put-in' destination. If the Navy unit was accompanying her, then why were they going to Vostok?

The Commander swayed, gripped the desk and nodded tersely. With a grimace he turned and shuffled drunkenly out of the room. Erica had had enough. She stood, much to the surprised expressions of the men around her, and followed the Commander.

"Dr. Daniels," said Roger. "We haven't finished the lecture."

"Dr. Rocheford is taking notes for me," said Erica with a grin. She saw the shock in Allan's eyes and then the scowl. "I need some air for a few minutes. I promise I'll be back."

Roger nodded, albeit reluctantly. Erica raced out the door. Commander Staten was a fast man, faster than one would expect with a head injury. He was already on the gritty path outside when Erica managed to catch him, thrusting on her parka and mitts in the frigid air.

"Commander Staten? May I have a word with you?"

The Commander swung around and blinked, the cold already making him start to shiver. "Certainly, *Dr.* Daniels."

The way he seemed to slur her title in a derogatory fashion made her cringe.

"But inside, please," he continued. "I haven't quite adjusted to this balmy temperature."

Erica smiled. "I thought you guys were SEALS or something. Aren't you supposed to be able to handle anything, the more extreme the better?"

His eyes protruded from their sockets and his teeth clacked together. "What do you know of us?" he growled.

"I only know the way you look. Here, let's head over to the bar to have a little talk." She steered him down the road, made a left at the Firehouse where the engines were snugly cocooned behind huge rollaway doors and led him into Gallaghers, the local sports bar and grill. It was a small construction across from the enormous Building 155 that contained the cafeteria, a store, a barber shop, TV and radio facilities, the local weekly newspaper office and some housing – basically a small indoor village. Gallaghers was the spur of the nightlife in McMurdo, such as it was. However, it was quiet at this time in the afternoon – the dance floor was empty, most pool tables racked up and bald of cue sticks and players, but there were a few scientists and maintenance personnel munching on some hamburgers around the simple wooden tables. Erica chose a table farthest from the other diners.

"Okay," said Staten. "What do you want to know?"

"Vostok," said Erica.

The Commander just blinked and folded his arms.

"Why is your team heading to Vostok? That's hundreds of miles from my volcano."

"There may be a connection," he said matter-of-factly.

"Such as?"

"Some of their scientists paid your 'volcano' a visit."

"They did?" said Erica. "Then why in the world am I here? They could have consulted with any volcanologist via satellite communications. I didn't even need to come here."

Commander Staten blinked again and just stared at her.

"Did I? What is it you're not telling me?"

Staten sighed. "When my team returns from Vostok, you will be fully briefed."

"Why can't I be fully briefed now?"

The Commander gave her a polite, terse smile. "This is above your security clearance, *Dr.* Daniels. Way above. So just sit it out, do the orientation, take the survival course and let me and my men deal with Vostok."

"I see," said Erica. "Sit my fanny down and let the big hairy men deal with all the bad stuff. Why does that sound familiar? Well, I have never sat on my ass and let anyone take my lumps for me. I'm going to figure out all your secrets before your little briefing, which I'm sure will leave out a hell of a lot." She shoved back her chair and marched out. As she flung a last look over her shoulder, she didn't like what she saw. There was a bemused smile on the Commander's face.

Erica didn't head back to the Chalet. Instead she tripped across the uneven street and dashed into the giant building that housed the science lab. She hardly glanced at the other facilities, making a beeline for the computer lab this time. None of the men and women in lab coats that were wandering in the halls seemed to question her presence there, which was a relief. She must wear that weathered scientist look well, as Rocheford would be happy to point out. When she finally reached the computer lab, she checked to make sure Cathy was nowhere in sight. She didn't relish a down dressing for missing a lecture that even the SEALS had shown up for. The station the NSF guide had used to call up satellite data was empty. The lab was still in a state of upheaval after the tremor three days before, but the broken glass from fragmented computers had been swept away, some of the debris had been cleared up and most of the scattered papers had been collected and stacked on various desks. At least the computer in front of her was still intact. Erica slunk into the cubicle and accessed the network with the codes she'd been given on her itinerary.

She requested the most recent satellite photo of the anomaly first, even though she was itching to investigate this Vostok connection. The 'hotspot' was unchanged - a strange cube of heat underneath a quiet blanket of ice.

She shifted her eyes to the northwest of the image. On the other side of the Queen Alexandria Range, where the Beardmore Glacier plunged into the Ross Ice Shelf, was a helicopter refueling station at a place called Plunket Point. Now this was interesting. Its proximity to the phenomenon made it an ideal place from which to investigate; yet no one had mentioned it before. Had someone gone out from there and, lacking the necessary scientific equipment, found nothing? But how could they lack the equipment? Mount Erebus was trussed up with seismometers and tiltmeters, actively monitored by the USGS (United States Geological Survey). Where was their resident volcanologist anyway? With the ground tremors during her first in depth look at the phenomenon, there hadn't been the opportunity to ask, but wouldn't he be right in the thick of things if there were something volcanic occurring? There were just too many questions and not enough straight answers.

Erica frowned and called up some data on Vostok. She knew all about the lake under 4000 meters (13,123 feet) of ice at Vostok Station. New technology had penetrated the ice and revealed that Antarctica was pockmarked with these subglacial lakes. It was situated in a rift valley, so there was probably sufficient geothermal heat from the magma under a thin crust of earth to keep the lake liquid even though it was squashed under layers of ice. Erica had heard about this strange lake, but had never studied it with any degree of interest. She was much too busy in the field and much too far away from Antarctica to give it any more than a cursory glance. Now, however, since Vostok was somehow connected with her 'volcano,' she examined it a little closer. The satellite image was interesting. In the midst of the wavelike drifts all around the station, the lake stood out as a smooth surface. Erica slipped the satellite image over again to the Beardmore phenomena. Little circular or oval splotches of smooth ice traversed the area, not on top of her anomaly, but not that far from it either. She blinked. She knew that they had found meteorites all along the Transantarctic Mountains on the inner side to the continent. The theory was that the ice sheet had collected them over the millennia and, as this glacial ice moved toward the sea, they became concentrated against the mountain range. Could it be? She looked over at Vostok again. Yes, glacial ice transformed and removed any details of an asteroid impact site, so everyone assumed they would never find any in Antarctica. But maybe they hadn't been removed, just covered up by the ice.

A hand came down on her shoulder and made her jump. Cathy Jones leaned over, copper curls framing a very stern square-cut face. "What are you looking at, Dr. Daniels?"

Erica put a hand to her chest. "You scared me to death. And it's Erica, please. We're going to be working closely together, so I think we can be a little less formal. Besides, there's enough starch from the military men to do a year's worth of laundry."

Cathy nodded, but she didn't smile. "I thought you were at the 'Day 3' lecture."

"Yes, well…" Erica ran her tongue over her lips. "I ran into Commander Staten and overheard them talking about going to Vostok. Major Ellis of the Air National Guard mentioned the station as well. But it seems I've been excluded. Tell me, what has Vostok got to do with any of this?"

As soon as Erica mentioned Vostok, Cathy's eyes grew wider and her lower lip began to tremble. She blinked a number of times, then sighed. "I've been sworn to secrecy."

"By whom?" asked Erica.

"The Pentagon."

"Excuse me," said Erica. "I was given to understand this would be a simple scientific investigation. What the hell does the Pentagon have to do with this?"

Cathy looked away, tucking a belligerent curl behind her ear.

"I think I have a right to know. I have a motley crew of men accompanying me on this investigation, and I need to know what's going on before I set foot on the Ice Shelf."

"I guess you do have a right. I've said it all along." Cathy met Erica's eyes. "These military men can be very persuasive."

"You mean threatening."

Cathy nodded. "Something very strange is happening at your 'hotspot.' At first there was just a little 'thermal wake-up' as Jimmy used to put it."

"Jimmy?"

"Our volcanologist." Cathy bit her lip and looked away.

Erica winced. She didn't like the words 'used to' being used in regard to a volcanologist. "And where is this Jimmy now?"

"I'll get to that. Anyway, NASA asked Jimmy to check it out. We have no idea why they were interested, but we surmised it had to do with their Earth Science Satellite picking up a thermal signal. Jimmy couldn't go right away, so he asked some of the geologists that were camped out at the Beardmore Glacier, by our helicopter refueling station, to have a look. There was about five of them altogether. John, one of our helo pilots, ferried them to the site and they radioed in on October 10th. We never heard from them again." Cathy closed her eyes.

Erica frowned. She didn't like where this was heading.

"Then the Russians at Vostok took an interest. Even though they were hundreds of miles from the site, I think they still have this drive to be the first in making new discoveries, just like during the cold war. Sometimes we're in league with them, sometimes it's competition, especially among scientists. So they sent a team in on October 12th. They said they'd look for our men so we didn't send a rescue squad. We didn't find out what happened."

"Why not?" asked Erica. "Didn't you radio them?"

"Yes. Of course. But they refused to answer our questions. They sounded scared. I don't know why. And after, this gets even stranger, we lost all radio contact with them."

Erica tilted her head. "Lost. Does that mean they switched off, or that they're refusing to answer?"

Cathy shrugged. "That was when Jimmy decided he had to check this out. Besides trying to find our lost scientists, he was intrigued and mystified by the anomaly. I mean there was never any volcanic activity that far in the ice sheet before. So he assembled a team and they left on the 14th. They took a Hercules, landed on the shelf and radioed us about some tricky wet spots and crevasses. They spotted some sort of tunnel in the ice near the thermal activity. They went in and..." Cathy stopped. Her eyes were glossy and her large hands started to tremble.

Erica waited. She didn't know if she wanted to hear the rest.

"They found some strange construction." Cathy swallowed loudly. "There were screams and then nothing. That was the last I heard from Jimmy." Tears were now streaming openly down her cheeks.

Erica gulped. "What about the rest..." She couldn't finish the sentence.

"Nothing. No response. We hailed them over and over. We still do, every day."

"Have you over-flown the area to check it out?"

"We tried, but the planes can't get right above it. There's a lot of electromagnetic interference that wreaks havoc with the instrumentation. They did spot the Hercules and some other planes and helicopters, but no sign of life. We really don't know anything else, except some people were there before us. They built something under the ice."

"Built something? You said that before. A construction of some sort." Erica's brows were knit. Could Allan's outlandish theory actually have some basis in fact? "What was it?"

"I don't know what it was. Jimmy didn't give many details except that it was massive. I thought they were heading into some hostile camp and I warned them, but Jimmy's never been afraid of anything. He wouldn't listen to me. Then, he mentioned ash and..."

"Ash?"

Cathy took a long shuddering breath. "That was when the screaming started. I think they might have been burned..."

Erica closed her eyes. "So no one thought to tell me that the little 'hotspot' is eating up people like a ravenous dinosaur."

"It's a dangerous mission," she said. "You have a right to know. The government wants to keep a lid on this, especially Vostok's involvement, or the conspiracy theorists and the UFO nuts will have a field day. But coercing you down here on the pretext of investigating a normal volcano is shameful. I wouldn't blame you a bit if you backed out now."

Erica scanned the computer image again, her eyes sliding over the undulating waves of ice and snow and the mar, the red spot at the center of this madness. "Ash and burning does sound like a volcano. Were they wearing suits?" she asked.

Cathy nodded. "Gas masks and thermo-reflective suits."

"Do you have any more?"

Cathy shook her head. "Jimmy took the last of them."

Erica sighed. "I'm not going in there without suits. There could have been an eruption below the ice. Is there anything else we can use?"

Cathy scrunched her forehead and looked up at the ceiling. "I've got it. The Moon suits."

"You have suits then."

"Yes. The astronauts train down here sometimes for missions to the moon and Mars. There was a geologist here not too long ago getting used to the cold environment and the suit. Marsh, I think his name was."

Erica's face flushed. "What? When was this?"

"It was at the end of summer. February or March. He was scheduled to take off this October. He must be there already."

A bolt of pain shot through Erica's temple. Her teeth were grinding together like grist stones. *He knew.* He'd already been chosen long ago, been training for months. The whole conference was a sham for her benefit. Someone wanted her in Antarctica. What for? To die like all the others? Maybe he wanted to get rid of her once and for all. No. She couldn't accept that. He was a cad, an ambitious egotistical jerk, but he wasn't a killer. In fact, he'd seemed as shocked to see her at the videoconference as she had been to see him. It was someone else. Someone wanted her here, but why? She looked back at the computer screen still displaying the smooth swept pockets. Perhaps the answer lay in who she was and what she knew.

Fourteen

Cathy left the science lab in a hurry. She didn't want to be seen together with Erica outside of regularly scheduled appointments in case someone reported her to Commander Staten. He would find out soon enough, but she hoped Erica would keep quiet until they were airborne. The last thing she needed right now was to lose her status in Antarctica, and lose the mission. She had to find out what had happened to Jimmy.

Jimmy was an awful lot like Erica. He had always been fascinated - no enthralled - with volcanoes. He was tough and smart, and always willing to take the extra risk to step one foot closer to a steaming vent or a bubbling lava lake. It was his job, of course, and a form of escapism, as he put it, but there was more to it than that. There seemed to be this *need* in him, as with many of the scientists she had met, to find answers to our existence within the dynamics of the earth. It was a raw determination that drove him to limits no one else would dare. She saw the same determination in Erica. She hadn't frightened the volcanologist with her tale, only intrigued her and solidified her *need* to find answers. Cathy felt a twang of guilt over not disclosing more of the gruesome details. She hadn't mentioned the bodies within the ice that Jimmy had described to them over the radio as plentiful and 'older' than their team. Erica should be told everything, but she didn't want to scare her off. Somehow, she knew she would need this woman if she ever wanted to find Jimmy back.

The snow was churning in out of the south on the wings of the katabatic wind driven by gravity out from the South Pole. She could hardly see as she weaved her way through the street, boxed and battered by hard pellets of ice and snow, when a white-clad man flitted in front of her. Since he was camouflaged and brandishing an MP5 'Room

Broom' – a little compact squirtgun that was a favorite with SEALS for short ranges with terrorists - she had no doubt to which company he belonged. He was heading toward the helo pad, so she spun around and followed him.

They hadn't gone five steps when he abruptly turned and faced her. "What do you want?" he asked. The hood of his parka framed his face, a dark wind-burned face with ice-greased chestnut hair. A livid scar arched above deep mocha eyes that chilled her with their intensity.

"I thought I told you g..guys about the laws we have r..regarding guns," she stammered out.

"I thought I laughed and said 'very funny.'"

Cathy took a deep breath that chilled her even more and said, "There is nothing that's dangerous here. You can stow your weapons until we leave for the anomaly."

"You think there aren't dangers here? People are dying."

"We don't know that they're dead! They're just…missing in action."

The SEAL nodded slowly as if he were placating a child. "Believe what you want," he said. "We're here to get them out, alive or dead."

"Is that why you're here?" she asked.

He frowned.

"Because if it were, you wouldn't be going to Vostok first, unless you suspect the Russians of something foul."

The SEAL's heavy brows drew over nebulous eyes in the swirls of snow. "The Russians are our friends now. We're on good terms with them." It sounded like a politician's speech.

"Yes, that's why you're going out there with MP5s and M16 assault rifles. And flying in on Iroquois attack helicopters." She nodded toward the helicopter pad where the 'thump thump' of rotors and the dark silhouette of a giant bird was dropping from the sky.

The lips peeled back from the Navy man's uneven teeth as he gazed at her. "For someone who hates guns, you seem to know a lot about them. And helicopters," he added as an afterthought.

Cathy stared him down, despite her desire to turn and run. "Yes, I do. My father was in the Navy. He flew the same type of bird in the last Gulf war. Six thousand pounds dry weight, two turboshaft engines with a maximum cruise speed of 110 knots. It has 2.75-inch rocket pods, a 16.50 caliber machine gun and a lightweight minigun. You're not taking her for a joyride."

The SEAL's cruel brown eyes were frozen in shock. Obviously he hadn't expected a girl from the NSF guide pool to have such extensive knowledge of SEAL operations. He shook his head. "He shouldn't have told you... Anyway, if you know this much, you should know that they're standard issue. Who is your dear old dad? Maybe the Commander should give him a call."

"My 'dear old dad' is dead," she said, "flying one of those deathtraps on one of your SEAL 'rescue missions,' if that's what you want to call them. But if you're heading to Vostok, it has nothing to do with saving our scientists, does it?"

He glared at her, his hand tightening on the MP5. "You have to learn to mind your own business."

"Is that a threat?"

"Take it however you like."

"Well, I've been threatened by the best in the business," she said. "Your buddies in the Pentagon have been working on me. I don't scare off that easy. I'm going to find out what happened to my friends no matter what. And don't think just because you're a crack team of special ops heroes that you don't need me. No one knows these mountains like I do. So if you want to get out alive, you'd better start listening to me and stop pointing your gun in my face."

She spun on her heel and left him, his jaw cracked a little wider than it should be if she hadn't made an impact. Of course, she didn't kid herself. These men were hard, and dangerous in their own way. She had to watch her mouth a little more. People were disappearing far too easily nowadays. Although she should trust these men – her father had been a part of their elite group at one time - she didn't. She knew that most of them had been trained to be automatons. Blindly following orders to the detriment of them all. That's what had killed her father and driven her mother crazy with overprotectiveness. No, there may be only one person she could trust – the blonde volcanologist with the same bold determination as Jimmy had. Together they might find the answers to too many lingering questions. They might even find Jimmy back, alive. It was like grasping at straws, but it was all she had.

Fifteen

"Marsh, get your butt out of bed." Chivas, the lunar base Commander ripped the velcro from David's sleeping bag rousing him from his dreams with a start.

David crawled out of his bunk and yawned. He bounced up a little too quickly, clunking his head into the ceiling, his superhuman strength a byproduct of the 1/6th earth's gravity here on the moon. He winced and rubbed his head as he sank back down to the floor in the squat habitat, or the HAB as the astronauts liked to call it in NASAese, although it had already been dubbed LUNA I by the establishment. David definitely needed to slow down in this new environment - make each movement deliberate - or he would be riddled with bumps and bruises by the end of the day. He walked toward the front of the habitat where the kitchen/dining area was situated, pausing as he squeezed through the confined lab and communications section. Leclerk was reporting in to Houston via teleconference through the satellite dish that was perched on a tripod outside. He smiled at the flight engineer, whose chilling nod was his only acknowledgement. The last area before the kitchen in this confined module, twice the size of a mobile home, was the airplane-sized bathroom and shower area and a small greenhouse to begin a closed-loop life support system, the plants interspersed between the exercise cycle and the treadmill.

It had been two days since the LTV – Lunar Transfer Vehicle - had made its translunar injection (TLI) of the latest payload and the Lunar Lander to the surface of the moon. David could still feel the adrenaline rush as well as the persistent nausea the journey from earth had produced as zero gravity took its toll. He had had a classic case of space sickness – dizziness, headache, cold sweats and that infernal queasiness. Leclerk had at least been sympathetic to his face, but he'd seen the astronaut exchange grins with Jing-Mei Wong as he'd turned away. Bosley, however, had experienced little of these symptoms, humming to himself and whooping like a child on a roller coaster as they left earth orbit.

"Take a look at that," he'd bellowed as the spectacular blue sphere of the earth glowed in the midnight void of space.

David had looked over, nodded appreciatively and thrown up.

It was so unfair that that emaciated twig of a man had come through his first voyage into space without a twitch of illness, and David, who'd spent the last two years hitching rides on fighter aircraft and braving the 'Vomit Comet' - NASAs equivalent to a giant switchback in a fairground - had succumbed. It was over now, thank goodness, and his stomach was almost back to normal. The minimal gravity of the moon had at least helped stabilize him a bit. Now he could fully appreciate the experience. He was a lunar resident.

After they had touched down with the final payload – the Lunar Roving Robot (LRR) and the last solar arrays - they had spent their first days on the moon assembling and attaching the solar arrays to further power the station. Vochenkov and Chivas, the two astronauts who'd started the colonization three months ago, directed the work – the Russian with a cocky grin and the Commander with a scowl. Now the base was fully operational with the appropriate oxygen/nitrogen atmosphere (20% oxygen and 80% nitrogen) and 14.7psi of pressure – the same as earth at sea level. The work had been supremely taxing in their robust EMU suits, the lower gravity giving them superhuman strength, but the bulky suits and awkwardness of adjustment to slow motion movement draining their energy reserves. David had fallen asleep as soon as his head hit the pillow and the result was this rude awakening from his commanding officer.

With bleary eyes David looked through the small porthole-like windows at the surface of the moon. Everything was a steel gray defined by the dust and regolith – chunks of rock – set in the black velvet of space. They were nestled in the Mare Imbrium, the dark volcanic sea below the North Pole, beside the Hadley Rille in the Montes Apennius mountain chain. This was close to the site where Apollo 15 had made its historic landing on the moon on July 30, 1971. At first David hadn't understood the reason for this location. It was still some distance from the pole, where they hoped to find water to sustain a colony and fuel flights home. It was a long way from the Aitken Basin in the South Pole where there was an area of constant sunlight and thus constant energy source. It was still on the near side, so setting up a telescope array on the far side would be some difficult. Finally he'd asked Dellows point blank why he'd chosen this site.

"Because of the Rille," he'd said. His left eye had twitched as he'd spoken.

David had stared at him, dumbfounded. He knew the Rille was a lava channel that resembled a deep riverbed. It originated in an elongated depression in an area of low domes, had a depth of 600 – 1300 feet and a width of one mile. There were many of these on the moon, but the significance was lost to him since he'd never really studied it in detail, more interested in mining the soil than exploring volcanic origins.

"You've visited it before," David had replied, stroking the fine bristle on his chin in puzzlement.

"Yes, but in no great detail. We want to determine if there are caves further down the channel. They've been conclusively shown to be lava tubes – wasn't that one of your theories in college along with the impact study?"

David had nodded, though he'd grimaced behind his hand. He had memorized every detail of that study when he had gotten his job in NASA, but through the years those details seemed to have slipped away.

"Anyway, if we do find some roofed over areas of these lava tubes, it would be an ideal solution to developing a colony."

"How so?"

"By sealing the caves and pressurizing them. They would be natural protection from cosmic rays and micrometeorites. We wouldn't have to waste valuable dollars constructing huge domes under the soil."

"I understand," said David. "But don't you have more pressing projects? Such as mining and finding water?"

Dellows had frowned and looked away. What was he hiding? But he'd continued his explanations as if to a child, still not meeting David's eyes. "You'll be close enough to the north to look for ice with the LRR (lunar robotic rover). We can set all the other projects in motion. But it will be a hell of a lot easier if we don't have to transport any more habitation modules or construction materials should you find an available resource at your fingertips."

So the decision had been made a year ago to inhabit the Hadley Rille in the Imbrium Mare. Who was David to question NASA's decision anyway? It was enough that he had wheedled his way into the good books of NASA's upper management, watched them send the first payload, the HAB, to the moon and made himself indispensable in their eyes to examine the mining potential of earth's natural satellite. Erica had never had a chance of getting on their team. He grinned at the bright circle of sapphire and swirling ivory on the horizon. The blot of white in the south was captured in the sun's radiance. That's how far away she was and how distant from thwarting him from his dreams. "I've won, Erica," he whispered.

"Who is Erica?" asked Vochenkov, the robust Russian cosmonaut and one of the first residents of LUNA I. He had a large square-cut face, a neatly trimmed golden goatee and expressive mauve eyes. He seemed to radiate barely contained mirth, but on occasion, such as when David made a minor error on the solar array hookup, he could abruptly switch to a stern, almost menacing demeanor.

"Just a girl I knew," David mumbled. He followed the Russian to the table set up for breakfast.

"It wouldn't be that volcanologist, would it?" asked Bosley, winking at David as he sucked his reconstituted orange juice from a bag. "I thought her name was Erica."

David scowled. "Miserable woman."

"Oh, yes," said Vochenkov. "I remember. She was the one on that video clip you sent me." He raised his brows pointedly at Bosley.

David's eyes narrowed suspiciously. "Why were you sending video clips of *her* to our team up here?" he asked the astrophysicist.

"I thought she was cute," said Bosley. "God knows the men up here have little enough to look at."

"But," David started to protest.

"It was appreciated," said Vochenkov. "She's a feisty one. And nice looking too," he added. "Nice round…" He emphasized with his hands at his chest, but was interrupted by a *thunk* as the airlock seal to Luna Cat I snapped open. In stepped astronaut Jing-Mei Wong, her sleek black hair cocooned around her tiny face. Intelligent eyes examined the men and knew instantly what they were talking about. How did women always know?

"I guess you're not talking about me," she said, eyeing Vochenkov's hands. The close-fitting uniforms they wore emphasized their physical features or, as was her case, the lack thereof. She smiled, so it obviously didn't bother her much.

"What we need to discuss is our assignments," said Chivas, who startled them all by the way he could appear in such a confined area from out of nowhere. He must have come from the storage area in the back for there was nowhere else to hide in the HAB unless you were in one of the Luna Cats or outside in a pressure suit. His Latin features were crinkled into a miniature scowl that gave him a 'no nonsense' appearance. It seemed a constant feature of his, along with tense, rippling musculature and a wrinkled brow. He took his job far too seriously. "I think it's time to do a survey of the North Pole for that fabled ice deposit. We'll send our little roving robot on his first expedition. Leclerk, will you get him prepped?"

"*Oui, mon capitaine*," said the Frenchman, offering up a mock salute.

David grinned and injected some hot water into his pouch of oatmeal.

Chivas frowned and shook his head. "I run a tight ship, but you don't have to salute. Now it should take the robot a couple of days to get there and begin drilling. In the meantime, Marsh and Vochenkov will check out the Hadley Rille."

David grimaced.

"Find out for us, Dr. Marsh, if there is a habitable cave in the vicinity. It could spare us a lot of extra work."

"I thought I'd be doing some surveying of the rocks in the area for the possibility of mining the soil."

Chivas's face flushed with an angry burn. "Are you questioning my orders?"

"No, of course not," he said quickly. It was hard to swallow his pride, since he'd never been in the military like most of these men and the woman as well, but it was in his best interest not to rub shoulders with the Commander just three days into the mission.

"You will have plenty of opportunity for prospecting, Dr. Marsh. Our priorities have been set. And since you're the geologist, you get the cave."

David nodded. They wanted him to go spelunking, he'd go spelunking. Although he'd never cared for fieldwork as much as Erica had, at least there would be no bats in these caves.

Chivas continued without dropping eye contact with David. "Wong and I will monitor the base and the rover. Houston will maintain radio contact with you."

David nodded solicitously.

"Is everyone clear on their duties?"

"Yes, sir," came the chorus.

"What about Bosley?" asked David. From the frown on Chivas face, he knew he'd stuck his foot in his mouth again.

"Bosley will be doing some preliminary work on the telescopes and looking for a crater deep enough to block sunlight continually so we can set up CAPS."

David frowned. He'd gotten used to the acronyms over the years of working for NASA, but some always sneaked past him. "What exactly is CAPS again?"

"The Comet/Asteroid Protection System," said Bosley with a smug smile. "Why I'm here."

"Oh yes. Sorry, I forgot."

"We all have our specialties," said Chivas. "Each of us is here for a reason. Dr. Bosley might have the most crucial job of all, if we're to prevent any major impacts on earth like we see all around us on the moon."

David blinked. "But these impacts are millions, if not billions of years old."

Chivas looked like he was losing his patience. He rolled his eyes to the ceiling and sighed. "There was one in 1953 seen by an amateur astronomer in Oklahoma."

"Amateur?" said David skeptically.

Now he could see Chivas very white teeth gleam against his tan skin. "The Clementine spacecraft we sent up in 1994 *proved* the amateur's find. We know of many impacts throughout the millennia on earth. Even though we have the LINEAR project…"

David frowned.

Chivas scrunched his face up even more in chagrin. "The Lincoln Near Earth Asteroid Research project that has telescopes set up on the White Sands Missile Range in New Mexico to observe asteroid orbits and determine which are a real danger to earth. Despite their constant vigilance searching our skies, they can't see as well as we could from our position on the moon."

"As you should know, considering your own work on impacts," said Bosley.

"Of course," said David quickly. He suddenly remembered reading about the project in order to keep on track with his 'supposed' specialty. Asteroids were hard to see because they reflect little light and they were always on the move. It was necessary to scan the same patch of sky over and over, looking for changing objects against a static background of stars. It would be easy to miss faint but potentially destructive asteroids from their position on earth.

"That's what your friend Erica specializes in too, doesn't she?" Bosley asked with a wink.

Red flashed behind David's eyes at the mention of her name again. "She's not my friend," he snarled. "I hadn't seen her in years until that conference. And I'm every bit as capable as she is for this assignment."

Vochenkov looked at Chivas and raised his eyebrows. Chivas just frowned. "Of course you are," he said softly. "No one is questioning that, unless you are?"

Damn. He'd done it again. "No, no. There's no one better qualified. I'll get the Luna Cat prepped and we'll head over to the Rille pronto."

"Very good," said Chivas. He turned away and stalked back to the communications console.

David gulped down his orange juice and spooned the last mound of oatmeal into his mouth. He looked away from his cabinmates, but he could still feel their eyes on him. Why did he have to be such a fool? They were already questioning his ability before he'd done one assignment, mainly because he couldn't keep his mouth shut about Erica. Why did he have to feel a tiny edge of guilt even though he'd worked for years for NASA to get this far? He was every bit as good a geologist as she was, and he was going to prove it.

Jing-Mei swept her long hair away from her face and swallowed her last gulp of juice. Her eyes never left his face – cool, penetrating eyes that threatened to dig beneath the surface. She'd already made it clear that she didn't trust him. Now he'd made it worse by exposing his own doubts. He watched her get up smoothly and carefully from the table. No abrupt movements. Life in this lower gravity was a lot like swimming for the first time. Some people had the knack - they propelled themselves evenly and efficiently through the water - while others fought from sinking with their frantic dog paddle movements. He needed to learn to stop fighting and go with the flow. David tried to copy her, rising slowly and following with measured steps to the Luna Cat airlock.

"I've checked all her systems," said the astronaut. "She looks good to go."

David nodded.

"Good," said Vochenkov. He had slunk up behind David in a smooth imitation of Jing-Mei, although he'd had more time to adapt in the three months he had already spent on the moon with Chivas. During that time the two astronauts had set up the HAB and the canopy to protect it from cosmic rays and micrometeorites and joined the Luna Cats to the HAB. They'd spent a lot of time working in the lower gravity until it had become almost second nature. However, knowing this didn't help David feel any less awkward and ill-suited to the environment.

His clumsiness became even more evident as he tripped through the airlock into the adjoining Luna Cat, feeling the Chinese astronaut's eyes drill through him like augers. The Russian didn't comment as he ducked in behind, effectively blocking her view of him. It was an added relief when Jing-Mei slammed the airlock home with a thud.

Vochenkov groped for the handle to open the secondary lock to the RV rover interior and twisted it sharply. The hatch popped in, clunking against the inside wall, and David entered their mobile home with a churning stomach – that fine admixture of eagerness and nervousness flooding his belly. The Rover was a masterpiece of NASA engineering. It was pressurized and had a couple of bunks with thin mattresses and sleeping bags perched on top, and some freeze dried food and water stores in cupboards over a small counter. They could be quite self sufficient for a number of days, even weeks, in the vehicle. David sat down in the passenger chair with a grimace that echoed the sentiments in his stomach. He left the driver's seat to Vochenkov. He wasn't about to take the lead in this assignment.

"I'll drive back," he said.

The Russian grunted. He gazed at the computer that gave them a map of their position and a heading for the Hadley Rille. A compass would be useless in the low magnetic field of the moon so he had to rely on computer tracking and the very detailed maps of the lunar surface in its hard drive to gauge where they were going and to direct their return. He started the engine and put the Cat into gear. The huge tires spun for a second on the loose gritty surface, but as Vochenkov eased up on the throttle, it bounced forward. The path they would take was around George Crater and Elbow Crater (referring to a bend in the Hadley Rille as it wound its sinuous course toward the highlands) and through some fairly level plains in the mare. They would continue on along the Apennine Mountains that rose 12,000 to 15,000 feet above the lunar surface and investigate a smooth area on lunar maps where the Rille disappears for a few miles beside Hadley C crater. It would be a 40-mile trip that would take them about two to three hours in the Luna Cat. The slow traveling speed was essential over the very treacherous lunar terrain, pocked with craters and jagged protruding rock. Despite his disappointment at this assignment, David began to enjoy the scenery. Where else could you see barren mountains etched against an inky black sky, scalloped craters of immense proportions and undisturbed dust for millennia? Where on earth could you find such solitude?

Eventually they reached the canyon walls of the Rille. The Rille itself was only five miles from the base, although it seemed like they were stationed a lot farther from it because perspective was different in this colorless terrain and unfiltered sunlight than it was on earth. Features that looked a few feet away could actually be miles and it was easy to become disoriented. Vochenkov kept checking his bearing on the computer, then he swung around to the south and headed along the canyon edge.

David's eyes widened as he stared at the U-shaped valley that yawned in the middle of the smooth soil surface. It was as if a giant worm had wriggled its way through the regolith and left an impression like a fossil on rock. Inside there were large black areas of shadow disturbingly contrasted to the white-cast of lunar soil in the long lunar day – fourteen earth days in total. David suppressed the urge to shiver. The view from the lunar surface was certainly different from the spacecraft. Although it was just absence of color due to the lack of atmosphere for light to bounce off of – a scientific phenomenon and nothing that should make the fingers of fear creep down his spine – he couldn't help but think of old science fiction films. Every shadow seemed a place that could hold back a flock of ravenous birdlike aliens with a penchant for human flesh.

But nothing leapt out of the dark pools of rock. Nothing slithered or flitted into sight. There was not even a shiver of dust ahead in the windless atmosphere. Only the steady plod of the balloon wheels over the grit and the wisp of dust they spun up behind them. David tried to shake off the weight of fear in this near weightless environment. It would certainly not endear him to these staunch astronauts if he succumbed to a panic attack. The moon was not empty of danger, but only carelessness might lead to a mishap. He had to adhere to all of NASA's strict protocols for spacewalks, or EVAs (extravehicular activity) as they liked to call them and he would be fine. His first experience in the open atmosphere of the moon was coming up. He was going to enjoy every second and forget about this ridiculous, irrational fear.

They trundled along the spur of conical mountains and the deep gully of the Rille in silence until Vochenkov finally spoke in his clipped Russian accent. "Like home?" he asked, nodding at the depression.

"What?" David blinked in surprise.

"The Rille. Is not like your Grand Canyon?"

David rolled his eyes. "I'm from Maine."

Vochenkov shrugged. "I was thinking every geologist had visited. A wonder of nature."

David nodded slowly. "I've seen it. But this isn't like it at all. There's no water gushing through the bottom, no fish or birds. It's like a dried up riverbed in a desert. Not that I'm not fascinated. No geologist on earth has seen this. I've beat them all."

Vochenkov frowned. "Is just a competition for you, isn't it? Not adventure of a lifetime. Not most fascinating opportunity for science. Just a race."

"Wasn't that what it was to you Russians during the cold war? As much as it was to the Americans?"

Vochenkov grunted. "That was then. This is new age. We are here to learn and broaden our horizons together. Race is over."

"Only because we won," said David.

The Russian sighed loudly. "I thought you were scientist. Most scientists I meet are interested in that alone – science. Knowledge and wisdom – something to take us beyond creatures of lust and ambition."

"Then you haven't met many scientists," said David. "Haven't you ever heard of the Nobel prize? Every scientist wants his theory to be 'the one.' How resistant they are to new ideas when they break down their own. Scientists are creatures of lust and ambition just as much as the average man, maybe even more so."

Vochenkov looked him up and down. "How far will ambition take you?"

"To the moon, of course."

"At what price?"

"Excuse me?"

"What have given up to reach the moon?"

"I don't know what you mean," said David. "I haven't given up anything."

"Really?" The Russian looked away. "I think we're almost here."

David swallowed and followed the pilot's gaze. He grasped the armrest to try to still his trembling hands. Damn this Russian and his noble ideals. Everyone had to sacrifice something to make it to the top. Surely this man had done something he wasn't proud of to become a cosmonaut. He remembered reading the man's background in a profile by Life magazine. Vochenkov came from an impoverished background – a farmer's son. Maybe in the former Soviet Union it would have been possible to become a cosmonaut from such meek beginnings – back then they had been guinea pigs anyway. But no longer. Somehow this man had pulled some strings, or plucked the right one out of a spool, just like he had.

The Luna Cat ground to a halt, jolting David out of his reverie. The deep canyon came to an abrupt end, as if a plug had been inserted into it. It was capped over with a mound of dirt and rocks, a solid wall on the top, but in the depths it was so black it was like an oil slick.

"We can't see bottom from here," said Vochenkov. "We won't know if it's solid or hollow unless we go down and have look."

David stared at the inky shadows and felt prickles of panic seep into his skin again. "Go down there?"

"We'll have to rappel down," he said. "You have rappelled before, haven't you?"

"Of course," said David. He could still picture himself dangling from a rope over a precipice with Erica hauling him up toward a steaming cauldron. He broke out into a sweat, despite the air-cooled interior of the Luna Cat.

Vochenkov spun away from the wheel and headed for the airlock. "We'll suit up and pre-breathe, then we'll take a look around."

It took David a good ten minutes longer to get into his multilayered pressure suit and oxygen pack. The first step was shinnying into the spandex body suit called the Liquid Cooling and Ventilation Garment (LCVG). This set of 'long underwear' was laced with spaghetti-thin water lines in order to circulate cooled water next to the astronaut's skin. It was essential since it could get as hot as 212°F (100°C) during the day up here on the moon. On top of that came twelve more layers of material. They ranged from the pressure bladder layer to maintain adequate pressure inside the suit outward through seven aluminized Mylar layers to protect the astronaut from the extreme cold in shadow or at night on the moon, -320°F (-195°C), to the outer shell composed of Gortex, Kevlar and Nomex. Kevlar was used in bulletproof vests and was needed to prevent the penetration of micrometeorites. After that it was the Hard Upper Torso(HUT) made of fiberglass and steel that was attached to the Portable Life Support System backpack (PLSS). The backpack contained the suit's oxygen, battery and water supplies for cooling and drinking. It also had dual radios to provide communications back to the HAB and to Mission Control. Then it was just a matter of snapping on the clear, double-pane helmet made of high impact Lexan – an ultra strong kind of plastic. *Et voila*, he was trussed up like a turkey for Thanksgiving.

Vochenkov had already contacted Houston to tell them of their plans, just in case they ran into trouble. Houston was monitoring their progress, but seemed much more interested in how the robotic rover was doing on its way to the North Pole. David took a full two minutes to pre-breathe pure oxygen so they wouldn't get any nitrogen bubbles in their blood in the lower pressure like a diver who swims up to the surface too quickly. The Russian activated the switch to depressurize and counted the standard thirty seconds - so they wouldn't be blown out of the Luna Cat - before he opened the airlock. He jumped down and grabbed the cable from a winch on the back of the Cat. David attached the belt and loops that would hold them on their climb down the wall of the Rille.

"Ready?" Vochenkov's voice crackled over the COMM – NASAese for 'communicator.'

David nodded, unable to trust his voice. He was breathing a little too quickly, so he made a conscious effort to slow it down. It wouldn't help his situation if he passed out on the way down into the nether regions of the moon. He clipped onto the nearest link on the cable, closed his eyes and took a deep breath. Vochenkov clipped on a little higher, so, of course, David would be the first to be lowered to the floor of the canyon. Placing a firm hold on the line with one hand, David backed over the edge, keeping his other hand out to avoid a collision with the rock wall. There was a jerk as the cable wound out. He had expected some sort of sound to warn him – like a whir from the mechanism – but there was no sound. The thick layers of his suit were barriers to sound other than radio communications and all he could hear was his own harsh breathing. Even if he were outside of his suit in the real lunar environment, there would be no sound. Sound waves couldn't move through a vacuum, which the moon's atmosphere was very close to being despite a small amount of helium, argon, neon and hydrogen picked up from solar wind or radioactive decay of the lunar surface elements.

He descended. The shadows grew long and abysmal. David couldn't see his clunky lunar boots below him. The line played out in a steady drop, but he couldn't avoid glancing off the wall every once and a while and bounding away from it in the low gravity. He had to keep his hands and feet in a constant defensive posture to prevent hitting too hard on the sharp spikes of rock and puncturing the suit. A definite hazard. It was good, though. It kept his mind occupied so he didn't dwell on the emptiness and the infernal shadow.

Finally his feet touched down on the shifty lunar soil. He unclipped and stepped away from the rope as Vochenkov descended right behind him.

David dug into a pocket of his suit and removed a short-stemmed flashlight. He flicked it on and started walking away, although he found it hard to take normal steps in the bulky suit and low gravity.

"Where you going?" asked Vochenkov.

"They want us to check out the plug, we'll check out the plug."

"You go too fast," said the Russian. "Use too much energy. Small jumps, like they taught us at home."

"It takes too long," said David, stumbling on a large boulder in his path.

"Please... and stick... protocol... Marsh," crackled a voice over the COMM. He'd almost forgotten - Mission Control was monitoring every movement the two of them were making now that they were EVA. He'd have to watch his words. It would appear, though, that the signal wasn't very strong down here in the trough.

"Copy that," he replied. Hopefully they didn't catch the lilt in his voice.

David dutifully mimicked the hops that Vochenkov was doing as he headed toward the plug in the Rille. The Russian had his own flashlight aimed at the wall, but it barely speared the syrupy darkness. They skipped forward like a couple of jackrabbits, running right at the wall of black and right through it. It was, after all, hollow.

"This is excellent," said Vochenkov. "It is lava tube, just like you predicted in your paper."

David winced. "You read my paper?"

"Had to. It was mission required reading. Houston, do you copy?"

There was blank susurration on the COMM.

"I guess roof of cave is blocking our signal."

David gulped and nodded, even though he knew Vochenkov couldn't see him in the thick shadow.

"Let's see how far this goes," said the Russian. "Then you take samples and make assessments."

David nodded again.

"Do you read me, Marsh?"

"Y..Yes," said David.

"Is something wrong?"

"No," said David. "It's a great discovery. Let's get the job done."

"Copy that," said Vochenkov. He played the beam over the walls and up towards the roof of the lava tube, but it couldn't really differentiate between the black of the basalt and the black of the tunnel itself. They kept walking for what seemed like hours over the uneven ground, David close on Vochenkov's heels, until the Russian grunted, fell back and knocked the geologist clean off his feet.

"What'd you do that for?" David snarled.

"Wall in front of us," said the Russian.

David dusted himself off and tried to get up. It was easier said than done in the EMU suit. He rolled off the oxygen pack to his side and gathered his legs up under him with a grunt. Then he tried to push off, but the push was too hard and he ended up sprawled the other way.

"Having trouble?" asked Vochenkov, amusement clear in his voice.

"No," said David as he bounced the other way again.

"Tsk, tsk. Too much pride." The Russian reached out and grabbed his arm, lifting David to his feet with steady but not too great pressure or he would have fallen over again.

David shook himself off and glared at Vochenkov. Lot of good it did, though, since the Russian could no more see his face than he could see the Russian's.

"Is this the end of the line?" he asked hopefully.

"It would appear so. Why don't you take some samples while I inspect the rest of this."

"Good plan," said David, relieved that he had the easy job. Just hammer out a few rocks while Vochenkov fumbled around in the dark. He reached into one of his multiple pockets in the suit stuffed with tools and withdrew a geologist's hammer with a tapered end and a vacuum-sealed plastic bag for sample collection. At the same time he was juggling his flashlight, creating a stroboscopic effect in the cave. Finally he managed to steer a steady beam at the wall. It was smooth black basalt, definitely a filament of lava that had dripped down from the roof and sealed the cave. He chipped away at it, delicately at first, but as the thin light of Vochenkov's flashlight flickered farther and farther away, he felt the weight press down on him again. He'd seen too many movies in his lifetime. He could have sworn he heard flapping wings or the hiss of acid-dripping teeth. The hammer dug deeper and deeper. Chips were flying everywhere.

There was a crackle on the COMM. David jumped as he felt a hand touch his arm. "You don't have to dig through the wall," said Vochenkov, emerging out of the shadow.

He fell back and clutched a hand to his chest. "Why the hell did you sneak up on me like that?"

"Has place got you spooked?" chuckled the cosmonaut. "Is very dark, but is also very dead. Nothing here but shadows and rock." As if to emphasize his point he pounded his fist into the spot where the geologist had been chipping.

David didn't hear anything, but he could feel a jet of pressure on the outside of his suit. He stared at the hole in the wall. It looked like it was breaking up, spider web streaks fanned out from the center. They cracked apart and a blowback punched into the men, propelling them thirty feet backward in a swirl of lunar dust.

Sixteen

Erica stomped over the McMurdo compound toward the Mammoth Mountain Inn, another squat housing structure beside the Hotel California with the same sparse accommodations. This was where Staten and his troops were billeted. She'd almost made it through the first set of doors when a hand clamped down on her arm and spun her around.

"Where the hell do you think you're going?" asked Allan, his face flushed despite the bite of the wind.

Erica's eyes narrowed. "I have to talk to Commander Staten." She looked down pointedly at the hand digging into her arm through the bulky scarlet parka.

Allan ignored the warning in her eyes and maintained his grasp. "You seem to be getting quite cozy with the Commander."

"What is that supposed to mean?"

"You left me in that bloody room all afternoon, jotting down notes for you, surrounded by a pack of military madmen so you could pursue the venerable Commander Staten. Now I'm finally released and where do I find you? Again, pursuing Staten."

"I would hardly call him 'venerable,'" snapped Erica. "What business is it of yours, anyway, whom I pursue?"

Allan looked steadily into her eyes and his grip tightened even more. His chest was heaving and his teeth gleamed through his clenched jaw. Erica thought he was going to slap her. She flinched as he raised his free hand; it swept down and grasped her other arm tightly. He pulled her toward him before she could prevent it and planted his mouth firmly on hers. The kiss was hot, electric and much as she hated herself for reacting, triggered a sizzle through her blood. She could barely feel the cold anymore as his tongue thrust into her mouth and dashed against her own.

She was slipping away, and she shouldn't, couldn't, *not with this scoundrel.* It was only when she felt the thrust of his pelvis and the hard knot at her groin – even through the many padded layers – that she came to her senses. She tried to pull away, but he held her even tighter. With a jerk, she jabbed her knee up between them and pushed him away.

"No, Allan," she said, gasping. "I don't want this. I don't want *you.*"

Rocheford grinned and slowly ran his tongue over his lips, freezing them solid no doubt, but he didn't seem to care. "Yes, you do."

"You bastard. You know exactly how I feel about what you stand for."

Allan shrugged. "You haven't given me half a chance to explain who I am and what I stand for."

"Really?" said Erica. He was looking at her with steaming eyes and she felt herself melting again. She had to strike out, or she would lose. "Why should I give you a chance? You'd only take advantage of me, like you did the Egyptian government."

Allan blinked. His jaw tightened and she could see, with some relief, that she had driven him back.

"You're like a cobra," he said. "You strike as soon as you feel threatened. Did he hurt you that badly?"

Erica gaped. "Who are you talking about?"

"You know exactly who I'm talking about. David Marsh. I'm no fool. I saw the look in your eyes when you saw him at the conference. At first I thought it was another woman. But it was more than that, wasn't it? He betrayed you where it hurt you the most. As a scientist..."

She tried to keep her face rigid, but her lower lip trembled. She blinked several times to prevent the tears from edging out, but an obstinate one crept out anyway and froze on her cheek.

He leaned toward her and gently swept it away with his glove. "Tell me," he breathed into her ear.

"You wouldn't understand." She tried to stop trembling.

"Try me," he said.

She took a deep breath. "H…he stole m…my thesis. He t…took away my career."

"With NASA?"

She nodded. "He pretended that he loved me. Then he stabbed me in the back." She stopped herself and turned away. What was she doing telling this man about her darkest hour? How could she make herself vulnerable to another man, especially a pseudo-scientist? It was crazy, yet the relief was like a noose lifted from her neck.

She raised her head and met his gaze. That hard, gritty mouth appeared for the first time to have softened. His eyes were moist with empathy as he touched her cheek again. "I'm not a threat to you," he said. "In fact, I'm giving you an opportunity instead of taking it away."

"What do you mean?" Erica frowned.

"I wanted you here from the beginning. Oh, they argued with me. They said there were better experts. I disagreed. And they needed me for this, so they had to go along with my recommendation."

"You wanted me here? What are you talking about?"

Allan took a deep breath and leaned against the flimsy metal wall of the hotel. A few parka-clad bleary-eyed scientists shuffled past them toward the door, peering out of the deep cups of their fur-lined hoods. They looked at them curiously – people rarely spent a lot of time talking outdoors in Antarctica unless they were in the field. He waited until they were inside. "It has to do with Atlantis."

Erica shook her head. "Don't spout that nonsense, please."

"NASA didn't think it was nonsense. Haven't you ever read the theories about Atlantis being on Antarctica?"

"Of course I've heard of them. When the ice cap got too big, the poles shifted and ripped the skin of the earth around, driving Antarctica into a deep freeze. And this happened, what? Ten thousand years ago?"

"Einstein thought is was possible."

"Possible that there had been a pole shift. Not that Antarctica was a green field only ten thousand years ago. The ice is thousands of meters thick, Allan."

"Okay, what about the Piri Reis maps – they were ancient, copied down through the centuries and most likely came from the library of archaic scrolls in Alexandria. They showed Antarctica without the ice sheet?"

"They're not as *accurate* as claimed," said Erica with emphasis. "And they don't take into account what the continent would look like in rebound from the massive ice sheet. It would have been raised over 3000 feet in the interior and 160 feet along the coasts."

"I guess I shouldn't debate this with a geologist."

Erica raised her eyebrows. "Any more questions?"

"There's still the fact that they found wooly mammoths instantly frozen in Asia, some with flowers in their mouths. That would suggest a catastrophic event like the slipping of the earth's crust."

"That's an easy one. I've read all the data, Allan. So many catastrophe adherents subscribe to theories without checking their facts. It was probably a catastrophe, but not global. The mammoths died of asphyxia, most likely from a landslide. They were not as well preserved as was claimed at first and radiocarbon dating showed that they were not all frozen at the same time. It's a lame argument. Antarctica is NOT Atlantis."

"Okay," said Allan. He turned away and looked at the door longingly. "I'm getting cold. Do you want to go in?"

"That's it? You give up already? I thought you'd have a hundred more arguments."

"I do," said Allan. "But not on the pole shift."

"Then on what?"

"My lips are turning blue and my teeth are chattering. Can we take this inside?"

"All right," said Erica. "We'll talk in the lounge."

"I was thinking of somewhere more private. Like, say, your room."

Erica choked. "Not on your life, although I wouldn't exactly characterize it as private. Besides, I still have to talk to Commander Staten."

Allan's ice-rimed eyebrows arched and his mouth set in a hard line.

"I might come clean on the Commander if you tell me everything you know."

"That's a tall order," he said. "I'll see what I can do." He steered her toward the door, and she had to admit, it was a welcome relief to escape the hypothermic wind and granules of snow that pelted them incessantly since they'd parted from their kiss. They stomped across the narrow strip of linoleum in the tiny foyer, shaking loose the crust of snow that had adhered to their boots, then glided over the threadbare carpet in the hall where they shed their outerwear on a coat rack beside the lounge. The lounge was a small room with a couple of cheap couches, a TV and DVD player and some posters of Sports Illustrated Swimsuit models on the walls. Erica tried to keep her eyes on the floor as she hung her coat on the hook. She could feel Allan's hot gaze rake over her body, and a bloom of color that had nothing to do with the cold stained her cheeks.

"You really are beautiful when you're not trying to tear a strip off of me," he whispered.

The color rose even higher and she caught her breath. She closed her eyes, steadied her trembling hands, and then met his eyes with a clash. "You wanted me here," she said. "I assume it had nothing to do with sex since you'd never met me before the flight to Orlando. So why are you doing this?"

Allan shrugged and fed his hand through his snow-streaked hair. "You're right. Wanting you here has nothing to do with wanting you. Maybe it started with the challenge of cracking that hard shell you've cast around yourself. But now that I have cracked it, I just want to probe deeper. It's no longer a challenge. It's a need."

He brushed past her, sending a zing of electricity through her veins as he headed for the couch in the corner of the lounge. There were two other people in the far corner opposite them – wind-burned scientists brooding over some mundane piece of data. They were so absorbed in their topic, however, that they didn't even notice the spring-loaded tension between the other two scientists. Erica followed Allan to the well-worn leather couch, looking for a chair she could pull up opposite him, but he snatched her hand and pulled her down beside him.

"I don't think this is a good idea."

"I'm not going to jump on you in a hotel lounge." He smiled reassuringly, but his eyes still held a smolder that wouldn't die.

Erica swallowed and nodded. "I just don't think we should get involved."

"Why not?"

"Because we're working together."

"Wow. Then you actually admit it. You've accepted me as one of your own."

"Oh, stop it. Are you going to tell me why you brought me here or not?"

He grinned. "Of course. But you'll have to bear with me and keep your skepticism to a minimum."

"I'll try."

"I guess that's all I can ask. Here goes." He took a deep breath. "The Atlanteans lived approximately 10,000 years ago. They built the Sphinx to align with the Milky Way and the stars and they built the pyramids over many years for some other purpose."

Erica raised her eyebrows, but kept her lips tightly sealed. How could she respect this man if he actually believed in fairy tales?

"They did not live in Antarctica."

"Then why are you here?" She couldn't resist.

"I said they didn't *live* here. That doesn't mean they didn't come here, just like Scott and all the explorers that ventured out a hundred years ago. They lived on an island, or, they lived on the coast – they were seafarers. That meant that they were almost completely wiped out by something cataclysmic."

"I thought you didn't subscribe to the pole shift theory."

"You can't help yourself, can you?" He was looking at her sternly, but there was a sparkle in his eyes.

Erica shrugged and grinned.

"I don't think it was a pole shift, but it was something that could cause massive tidal waves and devastating fires."

Erica's eyes widened. "You're not suggesting…"

Allan dug into his pocket and removed a very crumpled sheaf of papers. He read: "*the tektites in Australia* – basically rounded rocks from impact melt, right?"

She nodded, her forehead rippling up into her bangs. Her heart was pounding in her ears.

He continued to read: "*are dated at approximately the same time as the new impact site found in the Arctic tundra, 7500 BC, corroborating the theory of a shower of cometary fragments at this period. According to the size of the impact, it would have had global implications*." He looked at her.

Erica was frozen, her eyes welded to his.

"I subscribe to Marsh's theory."

The paralysis broke. She clenched her fists.

"Sorry, I mean *your theory*."

"You knew," she breathed.

"I suspected. My assumption was confirmed when I called him and asked him about the possibility of this cometary impact wiping out all coastal societies. He hummed and hawed and recited *your theory* verbatim, not giving me any new information."

"How did you find me in all this? David would certainly never mention me."

"It took a bit of investigating, but it wasn't too hard. Who were the geologists in his graduate school at Berkeley? Who was now an impact specialist? When I found you, I knew I'd found the scientist behind the theory. So what do you think? Could your comets have wiped out my technologically superior race?"

"Assuming this race existed, yes. But what is your evidence? And what has this got to do with Antarctica?"

"One question at a time. My evidence? *'As for the opening of the seventh seal, ...there followed hail and fire mingled with blood... and the third part of the trees was burnt up; and all the green grass was burnt up...*

'And the second angel sounded, and there fell a great star from heaven, burning as it were a lamp...

The fourth goes on to sound obscurity over the earth. The fifth angel ushers in yet another impact: *'I saw a star fall from heaven upon the earth... and there rose a smoke out of the pit, as the smoke of a great furnace, and the sun and the air were darkened.'"*

"You're quoting Revelations. That's your proof?"

"Possibly a prediction. More likely an event from history. There's much more - the remnants of humanity in the mountainous regions – the survivors – that somehow magically knew how to grow crops and so ushered in the age of agriculture. The text I found in the chamber beneath the sphinx."

"I read about your chamber. There was nothing in that text except a tribute to the gods."

"The gods of the primeval mound from which all life sprung. Couldn't that mound have been the huge lump of congealed mass that exploded in the Big Bang – the birth of our universe?"

Erica frowned, but she didn't interrupt.

"And if you'd read enough of the mythology you'd realize that what the Egyptians venerated above all else were the scholars. In my definition – the scientists. And the scientists built something of immense importance in Antarctica."

"They wrote about it?"

Allan shook his head. "Not in plain text, but numbers were scrawled all over the chamber. The language itself predated even Egyptian hieroglyphics, but it was sufficiently similar to cuneiform used in ancient Sumerian and Babylonian writing for me to decipher the numerical values. At first we couldn't figure out what they meant. It was just mumbo jumbo to an archeologist, so I consulted an astronomer. After all, the pyramids are lined up with the stars. He determined them to be angles. Angles from the pyramids to the constellation of Orion, from the Sphinx to the constellation of Leo."

"So you have proof of the theory that the Sphinx is aligned with The Milky Way. What has that got to do with Antarctica?"

"Those weren't the only numbers. On a separate wall, beside a strange diagram of a pyramid were totally different figures and strange oscillating patterns." He leaned over and drew some squiggly lines on a cocktail napkin on the squat coffee table in front of the couch. They looked something like ocean waves. "I had a whole slew of experts wade through them – mathematicians, astronomers, even some physicists."

Erica frowned.

"These people were geniuses, Erica, no matter how long ago they lived. They knew of star systems that we have only recently been able to locate with the new Hubble Telescope. It wasn't only Orion they were interested in. And the numbers were so confusing to me, but to physicists they had quantum implications. The number four seemed to be repeated over and over. I know the number four was always revered in the ancient world – the four seasons, the four directions in space. There were endless examples. But the physicists immediately linked the number to the four basic forces in the universe – the strong and weak forces of particles, the electromagnetic force and gravity. These Atlanteans, for want of a better name, seemed to know about things that I have trouble grasping even after studying a bit of quantum mechanics in college. But I digress. Well, no one could figure out these separate figures on the wall until I sent them to NASA and some low level consultants, a geographer and a geologist, came across them."

"Geographer?"

"They were simple coordinates on earth and somewhere else."

Erica tilted her head. "The coordinates were in Antarctica?"

Allan nodded. "Your little 'hotspot,' to be precise. I was the only one interested in these coordinates at first. You see, there had been no detection of any thermal activity prior to midwinter of this past year. I tried to convince a certain party to invest in an excursion to the site. They were very interested."

"Were they the same party you sold all the gold statuary to?"

Allan ignored the jibe and continued on. "But we were vetoed by the NSF. They don't encourage private excursions to their pristine wilderness. It wasn't until strange things started happening down here that NASA and the Pentagon became interested in those coordinates."

"Strange as in thermal activity, or strange as in people disappearing?"

"Oh, you know about that too."

"I know. When were you going to tell me?"

"Soon. Now, actually. I wasn't going to send you in blind."

"Right," said Erica, her mouth twisted sideways. Allan was about to open his mouth to protest his noble intentions, no doubt, when she cut him off. "It doesn't matter anymore. I know everything, about the science team, about the Russians."

"The Russians?" Allan frowned.

"Oh, there's something I know that you don't. Isn't that a corker? That's why I'm here, trying to pry more information out of the Commander and insist on accompanying him to Vostok."

"Vostok?"

"I'll tell you later, maybe. If you tell me what is supposed to be at these coordinates and why you would need me at all, besides to corroborate your theory."

"I don't know what the 'hotspot' is. A pyramid maybe."

Erica blinked. "You dragged me down here to check out a pyramid?"

"It's a very strange pyramid, Erica. As you can see, it's very hot. Under a sheet of ice, that's unusual, isn't it? Unless it's a volcano. I don't even think you believe that anymore. But what was really interesting was the drawing right beside the sketch of the pyramid under the Sphinx. It looked like a falling star."

"Okay, now you have me totally baffled. If what you say is true – if a comet wiped out the Atlanteans and this comet fell near your pyramid, then your pyramid would have been vaporized, unless..."

"Unless?"

"Well, there could have been fragments that impacted at various locations. That's sort of where the evidence stands right now. A small fragment might not have destroyed your pyramid, assuming it exists."

Allan grinned. "Yes. That could explain it. You see, that's why I need you. You're an expert on these earth impacts and you only believe in the empirically evident, so if anyone can prove or disprove my theory, it would be you."

"And if I prove it, then you will be vindicated in the world's eye. They won't remember that you were the greedy bastard that ripped off the Egyptians."

Allan winced. "That smarts. You won't believe me, will you, if I tell you I had to do it in order to get beneath the Sphinx. Only a lot of *baksheesh* – you know, bribes – in the Egyptian government's pockets would get me there, so I needed a wealthy backer. I didn't want to remove any of those treasures. But I still think the mathematics, the astronomy and those coordinates were worth more than all the gold in Egypt."

"Really?" said Erica. She gazed at his tense body. His lower lip wobbled just a fraction. Then she frowned. "You said there was more than one set of coordinates. Where were the others?"

Allan sucked on his lower lip.

"Allan?"

"You don't want to know."

"Allan!"

"The moon."

"What?"

"They were on the moon." His gaze slid off her and down the wall.

"The moon! They sent D...David...Ma..." She just couldn't sputter out the name.

"Your nemesis, yes. Along with a very competent crew to check it out."

"I hope they're competent," said Erica, "because with M...Marsh along they'll have to pick up all his slack."

Allan bobbed his head. "I couldn't agree more, having had a very enlightening conversation with him. But you don't have to be jealous anymore, Erica. We may be on the brink of the most exciting discovery mankind has ever made. Evidence of our predecessors – a technologically advanced civilization – made extinct by the same beast that wiped out the dinosaurs."

Erica sighed. "Is that a reason to rejoice or a reason to tremble?"

Seventeen

The door burst open to the hotel lobby and a swirl of snow accompanied the bulky form of the Commander in his Michelin Man Skidoo suit. Erica broke eye contact with Allan abruptly. Even though the cold air frothed against them, she was still suffused in heat as if her internal thermometer was frozen on the high side. She jumped to her feet and dashed toward Staten who was teetering on the beige linoleum by the door.

"Commander. Oh, Commander. I have to talk to you."

He lurched around and glared at her. "I thought our conversation was over, Dr. Daniels." Despite his harsh words and cold stare, his face was gray and he could hardly keep his balance.

"You don't look so good, Commander. Perhaps you should sit down."

"I'm fine, Dr. Daniels." He tensed his muscles to achieve a more rigid posture, despite rapid blinking of his eyes. "In fact, I'll be in tip top shape in a few days in order to accompany you on your mission."

Erica raised her eyebrows, coolly appraising his washed-out face. He didn't appear nearly as threatening when he was ready to pass out. "That's good," she said. "What about Vostok?"

The Commander's eyes narrowed. "I will not be going to Vostok. Neither will you," he added.

"What's in Vostok?" asked Allan, coming up behind Erica. He halted just at her right shoulder and crossed his arms complacently, his right eyebrow cocked in expectation.

Staten looked down at him, his beetled eyebrows nearly meeting. "There is nothing in Vostok," he snarled. He started to turn away, but Allan's words stopped him in mid-stride.

"Except a bunch of tongue-tied Russians."

Erica frowned and looked at him severely.

"I guessed," he flipped in her direction. "The Russians are never very forthcoming, and if the Commander's crew of crack troops is heading over to Vostok, it has to be because they've already investigated this phenomenon."

"Or perhaps created it," said Staten through gritted teeth.

Allan rolled his eyes. "Don't be ridiculous. They didn't scrawl its coordinates in a chamber that's been sealed for ten thousand years."

The Commander's eyes narrowed to tiny slits as he stared at the archeologist. Suspicion seethed in the air between them. "I know your role now in all of this. I've done a little investigating myself. You may try to come across as a scientist, but your work is pure fiction. Anyone could have scribbled some coordinates on a wall, especially if they were tipped off about some mysterious activity at this site."

"It was documented by a number of witnesses," said Allan dryly.

"So either you're in this for the grants and the notoriety," continued the Commander as if Allan hadn't interrupted, "or you're knee-deep in this Russian conspiracy. My guess is they're experimenting with nuclear devices beneath the ice. And we have to nip this in the bud before they start up a whole new arms race."

Erica's raised her brows and stared at the man in disbelief. "You're mad," she said. She opened her mouth to say more, but the door slammed open and Metzer, the SEAL with the warm brown eyes, entered. He was a head shorter than the Commander was, but he didn't balk from meeting the man's stone gaze eye to eye. He was followed closely by the scarred man with anvils for arms.

"The birds are ready to fly, sir," Metzer said crisply, but there was a slight lift to his eyebrow. "We have the refueling plane standing by."

"Full arsenal," added the scarred man, his eyes lighting up like ignited rocket fuel.

Allan frowned. "By birds, you wouldn't mean those Iroquois attack helicopters that flew in from that big naval vessel you have standing just beyond the sea ice?"

Staten glared at Allan, his hands curled into fists.

Erica sucked in her breath. She'd never imagined... The man was absolutely insane. "You can't be serious. You can't just descend on them like a swarm of locusts. This could mean World War III."

"Don't be ridiculous," said Staten. "I have full sanction for this action. The Russians are refusing to explain why our scientists are disappearing. In fact, their silence the Pentagon takes as an admission of guilt. They're murdering Americans and we can't just stand by and let it happen. Right, Bruzo?"

"Right, sir," replied the scarred SEAL. Strange how he'd singled out this man instead of his second in command.

"No," said Erica. "This is all wrong." She'd seen enough military strong-arm in her lifetime, but this was beyond her comprehension. Just because people were disappearing didn't mean you attacked a science station without any proof of culpability. They needed more information. She turned to Metzer, her eyes appealing to his warm side. "What if the Russians are disappearing too? Did you consider that? You can't do this without knowing the facts."

Metzer's lips twitched, but he remained silent.

"Then why aren't they talking?" asked Staten. "They've restarted their nuclear program, away from prying eyes. It's the only explanation."

Erica stamped the soft linoleum, which hardly made a sound. It wasn't exactly the impact she was hoping for, yet they all gazed at her expectantly. "We're not enemies anymore. We have a Russian and a Chinese astronaut up there on the Moon with us, for God's sake. Don't you understand?" She was pleading with Metzer, the only one who didn't seem brainwashed by fanatical dictates.

"I must obey orders," he said softly.

"What's wrong with you military assholes? You just can't stand the peace anymore, so you have to cross that line again. I won't allow it. I won't!"

The Commander crossed his arms, although he almost lost his balance while doing so. Bruzo reached out to steady him, but he brushed his hand away. "And what do you think you can do to stop the U.S. Navy?"

"I'll beat you there," she snarled. To emphasize her point, she spun on her heels and dashed down the hall to where her coat hung dripping on the rack. Allan paused for only a second before he flew up behind her.

"What are you going to do?" he asked as she jammed on her parka.

"Commandeer a Hercules transport," she said as if she were flagging down a taxi.

"That's a pretty tall order."

She ran back up the hallway, rudely brushed past the Commander who was shooting daggers at her through his narrowed eyes, and opened the door. A blast of frigid air and a haze of snow swirled into the hotel. "Not if I play my cards right," she slung over her shoulder, confident the archeologist was right behind her. She leapt forward and plowed through the drifts on the street, heading towards the Chalet. "You see, the NSF is a science organization and I don't think they would relish the idea of some trigger-happy yahoos raiding another bunch of scientists – the Russians – and starting a bloody war."

"Let's hope not," said Allan, pulling up at her side. "This is not what I came down here for."

Erica stopped and grasped his arms, shocking him with her intensity. "Whatever you came here for, money or prestige or vindication, if you help me on this it might be the best thing you ever did. It won't be lucrative and it won't ever make the papers, but it will make me change my mind about you."

"Really?" He grinned boyishly. "You make a very convincing argument, and I was going to do it anyway."

"Good. Then let's go. We have a race to win."

She dashed off into the snow, trying to erase the echo of his words in her mind. Could she trust him now? Could she ever trust another greedy self-serving man?

Eighteen

David twitched and stirred. He opened his eyes, but could see nothing. A bolt of pain zapped through his spine, exploding in brilliant Technicolor in his brain. His head was leaden, and as he moved, the weight of the enormous EMU suit held him back, wrapped around his body like a cocoon. The O2 purred through his helmet and brushed against his face. He was on the moon; that was it. He was in the Hadley Rille and something had hit him and hit him hard.

"Vochenkov?" he called. "Are you there?"

Nothing crackled back over the COMM. Was the cosmonaut dead?

He rolled over, ignoring the slice up his spine again and tried to sit up. It was a laborious exercise that took about three tries, but he finally made it. The next step was to find a flashlight. He felt around with his hands, but came upon nothing but scattered rocks and a layer of spongy dust. The hoarse grunting he made was loud in his ears. Gooseflesh popped up on his arms despite the multilayered suit. It was just so black.

"Houston, d…do you copy?" he stuttered over the COMM, hoping to get some assistance, some guidance as to his next move. There was no response from earth either. He was definitely cut off. He needed to find a light.

David felt around some more, crawling on his knees and grunting in near panic. Finally his hands made contact with something solid and thick. He felt upward and found the round capsule of a helmet. "Vochenkov," he yelled over the COMM again. There was no response from the Russian. No movement whatsoever. "Damn you, Vochenkov. Wake up." He shook him harshly, but the man merely flopped around like a rag doll.

What was he going to do now? The cosmonaut was undoubtedly dead. He probed around the suit in case one of the flashlights had fallen somewhere beside Vochenkov. To his surprise, his fingers curled around the stout cylinder that was still clutched in the cosmonaut's hand. He ripped it away and flicked the switch. There was no light. Nothing. The explosion must have shattered its face.

Explosion! That was what had happened. But how and why? They had just tapped through some rock in the basalt wall. Could there have been gases trapped behind. It was impossible. There was nothing organic to cause a pocket of natural gas or methane to have built up behind the cave. Sulfur maybe. But that would mean an active moon with magma still circulating, which was ridiculous. Everything about this situation was ridiculous. He wasn't trained for this.

Low lunar gravity. Mining oxygen. Setting up a habitat. That was what they'd trained him for. Not dealing with explosions in a pitch-black cave with a dead cosmonaut beside him. He had to get out of here. It seemed as if the low hiss of oxygen circulating through his helmet was diminishing; he knew time was ticking down. How long had he been unconscious? He had about six hours of oxygen in the suit, no more. David searched the cavern for some shimmer of light. Some meaningful ray he could head toward. There wasn't a photon in the tarry blackness. Then he had to use logic. The explosion had blown them backward. If he turned and headed in the same direction the Russian's head was pointed he should make it out. Slowly he scrambled to his feet, a little unsteady, but with better success than the first time he had fallen. He took two steps, then stopped.

What about Vochenkov?

The man was dead. He'd just burden himself by trying to carry him out.

What if he wasn't? If he left him for another crewmember to pick up, his oxygen would run out and he'd be dead for sure. David was his only hope.

He wasn't capable of carrying a man out the long tunnel and up the side of the Rille by himself. It would require superhuman strength.

But he had superhuman strength – at least it seemed that way with the low gravity. It would be a burden, but it wouldn't be impossible.

David turned away. He had never been a noble man. Save himself, that's what he would do. Walk away and make it out alive. That was his philosophy – win at all costs, and winning in this situation meant life.

He took another two steps, then stopped again. The memories rained down on him like a flashflood. Erica with her stunning blue eyes and wavy blonde hair tumbling out of bed to make a class. She'd draped on a silk blouse and pulled skintight jeans over her hips as he watched from his lax posture on the four-poster. As she smiled and leaned over to kiss him goodbye, he'd reached out and fondled her breast through the thin fabric. Then she was gone, the silence unnerving with her absence. It wasn't the silence, however, that itched as he lay there. It wasn't the absence that left him short of breath and gaping at her desk. The document was sitting benignly by the computer – printed and packaged, ready for review by the professor and most likely for publication in a journal. Two years of painstaking work - field studies, lab examinations and consultation. She'd spent five months up in the bitter arctic wind to scour an impact site for shocked quartz and iridium – things he barely understood and could care less about. He'd blinked and blinked. NASA was looking for impact specialists to work for their moon base program – a ten-year study with preliminary satellite and robotic excursions on the moon's surface to determine the perfect site for a future moon base. It was the opportunity of a lifetime. Erica would get the job, he was sure, with this thesis. Something he could only dream of. He got out of bed and stood there, naked, riffling his thick mat of auburn chest hair. The paper was there and what would it cost him? Just one steamy affair. One woman he couldn't compete against because she was too darn good. He reached out and grabbed the document. There'd been no chill, no foreboding wind; just a little stab at the back of his brain. That pain had lessened after ten years, but now it suddenly throbbed as if a red-hot poker had seared the gray matter.

He turned back. It was difficult to bend over in the suit, but he managed to grasp the cosmonaut under his arms and lift him from the spongy surface. With a little shifting, he was able to fling the limp body over his shoulder. The pain eased up immediately, even though this was the heaviest burden he had ever borne.

"I'm not what you think I am, Erica. I'm not."

He stumbled in the direction he had gleaned from Vochenkov's position. Each step was a tortuous trial, laden with jumbled regolith and the occasional slippery smooth surface of basalt. It seemed that the tunnel went on forever, but when his strength started to fade, a harsh slant of light broke through the blackness. He'd made it out.

A bit more stumbling brought him outside, on the far side of the Rille, his eyes tearing in the whitish glare of the sun. He eased Vochenkov to the ground, and stood there heaving. The cable and winch was five hundred feet to his right, blacked out in the dense shadows of the canyon.

"Houston," he gasped into the COMM.

"I copy you, Marsh. Where the hell have you been?" The signal was strong now that he'd cleared the cave.

"We ran…into…some trouble."

"Copy that. What sort of trouble?"

"Some kind of explosion. We were knocked unconscious. I'm not sure if Vochenkov is alive. Can you read his vitals?"

"Vitals are stable, Marsh. He must be concussed. Can you get back to the rover?"

"Think so," said Marsh. "I just carried him out of the tunnel and I'm… a bit winded. I'll try to hook him up to the winch. Stand by."

"Standing by."

David pulled Vochenkov backward through the darkness to the cable and latched him on. He connected to the same loop and pressed the hydraulic switch. With a jerk the line ascended, bumping them again and again against the rock wall. This time he could care less how many times he hit, even if it punctured his suit. He was just too tired. Finally the length of cable they were attached to drew level with the plain above the canyon, drawing them both over the lip. David flicked the switch and the winch stopped pulling. It took a couple of seconds to detach Vochenkov and himself from the line.

"Just outside the rover," he said.

"Copy that."

He opened the hatch and swung Vochenkov inside. "Hatch closed. Pressurizing now."

"Way to go, Marsh. We'll let you get out of your suits and examine Vochenkov before you give us a complete run-down of what happened."

"Roger," said David, rolling his eyes as he waited for the anteroom to fully pressurize. He'd just made it through the most harrowing experience in his life and they'd hardly give him time to breathe before they demanded explanations. He felt the strong magnetic force suck the moon dust from his suit as the oppositely charged walls of the anteroom activated, a practical solution to the invasive dust that could clog and disrupt electronics on the Luna Cat. The instrument panel blinked in front of him - the ideal pressure had been reached. He unlocked his helmet, ripped off the first layer of his suit and bent down to do the same for Vochenkov. The man's face was gray; a grisly open gash ran from the top of his ear around to the back of his head, thick streaks of blood coating his straw hair. David grasped the Russian under his arms and dragged him into the Luna Cat. Gently he picked him up and laid him on one of the cots. Then it was just a matter of simple first aid. It was one thing he was good at. He'd wrapped up so many of Erica's war wounds in her bushwhacking days, which hadn't ended yet from what he'd observed, that he'd felt like a surgeon in a MASH unit. Antiseptic, gauze and a Kling wrap around the Russian's head. Vochenkov moaned, which was a good sign. He'd be stirring soon, but probably be in no condition to drive the Luna Cat back to base. It was all up to David now, to complete the mission, such as it was. After he'd patched up Vochenkov, he finally lay back on the other cot and rested.

"Marsh, do you copy? Marsh?"

David slowly pried his eyes open again. He didn't know if he'd just had a brief catnap or he'd fallen asleep for an hour.

"Marsh? Do you copy?"

"I copy, Houston," he replied groggily.

"It's Chivas, Marsh. We're in 'hot mode' now. Houston opened all channels after they told us what happened. Are you still breathing?"

"Sort of," said David. "I guess I conked out for a minute. Quite the first excursion you sent us on, Commander."

"What happened? Dellows said something about an explosion."

"That's my best guess. Something blew us backward after I hammered into a solid wall in the cave to get some samples. It must have been an explosion."

"But..." said Chivas doubtfully. "What could cause an explosion on the moon?"

"Beats me," said David. "Unless we hit a pocket of gas – an active vent sealed off in the lava tube?"

"Hmm." Chivas mused. "It's possible I suppose. Although we haven't discovered any volcanic activity in all our robotic and satellite surveys."

"But there was Aristarchus in 19... Oh I forget the year. That transient lunar event."

"But we didn't find any fresh flow from the satellite data. I'm not trying to dispute your claim, Marsh. It just seems so unlikely."

"Something threw us backward," said David. "And it wasn't the wind, since there isn't any here and it wasn't an alien. The only way to find out for sure, I suppose, is to go back in. Not today, though. I'm exhausted and Vochenkov isn't even conscious."

"How bad is he?"

"He's breathing normally. His vital signs are stable. I'd say a mild concussion. He should come around in a few hours."

"That's good," said Chivas. "Do you think you can navigate the Luna Cat back to us by yourself?"

"Sure," said David. He wrinkled his nose. "Piece of cake."

"Good. Get back here as soon as possible. Our robot has found some other strange phenomena on his excursion."

"What has he found?"

"You're not going to believe it. I'll tell you as soon as you arrive back at the HAB. If you get into any trouble, keep a line open on the COMM. Houston will help if I get tied up. See you soon, Marsh."

"Sure." David frowned as he headed to the front of the rover and turned the ignition. The smooth purr of the engine was a soothing sound after everything he had been through. Just a few more hours and he'd be safe, back in the HAB, if there were a safe place at all in this alien environment. He was as doubtful about the gas theory as Chivas, but what other explanation could there be? Explosions didn't happen everyday on the moon. For the first time in a long time he actually wished Erica were with him. With her extensive knowledge of volcanism, she might have the answer right on the tip of her tongue. It would be comforting to have an expert dealing with this and not be considered the expert himself.

David ground the Cat into gear and spun the wheels, spitting opaque lunar dust behind. He headed back the way they had come, following the tracks the rover had made on the outset. It would be easier to get back to the HAB - since there was no wind to dust away the tracks he wouldn't even have to rely on the computer navigation system. He just had to stay awake and not slip over the edge of the canyon to his left. He rolled the sun visor over the window of the rover to protect his eyes from the harsh glare and puttered away between looming basalt mountains and the deep gutter of the Rille.

Nineteen

The dash through the blinding snow had scoured any doubt from Erica's mind that she was taking the right course. Cathy had winced when she'd first demanded a Hercules aircraft to take her to Vostok, but when she'd finished explaining about the war-hungry Commander and his trigger-happy troops, the guide had grabbed the phone and had a very fierce conversation with Gottlieb, the NSF Section Head of Antarctic Sciences. Somehow, although it had seemed the man was very skeptical at first, she'd convinced him to issue them a plane. At the moment it was being prepped for take-off.

"Grab your survival gear from the Berg Field Center," Cathy shouted over the wind. "I'll meet you in a few minutes and we'll head to Williams Field."

Erica nodded and raced for the building Cathy had indicated at the far side of the station, another gray rectangular structure facing a brown-gray heap that was called Observation Hill. The hill was on the opposite corner of the Station to Hut Point, just another volcanic mound of hardened lava. However, she didn't pause to consider the geologic background of the terrain. Erica burst through the double doors into the large warehouse, Allan close at her heels. The Berg Field Center was the supply depot for the expeditions of the Antarctica scientists. Everything from camping gear – tents, stoves, sleeping bags etc. – and mountaineering gear – ropes, harnesses, ice axes and crampons – to basic tools such as GPS receivers, binoculars, backpacks and dishes were issued here. Erica thrust the requisitions Cathy had signed and stamped into the hands of a stunned man with the nametag 'Jake' pinned to his chest. He was a large man with a thick chest, extremely wide shoulders and a flat, squashed-looking face. He grimaced at their abrupt entry and stared at them hostilely. It was clear he had been sorting out medical supplies into a knapsack on the front counter; gauze and iodine, tape and scissors were spilling from the lip. However, there was hardly time to be concerned about interrupting the man's work. The fragile peace of the continent, even the free world was at stake.

"This is an emergency," said Erica. "I need this stuff yesterday."

The man studied the requisitions with a frown. They requested typical survival gear for a field operation – mountaineering tent, four person kitchen box including a snow melting pot and stove, a basic tool kit, a sledge, some flashlights and batteries, matches and flares along with emergency food provisions – chocolate bars being a staple. Jake nodded reluctantly and loped off into the next storeroom, grumbling under his breath. Erica tapped her toes and Allan leaned against the wall, grinning.

"What are you smiling at?"

"You," said Allan. "Petite woman scientist trying to take on the big military machine."

"They don't know what they're up against."

"Obviously. I just hope we don't get shot before we find out what's hidden behind door number one."

"We'll find out, Allan. Maybe the Russians do know something – something that we should be apprised of before we set foot on that 'hotspot.'"

Allan nodded. "I hope you're right and the Commander's wrong, or we might be heading into an ambush."

"The Commander is wrong," she said sternly.

The grumbling distributor traipsed back into the room tugging knapsacks and polar gear. He tossed them over to the waiting duo.

"Thanks," said Erica. "Oh, and we'll need your moon suits."

Jake frowned. "What moon suits?"

"The NASA EMU suits that their trainees have been wearing down here."

His thick eyebrows met as he stared at Erica. "They're the property of NASA."

"Good," said Erica. "Because I work for NASA – at the moment," she said under her breath, " and I need them."

Jake crossed his arms. "Not without express permission."

Erica crossed her arms. "Do you want to be fired?"

He just glowered, obviously determined to stand his ground.

"Let me handle this," said Allan. He shuffled over to Jake and whispered in his ear. He drew his coat back from his waist, although Erica couldn't see what he was gesturing at.

The field distributor turned visibly white and bit down on his lower lip. "OK," he finally said. "You can have them, although I'll have to use a forklift to move them to your plane."

"That will be fine," said Erica.

Jake turned away and headed toward the back of the building, still grumbling but with a little more haste. Erica could just make out the words "bloody make-work scientists." She grinned as she grabbed one of the stuffed knapsacks and threw it over her shoulder. With her hands now free, she gathered up the polar gear. "So," she said quietly. "How did you do it?"

"Some things are best kept secret," said Allan, winking.

"No, really. I need to know how you can make people hop when they just roll their eyes at me."

Allan flipped his own knapsack over his shoulders. "You won't like it."

She lifted her snow-dusted eyebrows.

"I acted like the Commander. I told him I would shoot him."

Erica coughed and sputtered. "You... you threatened him?" She bit her lower lip, then started to grin. "Why didn't I think of that?"

"Because you couldn't back it up," said Allan, pulling away his coat back just the same way he had done when he'd talked to the distributor. The black hub of a Colt .45 revolver poked out of his belt.

Erica took a step back. "What are you doing with a gun?"

"It comes in handy when you get into sticky situations. Believe me, Erica, we're headed for a tub full of syrup."

She met his eyes again and drew in a shaky breath. "I know. And I'm glad you're with me."

He touched her cheek, whispered over it with his electrified fingers and dropped his hand. "We'd better go."

She nodded, not trusting her voice.

They turned as a unit and headed for the door. As she unlatched the handle, the door flew open and frigid wind swept in, making Erica's eyes water and freezing the tears as soon as they dripped into her lashes. It crystallized the droplets in her nasal passages so each breath she took seemed to tinkle. But it couldn't freeze the rush of blood in her veins. It couldn't suck the heat out of her cheeks.

Allan didn't seem to notice. He was looking left and right, up and down the deserted street, where the only sound should be the sifting of the snow. But it wasn't. They could hear the heavy thump of rotors in the distance.

"They're taking off," he yelled in her ear.

She nodded. "We can still beat them."

"Not if we have to walk all the way to the airfield."

"We won't," said Erica, nodding in the direction of a new sound. It was the heavy putter of a Snow Cat's engine – a huge tracked vehicle that was a cross between a John Deere tractor and a monster truck. It pulled up to them and Cathy kicked open the door.

"Get in," she yelled. "Sam is loading the Herc for us and I have a pilot and copilot on standby. Cartwright and Sandwich."

"Sandwich?" said Erica.

"You'll understand when you meet him."

Erica and Allan jumped up into the monstrous machine, Allan ceding the front seat to her as he plunked down behind.

"We can still beat them," said Cathy. "A Herc can beat helicopters in a heartbeat. I just hope the Russians are as friendly with our intrusion as you think."

"If they let us talk, they'll appreciate the heads up," said Erica.

Cathy put the 'Cat' in gear and they trundled off to Williams Field over the windswept ice shelf crusted with wavelike sastrugi. The big balloon tires crunched over the crisp snow and made good time to the mighty Hercules that took the battering of the wind without the slightest movement - like a mountain.

They piled out of the Snow Cat and dashed up the ramp into the cargo hold, through the pressurized doors and further forward to the strung out seats along the side. Erica winked at Allan as she saw sour-faced Jake slamming the moon suits behind some rope mesh to hold them snugly in place. So far, they were winning the race. It didn't matter that she could see the Iroquois helicopters flit up through the swirling snow. The Herc was faster. There was no way she would let them start a bloody war. They would have to go through her to reach the Russians. She couldn't help the smug supreme smile that latched onto her face. Until…

There was a thud and then another into the ice shelf, just behind the Hercules.

"What the hell…?" said Allan

"Those were missiles!" screamed Cathy. "They're shooting at us!"

"They couldn't. They wouldn't," said Erica.

"They are," said Allan as another thud slammed the ice field and threw up clods of snow and spears of ice over the Hercules. "We could turn back. I don't think they're trying to hit us, only stop us."

"No," said Erica. "This is much more important than any one of us."

Cathy nodded, her eyes bright and feverish. "Go," she screamed at the pilot. "Hit the runway while there still is one. They can't catch us once we're in the air."

Cartwright, the slim, bearded copilot frowned, but Sandwich, the pilot, turned immediately and closed the ramp. Erica could see now why he had that name. He had a tiny nose and pinched lips sandwiched between enormous jowls and wide cheekbones and an impossibly high forehead. Even his body was disproportionate, sunken chest and narrow pelvis with giant appendages. He grinned as if this was a holiday with adventure travel instead of a nightmare flight from attack helicopters.

"Don't worry," he yelled back at them. "Once we're in the air we can out-fly those gnats like an eagle. The Hercules has a cruising speed of 300 knots. That's 345 miles/hour. Those Iroquois can't go any faster than 110 knots. We'll breeze past them like they're standing still."

The engine ignited into a deafening roar and the Hercules spun forward, still torturously slow despite the pilot's speech. There was another scream and eruption just to the right of the runway. The plane canted to one side but managed to pull forward and jounce over the pebbly snow and ice. Erica looked out the window as the next attack sprang at them. It was a black hornet, coming right for them. She could see into the side of the helicopter as it veered left. Bruzo, the scar-faced man, was grinning widely and hanging half out the open door as he peppered the skin of the Hercules with bullets from his MP5 submachine gun. Yet the Hercules pulled forward, out of the hail, and leapt awkwardly into the sky. She could hear another whistle through the air. She closed her eyes. Were they finally aiming true since the Hercules was airborne? She waited for the explosion, the flash of flames and death.

Twenty

Cathy let out a sigh as the missile narrowly missed the wing of the Hercules. She looked over at Erica, eyes pinched shut, forehead creased up into her hair. "Hey!" She yelled and shook her arm. "We made it!"

Erica opened wet lashes and stared at her. "Are you sure?"

Cathy nodded, although she had to lip read to understand what Erica had asked. The drone of the engines obliterated all other sound. This was no good. She stumbled to the front of the plane and tapped Cartwright on the shoulder. He slipped off his earphone and raised his dark eyebrows.

"Headsets?" she asked, touching his own.

"Sure!" he yelled, digging into a shelf just behind his seat. He shoved a handful of communications equipment into her hands.

Cathy weaved back to the group through the vibrating body of the aircraft. She handed out headsets, which made Erica's pale face flush approvingly. Once they were all connected, Cathy began again. "The SEALS missed, although I don't think they were really aiming at us. Just trying to scare us. They might risk an international incident by attacking the Vostok Station, but they wouldn't dare shoot down American citizens."

"Well, that doesn't make me feel any better," said Erica through her mike. "I'm actually Canadian."

Cathy grinned. "Same difference."

"I don't understand how they can do this," said Erica. "We've been walking hand in hand with the Russians since we built the International Space Station together. Why the sudden suspicion?"

"Hand in hand on some projects. Not on others."

"What do you mean?"

"I mean that the U.S. Antarctic Program had a camp at Vostok a few years back. It was called East Camp and it was a support base for the joint Lake Vostok drilling program – into the pristine Lake Vostok. They were going to investigate microorganisms in the lake together. NASA had a hand in it in hopes of using the lake to test methods for detecting life on other planets, microorganisms that might have survived in the frozen moons of Jupiter, let's say."

Lean handsome Allan Rocheford turned away from the window and gazed at Cathy with his penetrating eyes. "What is Lake Vostok? I thought the station rested on the polar ice sheet."

Cathy grinned shyly. "Well, it does. But back in the '70's some British, U.S. and Danish researchers flew over the area and, using radar, discovered that a lake must exist under the ice. You see the surface is flat, while the regions around it are barreled with sastrugi – you know, ice waves - and ice ridges. Then in the '90's improved satellite imagery and radar data made it possible to map the entire region. It's about the size of Lake Ontario and all contained beneath the ice, collecting bacteria and preserving sediment from millions of years. It's a researchers' paradise."

Allan frowned. "But how is that possible, to have a lake beneath the ice?"

"Four thousand meters beneath the ice. It is incredible. But I bet Erica could explain better than I could."

"I wouldn't be so sure," said Erica kindly. "You've been doing great." She smiled.

Cathy felt a warm glow inside. This woman wasn't your typical beaker. She actually conceded to others once and a while. It reminded her with a renewed clamp on her heart how much she was like Jimmy.

Erica turned to Rocheford beside her. "They assume the lake exists because of a rift valley – two plates moving apart and allowing magma to bubble up to the surface and feed hydrothermal springs. It's a distinct possibility, but I'm not so sure."

"Not sure?" asked Cathy in surprise. "Every scientist that has ever theorized about Lake Vostok has concluded that it was a rift valley."

"It may very well be, but why the thin surface? Most of the geological evidence for this region indicates the crust is old and dead. I'm not disputing that it is a thin crust, only the reason why."

Allan raised his eyebrows. Cathy waited expectantly.

"I think it might have been caused by an asteroid or comet collision."

"But," said Cathy, "the lake is huge."

"Yes," said Erica. "The way it's shallower on one end and deeper on the other could very well indicate an oblique collision. The subsequent heat and melting of the ice could have made it a greater size."

Cathy blinked. Where did they come up with it? "The NSF hasn't found any evidence of impacts in Antarctica."

"With good reason," said Erica. "Everything is iced over. The ice sheet accretes over a site and scours away evidence. But you have found tons of meteorites right along the Transantarctic Mountains. With the moving ice sheet stopped and diverted around the range, the theory is that they fell all over the sheet and were deposited in the mountains. So why are there no impact sites? There probably are. They're under the ice."

"And they were covered over? Let me get this straight. The ice moves?" asked Allan slowly.

Erica nodded. "It's basically a gigantic glacier. It creeps about four meters per year."

"That's not that much," said Allan.

"Not if we're talking a decade or even a century. But the ice sheet is about 3 million years old, at least. These impacts could have happened anywhere in between then and now."

"Such as 10,000 years ago?"

"We won't get into that," said Erica.

Cathy frowned. Now what were they talking about? Asteroids and meteorites? This was way out of her depth.

Even Jimmy had never suggested such an outlandish theory for the subglacial lakes.

"These impacts vaporized the ice," continued Erica. "And when they hit, they punched through some of the crust, making it thinner, then they were covered over again when the ice grew and moved in its continuous easterly direction. I'm not saying that's the cause of all the lakes under the Antarctic Ice Sheet. There are over 70. But yet, for some reason, meteorites tend to concentrate down here, so anything is possible."

"I suppose," said Cathy doubtfully. "But it's really irrelevant to what happened there a few years ago. You see the U.S. scientists were never able to extract a sample from the ice. There were some arguments with the Russians. Who would be first to reveal any finds to the world and claim the credit? Since it was their station, they didn't feel the NSF scientists should have priority, but in their arrogance our scientists disagreed. So they were booted out, plain and simple. The NSF has never been welcome in Vostok again. Now I think it was just a matter of egos. I mean, there are far more men down here than women and egos are always a problem."

"What do you mean by that?" asked Rocheford, arching his eyebrows in mock offense.

Cathy ignored him. "But to the U.S. government, it was a kick in the teeth and probably a reason to renew old suspicions. I mean some organizations were never comfortable with the new alliance with the Russians after the disintegration of communism. They weren't happy unless they were spying on someone, and although there are enough terrorist organizations in the world to keep them busy for many years, it wasn't as glamorous to infiltrate those radicals as it was to pursue a country. I believe our Commander Staten has been waiting for just such an incident as the disappearance of our teams in order to restart a cold war and rebuild a nuclear arsenal. Jimmy was always afraid of something like this. To look at him, you'd think his only obsession was volcanoes. It would take his breath away when he stood on top of a crater and looked down on the percolating mass of lava. But he also had his neck craned when it came to politics. You really can't help it when you live down here. There are so many countries, supposedly working together for the good of mankind, but that's too utopian. The truth is, when there are so many different backgrounds and opinions there's bound to be strife, despite the fact that they're all scientists."

"Or maybe because of it," said Erica.

Cathy nodded slowly. She'd lived with scientists enough to know of the rivalry.

It was Allan who looked perplexed. "Because of it?" he echoed.

"It's that Nobel prize thing," said Cathy. "Always jockeying for position and funding."

Erica grimaced and looked away. Had she hit a nerve? Allan looked a bit discomfited as well. There was something here that she didn't know. Something intensely painful that made stoic Erica's face drain of color until it was as pale as the blinding white ice cap below the plane. She cleared her throat and continued. "Anyway, Jimmy foresaw this problem with the Russians getting deeper, even though he agreed with their position. After all, they'd lived at Vostok – the coldest place on the planet – since 1957. They certainly should have some rights. I just don't understand why they're not talking to us. They leaped forward to help our team when they got into trouble. It was as if the spat hadn't happened at all. Then, nothing, as if they'd slipped off the face of the planet as well. It's just so bizarre."

"Well, we'll find out soon enough," said Erica. Her gaze drifted to the window.

Cathy felt her own eyes wander that way. There wasn't much to see on this flight, except on the pass over the Transantarctic Mountains. There the glaring chalk gave way to half-buried peaks – black ribs in a white body – and glacier falls that flowed off the polar plateau like a still-shot river. The incredible power of the scene – something only captured in black and white – made her feel smaller and lonelier than ever. They'd left the choppers behind, but somehow she knew they were dogging them like bloodthirsty mosquitoes. This was more than she had ever expected to experience in Antarctica. Sure, she'd come here to escape the real world and chalk up her own thrills, but not even on the icy slope of Erebus looking down at the churning pit of lava had she felt this frightened. Of course, then she'd had Jimmy beside her. Now she was alone.

A cool draft knifed through her coat and into her heart. She looked down over the barren plain, the Transantarctics far behind, leaving a bleached endless view of nothing. The cream of the snow ended in the arc of aqua-blue that never seemed to feel the sharp rays of the sun, despite their blinding presence. She felt the heat bleed from her body just by looking into that void. Suddenly she started as she felt prickles ripple over her. It was as if someone were watching her, stripping away the many layers of clothing and leaving her naked and exposed. She looked back into the plane and caught the archeologist staring at her. His eyes that had seemed so deep and encouraging moments ago had taken on a glassy appearance. It was as if the warmth had fallen away from him as well with the dipping thermometer. He nodded coldly to her, then looked away, his eyes crawling over Erica. The volcanologist turned away from the window and smiled at him. Encouraged, he grasped her hand and kissed it, gentle and seductive. His eyes were tender and caressing as he bathed her face with warmth. Cathy must have misread him. She desperately longed for just such a look, or a touch, but not from this man. She shivered. It seemed that Antarctica had grown even colder.

Twenty-one

The Luna Cat hatch connected with the HAB rim as David backed the rover into place. He sighed with relief and rested his head on wheel for a few minutes before reaching over to switch off the engine. It was over. He'd made it back from one of the most harrowing experiences of his life with only a bruised spine and a small lump on the side of his head. Finally he got up from the seat to check the seal on the hatch. The connection was sound, so he cranked the lever and waited for the door to crack open. The crisp *clunk* of the release announced his arrival to the crew inside, although they were probably already aware he was back by the vibrations from his approach and the warning lights of the seal on the monitoring equipment inside. As David traipsed into the HAB, Chivas greeted him without his usual frown and Leclerk nodded instead of sneering. They were both hovering over the communications console just beside the rover seal.

"Glad you made it back in one piece," said Chivas.

"Good to be back," said David, giving a halfhearted smile. "I could use some help with Vochenkov though. He's still out."

Chivas looked at Leclerk and jerked his head to the side. The astronaut quickly sprang forward, almost thumping his head into the ceiling of the HAB – which made David's smile grow substantially - and disappeared into the rover. In minutes he came back carrying the large Russian as if he were a sack of soil. He gently laid him down on a bunk in the sleeping quarters and returned to where the men were standing, David, barely awake, but not willing to reveal this to his Commander.

"We're still trying to wrap our brains around this explosion," said Chivas. "Do you think you're up to another EVA tomorrow?"

"Tomorrow?"

"The sooner we get to the bottom of this, the better. Wong will go with you this time and I'll monitor you from the rover."

David nodded hesitantly. What could he say? He was the geologist, after all.

"Now let me show you what we found," said Chivas gleefully. This was a new emotion from the staid Commander, and it would have given David a reason to ponder, but he was so damned tired he didn't care.

"You mean the RRV?" The dryness of his voice was almost grating.

"Yes, the little rover was on his way up north to find us some ice," said Chivas, seemingly oblivious to David's tone.

"Did it find any?"

"That's just it. It found the mother-load, and not even 100k from our position. He was crawling over the rim of Plato – the dominant crater at the tail end of the Jura mountain chain. There was a large dark swath that's never seen sunlight. So Leclerk thought, 'What the hay, let's check it out.' And sure enough, when we aimed the spectrometer at it, ice – enough to support a colony of a thousand inhabitants for a thousand years. Come and see." He clapped David on the back.

"OK," he said, none too enthused. It *would* be an incredible discovery, but what he craved now above all else was sleep.

The Commander beckoned him to the computer console and the video portrait on the screen. It was another dark hollow in the specter of dark hollows, but when the light from the camera panned over it, the gleam of a multitude of crystals glanced off the rock. The rover was digging into the dense soil and extracting samples of the frozen regolith. This was a tremendous discovery, a sigh of relief for NASA with its gargantuan plans of colonization of the moon and then Mars. Yet it was a tiny spark compared to the fire of the mystery of the cave. It was expected. Maybe not on this scale or this close to the first habitat, but all of NASA's plans hinged on it. What they hadn't expected was an active planet. What might change all those plans was the close call that David had experienced today. And tomorrow, everything would hinge on him. He could be the hero or the fool.

His shoulders sagged at the mere thought of it. This was a time where he could shine, but was he up to it? Would he ever be that good without someone else's brain to pick? The weight became crushing and he could barely stand. He staggered and held onto the wall of the HAB for support.

"I guess you're a little tired," said Chivas, finally noticing his exhaustion. "Why don't you sack out while we wait for the RRV to bring back our samples. You've had quite a day."

David nodded. "I'm still a bit shell-shocked. A little sleep and I should be fine, ready to go back," into hell, he added silently.

Chivas dismissed him with a wave of his hand. "Good. Sack out."

Finally... He stumbled to his bunk and zipped into the sleeping bag, his eyelids collapsing as soon his head hit the pillow.

It was a glowing spectacle. The splash of orange lava pluming into the air and splattering down on the ashen surface of the moon. It had to be a dream, yet it seemed so real. He could feel the heat as the molten rock danced out of the lava tube and gushed down the Rille, filling it up to the banks like a river in flood season. He stepped back from the edge, feeling the blistering heat through the EMU suit despite its cooling coils.

"I guess I was right." The voice was sultry and melodic. It was unmistakable. He turned to his left and caught a glimpse of her blue eyes through the arc of her helmet.

"Erica! What are you doing here?"

"Came to watch the show. You always try to steal it from me, but not this time."

David winced and took a step back. "I never meant..."

"To be a bastard. Well, it's a little late for apologies now. You are who you are. Nothing can save you from yourself."

The lava inched closer, but he didn't move back. "I'm in over my head this time, aren't I?"

"You're drowning," she said matter-of-factly.

"But it isn't too late. It can't be."

He turned back to the streaming liquid fire. It swept up and over the banks of the Rille, rising over his boots and eating right into his suit. The pain seared his legs. He screamed...

And woke up.

Sweat beaded his face and trickled down his back. Damn, it was hot in here. He sat up, ripped open the sleeping bag and dashed to the bathroom. This method of frantic traveling ended in a series of thumps and bumps into the ceiling and crashes down to the floor of the HAB, but he couldn't care less. He grabbed a towel from the rack and sponged off the lather. "It's not too late," he muttered. "Never too late."

It was good everyone was sleeping now, even the tireless Commander Chivas. They would think he was mad, or concussed like his partner, Vochenkov. He was even more thankful that he could access Houston without any queries from the team. He crept up to the communication console and issued a patch.

"Houston, this is Marsh on LUNA I. Do you copy?"

A groggy voice from the CAPCOM chair answered. "I copy, LUNA I. This is Swenson. Do you have a problem, Marsh?"

It was always their first response. They'd had enough problems in the history of spaceflight to expect the four A.M. call.

"Not exactly," he said. "But I have to reach Erica Daniels."

"Who the hell is that?" asked Svenson, waking up a bit but sounding as if he wished he hadn't.

"She's a volcanologist. NASA sent her to Antarctica."

"You're kidding me, right?"

"This isn't a joke. I'll be heading into some pretty dicey territory tomorrow and I need her expertise."

"I thought you were the expert," he said, the sneer obvious in his voice.

"She's better than me," said David, hardly believing he was uttering these words.

Svenson sighed. "So you need her. And you want me to find her, in Antarctica, of all the godforsaken places on earth."

"That's about the size of it."

"It's pretty damn big. I'll see what I can do."

David sat back in the swivel chair and closed his eyes. He'd taken the first step. He wouldn't shine, but perhaps he wouldn't stumble either, and for the first time in his life he'd invited Erica to her own show.

Twenty-two

"You're not going to believe this." It was Captain Sandwich talking in her head.

Erica jolted from the mesmerizing landscape and looked toward the front of the Hercules.

"You've got a call from Houston."

"What?" said Erica, finally realizing that he was talking though the headset. "Houston?"

"Lana, at McMurdo, rerouted the call through the radio. Here, I'll connect you."

"Hello?" said Erica, frowning. Why would Houston be calling her?

"Is this Erica Daniels?"

"Yes."

"We have someone here who'd like to talk to you. Hold on."

Erica held her breath. Had they found out about her commandeering a Hercules and trying to stop Commander Staten? Well, she didn't care. They couldn't stop her, no matter what they said.

"Erica?" The voice was crackled and distorted.

"Yes, sir. You have to understand why we're doing this. The Commander is a madman. We can't let him start a war."

"Erica. It's me. David."

She stopped. Her heart skipped a beat.

"Are you there?"

"Aren't you supposed to be on the moon?"

There was a slight delay in his response, even longer than the standard satellite transmission delay. Then he came back on. "I am. I'm in trouble and I need your help. Although it sounds like you might be in trouble too."

"You could say that," she said. "Is this the kind of trouble in which I bail you out and you take all the credit?"

Another pause. Of course, if he were really calling her from the moon, there would be a two-and-a-half-second delay. "Erica, please." There was pain in his voice. Actual pain.

"What's going on, David?"

There was a longer pause this time. "I'm not... quite sure. I was exploring a lava tube, tapping a wall to collect a sample and there was an explosion."

"Explosion?"

"Something blew us backward. Vochenkov was knocked unconscious and I had to carry him back to the Luna Cat. I don't know what really happened and... I'm not... qualified to come up with a theory."

Erica blinked. Had he just admitted his inferiority? Over an open channel, through Houston, where everyone was listening and recording? It just wasn't possible. "Do you want one from me?"

"Yes, and no. I want you with me."

"What are you talking about?"

"I want your theories, openly recognized, but I also need you with me tomorrow. I'm going back into the tube and I would like you to keep an open channel with me. I want you to talk me through it."

Erica took a deep breath. "David, I'm a little busy at the moment."

"Trying to stop a war? Sounds like you."

"You don't even know me."

"You're right. I've been the biggest jerk in the world. It should be you up here and not me. I can't change that now. But I can start being a scientist instead of a stage-hog. I need you up here. NASA needs you."

She closed her eyes. "Okay. I'll keep my satellite phone on, and barring a full-scale war down here, I'll talk you through tomorrow."

"Thanks," he breathed. "I'll call you in five hours from the Hadley Rille. You won't regret this."

"I do already."

"This is a new beginning. Trust me."

She couldn't bring herself to answer.

"And Erica?"

"Yes?"

"I'm sorry." The line sizzled into empty static.

She sighed and pulled off the headset. With trembling hands she reached up and massaged her tired eyes. When she blinked them open, he was staring at her with tight lips. He took the headset from her hands and placed it firmly on her head again.

"Mr. Marsh, I assume."

"How did you know? Of course, you were listening on the headset."

Allan shrugged. "It wasn't intentional."

"He's actually asking for my advice," she said in way of an explanation.

"Or setting another trap..."

"Maybe. But I don't think so. In any case, this is too big for me to deny him. An explosion on the moon? It could be a gas pocket, which would mean an active planet. But it just doesn't make sense. If he opened up a pressure valve, there more than likely would have been lava ejected out as well. What has he discovered? I wish I were there."

"It's probably nothing," said Allan. "What we discover here might be far more momentous."

"You still think we're going to uncover a piece of Atlantis?"

"After we stop a war." He grinned.

Erica couldn't help but smile back. Allan knew how to warm her heart when all David had ever done was shatter it into a billion pieces. Even though he'd finally called, and invited her back into his life, she could still feel every crack in the very fragile organ it had taken her ten years to piece together again. But it was healing, slowly. She was finally sloughing the hold he had on her. Now she could reach out to the swashbuckling pirate without any more doubts.

She leaned over and kissed him. The startled look in his eyes told her he hadn't expected it. He grasped her by the back of her head and thrust his tongue into her mouth, thrashing and kneading it until she could hardly breathe. She wrapped her arms around him and crushed him to her chest, the pounding of his heart making all her nerve endings fire. His hand trickled down her neck and slipped in between their bodies, unzipping her parka, and she just wanted him to...

"Erica! Erica!"

Cathy's voice woke her from her swoon.

"We're landing in Vostok."

She pivoted in her seat, breathless, and tried desperately to straighten her rumpled sweater and zip up her coat again.

Allan gave her a lopsided grin and smoothed his own shirt.

Trying her best to regain her composure, Erica focused on slowing her rapid respiration and turned deliberately away from him to take a gander out the window. It was true. The ocean of white held a tiny splotch of color that gradually took on the dimensions of rectangular boxes and one immense chimney – the deep core building. Vostok Station was built around that structure. It was essentially a gigantic drilling rig that burrowed into the ice and extracted cores for scientific study. Beside the haphazard collection of shacks – which was basically what all buildings resembled on this frozen continent - she could make out an array of miniature telescopes, like the compound eye of an insect. They formed the DASI instrument – the Degree Angular Scale Inferometer. It was used by astrophysicists to read interference patterns of microwaves that would determine the universe's geometry and composition. Way cool stuff, but it seemed so quiet in the swirl of snow. The Hercules glided to a landing on its skis and halted on the ice shelf not far from the main drag - a snowmobile track. Erica hunched into her polar gear and prepared for the real experience of cold.

"Vostok has recorded the coldest temperatures on the planet," said Cathy.

"How cold are we talking?" asked Allan, pulling on his red toque and goggles.

"Minus 89.6 ° C was the coldest yet. But it averages around – 50. You'll get used to it, maybe."

Allan's eyes widened. He tugged up his hood as well. "A little different from Cairo."

"I imagine," said Cathy.

Erica couldn't help but grin. Despite her newfound affection for Allan, she could still take great pleasure in seeing the man squirm for a change while the women took everything in stride.

Sandwich lowered the ramp at the back of the plane, allowing the wind to swirl in and numb their faces instantly. Everything flash froze, despite their polar gear, from eyelashes to toes. Allan gasped as the cold grabbed him like a bear and squeezed the warmth from his body.

"We're at a much higher altitude here," said Cathy. "About 3500 meters above sea level. That's about 11,500 feet. So watch for any signs of altitude sickness and let us know." She looked pointedly at Allan. She must have guessed that Erica's long history as a volcanologist would make her acclimatize quickly to the thin air. "Dizziness, shortness of breath, brain hemorrhage. That sort of thing."

Allan scowled. "I'm not an idiot. Brain hemorrhage, indeed." But he did respond rather breathlessly.

"I'll keep an eye on him," said Erica. "We'd better announce ourselves to the Russians before they get suspicious. I don't know how much time we have before the helicopters arrive."

They walked down the ramp and stared at the station, a humble jumble of buildings sprawled across the blue-white icescape. It was a concoction of mustard yellow and aquamarine with the thrust of the rust deep core building dominating the tiny community. There wasn't a sign of anyone slogging from one construction to another. Of course she didn't expect an open-arms greeting. In this cold, everyone would be hibernating in the buildings, but there was an eerie aura to the station, with the wind whipping snow around like tumbleweeds and the vast empty ice sheet like a desert beyond. It was as dry as a desert too. Rarely did new snow fall on the sheet. She could feel her skin shrivel and her mouth become parched, but she resisted the urge to lick her lips - her tongue would probably freeze to them.

They advanced toward the buildings quickly; there was no other speed when you were seeping warmth from your body. Yet there was no sign of life anywhere. The first place they came to was the communications building. Cathy drummed on the door loudly and walked in. Allan stumbled in close at her heels, desperate as a hare fleeing a fox to escape the cold. Erica took up the rear. She closed the door soundly and looked around at the crammed center in dismay. There was the standard bank of radio and satellite equipment with various dials and knobs, with the standard swivel chair for the technician, a little damp and grimy but serviceable, yet nobody was home. It was essential in Antarctica to have someone monitoring communications twenty-four hours a day in case of an emergency. Considering the conditions on the polar ice cap, there were a fair number of emergencies. Yet Vostok was unmanned.

Erica stared at the flashing light at the top of the array, a tickle of fear brushing the hairs up on her arms. She lifted a headset from its perch on a large manual and settled it on her head. There was a blank hiss in her ears, as empty and alarming as the quiet in the room. She laid it back on the manual.

"This doesn't make sense," said Cathy. "There's usually twenty-five people at this station. They wouldn't have left the radio unmanned."

"It would appear that they did," said Erica. "Is this a record and playback button?" She pointed to the knobs that had symbols resembling their equivalent on the radios she'd manned on occasion in the USGS communications van. "My Russian isn't very good."

"I think so," said Cathy. "But anything you hear will be in Russian. I won't be any help there either."

"Move over," said Allan, brushing Cathy aside rather harshly.

"You know the language?" asked Erica, her eyebrows sweeping up despite her swift attempt to stop them. She didn't want Allan to think she doubted his abilities as much as she doubted his theories.

"I know some," he replied. "You don't study ancient civilizations and the roots of language without picking up the variations. I'll see what they recorded." He donned the headset and hit the 'apparent' playback button.

Standing so close to Allan, Erica could just pick up a brusque conversation and what sounded like distinct yells.

Allan frowned and removed the set from his ears. "They said something like 'It's a graveyard.' Then, 'We're going in.' The last part was some yelling, then dead silence."

Erica looked over at Cathy who was shivering visibly, her hands hugging her arms and her whole body hunched together. "Sound familiar?"

The guide nodded and bit her lip. A tear squeezed out of her eye, but she briskly swept it away. "So there was a conversation. There must be someone around."

Erica agreed. "But there's no one here. Let's check the deep core building and the dorms."

Allan dropped the headset on the thick manual with a thud. "The galley," he said suddenly. There was a wild light in his eyes. "I'll check the galley."

"I don't think it's wise for us to split up," said Cathy. She had stopped sniffling and was standing erect again, trying to get a grip and resume her duties. "We don't know what kind of reception we're going to get."

"You're right," said Erica. "We should check the galley together."

"I'll be fine," said Allan. "You girls check the dorms." He had a stern set to his lips, but his eye twitched a bit.

"Are you feeling okay, Allan?"

"Never better." His eye twitched again.

"Dizziness? Headache?"

"No!" he said adamantly.

"Just the same, I think Cathy's right. We'll do this together. First we'll investigate the galley, then we'll head over to the dorms." She walked out into the blistering cold, ignoring Allan's protest. The thin air was definitely affecting him. His rattling breathing behind her was enough to confirm her suspicions. She'd have to watch him closely and maybe they could find some medical supplies in the station. Otherwise it was back to the Hercules for an O2 tank.

The galley was another blue and yellow trailer of prefabricated metal not far from the communications shanty, although it seemed miles when the vitreous humor in your eyes was freezing. This time they didn't bother to knock. Cathy thrust the door open and tramped in, followed by a growling Allan. Erica brought up the rear, fumbling for a light switch. The standard couple of windows hatched in the side of the aluminum crate did little to dispel the gloom. When she flicked on the light, it was a relief it actually worked. From the chill inside, she was expecting that the generators weren't working at all, but the hollowness of the place still gave her the creeps. There were pots and pans, shelves full of dishes and a small area for dining set up with dark wooden tables and chairs that were scuffed and worn. There was even a full pot of coffee sitting idle and cold on the stove, a half-empty cup and half a sandwich on one table. Erica couldn't get over the feeling that the Clanton gang had come to town and everyone had fled.

"I guess we try the dorms," said Cathy, her voice dry and despondent.

Erica nodded forlornly. "What do you think happened to everyone?"

"Maybe they abandoned the station."

"Why would they do that?"

"Because of what they found at our anomaly," said Allan. His voice sounded quite rational now, although there was still a strange glow in his eyes. "Evidence that they want to keep hidden from us. Maybe Staten was right about their motives, but not about their activities."

"Stop it, Allan," said Erica. "We don't know anything yet. Let's not jump to conclusions."

"Let's check out the dorms," said Cathy again. Erica could tell by the slight tremble in her lower lip that the guide was unnerved by the ghost town, and Allan's insinuations weren't helping matters.

"Good plan," said Erica. She shuffled out the door before Allan could add to the tension.

The dorms were snowed in, access possible only through a tunnel cut in the firn like a long igloo entrance.

"I didn't think there'd be this much snow," said Erica, trying to keep things light.

"From windstorms, not snowstorms," said Cathy. "It just blows around up here. Some gets in from the coast, but there's never much accumulation."

"Then how the hell did they get an ice sheet that's... How deep is it again?" asked Allan

"Four thousand meters," Cathy and Erica said in unison.

"Four thousand meters. Don't you need snow to make a glacier?"

"There have been different climates over the millennia," said Erica. "This is millions of years worth of snow we're talking about, Allan."

Cathy punched open the door, leading into a long hall with tiny rooms adjacent each other like a college dorm. The rooms each held a bunk, a desk and a miniscule closet. They were strewn with clothes, books and tapes both in Russian and in English.

"It really does remind me of college," said Cathy.

"I don't want to be reminded of college," said Erica under her breath. She could still see the empty spot on her desk where two years worth of work had effectively vanished.

Allan put a hand on her shoulder and gently squeezed. Perhaps he was starting to adjust to the climate. His sensitivity to her pain was heartwarming. However this barren dormitory, despite its obvious lived-in appearance, made her extremely uneasy. It looked as if the scientists had just gone out for a stroll and never come back.

"There's no one here," said Cathy, coming out of the last room. The howl of the wind outside seemed to emphasize her point.

"There's one more building to check out," said Erica. "The deep core."

"Well, if there's no one in the communications room, there shouldn't be anyone there."

"It's still possible. If not, there might be some clue as to what happened here." Erica spun on her heel and practically ran out of the dorm. She had to get out of there, not only to escape the void, but to escape the memories as well. She couldn't believe she had let David back into her life, even on a professional level. She'd be walking beside a cliff with a knife at her back at all times. It was stupid and dangerous. Yet his words still echoed in her mind. 'I'm sorry.' Could she ever really forgive him and move on?

Allan was close on her heels, gasping a little as he ran, but cloaking her too with his shadow. He'd also done something he wasn't proud of, but he'd owned up to it right away. Despite his outlandish theories, he had discovered something in the anomaly. Pursuing it like a driven scientist. Like her. They were suited to each other. There was a chance she could be happy again. As happy as that summer in Hawaii…

Erica approached the deep core building. It pierced the electric-blue sky like a lighthouse on a barren rocky coast. She flung open the door and hastened into the dimly lit interior, driven herself to find out why this station had been abandoned. It took a few moments for her eyes to adjust from the blazing sunlight outside to this dingy warehouse, but when they did she could clearly make out every detail within the construction. The rig was a massive metal contraption that pierced the ice with an enormous bit and dug down as deep as 3600 meters. Beside the rig were a series of cylindrical ice cores housed in plastic containers, neatly stacked and labeled with depth and position coordinates. In the far corner of the building was a separate office where she could see, through the glass panes along the wall, a couple of computers and printers. Stacks of paper filled every available space in this room, a testament to the amount of data the Russians were extracting from the deep core samples. The interior of the building was cold. Not hypothermic like outside, but cold enough to keep the cores frozen, so the only heated section of the building must be the office in order to keep the computers functional. Erica spun around, surveying the entire housing, but there wasn't a soul manning the deep core building.

"There's no one here, either," said Allan faintly. His hand came up on her shoulder again, but this time she shrugged it off.

"No *one*, but maybe some *thing*." She walked over to the office and heaved open the thick metal door. Without a glance over her shoulder, although she knew Allan and Cathy were following by the heavy thuds of their boots, she picked up one of the sheaves of printouts and started reading.

"What are you doing?" asked Allan sharply. "This isn't a scientific study we're into right now. We're trying to find the Russians before the U.S. Navy blasts them to hell."

"There are no Russians to save," said Erica, "but there is this data." She tapped a paper with listings of core samples and age correlations.

"Did they find anything?" asked Cathy. "Some new strain of bacteria? Something dangerous perhaps? The conspiracy theorists always thought they had something to hide here. Maybe it wiped them all out."

Erica laughed. "Conspiracy theorists always find something to feed their paranoid delusions."

"Sometimes they're not that far off the mark," said Allan.

Erica ignored him as she shuffled through the data. Imagine, giving credit to a bunch of lunatics. It didn't surprise her, though. This man believed in myths. Oh, she could kick herself. What was she doing, getting involved with a pirate with delusions of grandeur? Her eyes scanned the papers, speed reading through the wealth of information about past climate and environmental changes deduced from the cores. It was amazing that the data was in English, but she noticed a translation program on the computer. The scientists were probably getting ready to publish their findings internationally. As she read through a highlighted page on the bottom of the stack, she paused and blinked, unable to believe her eyes. "Not bacteria," she said quietly. "Nothing to explain their absence. Just some iridium, shocked quartz and tektites." She looked up and met her companions' eyes.

Cathy frowned.

Allan raised his eyebrows, comprehension flooding his face. "Asteroid?"

Erica nodded.

"I don't understand," said Cathy plaintively.

"It's really quite simple," said Erica. "Iridium is an extremely rare element on earth, but much more common in the meteoric dust that constantly rains in outer space. To find it in sediment on earth is a clear indication of an asteroid or comet impact. Shocked quartz means the rock has been altered by an impact – the grains become crisscrossed by the extreme pressure. And tektites are rocks with rounded shapes. The consensus is that they are drops of impact melt sprayed about when the asteroid hit the earth causing them to them to spin and solidify into their rounded shapes during their brief flight through the atmosphere.

Often they're quite glassy. That's why there are so many glass beads on the surface of the moon."

Cathy nodded, the lines in her face smoothing out. "So they found some here?"

"Yes. Lake Vostok has clear signs of being the product of an asteroid or comet collision." She shuffled some more papers and stared at the core sample data. There it was, right in front of her eyes. "I have to sit down," she said. She grasped the back of the swivel chair by the console and sank into it.

"What? What have you found?" Allan spun the chair toward him and gazed deep into her eyes. "Tell me."

"They've found some fragments from your Atlantis era, Allan. Tektites and diamonds. Diamonds can also be formed by an impact. And in the interior, it rained iridium. It would appear that cometary fragments have impacted even down here during that time period. I guess I wasn't far wrong, but I never thought that you might be right."

"Archeology is a science too, Erica." He had a smug grin that almost made her laugh. "Do you think I based my theories on half-baked myths. I have the coordinates. We just have to check it out."

She nodded, the knot in her chest at the thought of this new relationship suddenly loosening. Maybe he wasn't so crazy after all. She met his eyes and felt an electric shock again. Smiling, she touched his hand. "We could go right now, before the troops arrive."

"Are you thinking of going to the thing?" a deep gravelly voice interrupted from the half-open door to the office. "In Transantarctic mountains?"

Erica leapt to her feet. Cathy and Allan spun around.

A black-bearded man in a bright orange polar snowsuit and frosted eyebrows stepped into the room, wringing his hands and directing shy glances at each one of them in turn. "I would not go there if I were you. You will not come back." Although he had a distinct Russian accent, his

English was impeccable. He shuffled slowly toward them, puffing as if the small effort were too much.

"Who are you?" asked Allan.

The man focused on the archeologist and took a deep breath. "My name is Dmitri Laryonov. I am an astrophysicist. I set up the telescopes outside." His finger pointed in the direction of the array of miniature telescopes that formed the DASI instrument. "I was also manager of the other scientists. Now I am sole survivor of Vostok Station."

Erica blinked. "What happened to everyone else?"

Dmitri shrugged. He brushed the frost from his beard and shook his head. "We sent one team to the thing – 'hot spot,' you call it. Within minutes, we lost communication, just like the American teams. But Russians do not lose teams on the ice. It's not possible. We have too much pride." He tapped his chest. "We sent another team and lost contact with them too. Two teams of six - twelve people - all lost. The others became frightened. They thought they might be blamed for this foul-up. They stole my plane and left. Where to, who knows? Only I was left; only I can take the blame. Is only fair, I sent them there. If you go, you will die too."

Erica couldn't believe her ears. Twelve more people, gone. It didn't seem possible. "It could have been volcanic gases," she whispered.

Dmitri frowned at her.

"Well, it could. Anyway, I don't intend to die there. But I have to find out what's going on. We can't just abandon those people. It's possible they're still alive."

Dmitri's frown creased his entire face. He sighed loudly. "You may be right. Either I stay here and face the music or I go with you and find out what happened to my people."

Erica nodded. "We could use your help."

"You may have it," said the Russian, "but I still do not know who you are. I assume you're scientists from the American station."

"Oh, I'm sorry," said Erica. "We were just so glad to see someone still alive here, we forgot the introductions." She promptly pointed out the small team – Cathy Jones from McMurdo, Allan Rocheford from Cairo – he frowned at that one – and the 'very stunned with the ice core data' impact specialist – herself.

"Yes, you would be very excited by our discoveries. We didn't have time to post them yet," said Dmitri.

"This is all very pleasant," said Allan. "Exchanging scientific ideas and theories. I'd like to do it all day, but aren't you forgetting something?"

Erica turned toward him. "This is a momentous discovery, Allan. You, of all people, should be pleased."

"I am," he said. "But we can't sit around and chat about it when a crack team of Navy SEALS are heading this way in attack helicopters."

"Attack helicopters?" Dmitri echoed.

"Heading this way," said Allan again.

"They think you didn't respond to their communication attempts because you were up to something on the ice," said Erica.

"Up to something?" Dmitri's eyebrows almost met.

"Nuclear. It's always their first thought. Why our teams disappeared. Why you jumped at the chance to help, then no word from you afterward. They're coming in on gunships and they're not open to rational discussion."

Dmitri nodded. "Typical American overkill."

"Hey," said Cathy. "We're not all like that."

"Sorry, my dear. But there are men in your military and mine that wished the cold war never ended. I suggest we get out of here before they arrive."

He turned abruptly and headed for the exit to the deep core building. Erica and the others shadowed him through the frosty warehouse of ice cores. When the door opened, a blast of frigid air drilled into them like a million tiny rigs. Allan gasped again and Erica took his hand. "Come on," she yelled over the scream of the wind. At the same moment, her phone jangled in her bag. "Not now," she hissed, but the thing persistently rang. She glanced at her watch. It couldn't be five hours already, could it? She punched the answer button rather violently. "David, this is not a good time."

"I'm heading out of the air lock now. This is the only time."

"But David..." She left the deep core building behind and swung into a gale force wind that seemed to push her backward.

"You told me you would help me. And it's not just for me. It's for NASA and science and life on other planets."

"Cut the crap, David. I said I would help you, it's just..."

There was a *snap* and a puff of snow chuffed into the air right beside her feet.

"Run," said Allan. "They're shooting at us."

Lowering right in front of her was a giant Iroquois with its rocket pods poised.

"Gotta run," she screamed and snapped off the phone.

Twenty-three

The click reverberated in his brain like the echo of a gunshot. David wanted to scream at her: *You promised!* Perhaps this was her way of getting back at him. He could hardly blame her, but he bloody well needed her right now. He felt like he was sinking in quicksand and the hand that had been extended to save his life had been suddenly retracted.

"What are you doing?" asked Chivas. His eyes were narrowed as he watched David climb into his EMU suit. "Why do you have Houston patching you to a satellite phone in Antarctica?"

David met his eyes with only a slight twitch to his lips. "I thought we could use a little more expert advice. Dr. Daniels is a leading volcanologist. She might have some theories about what's in there that I may not have thought of."

Chivas dark eyes narrowed even more. "I thought you hated her."

David looked away. "That doesn't mean I don't respect her opinion."

"You're a strange man, Marsh." He shook his head. "But I guess we're up against some strange stuff, so I'll let you run the show for now."

David's eyes widened as he looked back at the Commander. He'd just been given the reins, but he didn't know which path to take. He was hoping for Erica's tracks to follow once more. "Okay. Let's saddle up."

Jing-Mei nodded grimly and donned her PLSS backpack. "If we do need this Erica, perhaps you could keep trying to contact her," she said to Chivas, eyeing Marsh with a sharp, hostile look in her eyes.

Chivas frowned at the tiny astronaut, obviously frustrated. "Marsh is the expert. But all right, I'll remind

Houston every half-hour. Now, be careful in there. Don't get carried away by the mystery of the explosion. For all we know, there could be lava gushing into the Rille and you won't be able to hear it – no sound waves. You'll have to rely on your vision and thermometers. Any spike in heat, get the hell out."

"Gottcha," said David calmly, although he was feeling far from calm.

"I'll step out of the lock now. Good luck."

"See you later, boss."

There was a *thunk* as the airlock engaged. After the standard two minutes pre-breathing of pure O2, David tapped the button to depressurize. He counted thirty seconds, then clicked open the outer hatch. The dazzle of brilliant sunlight made him blink even through the sun visor on his helmet. It wouldn't be long before he was in darkness again, threading through the copious shadows with the thin needle of his lone flashlight. Where the hell was Erica?

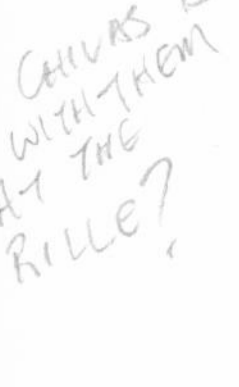

"Houston, do you copy?"

"I copy, Marsh." This time it was Dellows on the COMM. The bigwigs were screening this EVA.

"Can you try to patch through to Dr. Daniels again?"

There was a slight pause. "We've been trying for the last ten minutes, Marsh. She's not picking up right now."

"It sounded like there was gunfire. Is that possible?"

Dellows chuckled. "We're talking Antarctica, Marsh. There's nothing down there but penguins and some far-too-dedicated scientists. She probably just stepped out for a hike up Mount Erebus. You don't need her," he said pointedly.

"Are you still keeping tabs on her?"

There was a longer silence this time. He should have kept his mouth shut, but he had to know what was going on. Somehow he knew he couldn't do this without Erica.

"We don't keep tabs on our scientists, Marsh. They check in with us," he snapped. "Dr. Daniels is in the best of hands, I trust. When she's ready, she'll contact us. Focus on your job now. We need to find out more about this cave."

"Yes, sir," said David meekly. "Attaching onto the rappel line now."

He clipped his harness to the cable, far from ready for the descent into the dark underbelly of the moon, but unable to delay any longer. Glancing behind, he saw that Jing-Mei was hooked up as well. "Let's rock," he said.

"Spoken like a true geologist," Jing-Mei quipped over the COMM. David was surprised that her stern scowling personality had done a one-hundred-and eighty-degree turn.

"Did I hear you correctly?" David asked.

"That is what you are, isn't it?" she asked lightly. "You went to school for years, you worked for NASA for many more. Surely you don't need me to tell you that."

Now he got it. She was trying to instill confidence in him that he was sorely lacking at the moment, maybe because her life might depend on him, frightening as that was.

The line fed out and David sank into the gloomy canyon. Despite her words, the shadow evoked the illusions once more. Creepy spiders and hoar-winged bats. His imagination the product of Hollywood's finest science fiction classics. But he was on an airless world, a lifeless satellite, where the danger lay not in what was here as much as what he could contribute to what was here. Had he awoken a sleeping giant? The thrill of discovery was there, but he was still choked by his own inadequacy for the task at hand.

"In the shadow, the dark is absolutely thick," said Jing-Mei.

"We'll walk in from the far side - the lighted area of the canyon," said David. He hit the bottom of the Rille and detached from the line. "That way we might be able to see any blood trickling out of the cave before we even enter it."

"Blood?" queried Jing-Mei, coming smoothly down beside him.

"I mean lava. If you'd ever been close to a fissure in the earth that was spewing lava, you would swear it looked like a war wound spraying blood."

Jing-Mei nodded slowly. "If you say so.

David began to hop much more tidily over the rock-strewn channel than he had the day before. Jing-Mei leapt along beside him. There was an abrupt demarcation about five hundred feet in where the light chopped away the darkness, and there in the sunlight it was easy to see the beads of glass sparkling in the regolith, soil that had been shocked by countless asteroid and meteorite impacts. However, they could also see glimmers of polished basalt in the dusty rock. There was no doubt that lava had once flowed through this canyon.

"So what do you think?" asked Jing-Mei.

"Think?"

"*Your* theory. Why the explosion? Are we sitting on a volcano?"

Damn! His theory was dependent on a satellite phone in Antarctica. "Well," he said, struggling to dredge up knowledge that had been buried since graduate school. "It's possible. Any activity would be underground, since we haven't seen evidence on the surface. It's just..." He paused. "It didn't seem hot."

"In the cave?"

"Yes. Oh, I know that our suits are supposed to keep us cool. It's one hundred degrees Celsius out in the sun, but I still think a thermal vent might have seared our suits."

"Pressure but no heat," said Jing-Mei thoughtfully.

"Do *you* have any suggestions?" They were steadily drawing closer to the hollow crypt. At least that's what it felt like as the shadows swallowed the glare.

Jing-Mei shrugged. "Air lock," she chortled.

"Ya, right. From some alien, I suppose. I was hoping you had some scientific suggestion."

"Science would suggest you punctured a balloon," said Jing-Mei. "A pressurized pocket. If it's volcanic, that's exciting, because we could use the thermal heat to melt our ice and vaporize it for oxygen. We could also make hot tubs." She laughed heartily, which had a tinkling quality over the COMM.

"I'm glad you find this funny," said David. He was feeling the weight of the darkness as they stepped into the cavern. He flicked on his flashlight that was a pencil-fine beam that barely pierced the darkness around them.

"Come on, David. It's not every day you find a volcano on the moon." Jing-Mei snapped her light on as well. They crisscrossed their beams through the ebony cave, but couldn't penetrate too far in.

"It's a bit of a hike," said David. "Maybe an hour's walk into this thing. Are you up for it?" He played his beam over her face. She was grinning.

"I'm psyched," she said.

David pointed the light back into the hollow. "Houston? Do you copy?"

"A little better reception this time, Dave. Let's hope it holds."

"Any word from…"

"No," snapped Dellows. "We'll patch her through the minute we do. Concentrate on your mission."

"Yes, sir," said David. He sighed and shook his head. She'd truly abandoned him this time.

They traipsed silently through the tunnel, Houston occasionally confirming their position. David's own breathing was an obscene stridor in his ears. Finally the thin beam of the flashlight widened as it hit the rock wall. He scanned the ground intently, looking for an orange cast of lava or the smolder of gas escaping. There was nothing but impenetrable blackness.

"It doesn't look like a vent, does it?" said Jing-Mei.

"It's too quiet," said David.

"Let's scan the wall for your hole."

David grunted his agreement. It was hard to distinguish anything with that narrow beam of light, but they zigzagged down the wall in hopes of finding the gaping exit wound that would accompany an explosion.

"You go that way," said Jing-Mei, pointing to the right. "I'll study the left."

"Roger," said David, quietly acceding to the astronaut. It didn't really bother him, taking orders from a woman. He thought it would, but right now he was humbled by his own inexperience. He traced the wall carefully with his flashlight, searching every hollow and niche in the barrier. It couldn't have been more than fifteen minutes before he heard Jing-Mei's excited squeal over the COMM.

"I think I found it. Get over here, Marsh."

"Be careful," he commanded. "Look for any seepage and stay away from the opening."

"Yes, sir," she said, a grin in her voice. "It looks pretty quiet."

David made his way hastily over to the ray of light that was fixated on the wall. As he drew nearer, the jumble of rock and jagged toothy hole emerged from the gloom. He made one last hop and landed beside the tiny Chinese astronaut. "It looks like a blast wound."

"You like your medical metaphors, don't you?"

David shrugged. "My father was a doctor. He didn't like to lose," he added without even thinking.

"He didn't like to lose a patient, you mean."

David blinked at the soft brown eyes behind the helmet. "I suppose." He turned back to the hole. "I don't see any sign of lava extrusions. No gas visible. Did you check the thermometer?"

"Minus one hundred Celsius. She's cold."

"Like a lot of women I used to know."

"Really?" said Jing-Mei. "I guess you knew the wrong women. Or maybe you had that effect on them."

"Let's not get insulting. Shall we check it out?"

"After you."

David stepped through the aperture, his light panning the interior rapidly, looking for a gaseous mist or glowing molten rock. He stopped just inside the strange cavity, his eyes widening as he gazed at the wall.

"So, anything exciting?" asked Jing-Mei as she stepped in beside him. She caught her breath at the silver reflection on the beam.

Twenty-four

Erica scrambled over the frosted waves of snow, blindly dodging bullets that peppered the ice all around her. Allan was literally yanking her around the deep core building, using its proboscis as a shield from the pursuing chopper.

"The plane," she gasped. "We have to get to the plane."

Cathy rammed into her backside as she stopped beside a large drift. "It's over fifty feet of open snow. We'll be sitting ducks, especially with these bright parkas." She pointed to the vivid red, not to mention Dmitri's orange one. "They'll be able to pick us off one by one. We should have stolen some of their camouflage white. Then we'd have a fighting chance."

The rotors chattered around the chimney and a fleece-coated SEAL sent a new hail of bullets into the mound of snow right behind them.

"Maybe we have to make a last stand in one of the buildings," said Allan.

Everyone turned to look at him. "This isn't the OK corral," said Erica. "I don't intend to die here. If we could talk to them, we could explain that there are no Russians left, barring Dmitri. We need to get to the radio."

They looked across the compound. It wasn't farther than thirty feet to the communications building, but it looked like an ocean of open water. "Not possible," said Dmitri. "I don't think they want to talk anyway." A new puff of snow erupted around their heads.

"What about snowmobiles?" asked Allan. "I thought I saw some parked on the other side of the deep core. Would they be fueled?" He looked at Dmitri.

The Russian nodded. "Always kept fully fueled. They are brand new Ski-doo REVs with Rotax engines. They corner like they're on rails."

Erica tilted her head to gaze at him sideways.

Dmitri grinned shyly. "Russians have fun too, sometimes. Even Russian scientists."

"That's great," said Erica. "They're souped-up snowmobiles. But I doubt if they can outrun bullets."

"You don't outrun bullets," said Cathy sharply. "You outmaneuver them. Zigzag, stop suddenly. A helicopter can't turn on a dime. And so far we've only got one to worry about." All the scientists turned to stare at her, their foreheads creased up into their toques. Cathy shrugged. "My dad was in the Navy. I know about helicopters."

"Okay," said Allan. "So we dodge the copters in the snowmobiles. Only one problem. There's no snowmobiles in the desert and I've never driven one."

"You'll ride behind me," said Erica. "I used to race with my brother up in Sudbury."

Dmitri frowned. "Sudbury?"

"Yes. It's an old asteroid impact site in Canada."

Allan looked startled. "It is?"

She nodded. "Why do you think I'm such an expert? Oh, no. I think they're going to land and flush us out." The helicopter was lowering to the ground. "Maybe that's a good thing," Erica said with dawning comprehension. "Our window of opportunity. Let's go."

As the Iroquois settled to the snow, a couple of SEALS leapt to the ground and started racing toward them. Erica grabbed Allan's hand and fled after Dmitri around the building. They came to a sheltered recess where the snowmobiles were neatly tucked away, smooth sleek bodies of bright blue vividly contrasting to the stark surroundings. The Russian leapt on the first and turned the ignition, catching the engine and grinding it to life. Cathy sprang onto the seat of the next in line and had it purring in a second. Both of them were hurtling over the drifts as Erica jumped onto the seat of the third, with Allan jamming in behind her. She started the engine and opened the throttle wide, keeping an eye peeled for the pursuing men with their needle-nosed guns. The machine kicked forward and sped into the open, closely following the blur of Dmitri and Cathy's machines. Allan clung to her as she turned the throttle to maximum and the machine flew over the snow like a Sea-doo over waves. There were screams behind her and the staccato of the chopper's rotors intensified. The SEALS were licking their heels.

Dmitri swung left and Cathy bobbed right. Bullets again salted the snow and chipped near the front of Erica's snowmobile. She jammed to a halt. The Iroquois flew over them, breaking wind on their heads, but unable to stop its forward momentum quickly enough to hover. It swung off to the left and chased Dmitri over the wide expanse of ice. Cathy veered back to the Hercules, kicking the machine into high gear. Erica streaked forward again, gaining on her guide. She worried about Dmitri in those split seconds, though. The helicopter was shadowing him and only his pendulum path was keeping the bullets from crippling the snowmobile and ripping open his broad back.

"We have to draw their fire," she yelled over her shoulder.

"Are you mad?" Allan called back.

"We came here to save the Russians," she screamed. "Not sacrifice the only one left to save our own butts." She swung to the left and hurtled toward the bird of prey. "Hey. Over here, you scumbags!" she screamed as if they could hear her over the throb of the rotors. But they did see her. Dmitri had stopped and pivoted. Now Erica and Allan were plainly in their sights. The helicopter swung low and the gunman dangling out the side took a bead on their Ski-doo.

"Punch it, Erica!" screamed Allan. "He's made us."

Erica jammed the snowmobile forward, jerking them both back in their seats. If Allan weren't glued to her waist he would have flipped off the machine. They barreled toward the plane, puffs of snow misting behind them. Dmitri was already in front, hurtling toward the only refuge in the vast ice desert.

"Hold on, Allan. We're almost there," she screamed over her shoulder. Her heart hammered in her ears, louder than the sharp staccato of the gunfire. Louder than the thrumming of the helicopter. This was insanity. She was a scientist, not a soldier or a spy fleeing death at every corner. The ramp of the Hercules grew closer, waiting like the open mouth of a whale to swallow her. For the first time in her life she wanted to be Jonah. Explosions crackled all around them. The snowmobile leapt over the lip of the ramp and careened into the hollow plane. She jammed it to a stop and flopped forward over the handlebars. She heaved a sigh as the grind of hydraulics told her the ramp was closing.

"We made…it," she gasped.

There was no sound from behind. "Allan?" She turned around.

He was slumped over, his face chalky white, his lips a bleached blue. A dark stain was slowly spreading over his crimson coat.

"Allan!" she screamed. Then the bloody phone rang again.

"This is unbelievable," said David, playing his flashlight over the gigantic metal disc, then beaming it to the side where a series of red lights blinked incessantly beside a keypad of some sort.

"I told you it was an airlock," said Jing-Mei.

"But…but that's not possible."

"We're always so arrogant. We always assume that we were the first." She stroked the metal and looked at David as if to say 'this if what we deserve.'

"Are you talking extraterrestrial?"

The astronaut giggled. "Nothing so dramatic. Probably another country's been holding out on us."

David shook his head. "This is crazy. I have to reach Erica."

"What for? This obviously isn't a geological phenomenon."

DOES THE STONE WALL HE HAMMERED A HOLE HAVE A HIDDEN DOOR THAT IS EASY TO SEE ON THIS SIDE? IF IT DOESN'T THEN THIS METAL AIRLOCK SEEMS POINTLESS.

"No, it isn't. But she's dealing with Russians right now. And if anyone might be holding out on us, it would be them."

"Don't be silly. Vochenkov is with us."

"Maybe they kept him in the dark. Or maybe he knew exactly where to go and he directed the search here. Dellows didn't tell me why they were so keen on this location. And these letters on the keypad, they look sort of backwards."

Jing-Mei shuffled closer to the airlock control plate and stared at the keypad. "They don't look Russian to me." She blinked. "And they sure aren't Chinese."

David shrugged. "Could be some kind of code. Houston, do you copy?"

There was a muffled response, bracketed by static. "We co… Marsh. Lot….interference."

"Have you contacted Dr. Daniels yet?"

"We're still trying. What…say…airlock?"

"That's what this chamber is. A pressurization room with a rather large airlock. When we tapped it, it depressurized and punched us backward. What it leads to is an even greater mystery. I don't think Neil Armstrong and Buzz Aldrin were the first men on the moon."

There was silence from Houston. He didn't think it was because of the static. They were probably sitting back in their chairs, stunned beyond words.

"Shall we proceed inside?" he asked.

"Hold on, Marsh." It was Dellows. "We're trying to digest this."

"Tell me about it," said David. "What about the volcanologist?"

"Patching you through," said a COMM technician. "She just picked up."

"David..."

"Erica, you're not going to believe this."

"Look, I'm a little busy right now. We've... shot at. My… friend is bleeding... We have… missiles…damn Navy… Can you ask your NASA… to call off the dogs?"

"What are you talking about? I thought you were on a scientific mission."

"Oh God! There's another one." There was a loud crackle on the COMM that made him wince.

"Erica?" There was no reply. "Erica?"

"...still here, for now. I hope all you... at NASA are listening. The Russians are gone. All except one... They disappeared, just like our own team. We are heading to the anomaly... We're scientists, not terrorists. Call the Pentagon and tell them to stop firing at us. Now I have to go."

"Wait, Erica. I know this isn't a good time, but I have to tell you. The explosion wasn't caused by a volcanic event. It was the depressurization of an airlock. Erica, someone beat us to the moon."

There was a long rain of static. Then, "...crazy! I'll call you back, if I make it out of here alive."

"Erica? Erica!"

"She hung up, Marsh," said Dellows. "It would appear there's more going on in Antarctica than I supposed."

"Dellows? You have to help her. I took her spot in the moon mission. She should have been here. Instead we sent her to a war zone, not that we ever expected it to be. Or did we?"

There was no reply.

"You have to stop them. Call them off and do it now, or I don't set foot beyond that airlock."

"...blackmailing me, Marsh?" There was a note of incredulity in Dellows voice.

"Call it what you like. I don't proceed until I hear from her again and she says she's okay."

There was another long pause. David fidgeted with his flashlight. He tried not to look at Jing-Mei, but his eyes strayed to her helmet. She was gazing intently at him, reading him and digesting everything she'd heard. But she didn't argue. Her lips betrayed the faintest smile. 'I'm with you,' she mouthed.

It wasn't easy to influence a bureaucracy, let alone dictate up the chain of command, but David was in a position of power that he might never hold again. True, they could send other men down here, but what if the whole team revolted. They were on the moon, far out of reach and they could foil years of preparation and billions of dollars worth of equipment. All he could think of now was saving the one woman he'd done his best to destroy all these years. He always thought she was strong enough to survive anything. Now he wasn't so sure, and he couldn't imagine her gone.

He didn't need her anymore for this mission, but God, how he wanted her. Her strong impassioned voice in his head, exclaiming over this extraordinary discovery. He waited. Still no response from Mission Control.

"Dellows?"

"Five minutes," came the clipped reply.

He tapped his toes on the smooth igneous rock beneath his boots. His breathing sounded even harsher in his own ears, like the gurgles of a drowning man. What if they were too late? What if they came back on the line and said she was dead? Could he go on by himself? Could he ever forgive himself for taking every opportunity away from her and giving her death? He could still hear his father's words. "You have to win! Win at all costs! Life is meaningless in the middle of the pack." How he wished he were back in the middle and he could hear her voice, squealing with excitement over a bloody rock.

"David?"

He shook the memories from his head. "Erica?"

"Thanks, David. I never thought I'd say this, but I owe you one."

"You're all right?"

"Sort of. Allan has been shot. The rest of us seem to be OK." David bristled at the archeologist's name, and it wasn't out of sympathy. "Look, I've got to go."

"Wait," said David. "I don't want you to owe me anything, but I do want something from you."

"Yes?" Her voice had suddenly hardened.

He gulped. "Your forgiveness." The line seemed to be dead, hissing in space. The interminable two and half second delay for a return signal had passed. "Erica?"

"All right, David. I can't hold a grudge forever. I forgive you."

"Thanks," he gushed. "You'll never know how much…"

"I really have to go."

"But I need your advice."

"You don't need me, David. You never did. The discovery you just made will give you your headlines and all without my input. You're the best scientist they have up there. Take charge. I'll see you when you get back."

She was gone. David blinked back a tear. Somehow those words would have fallen on deaf ears if it were anyone else saying them. Even from another geologist, he would have doubted himself. But from Erica, it was the highest praise he could ever get. He'd waited all his life to look her in the eye again. He finally could.

Jing-Mei's eyes were boring into him, so he looked away. He traced the airlock with his gloved hand. "I guess it's time to take a second step for mankind, or maybe a third or a fourth."

"One thing for sure," she said. "It won't be the last."

Twenty-five

Erica closed her eyes as she hung up the phone. The steady drone of the Hercules should have had a soothing effect on her nerves, but she couldn't erase the adrenaline pumping through her veins. She took a deep breath and opened them again. Everyone was staring at her, unable to comprehend the sudden flaking away of the helicopters.

"They nicked our wing," shouted Cathy, "but I think we'll be okay."

Erica nodded. She turned back to Allan, lying on the floor amidst the fallen parachutes and crates, cushioned by a mound of extreme weather gear. His eyes were fluttering open. "Did we make it?" he asked.

"They veered off," said Erica. She knelt down beside him and unzipped his coat. Gingerly, she peeled it away from the bullet wound in his shoulder. A congealed mat of blood cemented his shirt to his skin. "Do we have some gauze?" she asked Cathy.

Cathy frowned and shrugged. She looked exasperated as she hunted around her seat. Finally she stood and slapped the headset back on Erica's head, hooked on her own and carefully placed one on Allan.

"Do you have any gauze?" Erica asked again.

"Yes." The guide immediately turned and rifled through some bags. She produced a handful of sealed sterile packages that she handed over to Erica. "How bad is it?"

Erica ripped a package open, pulled his shirt away from the wound and quickly thrust the gauze over it. There was a small squirt of blood before she had it covered. "Help me roll him over and we'll see."

Cathy squatted down beside her, but before she could slip her hands underneath Allan's shoulders to roll him, he growled, "I can roll over myself," which he promptly did.

"I think he'll live," said Erica, as an overwhelming wave of relief washed over her. She examined his back where there was a small round exit wound staining his shirt. "It looks like it passed right through. I'll just have to clean it and pad it well."

"See, bullets can't even stop me. Indiana Jones has nothing on Allan Rocheford."

"It did stop you," said Erica. "It just didn't kill you, thank goodness. Can you hobble over to the bathroom with me so I can clean you up?"

"Sponge bath?" he asked, grinning with a mischievous gleam in his eyes.

"That's the most you can hope for in the Antarctic. But you won't be getting it."

"What kind of a nurse are you?"

"Get up," said Erica. She propped his shoulder between her two hands, holding the gauze in place as Allan struggled to his feet. He was a bit wobbly, but Erica's body was a crutch for him as he walked slowly toward the tiny bathroom in the Hercules. With his arm hooked around her shoulder, Allan lowered himself to the toilet seat. Cathy slipped in the First Aid kit on the shelf by the sink.

"Isn't this quaint," Allan said, as the door slammed shut.

"Be thankful that it's still intact," she said. "Those missiles missed us by a hair." She grabbed a towel from the rack behind his head.

"Why did they break off the attack?" he asked. "I saw you on the phone but I couldn't hear your conversation over the blasting. Did you call Staten?"

Erica shook her head, slick tendrils of hair falling in front of her face. She swept them away and poured antiseptic solution onto the towel from a bottle in the First Aid kit. "I called David." She dabbed the towel to the rust stains around his wounds. His eyes bugged out, but she didn't think it was because of pain.

"David? As in Marsh?"

She nodded tentatively. “He’s my connection in NASA, such as it is. It was the only thing I could think of.”

“So you call the one man who literally tried to destroy your career. The man who took your biggest opportunities away from you.”

“I don’t think he ever wanted to see me dead.”

“Not to mention,” he went on as if she hadn’t spoken, “that he’s sitting up there on the moon, farther away than anyone else on earth.”

“Nothing’s that far anymore with today’s communications.” She tapped the headset. “And despite everything you just said, he did it. He got them to call off the dogs. I don’t know how exactly, but he has always found a way to win.”

“By cheating.”

“Whatever it took. His father drove him to it. He would wince every time his father called. It was never ‘Hi, son. How are you doing? I love you,’ sort of thing. It was more like ‘Are you making me proud? What awards have you received? Are you on the honor role? Call me when you’ve won the Nobel prize.”

“Am I supposed to feel sorry for the prick now?”

“No, Allan. I’m just telling you that it wasn’t *all* his fault.”

“But you hated him.” He looked deep into her eyes and she hesitated. How could she express how conflicted she felt about David? He wouldn’t understand.

Finally she said, “Yes, I did. Nothing he can do now will change what he did in the past. But he is different. He did save our lives.”

“By winning,” said Allan with a scowl. “He blackmailed NASA. Is that a noble course of action to get his way?”

“But it wasn’t selfish,” said Erica. “It was to save us.”

“To save you,” said Allan. “How do you know it wasn’t selfish?”

“You don’t think he really wants me back?”

"Of course, he does," said Allan. "He's kicking himself now. He wants your brain back, when he's in a jam, but he wants more than that. And who could blame him? The only thing I can't fathom is why it took him ten years to figure out something I realized the first minute I met you."

Erica pressed a little too hard on the wound and Allan yelped.

"Sorry," she said, backing off a little. "I'll just put the gauze on now." She leaned over him with the pads, his breath tickling her neck. She gritted her teeth and taped up the dressings. "There. You should be as good as new." She turned to go, but Allan grabbed her arm.

"What's the matter?" His fingers dug into her flesh and she flinched.

"Nothing."

"You can't be softening toward him."

Erica turned back and met his eyes. "You act as if you're jealous. Of David. And that's crazy. I only called him because it was a last resort. You have nothing to be jealous of."

"Prove it."

She stared at him. "We're in a 4 x 4 cubicle. And you're wounded."

"Those are excuses," said Allan.

Erica blinked. This was insane. Yet, why not? Why was she holding back? She'd just been through hell and who knows what lay ahead of them. Why the hell not?

Her breath seemed to quicken at the thought. She leaned over to kiss him, but the bar of the mike was in front of her lips, and, wouldn't Cathy and the pilots hear everything they said and did? She ripped it off violently and clicked off the connection. Allan watched her intently, but he didn't move.

"Do you want them to hear?" she said loudly, although the drone of the engine was blocked a bit in the tiny cubicle. They could actually talk without the headsets.

Allan just shrugged.

"Well, I don't." She grabbed the device from his head and tossed it down beside the sink. Then she leaned over again and kissed him, just a trickle over his lips. Her breath caught in her throat at the moist contact. He didn't respond at all. He was waiting.

Slowly, she peeled off her polar fleece and undershirt. There was a little flutter at the base of his neck. She reached behind and undid the clasp to her black lacy bra. It fell limply to his lap. His hand twitched, but he still didn't move. Erica thrust her fingers through his hair and leaned over him, her breasts dangling in front of his face like worms on a hook. He closed his eyes, then his tongue flicked out, nudging her nipple, tracing the circle of her areola. She leaned closer and he took her nipple into his mouth and suckled deeply. The sensation was exquisite and so much better because this was a man who hadn't betrayed her. Wouldn't betray her. His hands rose up at the same time and caressed her abdomen, tracing the skin around her navel, then diving beneath the elastic of her fleece pants. He touched her center, awakening the nerve endings. She moaned deeply in the back of her throat as her breath quickened. Her heart hammered against his face, now thoroughly buried in her breasts.

"Allan," she cried as he ripped down layer upon layer of outerwear. Finally he stripped her panties from her supple bottom and grabbed a cheek, pulling her closer. It seemed his pain was totally forgotten in the frenzy of their lovemaking. Her knees cracked into the metal sink. Her elbows became chafed against the tight walls, but she didn't care. She sucked in her breath as he leaned forward and flicked his tongue at her core. Her hands pressed against the walls, supporting her from collapsing in a writhing heap. Her hips gyrated with his persistent rhythm. Finally he couldn't contain himself any longer. He pushed down his own layers and released his rigid penis. It looked more swollen and painful than the bullet wound. He grabbed her around the waist and lowered her onto him. Erica gasped.

He thrust upward and she met him charging down. Her whole body quivered as the waves of sensation rose and fell until at last they peaked and crashed down in a final convulsion. She screamed and sank onto him, numb and exhausted, yet her eyes were fever-bright.

"Allan," she whispered, nuzzling his throat.

"Erica," he replied. He swept back her hair from her damp neck and kissed her. "You are fantastic. I think I love you."

Erica sighed, her brain as fuzzy as the rest of her body. "I love you too, David."

He tensed underneath her. "Allan," she said quickly.

"You said *David*." He spat out the words with a growl at the back of his throat.

"No, I said Allan."

"Damn him! You haven't gotten him out of your system, even after we…"

Erica shook her head. "No. I would never have said that to him. I despise him. It was just a slip of the tongue. After everything that happened, my brain was in neutral. Please, Allan. It's you I love. I really do. You're the only man I want to be with. Do you know how many I've turned down over the years? I couldn't trust anyone anymore. But I trust you, completely. Please, believe me. I didn't have any fantasies. It was you I made love to. It's you I want by my side when we investigate the anomaly." She paused. "Your Atlantis."

Allan studied her critically. He was taking in every word she said and matching it to her body language. Had she twitched or licked her lips, he probably would have shot her off him onto the floor. "Okay," he finally said. "That was some of the best sex I've ever had, bullet wound or no bullet wound. I hate to think that you believed I was someone else."

"Never for a minute. It was the pirate not the pickpocket that I saw. And still see." She leaned over and kissed him, rubbing her face against his day's growth of tawny stubble.

Allan grunted and shifted underneath her. "Give me a few minutes and I'll test you on it."

"Can't wait," she sighed in his ear. Her lips trailed down his throat, trying to expunge the suspicions that she could still sense in the tautness of her shoulders and neck. "Let me try to wake you up." She gently slid off of him and eased her hand down his firm belly. His muscles rippled and just as she felt him start to engorge, a fist hammered on the door.

"Erica. We're almost there." It was Cathy. "You guys better get ready."

She collapsed on his lap again. "I guess you'll have to test me later."

"I'll look forward to it." There was a sly grin on his face. The rigid lines of his jaw had eased up. It would appear he had forgiven her for now.

Erica rose shakily to her feet and slowly got dressed. Allan did the same from his cramped position. He had a little trouble buttoning his shirt. She quickly came to his aid. Then they stumbled out of the lavatory, looking a little ruffled. Two pairs of very squinty eyes followed them.

"It sure took an awful long time to dress that wound," Cathy yelled over the drone of the engine.

Erica shrugged as she walked past, although it was hard to keep from smiling. She felt refreshed, renewed. Now she could sweep all the crap from the past out the door, if only she could keep his name off of her lips.

She glanced out the window as she sank to her seat. The black ripples of the Transantarctic Mountains loomed closer, like rotten teeth in amongst the bright enamel.

Twenty-six

David tapped a key on the pad beside the airlock, his teeth clenched as he waited for the release. There was no sound – how could there be – no light, nothing. He frowned and looked sideways at Jing-Mei. A little more vigorously he punched the next one and then another beside it. He keyed in a whole series. "It won't open," he exclaimed in disgust.

"Uh, David," said Jing-Mei brightly. "It's okay if I call you that, isn't it? I'm a little past the scowling stage and we are in this together."

"Sure," he said. "Jing-Mei."

"I was just thinking. Maybe it's not so much a code as a failsafe system."

"What do you mean?"

"Well, you did blow a hole in the wall. If it is an airlock – and I certainly think it is – then it's not going to open until it's pressurized. Otherwise we'd have another venting."

David stared at her. He glanced back at the round aperture behind them. "I see your point," he said. "So, what do you suggest?"

"We have to plug the hole."

"With what?"

Jing-Mei frowned and chewed on her lower lip. "I got it," she finally said. She ripped down the velcro from her utility pocket and withdrew a long sheet of thick plastic. After handing it over to him, she opened her secondary pocket and pulled out some duct tape.

David's eyes narrowed as he watched her. "You knew all along."

She grinned.

"Do you think the plastic's strong enough?"

"It's the same material they used for the prototype Martian space HAB. It should hold." She beckoned him to the gap.

David opened up the sheet of plastic and fed her the other end. He held it firmly in place while she taped. "Ah, duct tape," she said. "Best invention ever made."

"I feel like I'm on a handyman show," he said rolling his eyes.

"First handyman show ever done in 1/6th g."

"I'll give you that."

She applied the last strip of tape and stood back to survey her handiwork. "It looks airtight. Let's give the airlock another go."

David nodded and turned back to the keypad. He played with it for a few minutes, then a light flicked on above the lock. They couldn't hear the hissing, but David seemed to feel, even through his pressurized suit, the air become heavier. The light went off abruptly. They waited, the tension in David's body keeping him rigid. There was a crack in the lock, then the door slowly shifted inward.

David stepped in first, pupils contracting at the bright illumination. He blinked and blinked until his eyes could focus. Jing-Mei came up beside him, shielding her face with her gloved hand.

"It sure is bright," she said.

"There appears to be power."

"Can you see anything yet?"

David blinked again and there was adjustment now and color. His mouth dropped open as the cave took on new dimensions. It reached the 1200 meters to the roof of the lava tube, but there was nothing but space above the canopy of the trees. *Trees.* Spread out in front of them like a regiment of stalwart sentinels were beeches and maples, giant ferns and wide-stemmed oaks. Forest flowers carpeted the ground - a deciduous garden of trilliums and dogtooth violets, wild daisies and jack-in-the-pulpits. Wild raspberries and blueberry bushes frothed beneath the canopy and in the middle – David had to blink at this one – there was a stream carving its way through the regolith and soil – there was even soil – until it disappeared underground.

Jing-Mei stood beside him, her jaw resting on the bottom of her helmet. Then she laughed. It was like chimes in his ears through the headset. She reached up and disconnected the seal to her helmet.

"What the hell are you doing?" asked David. He swung around to grab her arms.

"It's okay, David," she said, pushing his hands away. "There's trees and plants. A biodome. We can breathe." She twisted her helmet and took it off. With her eyes closed she sucked in a deep breath. "See?" She opened her eyes.

David shook his head. "This is incredible. Nobody could have done this in the last thirty-five years. How could they have flown all this soil up here – the weight alone – and some of these trees must be at least a hundred years old."

Jing-Mei grinned, breathing deeply. "It's fragrant. Here, you try it," she said, reaching for his helmet.

David backed away.

She took another breath, smiling like she was high on a drug. "It's perfectly fine."

"I'll wait for the lab results."

"There's plenty of lab results on biodomes. Take a chance. I'm not dead yet."

The COMM crackled and hissed. "Did you say biodome?" asked Dellows.

"It would appear so," said David. "We have a forest of plants and trees up here. Jing-Mei took off her helmet."

"That's not advisable. Wait until you scan the environment."

"See, I told you."

Jing-Mei shrugged. "Too late. It feels safe to me. I don't need a scan and lab analysis to tell me if I'm breathing. This is just too amazing."

"Too amazing is right," said David. He walked toward the stream, bent down beside it and dipped his gloved hand in the water. Of course he couldn't feel anything through the thick insulated material. "Water. Where did it come from? Oh, hell." He lifted off his helmet and took a breath.

"Oh, God!" said Jing-Mei. She clutched her throat and sank heaving to the dirt bank of the stream.

"Jing-Mei!" David yelled. He sprang toward her and lifted her up, but her contorted face suddenly crinkled into laughter.

"Thanks," she said. "But you forgot the cardinal rule of oxygen depletion. Save yourself first or you won't be any good to others. They even tell you that on airplanes."

David frowned and shook his head. "I guess I did," he grumbled. It hit him then. He had actually forgotten himself for a change. Even though it was the wrong course of action in the astronaut handbook, he felt a modicum of pride return to his shriveled ego. Maybe there was hope for him yet.

He took another deep breath and felt the purity of the air. It was undoubtedly a mammal-friendly oxygen-nitrogen mix.

"Marsh!" came the rebuke from Houston. "You didn't take off your helmet too? This is totally irresponsible of both of you."

He couldn't squelch the giggles. Jing-Mei grinned and winked.

Well, what was one rebellious act without another? He detached the gloves from the suit and threw them defiantly on the ground. It was time to find out how real this environment actually was. He bent down and dipped his hand in the flowing current of the stream. It was refreshingly cool, but not cold like the chill of the moon in shadow, nor was it hot like a thermal pool. He cupped his hand and brought the water to his lips.

"You might be pushing it now," said Jing-Mei.

He looked up at her and shrugged. He sipped. It was pure and clean. "H2O. But where did it come from? Where did all of this come from? It would take decades to build a biodome of this size on the moon."

"Centuries, even," she said.

David laughed. “Let’s not get carried away.”

Jing-Mei shrugged. “It’s a life-sustaining community without a soul in sight.”

His eyes followed hers, rippling over the forest. It extended far back into the cavern as far as the eye could see. Tall scraggly poplars and wide-based oaks that painted dappled light on the ferns and scrub. Maples that swung branches heavy with emerald leaves over the babbling brook. And in the distance, tall pointed spears – pines that thrust toward the roof of the cavern. She was right. The only movement was the soft circulation of air that made fronds and leaves shiver ever so slightly.

Then why did it feel like they were being watched?

He squinted at the trees until everything blurred except a single staring eye.

Twenty-seven

Hawaii. As the Hercules hurtled through the blinding brightness over the stark world of Antarctica, Erica's mind wandered back to a bliss that she had never quite reacquired, even now.

The little Bed and Breakfast just outside of Hilo on the active island. She could still see the lush tropical flowers in brilliant hues of lavender and pink, crimson and orange, swaying in the warm sun-drenched breeze. Erica walked through the garden of cream and butter orchids and tangerine bromeliads to the gently swaying hammock where David was sleeping, tied between two spiked palm trees. A scarlet Apapane was twittering near his head. The little honeycreeper kept brushing his nose with its tail feathers as it sipped nectar from an o hi'a-lelua, a pretty purple cluster flower. He absently twitched and dusted his hand over his face, still caught in the tight embrace of dreams.

"David," she whispered in his ear. She upended the hammock and sent him sprawling to the ground.

"W..what was that for?" he growled in mock anger, his orange eyebrows arched.

She bent down next to him and fluffed his unruly red hair. "You promised to hike with me to Kilauea today to see the new eruptions. You're not going to sleep all day?"

"Well, I wasn't exactly thinking of *sleeping* the whole day, but why don't we wait until tomorrow for your hike. I just patched up the burn mark on my flight suit from our last hike." He appealed to her with his enormous eyes, tenderly running his fingers through her hair. "Besides, I'm still wounded." He indicated the small blister on his thigh, just below the frayed hem of his cut-off denim shorts, where he'd been splattered by a miniscule globule of lava that had burned through his suit.

"Oh, poor dear," said Erica, allowing him to draw her head closer. His kiss was soft and lingering as his hands wandered down her long neck and under her thin cotton blouse.

"You could just stay here and nurse me," he whispered, probing a little deeper with both his tongue and his hands.

"A tempting offer. But I think you're pretty well on the mend and I need to see that crater." She pushed him away and stood up. "Let's go."

David sighed. "You know I don't care for volcanoes as much as you do."

"You don't have to come," she said quietly, trying to keep the hurt out of her voice.

He looked up at her, surprised, and from what she could see by the slight pucker in his forehead, considering. Finally he shook his head. "No, I won't leave you alone within Pele's grasp." Pele was the Hawaiian volcano goddess that spewed lava at the slightest character that angered her – namely the USGS volcanologists or Berkeley graduate students that persistently scaled her slopes.

Erica smiled, unable to contain her delight, not only at exploring the deadly world of lava and volcanoes at an active site but also at sharing it with the man she loved.

They drove thirty miles on highway 11 from Hilo on the eastern flank of the largest volcano in the world – Mauna Loa, some 17 km (56,000 ft) from seafloor to summit – to the most active volcano – Kilauea - on the island of Hawaii. Kilauea was 4,190 ft above sea level and had been spewing lava continuously since 1983. The landscape changed abruptly as they approached the more active zone of the island. The delicate greenery of the fern and bamboo forests, the twittering of the polychromatic birds and the scent of eucalyptus faded and transformed into charred vegetation, the stinging odor of sulfur and a barren moonscape that reminded her so much of her hometown, Sudbury, before the diligent greening-up program. Of course that moonscape had not been caused by volcanic activity, but by strip mining of the impact site – a man-made wasteland. This dead zone was created entirely by nature, which made it all the more intriguing. They detoured around the Kilauea caldera, Erica taking a dozen snapshots of the percolating Lava Lake in the center. Then they headed off on the Chain of Craters Road toward the most active flow from Pu'uO'o crater. A gaggle of brown and white striped nenes, native Hawaiian geese, waddled out of their path – the only sign of life in the lava desert - honking their displeasure at the disruption to their peaceful Sunday afternoon. Erica clicked off a shot of them as well. It was heartening to see another species as undaunted by the lava flows as she was.

David stopped the car abruptly where the folds of lava took out the road. Erica leapt from the jeep like a gymnast, her face beaming. David was a little slower, his eyes squinting at the ropes of charred rock, his teeth grinding together. This was closer than any tourist was ever allowed to get to the active lava flows, but David and Erica were hardly tourists, being in their final year of a doctorate in geology and volcanology. They donned their Nomex flight suits and thermo-reflective jackets. David still balked at the tight-fitting gas masks, but he relented quickly when he saw the venting steam on the horizon.

Trussed up and secure, they headed out onto the lava field. Their boots crunched over the shelly pahoehoe lava, which was gas-rich and left fragile crusts that flaked and shattered as they walked. Erica danced through the dark alien wasteland as if she had springs in her heels. This was crater heaven. She looked back at David with glittering eyes, but he merely raised his mask for a second and shook his head.

"Could you be a little less enthusiastic? I don't want to go as close this time. I don't relish being incinerated."

She giggled and lifted her own mask from her face. "Don't worry. I'll look out for you. I don't want any part of you incinerated either." She winked salaciously. "But isn't it a thrill to get so close to the fire?"

David rolled his eyes. "A thrill a minute. Now, really, Erica. The thrill is in winning the prize. Beating everyone to the finish line. And I can do that better back in the lab."

"In the lab," she said, "you only see a miniscule piece of the pie. A tiny slab of rock instead of the mountain. This earth, this whole universe, is so massive and mysterious, and I'm going to see it all."

"I suppose you will." He didn't look the slightest bit skeptical. She was grateful for that.

"The moon, David. I'm going to make it there. I know more about craters than anyone else on this earth, and they'll be begging for me soon."

He smiled.

"And you'll be with me, bouncing over the dusty surface and making oxygen from the regolith."

"And making love in the lunar rover?" He grinned lasciviously.

"In a pressurized lunar rover," she clarified. "Or it would be a little dangerous."

"But you live for danger." His grin widened before it quickly evaporated. David shoved his gas mask back over his face. "I think we're getting close." His voice was muffled, but she could still make out the change in it from amusement to taut anxiety.

Erica turned back to the ebony landscape speckled with craters where she saw the plume of amber and ruby fire. "Ohh." She breathed. "Isn't it beautiful?"

"Hot," said David. "Damn hot."

Erica smiled and trounced forward, hardly aware of the rising heat or the layer of sweat bathing her body beneath the suit. The plume jetted into the air and splattered to the right of the crater, sending a fresh flow of orange lava trickling down the slope into the surf of the ocean. The demarcation of the flow was only about fifty feet away from them, smoking black ropes solidifying on top of smooth basalt and the charred ruins of some unlucky houses. Erica couldn't keep her feet from edging closer and closer.

Finally she felt a hand grip her arm and pull her roughly backward. "That's far enough," said David.

"I have to take its temperature and gas measurements."

"The plume is getting higher." He nodded toward the climbing jet. "Remember what I said about being incinerated."

"All right, David. I'll plug it in here." She ejected her thermocouple probe from her backpack and stabbed it into a solidifying chunk of lava. "It's too old," she said, yanking it out. "I have to get closer."

"Last time you said that, I ended up with a burn."

Erica looked back at him and frowned. "Don't be a big baby. You'd have gotten more from touching a hot oven."

"Oh, really. Well, I..." He was interrupted by a loud belch from a spatter cone just to their left. "I thought the area we're walking on was inactive." A loud treble hiss drowned out the soft roar from the plume and steam clouded the air. At the same time the earth seemed to ripple beneath their feet.

This wasn't good, but she hadn't come all this way to turn around and go home without getting any data whatsoever. "I'll just get one reading," she said, " and then we'll go."

"Erica, we should go right now."

"Just one..." She hopped closer to the dense flow, raising the probe to jab it in a fresher area. There was a light popping sound and cinders started to rain down on them.

"Erica!"

"It's okay."

"You crazy woman."

She didn't have time to retract the probe. He'd grabbed her from behind, hoisted her over his shoulder and started to run.

"David! What are you doing?"

He stumbled and staggered over the uneven ground, but he didn't stop. The soft roar from the central crater was submerged by a deafening thunder right behind them.

"She's blowing a new crater," said Erica in amazement. "I've got to see this."

"Oh, God. We're going to die," moaned David. He staggered on, never turning around once to look at the show.

Erica couldn't help herself. She lifted her head from David's back and stared at the most profound sight she could ever imagine. The ground had subsided where the cone had once been, a perfectly circular crater with a geyser of white fire gushing from its center. The white-hot flow was rushing over the old black lava making a new stream that wound its way closer and closer to their path.

"David. Go uphill. Quickly."

She didn't have to tell him twice. He veered, climbing the buckled basalt and racing away from the leaping tongues of fiery rock with adrenaline-borne speed, his boots smoking beneath his feet. The lava inched closer, but David must have broken a record for land travel carrying an annoyingly death-defying volcanologist. He dashed uphill as the lava broke for the sea, leaving them behind. Finally he stopped, heaving and gasping, lowered her to the ground and sank there himself.

"We did it," she said quietly. "We won the race."

He tore off his mask and scowled at her.

"I'm sorry. I didn't think we were close to a vent."

David gritted his teeth, his face flushed, although he'd finally caught his breath. "I swear, if I didn't lo..."

She raised her eyebrows. "If you didn't...?"

It was over as quickly as it came. A mask fell over his face and he looked away. "If I didn't need you to help me with my thesis, I'd never go on these excursions. Look at my feet. My boots are practically melted. I don't know if you noticed, but we nearly died out here. You don't do that in a lab."

Erica reached out and touched his cheek. "You can't live in a lab, David. It's like living in a bubble and it's false security anyway. We didn't die."

"No thanks to you," he snapped.

Erica looked down and blinked back a tear. "You're right. You saved my life. I'll never forget that."

"I guess you owe me one." The harsh tone was starting to fade from his voice, but it still held a cold note.

"Of course, I do. If there's anything I can do…" She stroked his rough cheek and leaned over to kiss him, but before she could he stopped her with a hand to her lips.

"You can help me win."

"You don't need me for that," she whispered. She kissed his hand and wrapped her arms around him. They made love right there, in the black lava fields of Kilauea Volcano. It was a moment she would never forget.

"We're landing." It was Allan's husky voice over the headset jolting her back to the present.

She felt the hot blush on her cheeks and looked away guiltily. Why in the world was she thinking of Hawaii when she'd just committed herself to another man? Why did David always intrude on her most intimate moments reminding her of past joy and infinite pain? It was that moment when he'd almost admitted his love for her that everything had changed. He'd made a sacrifice, trying to save her, which was totally against his upbringing. He'd nearly paid the ultimate price and lost for good. Maybe he'd figured out that, despite some strong feelings for her, she wasn't worth it. That love was a losing proposition. Regardless of the reasons that she still couldn't fathom, she shouldn't care anymore. She had a new man, a new chance at something wonderful. She couldn't let David Marsh screw it up again.

Erica glanced out the window as the Hercules touched down on the ice sheet. It jounced over the scalloped snow on its skis like a jeep over deep ruts on a mud-caked dirt track. Finally, it came to rest next to a snow-covered Bell helicopter and a Russian cargo plane with streamers of ice hanging down its sides. Snow was being flung about by the wind making the vivid landscape dissolve in a thick haze. Erica could hardly make out the other plane – the other Hercules from McMurdo - about a hundred feet away, marooned on the ice like a frozen carcass.

Erica turned away from the ghostly scene. She quickly donned her thermal layers and polar suit, pulling the last zipper over her chin. Cathy handed her a pair of crampons to attach to her boots – it would be slick and treacherous up here between the pressure cracks and hidden crevasses that elbowed deep into the ice. She bent over Allan who was struggling with his own and adjusted the straps for him. He nodded his thanks and they stood, waiting for the ramp to lower.

There was a loud hydraulic hum as the tailgate opened and frigid air swirled in along with a fine dust of snow. This air was damper than at Vostok and a little warmer – you could actually breathe without pain. Allan didn't seem to agree by the way he hunched down in his polar suit and drew down the facemask from his toque.

"This is more like it," said Cathy as she walked down the ramp.

"What are you talking about?" asked Allan.

"It's warm here. Tropical almost."

"Is she crazy?" Allan turned to Erica.

"It is better than Vostok. You just haven't acclimatized yet."

"I don't think I ever will," he said, shivering and stamping his feet.

Dmitri came around beside him and clapped him gently, considering his wound, on the back. "This is vacation spot." He grinned. "We need lounge chairs and suntan lotion."

Erica laughed. "Maybe we will, considering the thermal data." She grabbed Allan's arm and pulled him close, determined to dash David from her head. "This is it, Allan. Your coordinates. The lost city of Atlantis."

They stepped off the plane, confronted only with the solid sheet of ice beneath their feet and the dark peak of a mountain protruding from the ice.

"Let's not get melodramatic," said Allan. "We'll find what we find. But I doubt it's the city of Atlantis. I've told you that."

Erica blinked, adjusted her tinted goggles and swung a 360-degree circle. "Where exactly is it?"

Allan dug into his coat and drew out a GPS unit. He flicked it on and waited for their exact location to pop up on the screen. "It should be right in front of that peak."

Erica nodded. "Under the ice."

They advanced slowly, ever wary of the empty planes and helicopter and their implications. Erica and Cathy prodded the snow with ski poles, looking for hidden crevasses. It wasn't long before they found one. "Hold," said Cathy, sticking out her arm to prevent Allan or Dmitri from walking forward. The ice was slushy and weak, although it did look solid where she stood, but Erica could make out a deep blue V just a few feet in front of them.

"Crevasse," said Erica, matter-of-factly. She leaned around Cathy and followed the crack into aqua-green depths – sheer ice on either side. "It's a deep one."

Allan crept in behind her and peered over her shoulder. "How deep is it? Can we climb down?"

Erica met his eyes and frowned. "You don't go down a crevasse. You'd just get stuck at the bottom and it's very difficult to get back up. The sides are sheer ice, you know."

"But it's right over the anomaly," said Allan, glancing at his GPS. "Can I have a closer look?"

Cathy backed slowly from the edge. "Be my guest," she said, but at the same time she was backing everyone further away. Allan tried to step around her, but she stopped him with a firm grip on his arm. "Wait until I secure you with a rope and a good piton in the ice."

He rolled his eyes, but did wait with crossed arms as she tapped a piton into a solid slab of ice, attached a rope and anchored it to him. "There. Now just because you have the rope on, doesn't mean I want you slipping over the edge. Be careful."

"Yes, ma'am," he said, saluting briskly.

It was Cathy's turn to roll her eyes. "I'm the guide. If you want to stay alive, I suggest you listen to me without the sarcasm."

Allan had already turned away. "Sorry," he muttered. He stepped closer to the abyss, his eyes crisscrossing the wide mouth, then looking down into the narrow depths. He sank to his knees on the edge and leaned way over.

"Stop it, Allan. You're making me nervous," said Erica.

"I don't believe it," he whispered.

"What?" She stepped closer, despite the hiss from Cathy that she wasn't secured.

"Can you see it? If you look at an angle, through the ice at the bottom of the V…"

She squinted and blinked. She could make out some rocks frozen in the ice, then she looked deeper and it seemed to loom out of the depths. It was a dark shape. A dark pyramid shape. "It could be a mountain peak," she said breathlessly.

"With no crags or jags. So fundamentally smooth. You know what it is."

"Let's not jump to conclusions yet."

"I'm going in," he sang, and grasped the end of the rope.

"No, you're not! That crevasse is a pit, not an access point. It's solid ice between. All you'd be doing is getting trapped in very tight quarters and we'd have to rescue you."

Allan stood up. "Do you have any better suggestions?"

"No, I…"

"Maybe you could use the tunnel," said a tiny voice behind them.

Allan and Erica swung around, crumbling some of the delicate ice at the edge of the crevasse. "What did you say?"

he demanded, wobbling on the disintegrating snow until Erica hauled him back.

"I said, maybe you could use the tunnel," said Cathy again. "Over there."

They turned and saw the yaw of a rather large hole in the ice that appeared to angle downward at about thirty degrees.

"It is a tunnel," said Allan. "Our way in."

"Probably the way the others went too," she said softly.

"So that's where I'm going," said Allan, a bold determination in his voice. He backed away from the crevasse, unclipped from the rope and strode toward the tunnel.

"No, you're not," said Erica, catching up to him and grabbing his arm.

"What do you mean? This is it, Erica. Our chance to discover the remnants of Atlantis."

"And the people who disappeared," said Cathy, hastening to join them. Dmitri was hot on her heels, but he had a lopsided tilt to his lips and an immensely furrowed brow.

"So we just follow them?" asked Erica.

"Yes," said Allan and Cathy together.

"No!" said Erica vehemently. "They might have died in there."

Allan turned on her. His face was flushed, and his eyes were narrowed to tiny ribbons as he grabbed her shoulders. "What do you suggest? We just leave. We've come all this way. We've found the entrance, then we just leave?"

"That's not what I'm suggesting at all. I think we should look for another entrance." She scanned the horizon, gazing intently at the mountain crest that seemed to magnetically draw her eyes. There was a crack of ebony near the center of the peak that looked darker than just shadowed basalt could explain. "There may be one in the mountain."

Allan squinted sideways at her. The angry blush was draining from his face. As he chased her gaze, his eyes widened. "You mean, a manmade entrance?"

"I didn't say that. I just mean that a melt water tunnel might not be the safest route to a 'hotspot' beneath the ice."

"You think they drowned?" asked Cathy, her voice very small.

"I don't know. I just think it would be wise to find another passage, if it's possible. And we have to wear the moon suits. If we do end up underwater, they might be the only things that can save us."

"Airtight, watertight," said Allan.

"Exactly. If we want to come out of the ice again, we'll have to do it a different way than the other teams. We'll have to be smart and we'll have to be cautious."

She turned before they could argue with her and headed back to the plane. She was pleased when she heard the trample of their feet behind her. Perhaps they had finally seen the error in blindly following the others like lemmings. The odds were, they wouldn't come back either. She knew Allan was driven by his passion for discovery and Cathy by love. Dmitri was so lost he would follow them anywhere. That left her, and her alone, to be the voice of reason. She drew them back to the plane where they dragged out the heavy EMU suits and Erica started to strap one of them onto her back.

"Are you telling me we have to carry these all the way to that mountain peak?" Allan asked, his lips curled into a scowl. "They're like two hundred pounds."

"Two hundred and eighty," said Erica.

"Are you forgetting that I was just shot."

"I haven't forgotten." She couldn't hide her smirk.

"Then what are you grinning at."

She pointed to the ramp where Cathy was loading a sledge with two of the suits. "We can't fit all of them on the sled, so we'll each take a turn carrying the other two." Dmitri was strapping the fourth to his back. "You'll be exempt, darling, considering your fragile condition."

"Oh," said Allan, somewhat mollified. "I'd like to do my share."

"It's okay. That you're up and walking is amazing enough."

"I can do more than walk," he said, "as you already know." He winked at her.

"Yes, I do. In fact, maybe you *should* be lugging this." She pointed to her back and the dangling EMU suit with the PLSS pack that was making her hunch already. "It's damn heavy."

"Soon as I'm healed."

He turned and started walking after Cathy who was already trudging forward pulling the overloaded sledge. Erica pulled up beside him, watching the man with renewed interest. Here he was between two women who were doing a substantial amount of the manual labor without protesting, whereas Dmitri kept mumbling, "I pull the sled. Too heavy for you," to Cathy. It was fascinating. Even David was never that secure in his masculinity. Allan swaggered forward, capable of taking a bullet in stride, a true Indiana Jones type of archeologist, yet confident that the women were just as capable as he was. She couldn't wait to be alone with him again.

This time they circled the path they had taken before, giving wide berth to the crevasse. They headed west toward the nearest mountain peak that was only fifty feet above the ice and a hundred feet away. Cathy pointed to the tunnel as they passed. It was a gaping hole that sloped downward into the ice at a gentle angle. But it did look slick and treacherous. There could be any number of ways that the teams had gotten into trouble, from deadly falls to being trapped in an underground lake as the ice melted over the thermal signature. Under the ice was the last place Erica wanted to go, but it was obvious that they could learn nothing up here on this barren plateau. Everyone seemed immersed in their own thoughts as they crept closer to the peak. There were only the sounds of the crunch of their crampons digging into the ice and their labored breathing.

The lone whistle of the wind sent a frisson down her neck. It was as if they were heading toward their doom.

Erica tried to focus on the black crags of the peak, so severe against the white glare all around them. But as the weight of the suit drained her strength and the moisture was sucked out of her by the dry wind, she began to doubt the wisdom of this option as well. What if she'd been wrong all along? What if the Russians did have a nuclear factory under the ice and Dmitri was in on their scheme. What if they were headed for a trap?

She shook her head. Maybe it was just her own naiveté, but she was inclined toward the more fantastic, unscientific explanation. She wanted more than anything to believe Allan now, maybe because she loved him – which was the most stupid reason a scientist could have to endorse a theory. She should know. She glanced over at him and found he was watching her, with his sensual lips curved into a delighted smile. His eyes were dancing.

"Don't feel vindicated yet," she said. "A structure under the ice doesn't prove it was the Atlanteans who built it."

Allan grinned back at her. "Who else would build a pyramid under the ice? Soon even you will have to believe."

Erica tilted her head and smiled. Maybe. She certainly hoped so.

They had almost reached the jutting peak of the mountain when the thump of rotors drummed across the empty sky. The tiny gnats were just at the edge of their vision, but they were coming on in a hurry.

"Let's go!" yelled Erica, punching forward as fast as her spiked feet would let her. They drew closer to the only shadowed area in this white world, the only place where they wouldn't be glaring targets. Erica slid to her knees as the Iroquois descended from the sky – a formation of warriors - but her team was steeped in shadow now, sheltered by the bleak crag. Allan gasped and shivered as he slumped against the rock. Dmitri and Cathy sank to the ice and watched with wide eyes as the helicopters disgorged the crack SEAL team,

blended white on white except for the black rifles they nosed out in front of them. They were moving cautiously – obviously schooled in mountain-climbing techniques as they spiked the snow in front of them searching for crevasses.

The final helicopter to descend delivered a white-suited African American with a lump under his white toque. "Commander Staten," Erica breathed.

"I guess he came for the show," said Allan.

"You mean the firing squad?"

He laughed. "You have a line in with NASA now, dear. He won't go that far, I doubt."

The Commander strode out of the helicopter, making a beeline for the crevasse they had abandoned not too long ago. He wobbled only slightly, his equilibrium much improved from the last time Erica had seen him at McMurdo. "He seems to know exactly where to go."

"He has the coordinates as well as we do, plus the thermal data. But just watch – he's not as smart as you are. He's going to head right into the tunnel," said Allan.

Sure enough, there was a yell from one of his men directly from the mouth of the tunnel, his white body cupped in the blue embrace of ice. "Over here! I found the entrance." His gruff voice labeled him as the bulky scar-faced zealot – Bruzo.

Staten mumbled something and headed toward his man. Erica leaned forward trying to make out his distorted words. She had to know what they planned.

"Do you think they've gone in?" he asked.

"There's nowhere else to go. They must have."

"Idiotic scientists. Leaping before they look again. Without backup. They're going to get themselves killed."

"Maybe they thought that's what we were going to do," said another familiar voice. Metzer had come alongside the Commander, his warm brown eyes suddenly hard as they locked with his superior. "It was a little dramatic, sir. Firing at them."

Staten shrugged off his comment. "We had to stop them somehow. Heading right into the lion's den. I'm amazed they're still alive. The Russians must have bugged out by the time they got there. Unless they're under here."

"Then so are the scientists," said Metzer. "*Many* scientists," he emphasized, tilting his head in the direction of the planes. "We're here to rescue them, aren't we, sir?"

Staten glared at his second-in-command. "Of course, we are. We will check our targets."

Bruzo nodded agreement, but the fierce look on his face made Erica wince. Sure, they'd check their targets. Maybe after they riddled them full of bullets. She held her breath, hugging the rock as Staten motioned his team down into the tunnel – all of them except for two SEALS guarding the entrance and a couple of helicopter pilots who remained bolted to their machines. They would freeze soon, though, if they stayed within the crafts. The steel frames sucked the warmth right out of you. They'd be warmer near the peak, out of the wind, but she wasn't staying here long enough to see if they figured that out.

"We have to move," she whispered.

"What if they see us?" asked Allan, his eyes still glued to the menacing bodies of the guards.

"We're in shadow. We have to find the entrance before they start scanning the horizon in their boredom. If they notice our flashy snowsuits, they'll come and investigate. I don't want to see anyone get shot again."

"Agreed," said Cathy. "We'll try to keep in the shadow and inch to the right."

It was a tedious process, to move slowly when she felt like running. She had to lift carefully and plant her crampons gingerly in the ice so the *scritch* wouldn't alert the guards. As she edged around the bulbous crag, the shadow became thicker and backed into a furrow. Erica crouched and kept slinking further and further back. It was inky, with icicles hanging from the lip above. She blinked because it was impossible to see after the blinding white of the ice cap, but she was sure her feet were drifting downward. She spun around and cracked her head against Allan, who was following a little too closely.

"Ow," he muttered. "What are you doing?"

"I think this is it," she whispered, only loud enough for the sound to carry to Cathy and Dmitri.

"It?" echoed Allan.

"The entrance. A tunnel that descends into the mountain. We've found the other way in."

Allan sucked in his breath. She could see the dim outline of Cathy and Dmitri nodding their heads, although she heard someone gulp loudly. "Does anyone have a flashlight?" asked Erica.

Cathy dug into her pack and flicked on a narrow beam. She played it over the dripping icicles and chiseled rock that dipped into the ground. "This doesn't make sense," she said, reaching for a melting cone. "The ice shouldn't be melting this much."

A sultry waft of air drifted from inside the tunnel and lifted Erica's hair from her neck. "It's warm down there," she said. "Our 'hotspot.' Maybe it is volcanic after all. Let's put on our EMU suits before we go any further."

No one argued with her. It was time to employ extreme caution, although, by the grimaces and muttering from the men, she could tell they weren't too pleased to pull on such bulky and heavy outerwear. They divested the parkas and fleece to be replaced by the Liquid Cooling and Ventilation Garment and the layered outer shell of the space suit. As Erica pulled on the orange garment, her hand ran over a lump on the shoulder section. She turned and saw a patch sewn into the fabric. Craning her neck, she could just make out the name: MARSH.

She caught her breath and bit down hard on her lower lip. Damn him for being everywhere, even attached to the bloody spacesuit she was wearing. Why couldn't she escape him when they were over 200,000 miles away from each other? Somehow she had to block him from her mind, despite the glaring presence of the patch.

The others were already donning the Hard Upper Torso with the PLSS pack. She quickly threw hers on as well and attached the Lower Torso Assembly – the suit's pants. Finally everyone pulled on thick gloves and attached them to the suit.

"Pressurizing now," said Allan as he initiated the oxygen flow from the PLSS. His voice was faint beneath the helmet. "Are you sure we need this. It's so damn heavy."

"We're not in space," Erica said, trying to keep her voice light. "But we still have to make sure we're airtight."

"Watertight is what you mean," said Cathy. "We'd probably be okay in scuba gear, not this incredibly bulky space suit."

"Yes, that would work if we walked into a flood. But if there's some toxic gases, or lava, you'll be happy for the suit. We won't be suffocated or burned alive." She screwed on her helmet and opened the communications link. There wasn't a sound from the other suits.

"Is everyone hooked up to the COMM?"

There was a chorus of "Yes's" in very grim tones.

"Perk up," she said. "If we don't find something very dangerous down there, we might find something fantastic."

"You're still hoping for a volcano, aren't you?" said Allan.

"Yes. But I doubt if that's what we'll find. Someone definitely blasted this tunnel. It's not in limestone and it's certainly not water-carved. I don't think the Atlanteans did this one, Allan. But I could be wrong."

"And as a scientist," said Allan," I'm going to prove you are."

Twenty-eight

David froze as he watched the eye examine him carefully before it disappeared behind the scrub in the strange lunar forest. "I…I think there's someone out there."

"Good," said Jing-Mei. "Someone had to create this biodome. It's about time he introduced himself."

"No, I don't think I want to be introduced to this one," he said. "It didn't look human." David bent down and carefully retrieved his gloves, all the while never dropping his gaze from the place where he'd seen the yellow eyes in the forest

Jing-Mei turned and stared at him openly. "What are you talking about? Did you see an alien?" She was trying to hide her grin and failing miserably.

"No," said David. "I think it was…"

A deep-throated growl interrupted and made both explorers jump. David grabbed Jing-Mei's hand and sprinted toward the far treeline, looking back only once to see the flash of gray fur and dagger-tips of white fangs. Hot breath must have singed his suit, the creature was that close, but he gave another giant leap through the ferns and overgrown shrubs, dragging Jing-Mei with him, and heard with some relief a yelp behind him. It wasn't gone, but it was held up. They kept running - it seemed for miles - until eventually the snarls receded. Still they ran for another good mile until the canopy of broad-leafed deciduous trees gave way to a mesh of white pines and Balsam fir. As they traveled, snakes hurtled themselves out from under their feet and chipmunks dashed between the deadwood on the forest floor. There was a flurry above their heads as birds trumpeted into the air leaving behind a snow of feathers. A disgruntled porcupine waddled out of their path just before they ran into its spikes and they came to a dead stop right in front of a snarling skunk.

"We'll just back away," said Jing-Mei slowly, tugging on David's hand. The skunk snarled once more, then swaggered into the forest.

David lowered his massive bulk – his body plus the EMU suit – to the ground, gasping and shaking his head. "This isn't just a simple biodome of plants supplying the O2 and humans supplying the CO2," he muttered. "It's an entire ecosystem."

Jing-Mei nodded, sinking down beside him. "Imagine the payload to seed this. Like Noah's ark."

"At exorbitant costs," said David. "What for? Why would you need wolves and snakes? Hell, why would you need skunks?"

"To complete the loop," said Jing-Mei. "A complete ecosystem would revitalize itself. And build soil. Decay from plant and animal sources to supply a living matrix, everything in balance. Eventually you wouldn't need anything from earth."

"I suppose. But wouldn't you need everything then. Worms and insects. Oh shit, I shouldn't have mentioned that."

A faint buzz grew louder and a sharp needle picked the back of his hand. "No," said David slapping and swatting. "Not mosquitoes! What were they thinking? What good are mosquitoes except to annoy us to death and spread disease?"

Jing-Mei swatted at her neck. "They're also food for birds and frogs, bats."

"Bats?" David squeezed his eyes shut and pictured his earlier fantasies of fangs and flocking nightmares. Maybe he hadn't been so far off the mark.

"A necessary evil," Chin Me continued, "I suppose, to an ecosystem."

"Okay," said David, opening his eyes and gathering his wits. "Either these people were very smart or very stupid. Imagine, introducing mosquitoes to a pest-free environment. But there's still something missing."

Jing-Mei raised her tapered eyebrows in mock alarm. "I hope you don't mean bears, or lions or man-eating sharks."

"Let's hope they skipped a few species. No, what are missing are the creators. There are no humans."

"So far," said the astronaut. "This lava tube goes on for miles. We've just tapped the surface."

"Rather thick surface," said David, looking at the prolific growth of trees.

"Shall we go on?" asked Jing-Mei. "Or do we go back? Perhaps we should ask Houston for orders." She paused and waited for a response.

"I don't think they can hear us."

Jing-Mei tapped the mike on her headset. "Houston, do you copy?"

Empty air and static. Maybe their whirlwind trip through the forest had jimmied the radio. David got up from the ground and brushed himself off. "Okay. Let's review our options. Either we go back and face the snarling, 'I'd like to rip your throat out' wolf, or we go on and find out who set the wolves on us."

"Let's go on," said Jing-Mei. "I kind of like it here."

"Ya, it can grow on you. If there weren't the bloody mosquitoes." He clapped his neck again as the buggers swarmed around his head.

They tramped onward through the forest, mesmerized by the richness of the ecosystem. They passed an open area overgrown with cattails and lilypads floating serenely on stagnant water - a bog, or, in other words, a filter for organic waste. Everything was lighted as if it were in daylight and not an underground tunnel. David squinted up at the high roof of the cavern. The lighting was mostly artificial, although he saw some reflected light from mirrors recessed in the shadows. There must be a glass partition up at the top where actual sunlight was beamed down during the 14-day light cycle of the moon. Down here the plants could harvest the sunlight, but not be harmed by the massive doses of radiation and ionized particles on the moon's surface since the roof of the cavern provided insulation for them. As they trekked deeper into the cave, the forest ended abruptly and gave way to groves. There were apple orchards and peach trees, grapes on snarling vines that seemed to snake up the rock walls themselves and cherry blossoms clouded one corner of the cave. Butterflies and birds hovered contentedly over the flowers and fruit, making the black lava tunnel a swirl of variegated colors. David couldn't believe that such an extensive project had been completed in just a few years. Jing-Mei was dancing through the orchards, her hands splayed, giggling like a schoolgirl.

"It's just so beautiful," she said. "It's like the dead planet has given birth."

David just shrugged as the groves fell away. Now there were fields - fields of corn and cabbage, beans and tomatoes, carrots and cucumbers - albeit they were overgrown and sometimes intermingled. The orderliness had long given way to savagery.

David shook his head and sighed. "I can't believe anyone could have done this much since the dawn of space travel."

"Well, maybe they could have seeded it and it grew at an exponential rate. There is less gravity." She plucked a ripe tomato from a chest-high plant. It was the size of a cantaloupe. "See. They can grow much larger without the constraints of earth's gravity. I wonder how it tastes." She bit into the fruit, expelling a gush of juice from the pulp and leaving a watery trail down her chin. "Delicious. You should try one."

"I think I'll wait until later. I want to explore further."

Jing-Mei nodded and tossed the remainder of the tomato into the tangle of stalks and leaves. Another quarter of a mile and the fields ended at a wall of what appeared to be made of brick the same color as the regolith. It was only eight feet tall and roofed over, but it extended across the entire cave. There were a series of recesses that flowed back into hallways spaced every ten to twelve feet.

"What do you think?" asked David. "Is this the brains of the operation?"

"Only one way to find out."

She advanced down the hallway without hesitating. She seemed to have forgotten their flight from the wolf. David followed, but with measured steps, squinting up the corridor and waiting for that unexpected flash of movement. Every fifteen feet there were intermittent doorframes that were slit through the middle, but nothing else.

"We have rooms," said David.

"Let's take a look. Jing-Mei approached the nearest doorframe and, just as David suspected, the partition drew apart like an elevator door. The astronaut walked through determinedly. David paused on the threshold, taking in the glass desk – the same dark color as the beads of shock glass in the moon's soil – the ceramic chairs, the flat plasma screen on the wall.

"It looks like a work station," said Jing-Mei. "This must be connected to a computer. There are thick cables running from the back into the wall." She pointed at the screen that had readouts printed across its width. "And these appear to be numbers, in different formats. There are some Roman numerals and what looks like Sanskrit. I used to study various languages and their origins," she said as David tilted his head. "I have no idea what the other characters are. It must be some kind of code. Anyway, it seems to keep flashing the number four."

David shuffled in closer as the doors sprang back behind him. He stared at the screen, but could make nothing of the flashing numbers scrolling across. Intrigued, he reached out and touched the screen, since there was apparently no keyboard, but jumped back immediately as a series of notes issued from the tiny speakers beside it. They were musical notes, harmonic at first, but interspersed with a discordant strum.

"What the hell is that?"

"Music," said Jing-Mei smugly.

"I know its music, smart aleck. Why is it playing music and why is it playing so badly?" He winced again at the dissonance. "And it keeps flashing four in digits this time and some other weird symbols that look numerical too."

"Maybe it's a joke. It's not any language I'm familiar with. But this is definitely connected to a computer somewhere else with those cables attached to it. Maybe we'll find the source if we follow the cables."

"Good idea," said David. "If we find the computer, we might find the programmer."

"It looks like they feed into the next room. We'll just follow the hallway down and check out where the cables go." She stepped back into the corridor and walked toward the next door in line, hardly hesitating for the retraction before she plodded forward.

David followed, swiveling his head from left to right. The room was laid out exactly like the last one and benignly empty, but a voice in the back of his head told him that this place was far from benign. "Jing-Mei," he said. "You should be a little more cautious. Things are functioning quite smoothly here. Too smoothly. What if the people behind this operation don't want us here?"

"Do you think this was meant to be hidden?"

"Why have we never heard anything about it? Why was NASA not informed? Maybe this is designed to support one race or one specific group of people only, and they don't want anyone else to take a piece of the pie."

"Now you've got me thinking neo-Nazi conspiracy. But NASA took all their rocket scientists away." She winked at David.

David was becoming exasperated. "You're too flippant. Regardless of who built this, there is the very real possibility that they're dangerous. Did you bring a gun?"

Jing-Mei swept her hand down to her utility pocket. "Got it right here with my duct tape." She grinned. "Really, David. A gun? We're on the moon, for heaven's sake. I'm not packing a gun, nor should we need one. If we don't come out of here, NASA will send the big guns on the next launch. Nobody's going to shoot us."

"Don't be so sure. This might be worth protecting."

"Getting rid of us won't be protecting it," she said, traipsing back into the corridor. "It will bring the whole shooting match to them. Right, Houston?" There was no reply. "I guess we're still on our own. This is kind of fun, though. I feel like Columbus."

"And just like Columbus," said David, "there's somebody occupying the New World."

"It's still a great discovery," said Jing-Mei. She stepped toward the next door. "After you."

"How gracious. Let me be the first one to lose a head." He stepped through and found the snake of cables attached to another screen in this room. The desk, chair and monitor were carbon copies of the last ones. He frowned and shook his head. "It's just like a giant corporation with cubicles for most of its employees. Only this screen seems to be displaying some video."

David trudged up to the image. It was focused on the moon's surface, only most of the image was hard to distinguish, steeped in shadow. "It must be a crater," he said. "But what is that?" He pointed to a large tube snaking along the surface until it disappeared underground.

"Water pipeline," said Jing-Mei matter-of-factly, coming up behind him. "They must transfer it underground to the habitat. They probably heat it with mirrors again, reflecting the sunlight on the ice, then send the subsequent H2O through the pipeline. The rest of the moisture in here is probably recycled. It's quite the efficient layout. But I still want to find the computer that's running all of this."

She plodded forward again, into the next cubicle and the next. There were workstations in every one with different functions. David stopped and his jaw dropped when he identified a series of telescopes again cradled in dark craters. Everything was so effectively hidden from the scans they'd done of the moon's surface before sending up the team. All the photographic and thermal data would not be able to identify an underground cavern or the water pipeline or even the telescopes that were banked in the dark corners of craters.

"This is just too much," he muttered, shaking his head.

"It is quite amazing," said Jing-Mei. "And humbling. We always thought we were the elite. The first to explore space. It was always a race between the Americans, the Russians and more recently the Chinese. But someone beat us to it, a long time ago."

"Then where is that someone?" asked David, cocking his head. "What happened here that left the plants, animals and mosquitoes as the lone survivors? Why is there only a computer running things?"

"Well," said Jing-Mei with a shrug. "We're on the moon. Anything can happen. An airlock breach. A malfunction in the environmental control. Maybe a computer error."

"The computer seems to be working fine to me. The ecosystem is intact and prolific."

"Point taken," she said. "Still, there could have been a virus that affected only the humans."

David shook his head as he came to the end of the long hallway. It angled back around to another series of cubicles. He poked his head in the first and found a functional, rather sterile bedroom. There was a mattress of white linen on ceramic tiles – the same black as the basalt – and an oak wardrobe and dresser. He pulled open a drawer and frowned. "Jing-Mei, take a look at this." He held up a long silk robe, an iridescent pearl color and angled to sweep over one shoulder.

"Sort of passé," she observed. She took it from his hands and held it up to her body. The material was so fine he could see her orange suit through the weave. A sudden smile breezed her lips and she whirled around, sending a cloud of material dancing about her legs.

"And risqué, as well," said David, grinning.

"Would you like me to model it?" Jing-Mei had a mischievous light in her eyes.

"No, thanks," said David flatly.

The beautiful astronaut shook her head. "Are you so smitten with a woman you're supposed to hate that you can't even respond to a harmless bit of flirting?"

"Smitten? I don't know what you're talking about."

"Ever since she said she'd forgiven you, you've been walking on air. Don't kid yourself."

"Fine. I was a bastard to her, and I regret it. Yes, I'm happy that she's forgiven me. That's a long way from smitten."

"Hopelessly smitten." Her eyes were dancing. "And you seem to have a lot more confidence in yourself despite the fact that we're embroiled in the greatest mystery of our time."

David shrugged. He headed back out of the room where the corridor seemed to extend the width of the Rille. Each room down this hallway encompassed the same sparse lodgings. "There must be accommodation for hundreds."

"There's more living quarters down this way," Jing-Mei called from the next corridor.

"I correct myself. Thousands. They really were far ahead of us." He turned around, gazing at the extent of the compound. They were almost at the end of the cavern, a thick wall of basalt dripping down from the ceiling and sealing the far end of the Rille. His eyes fell upon a gleam of metal – another circular disc like the one in which they'd entered the biodome. So, there was another way out. He turned back down the corridor and headed toward the rock wall at the side of the cave. It extended solidly from the depth of the canyon floor all the way to the dome ceiling of long-hardened lava, but at ground level, there was a small black hole right in the center of the wall.

"Where do you think this leads?" he asked Jing-Mei, who was creeping along behind him.

"Underground?"

"It looks like a small lava tube, but the markings around it are strange." He gesticulated to the backward scrawl that was etched in the wall. There were also pictograms of men in spacesuits constructing pipelines and seeding the ground-up glass beads into what looked like a giant furnace or smelting apparatus.

"Interesting," said Jing-Mei. "It has a certain caveman flavor in a high tech arena."

"You're not suggesting that the cavemen built this?" said David with a smirk.

"No, just descendants of cavemen. Let's take a look."

David nodded and proceeded into the darkened tunnel. He flicked on his flashlight and played it over the myriad markings that pointed the way deeper into the rock. "I still don't get it. Assuming these men traveled from earth in the last fifty or sixty years, how did they keep it hidden from the rest of the world? Surely someone would have noticed a spacecraft leaving the earth, let alone the dozens it would take to seed this project. And if they did manage to avoid detection, where is the evidence, besides the construction and these pictograms, of their presence here?"

"Are you asking where the bodies are?"

He nodded. The tunnel took an abrupt dive and David stumbled downward. His flashlight slipped from his hand, crashed and flickered out. He landed right beside the dying light and rolled with a crunch onto the ground. His head jarred against a rock, sending a spike of pain into his brain and a roiling cloud of darkness.

Twenty-nine

The tunnel descended into the muddy depths of the mountain beneath the ice shelf. It was slick with a stream running through the middle from the melting icicles above and the walls were close. Erica felt as if they were closing in on her. Or maybe it was just the exorbitant weight of the EMU suit. If not for Allan's excited chattering, she would have felt kin to Frodo on his journey into Mount Doom. She'd always preferred open craters to caves and lava tubes. She marshaled her courage, though, and led on. This team had somehow become *her* team. She'd been nominated the leader without even vying for the job. In fact, she'd rather pass on it, considering the unknown fate of the previous teams.

The tunnel must have reached 3000 meters in depth by now. The air was probably heavier since they were practically beneath the polar plateau, although it was hard to distinguish between the weight of gravity and the weight of the blasted suit. These things weren't designed for earth. They were tortuous in the extreme, but necessary. Somehow she knew they were necessary to their survival.

Suddenly the stone floor beneath them leveled off. The chiseled ceiling that she kept hammering her helmet against opened up. Erica stepped into a wide, hollow chamber. She held out her hands and halted the team.

"Let's stop here and have a closer look." She played the flashlight over the ground and open air. It picked up pockets of steam and bubbling water on either side of a narrow path through the center of the cavern. "We just stepped into the cauldron, my friends."

"Is it volcanic?" asked Allan, obvious disappointment in his voice.

"Most definitely," said Erica. "Probably a thin crust here and magma is heating the ice creating a thermal vent. But that certainly isn't volcanic." She pointed at some large metal discs attached to a shaft that ran beside the path and connected to a large squat cylindrical container. The discs were rotating at a tremendous speed and Erica could feel the vibration of power.

"What is it?" asked Allan, once again intrigued.

"It looks like a gigantic steam turbine." She aimed her light over the vast underground cave locating more and more units of the same components. "The thermal heat from the magma below melts the ice, then boils it into steam. The heat down here must be tremendous. Thank goodness we're wearing the suits, although I'm sweating already. The steam then causes the discs to rotate and drive electric generators."

"This looks like it extends for miles. Someone needs an awful lot of power down here. I take it this is a little more than a science station requires."

Erica nodded wordlessly. Had they actually walked into some terrorists' factory – arms productions, chemical weapons, maybe a nuclear manufacturing depot? What else would require this amount of energy and secrecy? She shuddered. Every step of this mission seemed to be putting more people in harm's way.

She stepped closer to the rotating discs, peering with narrowed eyes at the glistening metal that held an odd platinum tint. "It doesn't look like steel," she said.

"Of course, it's not steel," said Allan. He seemed almost gleeful. "It would rust after ten thousand years."

"Allan," said Erica sternly. "The Atlanteans didn't do this."

"How can you be so sure? The myth implied they had aircraft. What would be so hard about steam turbines?"

"Or blasting a tunnel through the rock until they found a thin piece of crust – not to mention the fact that they knew exactly where that thin segment was – and constructed a gigantic thermal generator? You give them too much credit."

"You don't give them enough. They built the pyramids, for pity's sake. How do you think they moved those immense blocks of limestone in the sphinx's temple? They were construction geniuses. There's even been suppositions that the pyramids were giant electric transformers."

"I've heard that one," said Erica, unable to keep the amusement out of her voice. "It was proposed by the same sort of people who think Antarctica was a grass field just ten thousand years ago.

"Laugh if you want," said Allan. "We'll see who gets the last laugh."

Erica turned away, a little deflated by the bite to his voice. She shouldn't have been so sarcastic. She hadn't proven him wrong yet. The scary thing was, she didn't want to prove him wrong. The other alternative seemed far worse.

"Okay, if it's not steel, what is it?" asked Allan.

Dmitri squinted and stepped closer to the turbines. "It could be a refinement of the new liquid metal. They say it's an alloy of titanium, copper, nickel, zirconium and beryllium."

Erica snorted. "I've heard of it. Metal that doesn't rust. Only it does melt. It's sensitive to heat. How hot do you think it is down here?"

"Very," said Dmitri. "But I did mention a refinement. Whoever constructed this could have found a way around that problem."

"Exactly," said Allan. He glared at her, almost daring her to challenge his belief again.

She couldn't burst his bubble. "All right. Whatever you say."

The hard edge seemed to melt away from his eyes, but they still hadn't regained the warmth she had seen on the plane. She shivered. "Let's go," she mumbled, taking her first heavy step onto the thin pathway. It was solid enough – hardly molten rock – but it was slippery and treacherous in the bulky suits. "Be careful here," she said. "One slip and

we could still fry, even in the suits. They weren't designed for exposure to this type of heat for any length of time."

They were halfway across when Erica heard Allan catch his breath and she knew he was slipping. She turned around and caught him with only one boot in the boiling water. Firmly, she drew him back upright. The boot was steaming, but otherwise undamaged. "You all right?" she asked.

He nodded breathlessly. When she met his eyes, she relaxed. He was smiling again and his eyes were twinkling.

"I'm sorry," she started to apologize for doubting him, but he cut her off.

"For what? You just saved me from a very hot bath. Literally saved my skin. I'm not angry about your doubts. Who wouldn't have them unless they were there with me, beneath the sphinx? That's why I wanted you here." He looked back at the others, then leaned forward and whispered, "before I just wanted you." They heard, of course. Everything was broadcast over the COMM. He seemed to know that, but it didn't faze him at all. "If I can get anyone to believe, I have to have an unbiased, totally scientific witness. I love you for being who you are." He grinned and squeezed her arm through the space suit. She felt hardly anything, except the intent. It was clear now that she'd been silly seeing something other than bold determination in his eyes. This was Allan, for goodness sake. The warmth in his voice seemed to flow into her body, making her flush.

"Okay," she croaked. "Let's get on with the witnessing, then." She turned and walked a little weakly toward the hollow exit at the other side of the path. It was clearly another tunnel. She tried to stop panting and focus once again on her job as leader as she approached the next pathway. It was difficult, with Allan trotting right behind her, breathing heavily in her ears over the headset. She was almost at the aperture when the flashlight flickered and dimmed.

"Oh, no," she said. "I hope we have spare batteries."

"Don't worry," said Cathy as the light snapped out.

It should have been pitch black, but there was an amber glow from the beneath the pool. Cathy stared at it apprehensively, trying to swallow the lump in her throat.

"It's a very thin crust," Erica answered her thoughts.

She looked up at the volcanologist and a splash of light haloed her head, coming directly from the tunnel that led out of cavern. "There's light behind you too. I guess we don't need this." She slid the extra flashlight she'd pulled out her pocket back in.

Erica turned toward the tunnel. The contrast of the white light to the dull glow of the chamber behind them was startling. She walked forward, Allan close on her heels, his eager pants like the annoying buzz of a mosquito in Cathy's headset. She grimaced. This man was hot one minute, cold the next, just like the inadequately insulated Hercules. She didn't like him. Even more, she didn't like this place. It was creepy, this steam bath beneath a cap of ice. Cathy held back from entering the tunnel, wanting to find out about Jimmy, but dreading it too. She didn't know if she could stomach what lay ahead. Dmitri caught her thick-gloved hand and drew her one step closer to the bald light.

"It will be okay," he said quietly in his solemn, sweet manner. "It's just the ice."

He was right. There were cracks in the rock here, some rather wide where the electric blue wink of the ice sheet shone through, even this far down, transmitting the light of the sun far above. She edged toward the tunnel, then stopped and swung around gazing at the spinning discs.

"What is it?" asked Dmitri, touching her shoulder.

"It's just, this is all so strange. What has Jimmy walked into? It can't be an ancient construction like Dr. Rocheford says, can it?"

The Russian scientist shrugged. "I doubt it, but anything is possible."

"If it were, why would we just be seeing the heat from it now?"

Erica had stopped up ahead and looked back at her. "I can't imagine that the steam turbines are ancient," she said, looking apologetically at Allan, "but the thin crust and thermal springs are not new."

"We never detected them before," Cathy protested.

"I can't tell you for certain why that would be," said Erica. "What I can tell you is that we've seen unprecedented melting of the ice shelves in recent years from global warming. Perhaps the thermal springs were so deep beneath the ice that they never registered before, and maybe now that the ice sheet is thinning, causing collapses and breakups above the springs and letting heat escape, it's finally being detected by our satellites."

Cathy sloughed Dmitri's hand and took a step toward Erica. "So you think someone found this out before us and used it to build a generator?"

"I don't know," said Erica, avoiding the sharp gaze of Allan Rocheford. "The only way to find out, I guess, is to explore further down this tunnel. We'll have to be careful here, though." She turned and started sloshing through some meltwater. "The heat from the thermal pool may have caused some flooding."

Cathy nodded silently. For once she was thankful for the cumbersome space suit. She plodded after the scientists reluctantly, the tide of meltwater splashing against her boots. Despite the tunnel keeping at bay the huge slab of ice overhead, she felt as if it were crushing her, that tight anxiety in her chest a warning that something was amiss down here. Dmitri checked his pace to remain at her side. The water rose to her knees and then her thighs, making the assumption that the others had drowned become more and more probable. Above their heads there were wider cracks in the stone ceiling and some areas of jumbled rock lying on the sodden ground where the cave must have buckled in from the enormous weight of the ice sheet. Cathy gazed upward, almost blinded by the light, until a shadow passed over her eyes. She blinked and tried to refocus, stepping away from Dmitri and halting right beneath an open window of ice.

Dmitri stopped and turned back to her. "What is wrong, Cathy?"

"I thought I saw something." She shaded her eyes and squinted, seeing only the blue-white sheen and speckles of rock and debris. "It was probably nothing."

She smiled hesitantly at him and splashed forward through the river in the tunnel. Dmitri gazed for a moment longer through the window too, then shrugged and joined her.

They trudged on for another fifty feet, the tunnel sloping slightly upwards and the water level dropping to a mere stream. Here they came upon another rather wide window to the ice. Erica and Allan plodded on, intent on approaching ground zero, the area where Allan had glimpsed the anomaly. Dmitri looked up, shook his head and traipsed forward. Cathy brought up the rear again. It seemed the closer they came to finding answers, the more she was repelled by that eventuality. She passed the window without seeing anything strange this time, but she couldn't keep her eyes leveled on the path. She kept glancing through the chinks in the armor of the tunnel. It was like walking beneath a canopy of leaves – from sun-dappled to shadow. Sun-dappled to shadow – with eyes.

She stopped and pressed a hand to her chest. Dare she look up again? But she had to. Slowly she raised her head and peered through the crack. There were ghostly gray eyes staring at her from the aperture. She reached up and peeled away the weak sliver of rock. It splashed to the ground, sending a jet of spray over her suit. Cathy caught her breath. "Dmitri," she said weakly. "Erica. Oh my God!"

"What? What is it?" The Russian hurtled back to her side. Erica and Allan were right behind him.

She couldn't speak. She'd thought she was prepared for this eventuality, but now, with it staring her in the face, it was as if a giant fist was squeezing her heart. Gasping, she raised her hand and pointed to the new window in the ice that she'd just created. There was the long dark shape of a body, the frozen eyes attached to a frozen head with rather small features, chestnut hair and honey-toned skin.

"Cathy," said Erica quietly. "I have to ask. Please forgive me, but is that Jimmy Albright?"

"N…no."

"One of the American team?"

She shook her head, her teeth sinking into her lower lip.

Erica turned to Dmitri. "One of your Russian comrades?"

Dmitri studied the man. "*Nyet.* Not one of ours."

"Then he must belong to the crew from the helicopter refueling station."

"No," said Cathy adamantly. "I knew them all. I had to stop there often enough when I guided scientists in the Transantarctics. This man doesn't look familiar." She chewed on her lip and looked away from the volcanologist. She couldn't meet her gaze. The woman was a keen observer and maybe she would read Cathy's foreknowledge of bodies in the ice in her rapidly blinking eyes.

Erica paused, her eyebrows drawn together in a perplexed frown. "This is rather odd. Especially since he's caught so deep in the ice. I imagine there must have been a melt-water incident. At least it's not one of ours. There's still hope."

Cathy snapped her gaze from the body and stared at Erica. Her voice had been strong with her last comment, but she'd looked away quickly. "You don't believe he's alive," said Cathy tremulously. "You don't hold any hope."

"Cathy," said Erica sternly. "There's always hope. One body means absolutely nothing in this frozen wilderness. You should know that."

She bit her lip and nodded. Erica was right. How many times had she participated in a rescue effort? It was easy to misinterpret the weather conditions down here and end up in dire straits. But it seemed that no matter how many bodies they pulled out of the ice, there were more survivors. Antarctica was chock full of survivors. She'd been one of them when her helicopter went down near Mount Kirkpatrick. A survival kit, a good barrier to the wind and a radio. That was all it took to survive if you were smart. And Jimmy was very smart.

She rolled her shoulders and strode forward, tweaking that little bit of hope and making it grow. They were ten feet farther up the tunnel when she caught sight of another pair of eyes. Then another. And another. Erica was backed up against the wall. Allan gasped. Dmitri just froze.

"Are any of them…?" Erica's voice was shaky, as if her teeth were chattering.

Cathy didn't want to look, but she had to. She examined each body in turn – a woman with auburn hair and hazel eyes, a squat man with rich carob skin and pudgy fingers splayed on the ice, an elderly woman with a stubby nose and chipped teeth. They were all wrapped in fur parkas and leggings, more Eskimo wear than the standard synthetic thinsulate and nylon. When her eyes strayed to the next one, she sank down to one knee and grasped her stomach. It was a child. A beautiful child of six or seven with silken strawberry hair and a fixed blue stare. Her mouth was an open oval - a frozen scream.

"A baby," she whispered. "These people aren't from a science team."

Erica nodded, but she didn't answer. It seemed words had finally failed her.

"There are so many," said Allan. "At least twenty."

"No," said Erica, finally regaining her voice. "There's more." She pointed ahead of her at the long tunnel of broken rock, ice and dark shapes.

Cathy sat down in the rippling stream, clutching her chest. She was finding it hard to breathe. All these dead people. Even though Jimmy had spoken of it, it didn't make any sense. She kept thinking that the next one would be him or one of the science team members, and even though she was relieved when it wasn't, it didn't make it any easier to look into the vacant eyes of the dead. Especially the children. She didn't understand why they were here. No one ever brought children to Antarctica. It was just too barren and isolated. Most of the scientists that came here seasonally left their families at home or they were loners without families, which was the case in most of the regulars. But, as her eyes flicked from one body to the next, she could identify entire family units. It was impossible, yet she couldn't deny the gruesome evidence in front of her. If these people had all died down here, what hope could there be for Jimmy?

"How did they die?" asked Dmitri. He was confronting Erica now. She was the leader and the only one who seemed calm enough to call on for answers.

"I don't know," said Erica. "It doesn't look like thermal burns. I would say they drowned. They were possibly in an ice tunnel like the one we identified on the surface and there was a sudden flood. The real question is, who are they?"

"I think you know, "said Allan.

Cathy frowned and stared at him. "Who?" she croaked.

"These are no seasonal scientists or terrorists." He looked pointedly at Erica. "They're Atlanteans."

"Oh, Allan…"

"Let me finish. Look at them. They have that honey-tan complexion of the Mediterraneans, yet they have some Caucasian features. They're shorter by far than your average man or woman today. And they were drowned."

"In Antarctica, Allan. There was no flood here."

"You said there was evidence of a comet shower down here as well in other parts of the world. It could have caught them unawares. It could have melted and flooded parts of the ice sheet."

"And what were they doing down here? Why in the world would they come to Antarctica?"

"Well, I guess that's the reason I'm here. To find out what's really hidden under the ice."

Cathy shook her head. "You people are all crazy!" she shouted. "That's not why we're here. It's supposed to be a rescue mission. These people are dead. More people may be dead. Jimmy..." She couldn't finish.

"It's okay, Cathy." Dmitri was crouching in front of her. He grasped her helmet and met her eyes with warmth that she'd never seen before in such a cold gray color. "If Allan is right, than these people are over ten thousand years old. Whatever happened to them happened a long time ago."

"Oh, that makes me feel so much better," she huffed. "The only hope I have that Jimmy is alive is if a crazy man's theory turns out to be true."

"I am not crazy," said Allan succinctly.

"Of course, you're not. And there are vampires and werewolves too. That's probably what killed these people." She knew she was babbling, but there was just so much death. Every time she looked up, they were screaming at her from their frozen grave. Their eyes spoke volumes about horror and agony. Then there was the one that was moving.

Her teeth sank down into her tongue as a shadow crossed over their window. She gaped, her eyes nearly popping out of her head. "T...there's somebody alive," she hissed.

The others turned together, following her trembling finger. There was a long, lean shadow about twenty feet higher than the bodies. It was moving past the window, a thin, sharp object projected in front of it.

"It's a tunnel above," said Erica, bringing Cathy back to earth. "It must be Staten's SEALS."

Allan nodded. "That's why they're hard to see. Their white camouflage suits. If it weren't for the blue tint of the ice, we wouldn't have noticed them at all."

The figures paused. There was a blur of gesticulating arms.

"They've seen us," said Cathy.

"No," said Dmitri. "They see the bodies."

Cathy nodded. It was impossible to miss the dark frozen objects that littered the ice below the SEALS. They were paralyzed by the discovery as much as she was. For a moment it seemed they would remain staring at the bodies, looking at each other but not really seeing past the graveyard. Then the SEALS moved on. They were heading downward toward the larger shadow that was tapered at the top and massive at the bottom. Cathy blinked. She hadn't really seen what was lying beyond the bodies. The men were heading toward a gigantic stone pyramid, as crazy as that was.

Thirty

Erica had stopped counting bodies as she continued down the tunnel. Every break in the stone walls seemed to add to the horror. There must be hundreds. It was astonishing and terrifying at the same time. What could have killed these people so violently and so suddenly that they didn't have time to flee? Nothing short of a nuclear blast or a full-scale eruption of a volcano could have melted the ice so quickly and extensively, but there was no evidence of lava or ash in the ice. That ruled out the most logical answer, considering the thermal vents. That left the nuclear blast, assuming this was something recent. She was thankful for the EMU suit, which would at least give some minimal radiation protection. Yet she had to consider the other alternative. Allan's pet theory. Could these people be over ten thousand years old? Had the comet shower – her discovery - actually killed all these people? She was still reluctant to believe the so-called Atlanteans were so sophisticated as to have constructed a pyramid beneath the ice with such a high-yield source of power.

Why? Why blast out miles of tunnels and cavern and most of all, a block of ice 4000 meters beneath the surface to build a pyramid? There was no doubt now that the looming shape they were approaching was none other than a replica of Giza's Great Pyramid. It had the same massive dimensions and carved blocks of stone. Staten's men were at least two stories above them in the crystal conduit heading for a large borehole in the structure. They kept gazing down at the bodies, but they had no idea the team they sought was right below them. Erica was happy to be taking an alternate route. So many people had disappeared down that rabbit hole. At least, they were taking the service entrance. It gaped in front of them now - a smaller square carved in bare rock into a passage of blinking red lights - like emergency warning lights. The flash was as disconcerting as a strobe light during a disco 'flashback' night in high school. Erica advanced slowly, glancing left and right at blinking pulses and a web of wiring that was strung out along the wall. She imagined a nuclear accident would result in just this sort of eerie periodic blinking of blood red lights, the people long since evacuated, or dead. Gritting her teeth, she shook off the fingers of fear that had tightened around her throat and stopped at a slit in the wall and a cage housed in the niche beyond it.

"What do you think?" she asked no one in particular.

"Looks like an elevator," said Allan.

"Which goes where?" asked Cathy.

"Probably to the same place our crack team of SEALS is investigating right now. We go on," said Erica firmly.

Everyone nodded. They trusted her judgment. If only she could trust her own instincts. Her mind was screaming 'don't go up there. If you want to stay alive, stay below.' So she went on, down a descending ramp of chiseled limestone. It was incredible that these people, whoever they were, had hauled these massive blocks all the way to Antarctica. Most of the mountains in the region were made of basalt, so they must have transported the limestone from elsewhere.

"What is it all for?" she wondered, thinking out loud. "Why build a pyramid under the ice cap?"

"Maybe it didn't work above ground," said Allan.

Erica whirled around. "What did you say?"

"Whatever this thing was supposed to do, maybe it didn't work on the surface. That's why they came here. It had to be underground."

"And it was easier to melt ice than to blast through miles of bedrock. The ice is an insulator. But for what?"

"That, I suppose, is the ultimate question." Allan raised his eyebrows, but his face was anything but quizzical. It was triumphant.

"You have an idea?" asked Erica.

"Not a one. That's why I brought you."

Erica frowned and shook her head. He was so sure he'd found something magnificent. What if it wasn't? What if it was like a Venus flytrap, enticing to the inquisitive and poised to ensnare? She tried to appear confident, all the while chewing on her lower lip as she traipsed further into the heart of the structure, following the long snakes of cables along the wall. Finally the passage opened up into a small chamber. The cables fed a series of monitors flashing again and again in a series of four.

"The cables must be linked to a computer," said Erica. She halted in front of a monitor and studied the graphics on the screen. It showed a pattern of waves. Absently she ran her fingers over the screen following the wavelength and frequency. Instantly the machine awoke, sending out a stream of harmonics that were powerful enough to penetrate their insulated suits. Erica stepped back, listening to the harmony and the discord of the sound waves, although it was entirely too faint to discern clearly.

"What in the world is this?" asked Allan, suddenly perplexed. It was obviously not what he expected to find in an ancient pyramid, Atlantean or not.

"A computer," said Erica. "Very sophisticated plasma screen. It must be detecting seismic waves or sound waves, but I can't hear it too well in this suit. I'm keying in the outside COMM. There we go." Her teeth clanked together as the notes jarred against her ears. She looked over at the others who had followed her lead and were listening and retracting their heads like turtles as the sound penetrated their suits. "The music is rather disturbing, isn't it?" she said.

"No, not entirely," said Dmitri, frowning. "It repeats. A pattern of four. It's telling us something in a language of mathematics and waves."

"What sort of language is that?" asked Allan. "I've studied a lot of ancient languages, but nothing that has to do with waves."

Erica stared at him for a minute, trying to dredge up a memory that was buried in her brain. "Yes, you did. You said in the chamber beneath the sphinx there were strange oscillating lines and four numbers repeated over and over."

"Well, yes. As I told you before, four was a special number to the ancients. Native Americans had a widespread numerical theme consisting of the four directions of space, the four divisions of time – day, night, the moon and the year – the four parts of everything that grows – the root, the stem, the leaves and the fruit. I could go on. There were others as well. The Greeks believed that everything consisted of four elements – earth, air, fire and water. But the physicists I consulted seemed to think the numbers had more to do with quantum mechanics."

"That's it," said Dmitri. "The music of the spheres."

"What are you talking about?" asked Cathy, looking as frustrated as a child tackling a Rubix cube.

Dmitri smiled. "It is really clever, and not likely, unless Allan is more correct than we imagined."

"You think this was created by an ancient race?" asked Erica, wrinkling her forehead into the tight-fitting headgear beneath her helmet.

"Anything is possible. The music makes it frighteningly so. You see, Pythagoras – the father of mathematics who lived in Greece around 550 BCE - developed the notion that each element of the universe played its own music. He and his followers were the first people to relate numbers with music. They supposed the elements of numbers were the elements of all things, and the whole heaven to be a musical scale and a number. In this way, music was number and the cosmos was music."

"So we're listening to the music of the universe," said Cathy, her face contorted in disbelief. "It isn't very good, is it?"

"Wait. Wait," said the astrophysicist holding up his hand. "There's a great deal more to it. First, we'll finish with Pythagoras theory. He defined music as consisting of three types. Of course, there was ordinary music made by plucking strings or blowing pipes. Then there was the continuous but unheard music made by each human being that reflected the harmonious and inharmonious resonance between the soul and the body. I won't touch that one. The third type was the one I mentioned – the music of the cosmos itself or 'the music of the spheres.' He broke down this music into a scale counting outward from earth – to the moon was a whole step; from the moon to Mercury, a half step; from Mercury to Venus, another half step; from Venus to the Sun was a minor third; from the Sun to Mars, a whole step; from Jupiter to Saturn, a half step; and from Saturn to the sphere of the fixed stars, another minor third. If you played it on a scale it would be C, D, E-flat, E, G, A, B-flat, B, D – the Pythagorean scale. The distance between the planets was believed to be a gigantic musical scale.

"Are you all with me still?" asked Dmitri, studying their frowning faces.

Erica nodded vigorously, although she still couldn't guess what this ancient belief had to do with the discordant music on the computer.

Cathy shook her head. "I never studied music."

"That doesn't really matter, dear. As long as you understand that sound, including music, travels through space in waves."

"I know that much," she replied.

He continued. "So what you're looking at now are sound waves transcribed from something else, I believe. Produced to signify what, you ask? Surely not Pythagoras' music of the spheres. I don't think so. Not exactly, but in a way he might have been very close to the truth that we are just now starting to realize. You see, Allan was right. The number four is very significant in quantum mechanics."

"Quantum mechanics? Are we getting into physics?" Cathy asked, now with a very distraught look on her face.

"Yes, Cathy," said Dmitri sympathetically. "A branch of physics that links our whole universe together. But first, we will deal with the number four. In quantum mechanics, the infinitely small particles that make up our world, there are four forces that come into play. The strong force that holds neutrons and protons together in an atom." He held up his hand. "Don't worry about it, Cathy. You don't have to understand everything."

"I was going to say, I do know what atoms are."

"Good," said Dmitri. "But atoms are not the smallest particles. They have a nucleus of neutrons and protons, surrounded by electrons, correct?"

Cathy nodded with a gleam of understanding in her eyes. Erica crossed her arms. This was far too slow for her taste. "We all understand about atoms," she said. "And most of us know that quarks hold the nucleus together. Can we get on with it? What has this got to do with the music on the computer?"

"Okay," he said, looking long and hard at Erica. "We are not all scientists," he remonstrated. "So," he turned back to Cathy, "of the four forces, the strong force would be Number One. I'm going by their strength now. Every other force is weaker than the strong force, so the force of the quarks," he looked pointedly at Erica, "that hold the nucleus together has to be exceedingly strong to overcome the natural repelling force of the particles. Remember how like charges repel each other. Now the next force would be the electromagnetic force that makes the magma circulate inside the mantle of the earth and powers our computers and televisions and the nervous system in our bodies, for that matter. The third force is the weak force, which has to do with particle decay. Please stop frowning, Cathy. There will not be an exam. Anyway, the only force that we should concern ourselves with is the final and fourth force - gravity."

"Number Four," said Erica with dawning comprehension.

"Exactly. The weakest force in our world, but of extreme importance. It keeps our feet on the ground, the planets circling the sun and the universe from expanding too quickly

IT IS PUSHING US DOWN AGAINST THE GROUND, NOT PULLING US DOWN AGAINST THE GROUND and killing the heat that gives us life. It is possible that these ancients are trying to tell us something about the gravitational force, maybe a fluctuation."

"Then why the music?" asked Erica, wincing again at the discordant notes coming from the tiny speakers beside the monitor.

"That's where it gets a little bit strange. Could these ancients have known about string theory?"

Erica blinked. "The Theory of Everything."

"This is really too much for me," said Cathy. "It's enough that you think the Atlanteans built this pyramid. But you're suggesting they knew about physics – something that I can't even grasp without a great deal of pain."

Dmitri looked at her patiently. "It does not seem likely, does it? Yet it does not seem likely that they could have built a structure such as this beneath the ice, let alone a computer. The music speaks to me in particular. An astrophysicist. String theory states that all particles in the universe – such as quarks, electrons and a very important one, the graviton - are themselves constructed of tinier units called strings. What makes it so wonderful is that it explains the universe in terms of music. Each particle's properties are a reflection of the various ways a string can vibrate – the resonant patterns – which give rise to the four forces, just as the different resonant patterns on a string instrument give rise to different musical notes. What we might be seeing now is the computer picking up from some other source the actual vibrations of the universe, particularly the force of gravity – Number Four."

"Then why is it discordant?" asked Erica, following everything, but still feeling her teeth jar each time the dissonant notes clashed.

"Maybe it's trying to tell us something is out of order," said Allan.

Erica turned to him and found everyone else staring too.

"What?" he asked.

"I do not like the sound of that," said Dmitri, " but you may be right."

"What could be wrong with gravity?" asked Erica.

"Well," said Dmitri gravely, "according to Einstein, everything with substantial mass warps space and time creating gravity. Maybe something is warping where it shouldn't."

Erica's eyes ballooned and she backed up right into the plasma screen. The music stopped instantly. She swung around and stared at the screen, now alive with video feed of a whizzing chunk of ice colliding with a large section of rock and metal, altering its normal course.

"An asteroid," she gasped. "It looks like its orbit has been skewed by a comet."

"Where is it heading?" demanded Dmitri.

She touched the screen again and a map of the solar system blinked onto the pixels. The flashing orb was careening toward earth from the asteroid belt between Mars and Jupiter. "Just beyond the moon, blocked from our LINEAR telescopes." She felt a ripple of terror pulse through her body. Could this be real? Could the ancients have been so intelligent as to have tracked an errant asteroid by measuring the harmonics of the universe? How she hoped this was all Hollywood, but somehow she knew as she studied the blinking dot on the screen that it was all too real.

It seemed that time itself had frozen. There was no sound anymore from the screen or from her team. She looked up into Dmitri's pale face. Cathy fidgeted nervously with her hands as she watched them both with wide eyes.

"Will it miss us?" asked Allan, studying Erica's face closely.

Dmitri sidled up to her and scrutinized the screen. His lips trembled ever so slightly.

"No," said Erica.

"What do you..."

Shouts and the hollow stutter of gunfire erupted from above. There were some rumbling yells and high-pitched screams. The thick stone barrier of the pyramid distorted the sounds, but they fed right into Erica's own sense of horror.

"It's the SEALS," she said. "I think they're in trouble."

She turned and raced up the companionway, heading for the wire cage near the entrance to the pyramid. "Where are you going?" called Allan, two strides behind.

"To try to help them," she replied.

"But you said it was dangerous to go up there."

Erica leapt in the cage and turned to face him. "It hardly matters now."

Thirty-one

David felt like he was swimming again. Drowning in long buried memories. Erica's words still echoed in his mind. 'You don't need me, David. You never did.'

How many times had she said that? How many times had he doubted her?

They were in the lab at Berkeley, a large hopper in front of them where the basaltic fines that contained ilmenite – the most common lunar mineral – were dumped to begin the process of extracting oxygen from soil. It was his baby. Erica was smiling at him as he explained in tortuous detail the process they would need to use on the lunar surface to produce oxygen for rocket propellant and life support. She smiled and nodded as if she weren't bored stiff, although he could see her chafing at the bit to get back out there into the field.

"From the hopper, it goes to the preheat chamber," he explained. "We'll use solar reflectors to heat the vessel and drive off the volatile gases."

Erica stifled a yawn. "Then you raise the temperature, right?"

"Well, you have to pump hydrogen in as well. Then heat it to 900°C. The hydrogen will reduce the ilmenite into iron and rutile (titanium dioxide) and gaseous water vapor is pumped on to the electrolysis vessel."

Erica blinked and nodded.

"I'm boring you to tears, aren't I?"

"No," she said. "It's very interesting."

"Really?" David raised his eyebrows. "Anyway, to make a long story short, we separate the hydrogen and oxygen by electrolysis (applying electricity) utilizing photovoltaic solar cells. You don't find this interesting at all," he added.

"Well," she smiled and moistened her thick luscious lips. "I find *you* interesting."

His breathing quickened as he looked into her deep blue eyes. "You do?"

"Fascinating. And I'll need you when we're living up there." She pointed out the window to the brilliant white ball in the night sky. "How else will I breathe?"

"You're making it hard for me to breathe right now." He loosened the collar of his shirt and looked around to see how many devoted scientists and students were looking their way. She nestled in closer and he found his heart thudding loudly against his chest, not to mention the swelling at his crotch.

"So what do you think?" he asked as his hand tickled around her back and crept under her tight-fitting sweater.

"I think it's brilliant," she whispered. "Just like you."

His hand fell away as he stared openly at her. Was she mocking him? "I'm not brilliant," he said. "This was someone else's idea. I'm just perfecting it."

Erica frowned. "Why do you sell yourself short? You always do this. No one else traipsed around the desert looking for the perfect twin basalt fines to the moon rocks. No one else put as much time and effort into design and construction of this facility as you did. This is your project and NASA will sweep you up as quickly as they will me."

"Right. They'll take the lab monkey over the impact specialist. They're crater crazy over there. Anyone can mine the moon."

Erica shook her head and her golden hair splashed against his face. "Don't be ridiculous."

Now he was ridiculous. She couldn't see what was right in front of her face. "Okay, say they like my ideas. Will you help me promote them? Will you put a good word in for me with the professor and during your interview with NASA?"

Erica tilted her head and gazed intently into his eyes. "David. You don't need me. You can do this on your own."

Blind fury rushed in and stole all reason from his mind. "So you won't. You won't help me, even though I've traipsed through the bloody mountains of hell for you. Even though I saved your life…"

"David."

"You really don't give a damn."

"David."

"You'd just as soon I failed."

"Listen to me."

"I don't have to listen," he snapped, heading for the door.

"I would do anything for you!" she screamed making every scruffy-headed scientist and bleary-eyed student turn their way. "But I don't have to do this. Don't you understand? You don't need me."

How many times had she said it? How many times had he turned away? He still could hear the slam of the door behind him and her tiny voice calling him. "David."

"David." This tiny voice was right in his ear and far sharper than the deep melodic tone of Erica's. "Wake up."

"Erica?" he slurred.

"No, it's Jing-Mei. You really are hopeless. It's dark and I lost my flashlight. Do you have yours?"

David groped around in the ebony chill, finally realizing where he was, the bulk of the EMU suit pinning him to a very uneven ground. "Found it," he said as his fingers grasped a long cylinder. He flicked the switch, but there was only an empty click with no corresponding beam of light. "Damn, I think it's busted. Are you all right, Jing-Mei?"

"I…I think so. Here, I'll try my torch." There was a flare of light and the dark cave came to life from paintings on the walls, delicate filigreed renderings of human endeavors.

David gazed around keenly, surprised at the artistic details. There were men with telescopes and lasers, men with microscopes and rockets, all centered round a pyramid laced with wires. "It's like a tribute to scientists."

Jing-Mei was silent.

He looked over at her, the sizzling torch poised in her hand, her eyes wide and frozen. She pointed wordlessly to the ground where shriveled, dusty mummies in tattered linen wrappings were lined up side by side across the rock floor. Some were even shrouded in EMU suits, like a space opera of the damned. She let out a whistling breath and whispered, "Now you know."

He caught his breath. "What?"

"You wanted to know where the bodies were," she said a bit louder. "Now you know."

David shifted his position on the ground eliciting a loud snap and crackle. He looked down and recoiled in dismay. He was sitting in the middle of a shattered ribcage, spear-point edges jabbing into his side. He scrambled to his feet, crunching through brittle bones and crusty leather skin. Bile threatened to eat up his esophagus, but he fought it back down.

"They're dead, all right," he muttered, seeking Jing-Mei's eyes. The astronaut had still not moved. She seemed transfixed by the horror of their discovery.

"Jing-Mei? Look at me."

She finally broke her gaze from the mass grave. "They're so old and shriveled," she whispered.

"They're mummies," said David. "They were probably left out in the moon's atmosphere. The heat of the sun would have mummified them in no time."

"I…I'm not so sure."

"Stop that," said David. "You're shivering. They're just bodies, for God's sake. Stand up and come over to the far wall with me. We can better gauge the situation when we're not standing in a heap of bones."

Jing-Mei still didn't move.

David rolled his eyes, exasperated. He walked swiftly through the densely packed bodies, crunching bones to dust under his boots, but he had no choice. When he reached her, he grasped her under the arms and hoisted her to her feet.

She wobbled and would have fallen had he not caught her to his chest. "Walk with me," he instructed.

Her head bobbled so he hoped that she was sufficiently coherent to place one foot in front of the other. Supporting her firmly, he drew her to the far wall where there was an empty space. She winced every time her foot fell through a pelvis or snapped a fibula. David found himself impervious. They were dead anyway.

When they finally reached the wall, Jing-Mei sagged against him. "Why are they all dead?" she murmured, still in shock.

David shook his head. "All these paintings are like a tribute to science. These people were scientists, and they were paving the way for habitation on the moon, but something went horribly wrong. Maybe that's why the ecosystem was abandoned and no one else was sent here."

"It doesn't make sense," said Jing-Mei. "Even if they all died, someone had to be last. Someone had to place their bodies in this tomb."

David nodded, his forehead scrunched up. "Maybe there was. These bodies were all preserved, mummified. That means they were probably left out on the surface for a period of time and then buried in this tomb. The atmosphere within the cavern is too moist for this kind of desiccation. So maybe the last one stumbled out on the surface to die. He's probably still out there."

"But we didn't see anyone," said Jing-Mei uncertainly.

"Maybe we came in from the wrong side. There was another airlock at the end of the lava tube, just beyond the living quarters. We should check it out."

"I don't want to go any further." Her lips were still trembling.

"What are you talking about? You were the one that took off her helmet first. You were the one who said follow the cable."

"I don't want to find any more…"

"Bodies? They can't hurt you."

"No. But something hurt them. I'm not ready to die yet."

"Fine," he said. "You go back. I'm not prepared to hand this over to someone else."

"Don't be ridiculous. I'm not leaving you alone. It's just…"

"You're spooked. So am I. Finding a cave full of mummies doesn't exactly give me nerves of steel."

"Could have fooled me."

"But I'm not ready to give up."

"You have to win," said Jing-Mei harshly.

"Yes." David licked his lips. "I have to win. Not for you, not for NASA, not even for Erica. I have to win for myself. To prove that I'm not a parasite any longer."

Jing-Mei shook her head and sighed. Finally she said, "I'll go with you. As long as there are no more bodies."

"No promises," said David. He gripped her hand tightly and pulled her up the steep incline out of the mass grave. The air seemed lighter here, less oppressive. Jing-Mei still looked very pale, but the tremors had ceased in her thin frame. He drew her back down the corridor toward the circular metal airlock.

"Before we release this, we'd better put our helmets back on, just in case."

He got no argument from the petite astronaut. She twisted on her helmet quickly and efficiently, as if she were expecting trouble. David sealed his own, re-pressurized his suit and released the lock. The door popped open.

They stepped into a glassed-in tubule that displayed a distorted view of the moon again, gray canyon walls, deep black space and a sliver of earth on the horizon. They were still in the Rille, but the roof of lava had broken at this juncture. It reappeared about 500 feet further on where the tubule punched through another rock wall. The strange thing about this glass tunnel was that it had a series of airlocks all the way along every twenty-five feet.

"What do you make of this?" asked David.

"I don't know. Access tunnel to another cave, perhaps."

"Then why the series of airlocks?"

She sighed deeply. The tension seemed to ease out of her body and her brain cells must have blinked back into action as she screwed up her face and pondered. "It could be because of...the possibility of a breach. It is made of moon-glass. Just an extra precaution, I assume. Although it appears to be mighty thick."

She *thunked* her hand on the glass. It was as solid as an aquarium at Seaworld.

"The computer must be in the next cavern. Our answers have to be there. Let's go."

Jing-Mei nodded, although she was chewing on her lower lip.

David opened the next lock and the next. There was the hiss and buzz of Houston trying to make contact. He heard scattered words over the COMM. "...you copy?"

Jing-Mei reached over to the controls on her arm.

He grabbed her none too gently. "Don't," he said. "They'll want us to go back."

"They're probably right," she snapped.

"We're almost to the end," said David. "If you want to, you can go back. But I'm going on."

"Full of bluster and courage till the end," muttered Jing-Mei.

"There's no end," he insisted.

"Oh, you'll be confident and carefree until we run into the next set of bodies."

"There won't be any more bodies."

"Sure," she said.

He groaned and punched open the next lock. Above the access a light was blinking like the hazards on a car, but he ignored it, too intent on reaching the other end of tunnel. As the door flipped open he was propelled by a blast of air into the next pod. Jing-Mei sailed in beside him, as if a wrestler had picked her up and flung her over the ropes of his ring.

They landed facedown in a pile of debris, winded and a little shaken.

"What was that?" asked Jing-Mei, shaking her head.

"Depressurization," said David in a grim tone.

"Are you sure?"

"Absolutely." He stood, slowly and carefully, blinking to try to focus his blurred vision. He reached down and helped Jing-Mei to her feet. As soon as she was upright, she gasped and squeezed David's arm painfully. He blinked again, the scene before him finally becoming more than amorphous lumps of debris.

There were at least twenty mummified corpses strewn over the glass-littered capsule. David gulped and took a deep breath. These bodies were shriveled tan and black with fragments of cloth scattered over their remains. The odd tuft of taffee or golden, ebony or chestnut hair was still adhered to their withered skulls. Six of them were positioned not far from the airlock, collapsed facedown with their fingers splayed forward as if they were grasping for the door but didn't quite make it. These were the ones they'd tumbled into. Down the pod there were another ten bodies, if one could call them that. They were lying on their backs, bones separated and muscles ripped apart, fragments of petrified flesh scattered all around them. Near the next airlock there were four more, lying in a heap as if they'd fallen on top of each other, although with the explosive remnants it was difficult to tell which body part belonged with which head.

"More bodies," said Jing-Mei through chattering teeth.

"I'm sorry I couldn't keep my promise," said David. "How do you think they died?"

He knew how they'd died. The glass fragments and large spider web hole in the ceiling spoke volumes. He just wanted to keep her mind from taking a nosedive.

"Meteor strike," she said. "There's a fracture in the glass." She drew a long shuddering breath. "Integument rupture. They weren't suited. They died."

"But they're in fragments," said David, pointing to the piecemeal corpses. "It could have been an explosion."

Jing-Mei shook her head. "The others are intact. They let out their breath as they tried to reach the airlock. The rest of them didn't. They exploded as the contained air volume inside their lungs expanded."

"Ugh. That's horrible."

"It could happen to anyone if they panic." The shudder encompassed her whole body now. "Need to be a diver on the moon. Blow out."

David nodded. "Well, I guess it's good we wore our suits. And now we know what killed these ones anyway. Although they don't look like the others."

"W…what do you mean?"

"They don't seem as petrified." He pointed to the nearest body, some of the flesh still thick and seeping juices. This must have happened recently."

Jing-Mei tilted her head and looked at the eyeless, lifeless creatures. "If you say so. Can we go back now?"

David closed his eyes. This was getting more and more difficult. If they ran into one more death scene, she was going to lose it. But he couldn't give up when he was so close. The other cavern was a mere six capsules away, and they had their suits on. They didn't have to worry about a breach.

Yet he hesitated too. Confronting dead bodies on a distant moon was a little unsettling to say the least. He didn't know if he wanted to find any more corpses. But the old drive to win took over again, before he could give in to his fears. If he were the first one to uncover this mystery, it would be his picture all over Newsweek and Time magazine for the next month. It would be tantamount to being the first man to walk on the moon, except he would knock the legends – Neil Armstrong and Buzz Aldrin – off their pedestals.

"No. We're going on. A lot of people may have died here, but they were all without suits. We have the ultimate protection right now. We're safe, Jing-Mei."

"How can you be sure?"

"I'm not, entirely. But aren't you curious? Don't you want to know who made this place and what makes it tick? How can you go back when we're so close?"

The astronaut studied him long and hard. "You're right. I'm stronger than this. I owe it to my people who gave me this chance to find out what this habitat is and if we can use it."

David smiled. He'd won again, although he was starting to wonder if winning this race was the wise decision. He elbowed the next keypad and proceeded into an intact capsule. As the lock sealed behind them, David felt the weight press against his suit. The tube was re-pressurizing. Before they made it to the next lock, the red light above the door stopped blinking and switched to a solid white glow.

"I guess that's what the blinking light meant," said David. "Depressurization."

"We'd better keep that in mind," said Jing-Mei. "In case we run out of air."

David looked back at her with a frown. "Let's not."

"If the next cave is sealed, we'll conserve. As long as we're in this conduit, I suggest we keep our tanks switched on."

David couldn't agree more. The last thing he wanted was to end up like an ancient Egyptian buried in this glass tomb. The airlock closed behind him. They were almost to the end of the tube, confronted with a giant wall of basalt again. The cables wound their way through the wall with an airtight sealant around their circumference. David approached the next lock with a return of that nagging fear he'd felt on his first trip into the Rille. Tiny beads of sweat broke out under his suit and were quickly absorbed into his spandex underwear. In every science fiction movie he'd ever seen, this was where the sideline figure bought it. Never the hero, mind you. But when had he ever felt like a hero even when he was winning.

David shivered. He was letting the eerie atmosphere get to him and he knew it. All the evidence suggested that these people had died as a logical consequence of a mishap in space. But their presence here didn't add up. It was all too secretive, too steeped in mystery. Something this elaborate could not have been constructed without someone knowing about it. All that space travel would have been noticed. Yet it hadn't. Someone had gone to a heck of a lot of trouble to keep it hidden. That same someone would probably not hesitate to take the next step. He doubted they would stop at murder.

"Jing-Mei, I think we should reconsider." He spun around, which almost upset his equilibrium in the low gravity.

She stopped his momentum by bracing herself against the wall and grabbing a hold of his arm. "Haven't you learned anything yet. No sudden movements."

"That means it would be awfully hard to dive out of the way of bullets."

"I told you before, there's no danger of bullets here."

"Why not? These people have kept a secret for so long, don't you think they'd protect it?"

"Only if they were suicidal. We're NASA, for goodness sake."

"Maybe they don't care. Maybe they programmed their computer with a deadly security system."

She frowned. "Then I don't think they would have let us come this far. You're being irrational, David. What happened to all that bravado you displayed when we ran into the bodies?"

"I'm not being irrational, just cautious. I was the one that was blown out of the first airlock, remember? I had a bad feeling then, and I have an even worse one now."

She grasped both his arms and glared at him with her midnight-black eyes. "For heavens, sake, you're a scientist.

You make decisions on theory, logic and investigation, not on gut instinct. Besides, wasn't it you who bullied me past those bodies and spoke of courage and exploration? I'm not going to turn back now. How can you? Don't you have to win?"

David gulped and slowly nodded his head. She was right. He was being a gutless coward. Somewhere between the last set of bodies she had regained her courage and he had lost his. The old David was creeping back in again.

He prodded the airlock button and waited. The door popped open to the gloom of another cavern. He bent his head to enter when there was a hollow pop from the other side of the wall. A chink exploded out of the side of the tube, cracking the thick glass. Then there was another pop and ping as something ricocheted off the metal door. David backed up too quickly and nearly fell on top of Jing-Mei. Another crack in the glass and he dove on top of her, bringing her far too slowly to the ground.

"No bullets?" he hissed.

She opened her mouth, then closed it. With a *snap*, the capsule cracked open, sucking David and Jing-Mei toward the hole.

Thirty-two

Erica began to pull the elevator door shut when Allan jammed his hand in between and planted himself beside her.

"What is that supposed to mean, 'it hardly matters now'?" he growled.

Dmitri and Cathy slammed into the elevator, faces red and chests heaving from the sprint down the tunnel. "You're not leaving us behind," snapped Dmitri.

"This could be dangerous," said Erica. "In fact, I almost guarantee it is."

"That doesn't matter anymore, does it?" said Dmitri.

"What the hell are you two talking about?" said Allan. "It's not that big, is it? It's not cataclysmic?"

Erica ignored him and pushed a button that she assumed was the lift control. The pulleys and cables were set in motion and the cage sprang to life, swaying gently as it eased out of its berth.

Allan grasped her arms and turned her to face him. "Tell me."

"Okay," said Erica. "This contraption is basically an asteroid detection facility. And it's detected something very close."

Allan raised his eyebrows and looked at Dmitri.

The Russian nodded sadly. "It's on its way. It looks at least 10 km in size. The trajectory should take it right into the continental shelf of North America."

"Are we talking mass extinction?" asked Allan with wide eyes.

Erica bit her lip and nodded. She hardly noticed the circuitry in front of her until the elevator emerged from its pocket of stone and opened up into a massive cavity that spun out to the very top of the pyramid. Her eyes enlarged as she saw the winking of charges and slithering worms of

THE SHOOTING IS TAKING PLACE WHERE?

wires all connected to softly lit solutions. The extent of the circuitry was unbelievable.

"This can't be happening," Allan groaned. "This isn't happening. Not now. Not when I was so close." His head was hanging. His eyes were pinned to the floor of the lift. Dmitri and Cathy were goggling at the flickering expanse of the pyramid.

"Allan," said Erica. "Take a look at this."

"What now?" he snapped. He fell silent as he glanced up and gazed all around in wonder. "What is it?" he asked when he finally found his tongue.

"I think," said Erica, "though don't quote me on this, that it's a quantum computer."

"*Da!*" said Dmitri, stamping his foot. "That's why it's under the ice. Too much interference above ground."

"I'm lost," said Cathy. Her eyes had a glassy glint of sheer confusion and fear.

"It's too technical to get into in any detail," said Erica, "considering our finite time constraints. Let's just say that while an ordinary computer makes calculations using two electron states, one and zero, a quantum computer uses all thirty-two quantum states of an electron. It's infinitely more powerful and in its infant stage in our laboratories back home. Somehow your Atlanteans," she looked pointedly at Allan, "constructed a computer decidedly more advanced than we have been able to create. But they must have discovered that it didn't work above ground because quantum technology is sensitive to cosmic rays and electronic fields. It needs shielding. I read something about water shielding, so I guess the next step would be ice." She grinned halfheartedly. "That's why they built it under the ice. We just found our answers a few days before it won't matter anymore."

Allan grimaced, but he didn't appear satisfied with her explanation. "So they built this massive cutting-edge technology to detect asteroids?"

"Maybe. The people outside were definitely wiped out by something massive like my comet strike. But it doesn't make sense unless you have something to prevent the strike." Erica stared at the tubular conduit in the middle of the pyramid that the elevator was advancing toward. The yells and gunshots had stopped. That wasn't a good sign. "An ordinary computer would be enough to transmit the data."

"But you would need something quite sophisticated to interpret string data," said Dmitri. "Just like you would need something pretty powerful to detect a disturbance at the quantum level."

"I suppose," said Erica. "But I didn't see a telescope topside."

"Maybe you don't need one," said Allan uncertainly.

Dmitri and Erica both tilted their eyebrows at him.

"Well, maybe," said Allan. "Various experts have found that the Cheops Pyramid has a constant 6.8 Hz frequency signal running through it. Nobody could ever figure out where it comes from or why it is present at all. But maybe it has to do with the construction of the pyramid itself. Sandstone has no magnetic properties, whereas granite, contained in the king's chamber has a great deal. Maybe the structure was created as an amplifier of certain signals, things we may not even be aware of."

Erica frowned, feeling overwhelmed by the brilliance of the designers and terrified by what these discoveries implied. Cathy was shaking her head miserably.

"What is it, Cathy?" She laid a gentle hand on her shoulder.

She looked up, exasperated. "None of this makes sense. Quantum computers. String harmonics. Asteroid detection. And steam turbines. Why would all this amazing, cutting-edge technology be powered by steam turbines? I though that was an old, dated source of energy."

Dmitri grunted and shook his head. "Not really. The latest in fusion energy technology still uses steam turbines to generate electricity. Instead of magma under the earth creating steam, they use the fusion of atomic nuclei to generate the initial energy to heat the water. It's not old technology at all – it's fundamental."

"Okay," said Cathy with a sigh. "I give up. It all makes sense." She was still frowning. "All of this to tell us we're going to die?"

This made Erica frown too. She was right. It didn't make sense at all.

The lift ascended into the slot just in front of the metal tube. There was a dim light that exposed the large pipe they had seen from the outside. There was no sign of the SEALS.

"And what would this be for?" asked Allan, a little too intensely. He seemed halfway between bliss at proving his theory and madness because it was too late.

"I have no idea," said Erica. "But I think they came this way." She pointed to a discarded pack on the ground, clips of bullets spilled from its lip.

"If we're going to die," said Cathy softly, "then can we take these darn heavy suits off?"

Erica shrugged. "I don't see much use for them here. But something happened to all those men. If we want to live a few more hours and solve this mystery before we die, it wouldn't hurt to hang onto them."

Cathy scowled, but she kept the suit sealed anyway.

Erica took the first step toward the conduit. She felt so tired now. Tired of being the leader. Tired of finding out things that she really didn't want to know. Tired of the darn weight of the suit. She wanted to fling it off as well. She reached for the airlock at the neck and twisted it half off when a loud gong sounded in the tunnel. It ripped through her eardrums and sent her reeling to her knees. She grasped the helmet and screwed it tightly back on, sealing off the sound until it diminished to throbbing pings. It was only then that she felt Allan's hands around her body, supporting her.

"What is it?" he asked.

"I don't know." She stood unsteadily. "I feel it vibrating through my body, sort of like an MRI scan. Have you ever had one?"

He shook his head.

"I did. It was after I had a car accident. They thought I had some spinal cord damage, although it turned out to be just some swelling of the tissues compressing the cord. It was just like this, only not quite as loud. I think we're being scanned."

"Scanned?" Allan stumbled and his support fell away as a massive jolt rocked his body.

"Maybe it's for security," she puffed out. "DNA analysis or something."

"They can do that in such a short time?"

"With a quantum computer, you bet," she replied. "Let's get through this thing and see if they try to stop us."

Erica reached out and grasped Allan's hand. She pulled him to the other end of the tube. As soon as they stepped out, the noise and vibrations ceased.

"Do you think we passed the test?" he asked.

Cathy and Dmitri stumbled out behind them. Cathy looked wide-eyed with shock, but Dmitri had a cat-that-ate-the-canary grin on his face.

"Okay," said Erica, glancing around at the huge chamber they were now in. "Spit it out."

"It was an MRI machine."

"I said that already."

"Hey," said Allan, spinning around and gazing at the massive red granite roof of the chamber. "This looks exactly like the king's chamber."

"Very nice, Allan," said Erica. "I'm waiting, Dmitri."

The Russian bared his teeth through his helmet. "To scan DNA."

"Yes?"

"In a quantum computer, you could store human beings and transmit their data to another quantum computer and reconstruct them there."

"Erica," said Cathy through chattering teeth. "We have…to get out of here."

"In a minute, Cathy. Dmitri, are you talking about quantum teleportation?"

He grinned. "The computer would have to be very big though."

"I'm not kidding," said Cathy. "Jimmy talked about…"

Erica raised her eyebrows and held up her hand to the babbling guide. "You mean, like a pyramid. I've heard about the theories. It works something like a fax machine. The DNA is recorded and copied at the other end of the fax – the receiving end."

Allan frowned. He seemed to have stopped spinning and admiring the chamber. "A fax machine? But in a fax machine, isn't the original information destroyed?"

Erica froze, her heart pounding. She looked at the crisp layer of ash at her feet. She raised her head to the slim barrels projecting from the ceiling.

She screamed, "Run!"

Jets of flame rained from the roof, crisping the outer layer of their suits, eating through the inner mesh, melting the coils of coolant and chewing up human flesh. The suits were strong, but they were never designed for an inferno.

Thirty-three

David felt the drag on his spacesuit, the inexorable suction that was trying to pull him out of the capsule along with all the pressurized air in the compound. He adhered to the wall like a fly on flypaper, but the hairline cracks in the glass were expanding, taking more air into the vacuum outside.

"Jing-Mei," he croaked. "Do you still have more plastic and duct tape?"

"No." She was wedged in beside him, partially plugging the hole, but not enough. "But you do. Check your utility pocket."

David reached down and ripped up the velcro. He dug out the plastic and tape and tried to turn around. It was impossible. The suction was too great. Out of the corner of his eye he saw a man in a white polar suit stagger from the cavern through the airlock, desperately grappling for a support to stop his momentum. He was gasping for air. If the capsule exploded outward, he'd be dead in seconds. David hardly cared about that, since this guy was probably the asshole that was shooting at them – which gave him an idea.

"Jing-Mei, listen. On my count of three, push away from the hole with everything you've got."

"I don't think we can slap the plastic on fast enough."

"Trust me," said David. "One, two, three."

He pushed himself away from the hole, grasping an overhead support beam. Jing-Mei did the same thing. The white-clad idiot flew right at the aperture, splayed on the glass like a toad ready for dissection. The pull was still there, but they could move against it to a certain degree.

"Now, let's try to plug the hole."

"Do you think this is the guy that shot at us?" asked Jing-Mei.

"I'd bet my life on it."

"Should we plaster him to the wall with the plastic and duct tape?"

David grinned. "What a great idea."

The man was keening and sputtering, red-faced as the air was sucked out around him. It was tempting, but David could hardly use a human being as a sealant. "Let's shove him out of the way and hold the plastic in place.

Jing-Mei nodded, a little reluctantly, it appeared.

He shook out the plastic and handed her the duct tape. "Okay, let's do it." He rammed the bastard out of the way and slapped the plastic over the hole at the same time. Jing-Mei worked deftly with the duct tape, stripping and sealing, stripping and sealing. Finally the seal was intact and the pressure eased.

David fell back against a support beam and blinked. "I think we did it."

Jing-Mei leaned against him. "For now," she breathed. She turned to the black-haired white-clad menace that was sprawled on the floor and growled deep in her throat. "You bloody bastard! Why the hell were you shooting in here? Are you totally daft?"

"Uh, Jing-Mei. I don't think he can hear you." David pointed to her helmet.

"Oh." She keyed on the outside COMM. "You bloody bastard," she started again.

The man was shuddering and taking deep breaths. He looked up at her, startled. "You…speak English?"

"What do I look like, Chinese?" She chuckled. "Who are you and why are you shooting in this very delicate environment on the moon?"

"Moon?" The fellow's eyes widened. He gazed out the translucent glass to the gray-coated regolith and bare rock of the canyon walls. "What do you mean, moon?"

David and Jing-Mei looked at each other. They both bent down at the same time, grasped the bewildered man under his arms, and hauled him to his feet.

"What does it look like? Disneyland?" David growled.

He merely shook his head and blinked. "I wasn't on the moon a few minutes ago. I must be dreaming."

"What do you think?" asked Jing-Mei. "Oxygen depletion? Pressure sickness?"

"Maybe," said David. "But it couldn't have been the reason he was shooting at us. He *caused* the blow-out."

"Let's go inside and find out where he came from."

David agreed. He pulled the man harshly by his arm. "You got a name, dizzy?"

"Bruzo," the man replied. "Lieutenant Bruzo."

"You sound American," said David as he tugged Bruzo toward the airlock. "Which has me even more confused."

"I *am* American."

"Then why were you shooting at another American?"

"Because it's crazy. Too many people have disappeared in this damn pyramid."

"What are you talking about?" David stepped through the airlock into the next cavern. He halted and looked up. A colossal pyramid of perfectly merged lunar brick occupied the entire width and height of the cavern. "Oh, this just gets better."

Jing-Mei had come abreast of him. She was speechless.

There was an archway about fifty feet in front of them and twenty feet higher that led into the structure from a ramp at ground level. White bodies littered the ground of the cavern in front of the ramp, gasping and breathing heavily, although one thick-faced man with bushy eyebrows was staggering to his feet and raising a long-barreled rifle.

"David, look out," screamed Jing-Mei. She bounced against him and knocked him to the ground.

David let go of their prisoner and rolled. The rock around him was peppered with bullets. He reached - damn, everything was so slow in this low g – and punched his external COMM again. "Stop shooting, you idiot! Don't you remember what happened last time!"

The stocky man hesitated. Another man dressed in the same sort of puffy white snowsuit rose from the ground. He had coffee-colored features, a slender build and an air of authority. He grasped the barrel of the brute's rifle and pushed it down. "The man is right," he growled. "Shooting in here is a bad idea."

Another lean fellow with thoughtful brown eyes clambered to his feet. "Shooting is a bad idea when you haven't identified your target, either," he said.

"Lieutenant," snapped the first man who was obviously in charge. "I'm getting tired of your interference."

The Lieutenant clipped the safety clasp on his rifle and glared at his superior. At least one of them had no intention of shooting them.

David shook his head and slowly got to his feet. The suit seemed to be growing heavier even in $1/6^{th}$ g, but he was thankful for it with its Kevlar layer around these trigger-happy marines. They had the air of a military unit. And they were American. What the hell were they doing here? He might as well ask.

"What the hell are you doing here?"

The dark man frowned and eyed him harshly. "What the hell are you doing here and dressed like that? Are you the scientists that disappeared?"

It was David's turn to frown. "Disappeared from where?"

The creases in the other man's forehead deepened. "The anomaly, of course."

"Of course," said David. He turned to Jing-Mei and shrugged.

"The 'hotspot,'" the man said impatiently.

"Something tells me we're not speaking the same language. Who are you anyway?"

"I'm Commander Staten," he said briskly. "That's all you need to know. We've come to rescue the scientists."

"I'm the scientist," said David. "And I don't need any rescuing. Jing-Mei here is an astronaut. Our astrophysicist is back at the HAB. How did you get here?"

"We flew," he snapped.

"Obviously. But we didn't see any spacecraft."

The Commander's forehead disappeared entirely into his white toque. "We came in helicopters. What are *you* talking about?"

David looked back at Jing-Mei again. They connected as only two sane people can when they're talking with the insane. He turned back to the Commander. "Helicopters. Well, that's special. They must be uniquely crafted to fly all the way to the moon."

Staten lifted one eyebrow. "Oh, I get it. That's why the spacesuits. What little game are you trying to play with me?" Some more of the other men had risen to their feet now and were holding their rifles at the ready.

"Call off the dogs, Commander," said David sternly. Even if the man was mad, he had no intention of being shot at again. He was too angry after being nearly blown back into the moon's atmosphere. "Don't you understand anything yet? Maybe you don't remember how you got here, but you sure as shootin' know what happened last time that you opened fire. This is the moon - low gravity - or can't you tell by the way that you can bounce right up off the ground. There's no air or pressure outside the dome either. That's why we're wearing the spacesuits. That's why you nearly died when you punched a hole in it. Where do you *think* you are?"

The Commander glowered at David. "I didn't hit my head that hard. This is still Antarctica."

"Antarctica?" David blinked and gazed at the man in disbelief. "You think you're in Antarctica?"

"I know I'm in Antarctica. We flew in to rescue the scientists that disappeared in the anomaly. We found this pyramid under the ice."

"Erica?" David mouthed.

"You know Dr. Daniels?"

"I know her."

"Well, she's caused me a hell of a lot of problems. Commandeering a Hercules without my permission. Flying on her own to the 'hotspot' without our backup. She's in here too."

"She's here?" said David, trying to come to terms with this strange man's story. "Where is she?"

"Well, if she isn't out here, she's still in the pyramid."

David couldn't believe it. Could Erica be on the moon? No, this man wasn't playing with a full deck. Either he was totally deranged or he had some knowledge of David's association with Erica. It seemed that the residents here were playing a game with him. They'd probably draw him into the pyramid and then attack him again, away from the thin outer walls.

"I'm not buying it, Commander. Who do you work for and who built this pyramid and ecosystem?"

Staten's eyes narrowed. "I work for the U.S. government. I suggest you ask the archeologist who built this pyramid. He seemed to think it was the Atlanteans."

David coughed. "The Atlanteans. How interesting? Did you hear that, Jing-Mei? This pyramid was built, what, ten thousand years ago by a mythical race."

Jing-Mei didn't answer. David turned toward her. She was tilting her head, examining the cavern and the gigantic structure of the pyramid.

"Jing-Mei?"

Finally she sighed and met his eyes. "Some of the mummies we found seemed quite old."

"And the others were quite new."

"The trees are ancient and overgrown, maybe re-seeded many times over. The fields, the groves have been here for a long time."

"You can't be suggesting…"

"David. I don't know how these men got here. They probably have nitrogen bubbles in their brains right now.

One thing I'm sure of is that they don't belong here. They're not the builders. Those mummies back in the other cavern, they were the builders."

David sighed and shook his head. "You're both crazy." He stared at the strange pyramid of lunar brick and decided to throw caution to the wind – if there was any. He was going to go in there. It seemed the key to this entire mystery lay in there. Not that he believed for a second that he would find Erica ensconced in those tilted walls. She was in the frozen wasteland back on Earth, but she had given him the courage to do this. Her forgiveness was all he'd needed to find answers in the name of science.

"I'm going in," he said softly.

Jing-Mei nodded. "I'm with you."

"We're going with you as well," said Staten in a no-arguments tone of voice.

"Whatever," said David. "Just keep the safety clips on your guns. Right now, they're the biggest threat I can see."

The Commander nodded briskly and motioned for the men to stand down their weapons. The Lieutenant that had opposed the Commander nodded his approval, which brought a renewed scowl from the older man. The rest of his team obeyed the order rather reluctantly.

David bounced slowly forward, finally adapted to the low gravity environment. He was as sure-footed in the regolith as a mountain goat in the Himalayas. Cautiously, he edged into the mammoth structure, blinking his eyes at the myriad circuitry that slurped through the walls in electron baths. Raising his eyebrows, he looked back at Jing-Mei.

"Computer," she whispered.

"Rather big," said David.

"Quantum," she replied.

David sighed. "You still think some ancient mythical tribe built something this complex?"

"We went from steam engines to nuclear fission in sixty years."

"Right."

"Horse drawn carriages to rockets in less than a hundred."

"I get your point."

He hastened forward so he didn't have to listen to her nagging logic. He walked beneath gigantic support pillars between the suspended wires of the circulatory system of the computer. But what he sought was the heart. The path led toward a closed tunnel in the brickwork that angled upward. David advanced more quickly, as if drawn by the power of the beast.

"Have you been up there?" David asked Staten. The Commander didn't reply. David turned around and faced the stalwart military man who seemed to be quivering in his boots right about now. "What's up there?"

"I…I don't know," said Staten.

"So you weren't there."

"I…can't remember."

"What can you remember?"

"B…big round tunnel. Lots of noise. Then…lack of cohesion."

David frowned. "What the devil are you talking about?"

"You can go on from here," said the Commander. "We'll watch your backs."

David shook his head and keyed off his outside COMM. "Jing-Mei?"

"I heard."

"Something really spooked a bloody war veteran. Should we go on?"

"Your call."

Strange, she really had given over to him. Maybe she was spooked again too. The glazed look in her eyes when they'd found the mummies was reappearing. It was strange, but for once, he didn't feel shaken at all. He was too close to finding out what this mystery was all about. He was too close to winning on his own, although the thrill was the confidence he felt in his own ability. He'd dealt with an explosion and saved a man's life. He'd dealt with mummies and grisly bodies that had been torn apart by the dynamics of space. Most of all, he'd dealt with his shame and finally been forgiven. Now he was one step away from unearthing the truth about the moon. "I'm going up. Maybe you should stay here."

"Whatever you say, boss." She didn't look him in the eye.

David turned away. He was on his own. Onward he plodded, through the rectangular shaft of glazed brick into the vast chamber at the top.

He halted just inside, gazing at the network of wires and tubes bubbling with solutions. There were glaring lights that illuminated glass cylinders that in turn were connected to the circuitry. He felt a distinct pull in the air as if it were fraught with electrical disturbances. David walked toward the nearest cylinder and reached out to touch it with his gloved hand, but an invisible force seemed to push him backward. The barrel slowly rotated on its base, gradually spinning faster and faster. What was this? There wasn't a soul in sight directing this activity. It seemed to be all computer-controlled, but what for? Maybe Jing-Mei was right. This was advanced technology far beyond NASA's present capabilities. Who had made this place? Was it earth-generated at all?

Flecks danced in front of David's eyes as lights flashed within the glass capsule. He shielded his eyes with his fingers, but squinted between them to try to discern what was happening now. The solutions were boiling into the cylinder along with a blue-white light. The empty jar was filling with speckles and color. There was an amorphous lump within that seemed to gradually gain shape. Opaque white bones and a skull, strings of muscles, slithering veins and arteries in ropes that encircled the musculature, smooth, sleek organs and a pulsating heart. It all happened so quickly, but he saw it take shape – human form that finally filled in with paper-thin skin. He didn't want to believe it as the shape grew more and more familiar - long slender legs, gently rounded hips, taut smooth belly, furls of kinky ash blonde hair, firm, tapered breasts, delicate heart-shaped face, thick golden waves of hair.

"My God!" he cried.

Spandex underwear was drawn over the body like an artist filling in the details. Then a bulky EMU suit and finally a helmet capped her silky head. She gasped and clattered against the side of the receptacle. It opened up and she fell, right into his arms.

"Erica!" he exclaimed.

"David," she sputtered. "You're supposed to be on the moon." A spasm ran through her body and she went limp in his embrace.

Thirty-four

She was lost in a swirl of energy and color. Traveling through circuitry like a jolt of electricity, but somehow in limbo with no cohesion, no substance. It was as if Erica, mind and body, had disassembled and Erica, pure information and energy, was the only thing left. Slowly the atoms came together and then the molecules and cells, rewiring of the brain and memory engrams. Sensation returned and sight. She was in some receptacle, no longer in the gongs of the MRI machine. Through the glass she could see a man gaping at her. He was also in an EMU suit, and at first she thought it was Allan Rocheford, but on second glance, his eyes were too dull a green, his nose too wide and flared, his chin too square. He couldn't be real. She had to be dreaming. Then she gasped for air like it was her first breath and the receptacle opened. Her legs were too weak to stand. This was crazy. It was as if she had just been born. She fell straight into his arms.

"Erica!" he exclaimed.

"David," she sputtered. She tried to fight the misfiring in her musculature, but she couldn't stand, could hardly breathe. She slumped in his embrace, even though she'd vowed years ago that she would never let him touch her again. "You're supposed to be on the moon. What are you doing here?" she finally managed to croak.

"I'd like to ask you the same question. What are you doing on the moon? And how did you appear out of nowhere and nothing? I thought you were a hologram, but I can feel that you're not."

How did he do that? Even through thick layers of spacesuit material he made her feel as if she were naked. She tried to struggle out of his arms, but her muscles were still too flaccid. More brain cells awoke and her thoughts seemed to clear. Did he say moon?

"Get your hands off her!" Allan's weak voice still managed to rumble through the COMM.

Erica was able to lift her head just enough to see the archeologist's body sprawled on the ground in front of the next receptacle. Dmitri and Cathy were similarly incapacitated beside a series of glass tubes. David seemed startled to see the other members of her team.

"I guess you're not alone," he said quietly. He tried to help her to her feet, but she still had to lean on him like a rag doll.

"I said 'get your hands off her!'" Allan was still struggling on the ground.

"If I let her go, she'll fall," said David.

"Why are we so weak?" asked Cathy.

Dmitri was grinning despite his awkward sprawl on the floor. "Because you've just been born."

"What?" asked Erica, shifting her head in David's broad arms to see the Russian. "What do you mean?"

"The MRI machine. It recorded our bodies' makeup into the computer, right down to the DNA structure. Then it stored the information in the quantum computer and made copies of us like a fax machine."

Erica blinked. "Are you talking about quantum teleportation?" Strength was slowly oozing into her body so she could probably support her weight now, but she forgot all about that as she rattled this new revelation through her brain. It was new, wasn't it? David's arms tightened around her as he stared at Dmitri. He was starting to see the implications too.

"Exactly," said Dmitri.

"So you're saying that we were teleported from the pyramid in Antarctica to the moon?"

"No," said Dmitri. "Our information was transmitted and copies of us, with the same memories of course, were created on the moon."

"Then what happened to the originals?"

Dmitri shrugged. "In fax machines the originals are usually destroyed."

Erica's eyes widened.

"It hardly matters," he continued, "since all life on earth as we know it will be wiped out in a matter of days."

David's arms tightened even more until it was getting difficult to breathe.

"I'm okay," she said firmly, looking into his eyes. He loosened up a bit, but he didn't let go.

"Will you stop with the bloody impact nonsense!" said Allan. His face was flushed. His hands tightened into fists. He scrambled to his feet and bounced a foot off the ground. "What the…!"

"One-sixth gravity," said David smugly. His eyes had narrowed as he gazed at Allan. The look surprised Erica, since he could hardly know who the man was.

"Sure," he said. "So we are on the moon. But that doesn't mean that the earth is going to be devastated. It can't be. Not now!"

"I don't want to believe it either, Allan," said Erica softly. "But it was your Atlanteans that built the warning system. They also build a quantum computer to teleport human beings to the moon." Her voice had petered out as she mulled this over. "An escape hatch," she whispered mostly to herself, although everyone could hear her over the COMM.

"They knew," said Dmitri, joining in her speculations.

She nodded. "If they had technology to build a quantum computer, then they must have traveled to the moon and built the receiving end of the fax machine. They had experienced some asteroid events, and they figured out how to detect them. They knew, just like we did only recently, how catastrophic a large comet or asteroid impact could be. This was their escape hatch."

Erica looked up into David's eyes. "What did you find here? Were there any people?"

He shook his head. "Only mummies – some in catacombs in the other cavern, some in the connecting pipeline to this cavern. There weren't many."

Erica nodded sadly. "They were too late. That's why we found so many dead bodies beneath the ice. They didn't make it to the teleporter." She fell silent. Her body now felt entirely restored, powerful, invigorated. She shouldn't stay wrapped around her former lover like this.

"David. You can let go of me now."

His arms fell away, somewhat languidly and reluctantly. He was staring at her with an intensity she'd only seen once, when he was exploring his thesis on making oxygen from rocks. He was working under his own power, a brilliance that he never acknowledged he had as he cheated his way to the top. Something had changed since that last call – when he'd asked her forgiveness and she'd finally given it. He didn't seem so small anymore.

She moved quickly away, almost flouncing on her face as the momentum took over in the low gravity. Allan moved forward and caught her this time. "Are you all right?" he asked.

"Fine." She didn't feel fine at all.

"Well, I've listened to quite enough to these half-baked theories," he said loudly. His arm went around her tightly as he looked defiantly in David's direction. "I've just made the greatest discovery an archeologist ever could make."

Erica frowned.

"And I'm not going to lose it because of some silly musical notes on a computer monitor. It wasn't absolute proof, was it Erica?"

"Well, no."

"But you're convinced that the computer and the pyramid, even this miraculous transporter – what did you call it?"

"Teleporter," supplied Dmitri.

"Yes, teleporter," he rolled it over his lips as if the word was delicious, "were created by the ancients?"

"Everything seems to point to that," said Erica.

"That's exactly what I needed from you - corroboration from a skeptical scientist. Among other things." He grinned lasciviously and winked at David.

Erica had never seen David's eyes so marble. She was stiffening herself at his words. Where had all that kindness and tenderness from the last forty-eight hours gone?"

"This will be my shining moment, Dr. Marsh. Your moment in the sun was tainted from the beginning. Mine will be triumphant, for it was *my theory* that was proved and *my name* will be etched in the history books for eternity."

"I'm sure there'll be riches to go with it," said David in a deep menacing tone.

"Undoubtedly," said Allan. "And, of course there'll be Erica."

"That's quite enough," said Erica. "What's gotten into you, Allan? Don't you see how meaningless all this drivel is about riches and fame? Has David finally gotten integrity and you lost it?"

This seemed to cut him to the quick, because his arm nearly crushed her body to him.

"Stop that." She pulled away. "Don't you see how empty all that is when there may not even be a habitable earth in a few days? Wake up!"

"I don't believe it," said Allan.

"You were quick to believe her when she corroborated your theory," said Dmitri. He had moved closer to David as if suddenly repelled by Allan.

Erica wanted to do the same. Yet she wanted to hug him and shake him at the same time. This was not the man that she'd made love too only a few hours ago. She'd trusted him. Now he was becoming the bloody pirate she'd first accused him of being, one that would yank her by the hair and claim his prize. It was too crazy. She couldn't have been deceived like this again.

"Are you feeling okay?" she asked tenderly, trying to rekindle the warmth in his eyes. "Do you have a headache?"

He laughed scornfully. "I'm the same person, even if I'm a copy, Erica. This machine didn't scramble my brains. I have no intention of letting the Earth erupt in a fiery ball. I'm going back. And you're coming with me."

He grasped her arm painfully and yanked her toward the tube.

"Let go of her!" said David with more authority than she had ever heard in his voice before.

"I don't think so," said Allan. "We're going back to Earth." He stepped into the cubicle and pulled her with him. "And if there is an asteroid, your brilliant little impact mind, Erica, is going to find a way to stop it."

David strode toward her on lightly bouncing feet, faster than Allan could move by far. He'd adapted to the environment and he was in command. There was no doubt in her mind anymore. He was right in front of them when Allan ripped open his utility pocket and pulled out a gun. Erica's eyes widened in terror. She reached for it, but she was too slow. His arm came up, but David's reaction was quicker. He dodged and rolled, as if he were used to evading bullets. There was a hollow pop and a flurry of sparks in the corner of the chamber. Erica grabbed Allan's arm and fought him for the gun. He held on tight and yelled, "Beam me back, Scotty."

"It doesn't work that way, imbecile." That was Dmitri. He was heading toward them, his eyes burning with fury. "And you might as well put down the gun. These suits are lined with Kevlar for micrometeorites. They'll work for bullets too."

"I know that," snarled Allan, struggling with Erica for control of the gun. "That's why I loaded it with armor-piercing bullets."

Erica pulled Allan's aim away from David. He just grinned and pulled toward the Russian. There was a loud crack as the gun fired. Dmitri fell in slow motion to the ground, a bright splatter of blood on his thigh. "Damn American cowboys," he mumbled.

"I'm British," said Allan. He'd managed to wrench the gun from Erica's grip. "How does it work, bloody boorish Russian?" He pointed the gun at Dmitri's head.

David was standing up slowly, edging toward him. Allan swiveled and aimed at him. "I will kill you all," he said. "But that doesn't seem to stop you. So I'll kill her."

He planted the gun on Erica's breast. All the men stopped.

Cathy was still shivering on the floor. She looked tearfully at Erica. "I'm sorry," she said. "I should have told you."

The gun dug into the mesh of the spacesuit. She was painfully aware of it. "What do you mean?"

"I thought he was a cold and calculating bastard. The way he looked at you like a shark toying with its prey. I should have warned you."

Allan grunted. "I guess she was smarter than you, cookie." He jabbed Erica with the gun. "Now how do we reverse this thing? How do we go back?" He looked pointedly at Dmitri.

"The computer has to send the information back," said the Russian through gritted teeth. "Then it destroys you." He grinned rather wickedly.

"Then let's tell the computer to do that," said Allan. He didn't seem the least perturbed about being destroyed. Again.

"That would be easy," said David, "if we knew how to program it. It's all a jumble of musical notes and numbers."

Allan blinked. His face cracked into a self-satisfied grin. "Well, it's good someone here understands the language." He looked at Dmitri again.

The physicist scowled. "Just because I have theoretical knowledge of what they might have attempted, doesn't mean I can program the computer."

"You're lying," he said. "You will help me, or I'll kill her."

Erica struggled against his arm, and let out an exasperated yelp as he dug the gun into her chest rather forcefully. "Don't you get it?" said Erica. "There's nothing I can do. I can't divert an asteroid of that size with so little time left. We would need to send nuclear weapons into space and change its trajectory. It's too late to get them there in time. The best thing to do is evacuate. Your Atlanteans knew that..."

"Shut up!" screamed Allan. "Just shut up!" She felt his arm tense and, for a moment, thought he was going to hit her. "You don't get it," he said menacingly. "I am not going to lose."

Erica blinked. Why was this feeling of déjà vu slapping her in the face? She looked over at David who was actually wincing.

"You bastard," she said quietly.

He didn't seem to hear; his eyes looked so wild and frantic. But the gun pushed insolently closer to her heart. "So let's find the computer console and get to work." He motioned to David. "I assume you know where it is, since you've explored this complex quite thoroughly."

"Go to hell," said David.

"I guess I read you wrong. I thought you'd retained some feelings for the girl, despite the way you stabbed her in the back. I'll just kill her then." He jabbed the gun in her ribs.

"Wait." David said through gritted teeth. "I'll show you." He spun on his heel, a delicate deliberate turn that didn't end up over-rotating, and headed for the square-cut gap in the wall.

Allan nodded at Dmitri and Cathy to proceed in front of him. Cathy scrambled to her feet and helped Dmitri up. He limped forward awkwardly, his leg wobbling as a fresh fount of blood gushed from it.

"He can't walk," said Cathy pleadingly.

"He has to," said Allan. "I need him for a few more minutes."

Cathy shook her head, tears squeezing out of her eyes. "It's too cruel. He'll bleed to death."

"Boo hoo."

"Here," said David from across the room. He shot a roll of duct tape over to Cathy. It floated through the air until it landed calmly in front her. "Tape up the hole and re-pressurize his suit. It should stop the bleeding for now."

She nodded and peeled a strip of tape from the roll. After she'd bound him and activated the pressure, Dmitri nodded and rose to his feet again. "It's better," he assured her. They hobbled toward the exit where David waited.

Allan prodded Erica forward, the gun still tucked in at her breast. They walked awkwardly, huddled together in their massive suits. She had never felt so angry or scared or utterly defeated. She'd fallen for a madman this time.

"By the way," said Allan. "How's the air here? I noticed you're wearing your little spacesuit still."

"In fact, it's quite fine," said David, unscrewing his helmet. He popped it off and took a big whiff. "See, good old oxygen/nitrogen blend. Your Atlanteans built an entire ecosystem up here. All kinds of plant and animal life. Very earthlike. Did you know that?"

Erica frowned. What was he up to?

"Really?" said Allan. "I didn't know that. They were quite clever, weren't they?" He reached up and uncorked his own helmet, still playing the gun miserably close to her heart. He breathed deeply in and out. "You're right. It's quite breathable." He forced the helmet into Erica's hand. "Hang onto that, love, or I'll have to mess up that pretty face."

Erica snatched the helmet, seriously considering elbowing him in the gut. By the look in David's eyes, she knew it was too risky. She had to contain herself.

No one else took off his or her helmet. They weren't in the game. Erica just hoped this game ended well. She hoped David was as clever as ever at duping the other guy.

The tunnel sloped downward through the magnetic barrel again. It was identical to the pyramid in Antarctica. They emerged out of the massive MRI machine and traipsed onward through the large tunnel that resembled the grand gallery in the Giza pyramid. Halfway to the ground there was a hollow rumble and the stone beneath their feet began to quiver.

"What the…?" said Allan, losing his balance and falling to one knee. He drew her with him, the gun still leveled at her chest.

Dmitri lost his footing immediately and sprawled on the path. Cathy stumbled beside him, but David maintained his balance although the entire complex was vibrating and rattling loose some mortar.

"What's going on?" demanded Allan, jabbing his gun purposefully at Erica although his eyes were glued to David.

"I'm not sure," said David, shrugging. "Could be another moonquake. We never figured out what caused the first one."

"It's pre-impact debris," said Erica solemnly. Ice and rock was chipped off the asteroid and comet during their collision in the asteroid belt and sent hurtling ahead of the asteroid itself. There'll be some chunks hitting the moon now and more traveling towards earth. What more proof do you need, Allan?"

The archeologist growled as the quake subsided. He tortuously regained his feet in the bulky suit, using Erica for leverage. The gun never wavered from her body. "So it might be true," he snapped. "You're still going to stop it for me. I'm not going to lose everything at the moment of my triumph. Get going, Marsh."

David turned and hopped forward again, down the slope for about fifty feet where he emerged in a level conduit beneath wiring and solution baths. A large archway led into a forward compartment. As soon as they stepped through, they were met with the long slim barrels of eight rifles pointed at their heads.

"Well, well," said Allan. "Commander Staten. So we meet again."

"What the hell is going on?" asked the Commander. "Lower your weapon, Rocheford."

"I think not. I know any one of your SEALS could put a bullet through my brain in a split second, but she'll still be dead before I am."

Staten glared at Allan, but he saw the tight grip on the gun. Finally he shook his head and held his hand up, ordering his men to stand down. The rifles were lowered, only slightly.

"David?" The petite Asian astronaut Erica had seen in the conference room in Houston a couple of weeks ago had stepped toward him. "What is going on? Who are all these people." Her eyes scanned their motley crew and finally came to rest on Allan with a look of consternation.

"Jing-Mei," said David calmly. "It would seem that these people have teleported from Antarctica with the help of this rather amazing computer."

"I hate to break up your little reunion, but where is the amazing computer console, Marsh?" asked Allan.

"It's in the next cavern," said David, pointing to an airlock.

Erica sneaked a sidelong glance at him. It seemed unlikely that the console was in the next cavern, since the computer was in this pyramid. David was meeting Allan's gaze, his face a complete mask of sincerity. Allan really had no choice but to follow him. Where was he leading?

"David?" said Jing-Mei again, a little quiver in her voice. "What's with all the guns?"

There was no quiver in his voice when he replied, "That's a very good question. You remember how I was always concerned about winning. Well, it would appear that I wasn't the only one. It's like a disease. This man thinks he can grasp all the glory this creation alludes to by betraying the one woman who can save him. Sound familiar?"

Erica sucked in her breath and swallowed hard. This was too ironic, and David seemed to be the first to recognize it as such.

"You're breaking my heart," said Allan. "Now open it."

David walked toward the lock and keyed in a command.

"Wait," said Allan. "You wouldn't be opening an airlock onto the moon's atmosphere, or lack thereof, now would you?"

"I'm not into committing suicide," said David, pointing to his helmet-less head. "Nor murder." He looked at Staten's team.

"All right," said Allan. "You're too self-serving a prick to do that. Open it."

"I guess it takes one to know one," said David. He punched a key and the lock popped open, leaving a view of the splintered glass tunnel and patchwork quilt of plastic over it.

Erica frowned, but David seemed to be breathing normally. Whatever had happened here, the tunnel was sealed again. David ducked through the lock and walked into the tube. Dmitri hobbled after him leaning heavily on Cathy. He groaned quietly as he bent his leg and stepped over the threshold.

Metzer started to follow when Allan stopped him. "Not any of you." He backed Erica and himself towards the wall beside the lock so he could see both in front of him and behind. "She's dead if you follow. And I'll shoot the next person who comes through this door behind me."

Allan walked through the lock, cradling Erica to his chest and angling sideways so he could keep an eye on Staten and his men, and David as well.

Metzer scowled at him. The other men were as stone-faced as ever.

"Close it, Marsh," he barked as soon as they were fully encapsulated in the first pod. Erica stared around, as much as she could in Allan's clutch. The pod was constructed of a translucent glass – it looked lunar in origin – but despite the distortion, she could still see the gray blanket of regolith and the sharp walls of the Rille beyond. She hadn't quite grasped the reality of being on the moon until now, despite the low gravity. They were in an actual lava tube where some ancient very wise individuals had constructed a habitat. A trill of pure joy ran through her body until she felt the weight of the black Colt pressed against her ribcage. In reality she could hardly feel it through the thick layers of the suit, but the fact that it could punch a hole through the Kevlar, just as it had with Dmitri, made the gun seem extremely heavy.

David keyed the lock and the door sealed. "There's twelve separate locks," he said, "then we're in the next cavern."

"And how do we keep the good Commander from following," said Allan. "Oh, I know." And he shot out the control pad sending sparks flying.

David winced, but he didn't seem overly upset by the destruction. He must have something else up his sleeve. At least, she hoped he did.

"Lead on, Marsh," said Allan. "You don't want to see your former lover's blood spattered all over the glass, now, do you?"

"I'd rather see yours," said David, opening the next lock. He walked through with those agile short hops that looked so strange yet moved him much more efficiently than the unwieldy walking steps that the rest of them were taking. He looked in his element even though he was being ushered by a madman with a gun. Something extraordinary must have happened in the short time since their last exchange. David exuded confidence, whereas the suave, formerly intrepid pirate of Cairo was slipping by degrees. His face was beaded with sweat, his lips and eyelids twitched, and every muscle in his body looked tight and drawn. Unfortunately, his gun hand was incredibly steady and controlled.

Erica watched David's back recede into the next capsule of glass. Dmitri followed, supported by Cathy's steady arms. He looked somewhat ashen beneath the helmet. How long would he be able to keep going? He'd definitely be no help with David's plan, if David had one. Again they drew up the rear, Erica and Allan - her Siamese twin - attached at gunpoint. This pattern continued for the next five pods in silence except for Dmitri's heavy breathing in the COMM, David's brisk patter over the brick floor, which she heard through her external COMM, and Allan's harsh croak behind her head.

David came to the seventh capsule and reached for the airlock release. The light above the door was blinking.

"Wait," said Allan.

David paused, turned back and crossed his arms over his chest.

"Why is that light blinking?"

"How should I know?" said David. "It was blinking the last time I came through too."

"Really. I suppose you had your helmet on that time."

David rolled his eyes. "I've told you before, Rocheford. I don't intend to commit suicide. If the structure weren't intact, it would kill me within seconds."

"Nevertheless," said Allan. "I'll be putting my helmet back on now. You can keep yours off." He reached for the helmet that Erica instinctively held away from his hands. "Give me the helmet, dammit!" he exclaimed.

Her fingers loosened and it slipped away, falling excruciatingly slowly to the ground.

"You bitch!" Allan kicked her effusively in the back, which she hardly felt. "Pick it up or, I swear, I'll kill you. Sex was fun but I can always get another bitch."

Erica looked over at David, expecting a flush of anger or at least a little protest over the words, but there was nothing. More than that she was expecting him to be jumping Allan while she gave him those few seconds of distraction. But David was far too busy, moving clandestinely backward, his fingers reaching for the airlock release. What was he doing? His helmet was gone - tossed off back in the pyramid. Even if he'd changed, would he willingly give his life for her? Had that been his plan all along? Kill himself, but take Rocheford with him? She couldn't let him do it.

"David," she cried.

It was too late. Allan's head flew up, the helmet dangling from his fingers but far from his head as the airlock popped out, evacuating all the air and pressure into the vacuum of space. Erica felt the dramatic pull toward the door. Her eyes were bulging as she watched David, blown out into the next cracked capsule. He had a smile on his face. It was madness.

It all happened in seconds.

Cathy and Dmitri were pulled into the next chamber by the force. She and Allan next. The man's hold on her body relaxed. The gun fell out of his hand. He was clutching at his throat, holding his breath, only conscious of the fact that there was no breathable air. It was the worst thing he could do, she knew.

She threw herself away from him as his eyes bulged and his cheeks expanded. He was grasping for the helmet that was still in the other chamber when his head blew apart and his body fragmented.

"Oh my God!" screamed Erica.

She turned her head and found she was in the open now, the earth a blue crescent above her. Cathy was stumbling toward the next airlock, looking around her in bewilderment at the jumble of bodies on the glass floor. Dmitri was closer to her, sprawled where he'd fallen among a mound of body parts. Where was David? She didn't want to see him, not like Allan.

Movement further along the capsule caught her eye. It was the suited redhead, hopping vigorously toward the next lock. He was still intact. He wasn't holding his breath, but he was running for his life. She needed to help him, but what could she do? Then the helmet that had slipped from

Allan's grasp wobbled into view as it settled down on the ground. She grabbed it and hopped with all her strength, just the way David had done it, smoothly and quickly with ultimate balance, because if she slipped now, it would be too late.

"David!" she screamed, but of course he didn't hear her. He was slowing down, though. That wasn't a good sign.

She tore forward, digging in and sailing through the air. She landed right behind him, grasped his arm and spun him around. He would have continued spinning if she hadn't thumped right into his chest. Erica raised the helmet and plunked it on his head, screwing it tightly to the suit. His eyes were glassy. His skin was pale and colorless, like a cancer patient taking his last breath. She could almost feel the in-drawing of his ribcage on the absence of air. She keyed in oxygen and pressure from the controls on his arm and the suit ballooned out. David slumped against her shoulder and slowly sank down to the ground, taking her with him. She could hear his harsh rattling breath over the COMM. She held him cradled against her, his chest rising and falling rapidly. His eyes were gradually regaining clarity as he blinked again and again, watching her as life returned to his oxygen-parched body.

Erica closed her eyes and rocked him. There was a whisper in her earphones, faint and barely discernible. She opened her eyes and gazed at him through the clear pane of his helmet.

"I'm sorry," he said again.

Thirty-five

Cathy turned around a little too abruptly as she heard Erica scream and continued spinning until she crumpled to the ground. She stared at the eruption of flesh and blood of the archeologist, feeling nothing except revulsion. She hardly felt sorry for the man who'd shot Dmitri and tried to kill Erica. Of course, one wouldn't wish such a horrible death on anyone, but she couldn't help feeling relieved. She looked over at the other helmet-less man, dashing for the next airlock. He hadn't exploded, which was good, but she couldn't understand it well. She supposed it had to do with physics or something. She'd never been in an airless environment, nor studied anything about space, but there was obviously something the clever man had figured out that the fool had not. He didn't look in good shape though. She should follow him and try to help. But there was still Dmitri. She'd lost him in the explosive suction and he was in trouble too.

Cathy was happy to see Erica sprinting toward the Marsh fellow. She'd take care of him. Now, what had happened to Dmitri?

She turned back and studied the ground. Where was that orange spacesuit? She saw a sliver of it back by the door among a jumble of...

Oh, no! These weren't mounds of debris. They were torsos and skulls, tibulas and fibulas, femurs and pelvises meshed with globs of torn flesh.

She drew in a shuddering breath as she took some tentative steps back toward her fallen comrade. She'd gone only a few feet when her boot got caught in a web of torn fabric and bone. She looked down apprehensively. There was a leather strap and ripped metallic material attached to long withered digits that seemed to be grasping at her ankle, although that was just horrified imagination. She caught her breath, fully realizing this was one of the mummies Marsh had mentioned, but unable to stop the slithering fingers of fear up her spine. *Get a grip on yourself, Cathy, old girl. It's just an old piece of leather now. It can't hurt you. Not even the bloody archeologist can hurt you now. You have to help Dmitri.*

She tried to pry her eyes away from it, but more of the body seemed to assemble itself in her head as she gazed at it. There was a forearm, a withered ribcage, a half a skull and again the steely fabric. It was a longer swath with a patch on it. She wanted to run, but at the same time she was drawn to this body. Grimacing, she shook a ball joint from the material. It had a crisp white logo on the flame retardant weave. USGS.

"No," she gasped. It couldn't be.

She stared at the sunken skull with a few threads of black and white hair encrusted with old blood still adhering to the white bone.

"Jimmy?" She bent down, blinking incoherently at the empty skull. She reached out and tentatively touched it, then stroked it. "How can you be dead? We made it through alive. Why couldn't you?"

Erica screamed, "David!" over the COMM, but it seemed faint and far away as the enormity of her discovery hit her. She curled up on the ground and rocked back and forth.

"Jimmy. Oh, Jimmy," she moaned. It just wasn't possible that he had survived the incineration on the planet, or at least a copy of him had, but had died in this unimaginably horrible way. All this time she'd held onto hope. There was no more hope.

A harsh grunt echoed in her ears. She supposed Erica had saved the geologist. All well and good. She'd saved her man, but it was too late for Jimmy. Too late for the man she loved. It was so unfair. As far as she could tell, this David was a man that Erica had despised because of his treachery. Yet he had been spared. Why did the man she loved, the man who'd never done anything but shine in their world, have to die?

Suddenly the moon awoke in clarity. The gray dust and grit, the barren sweep of rock and the body parts. Dozens of body parts.

My God, had they all died here? There were glowing bits of metallic cloth entwined with the shriveled flesh – Jimmy's team – scraps of dark material – helicopter patrol? – and tattered patches of a lighter gray polar fabric – maybe the Russians? They'd all been blasted out of the airlock into instantaneous death.

They'd been alive before. They'd had a chance, all of them. Why hadn't Marsh come sooner? Why was it too late for them, for Jimmy and her? A pain sizzled through her brain. Wake up! There is no hope. There never was. The world ended ten thousand years ago, but even those people who had a plan to save themselves were too late.

Nothing mattered anymore.

She reached up and started to unscrew her helmet. "I'll be with you soon, Jimmy."

"What are you doing?"

She looked up at a gold-coated visor, blinding her to the face beneath, but she recognized the voice. "Dimtri. It's over. Jimmy's dead." She pointed to the skull at her feet. "The world is going to be destroyed. What's the point anymore?"

"The point is, that *you* are still alive. *I* am still alive. *They* are still alive." He nodded at the couple still lying on the ground in the rubble of glass and bodies.

"So what?" she said. "Are we supposed to live here on this godforsaken moon?"

"Why not?" said Dmitri. "It was built as an escape hatch and we used it. We escaped. If they constructed an ecosystem, as Dr. Marsh said, then we will have enough to survive for a very long time. Why do you want to die?"

"Because I don't want to *just survive*. The man I love is dead."

The Russian growled deep in his throat. "Maybe. Maybe not."

Cathy paused and frowned. She stared at him as he slid open the translucent visor and knelt beside her.

"This is not the end," he said quietly. "This is the beginning." He took her hand and even through the thick glove she could feel him squeeze her fingers.

"I…I don't understand."

"We were reconstructed by a computer. Think of the possibilities."

"Jimmy?" She stared at him with wide eyes, comprehending but not really believing.

"Your Jimmy was reconstructed by the same computer. The information must still be there. What happened once could happen again. I told you this before, you must not lose hope."

"But what about Earth? Erica says our planet is doomed. What kind of hope is there if everyone dies and there is no home to return to?"

"The hope of survival – what these Atlanteans clung to as well. Don't think of this as the finale, just the end of one chapter of our existence. It's not over. It's never over until the last human stops breathing."

David couldn't believe he was still alive. It really hadn't been his intention to survive, even though he knew he had a slim chance if he didn't hold his breath and beat it for the other lock. It was strange that he'd been willing to sacrifice himself for the others, particularly Erica, after living a life of greed and ambition. That life had gotten him to the Moon, but without ever instilling confidence in his own abilities. Now he'd finally achieved that confidence in mankind's darkest hour. He gazed up into Erica's enormous cobalt eyes, frothing with concern, or was it pity?

"I'm sorry," he uttered again.

She shook her head vigorously. "It's all in the past, David. You've more than redeemed yourself. I'm just happy you're still alive and that bastard that sucked me in finally got what he deserved."

David took another shuddering breath as oxygen-rich blood languidly flowed back into his weak body. "I think I can stand now." He grabbed a hold of her hands and dug his feet into the ground. He wobbled - would have toppled had she not supported him – and finally rose from the glass-littered floor. "What about the others?" he asked.

"I heard Dmitri and Cathy on the COMM. I think they found their science teams." She gestured sadly to the corpse-ridden ground.

David shook his head. "We found them on our way into the pyramid-complex. They looked much fresher than the mummies we found in the cavern, but we couldn't place them. Why would they have opened an airlock without wearing an EMU suit?"

"They didn't know," said Erica. "They thought they were still somewhere on Antarctica. How could they even assume that they were on the moon, despite the terrain?"

"But *you're* wearing a suit."

"It was the only protective gear we could find for a potential volcanic eruption. These guys had the thermal protection and gas masks, though it did little good up here. You left the suits we're wearing behind from your training missions."

David winced. So she knew about his last betrayal.

"See. It even has your name on it." She indicated the patch on the sleeve with Marsh printed in neat block letters. "I must admit, I wasn't too keen on wearing it at first. Now I couldn't think of a better suit to wear." She raised her eyebrows behind the reflective glass of her helmet.

God, how he wanted to kiss her. She really had forgiven him. He felt light and airy, not just because of the $1/6^{th}$ g. But he was forgetting something. An asteroid bearing down on their home planet.

"Erica, is there anything we can do about this asteroid?"

She looked intently into his eyes. “No, David. It’s too late. We couldn’t get a nuclear device launched in time, and I doubt it would do any good.”

“I mean, can we evacuate some people? We have a transporter device.”

Her delicate blonde eyebrows crushed together in deep thought. “It’s possible. Let’s get back to the complex. Are you in touch with Houston?”

“Not really,” said David through the corner of his mouth. “But I can get back in touch with them.”

“Then at least we can try.”

David nodded. He opened up a channel to Mission Control, and received a right proper blast from Dellows and company. When he started to explain the situation, though, the shouts and harangues tapered off. There was dramatic, cold silence at the other end of the link.

Finally Dellows said, “Are you sure about this transporter thing?”

“Teleporter,” said David. “Would you like to speak to Dr. Daniels? She went through it.”

David watched in admiration as Erica calmly explained the construction and function of the teleporter. However her patience started to wear thin as the skepticism in their voices became clear.

“Look. I don’t care if you believe me or not. If you track the asteroid – it should be in range of our telescopes by now - you’ll realize that time is of the essence. Send the people closest to the teleporter through as soon as possible, or there will be no human race to speak of except a few grizzled and pathetic scientists on the moon.”

“Hey, I’m not grizzled,” said David, not caring to comment on the pathetic.

“You will be after we set up a community to live here indefinitely,” said Erica.

“Can we get the president there in time?” muttered Dellows.

Erica rolled her eyes. He knew what she was thinking. Why did the politicians always come first when so many others were just as worthy?

"You figure it out," said Erica. She signed off.

"I hope they make it," said David.

"It's out of our hands. We'll go back and tell our nice Commander…"

David grunted.

"Oh, you had a run-in with him too?"

"He likes to shoot first and ask questions later."

"I know," said Erica. "We'll have to train him to be a little more pacific since we're stuck with him."

"We can let Jing-Mei deal with him. She's good at straightening out fools."

"Really?"

David nodded. "Almost as good as you."

Erica sighed. "I hope she doesn't take as long as me. Anyway, we'll get Jing-Mei, is it?" He bobbed his head again. "And the Commander to monitor any incoming escapees while we track the asteroid. Then, I hope you can show me Eden."

"Eden?"

"It's appropriate, don't you think?"

David nodded as he slipped his hand over hers. "And will I be Adam and you Eve?"

"Let's not get ahead of ourselves," said Erica. "Just because I've forgiven you, doesn't mean I'm going to jump in the sack with you."

"There won't be a lot of choice, Eve."

"Are you kidding? There's a whole unit of Navy SEALS waiting in the lobby."

"Now I know that you're kidding."

"What do you mean?"

"They're not your type."

"My type? Maybe I've been looking at the wrong type."

David winced at the lash, but he deserved it. "Yes, you're probably right. Your last choice wasn't much better than your first."

She scowled.

"But there's something you should know about your first. He's changed."

"Has he?"

David smiled as he reached over and caressed her helmet, aching to feel the real flesh underneath. "You see, I've spent my life trying to win."

"I know."

"But when I did win, I didn't enjoy it. I couldn't embrace it, because I never could do it on my own. It made me small instead of large, stealing scraps of success instead of earning them. It's taken my whole life to figure out that there's only one thing I really want to win."

"David, it's not always about winning…"

"Wait. Let me finish. The only thing I want to win is your heart."

There was a deafening silence. Erica blinked and tilted her head. "You broke my heart," she finally said. "How can I trust you with it again?"

"You can't." He closed his eyes and sighed. "I'll have to earn it and I know it might take the rest of my life, but it will be worth it."

Erica leaned forward and rested her helmet against his. Their faces were six inches apart, but her voice was right in his ear. "You've taken the first step."

Thirty-six

The ten-kilometer wide asteroid hurtled toward Earth like a demon from the depths of Hell. The global intensity of the blast was equal to the asteroid's kinetic energy which was half of its mass multiplied by the square of its speed ($E = \frac{1}{2}mv^2$). With a mass of roughly one thousand billion tons and a velocity in excess of 20 kilometers per second, it created an impact energy of 10 to the 24th power joules - an energy equal to one hundred million megatons of TNT, 10 000 times the explosive energy of the world's entire nuclear arsenal.

The atmosphere was literally blown away as the asteroid plunged into the continental shelf of the Atlantic Ocean off the coast of North America. Shock waves spread throughout the atmosphere and ocean waters. There was a formidable outward rush in the atmosphere at a velocity close to the incoming projectile gradually decreasing with time and distance from ground zero, but still within a radius of 1000 km having wind velocities stronger than the worst hurricane winds on record. Then the outward blast created a vacuum in its wake, causing the wind to reverse direction and develop a two-way hurricane effect. Forests were flattened, structures obliterated and human and animal life blown away. Tidal waves in the range of 100 meters hit the coast near the impact. Smaller impacts were felt all across the Earth caused by the debris trail, in turn causing monstrous waves that wiped out coastal societies.

Yet the oceanic and atmospheric upheaval only represented one percent of the energy unleashed by the impact. The remaining 99% went towards melting and vaporization of the asteroid and target area – the ejection of ejecta from the crater and seismic shock waves that plowed through the planet like a bulldozer.

The earthquakes were phenomenal – an unprecedented 10 on the Richter scale – triggering fault movement and landslides. The impact itself sent a blast of flaming ejecta from the site firing back along the asteroid's incoming trajectory, then dispersing high in the atmosphere. It released an iridium-rich fireball that wrapped its deadly fist around the globe.

There was also a spray of solid, pulverized ejecta moving outwards, 300 times the mass of the impactor. Nearly 200 000 cubic kilometers of target rock were blown out of the crater leaving behind a gaping hole reaching a depth of 30 km. Immediately, the steep walls collapsed forming a crater 200 km wide.

At the same time, the lethal extraterrestrial missile released a heat pulse from the ejecta plume that torched the upper layers of the atmosphere in a blazing inferno. Within an hour of the impact the surface temperature of the soil was raised to 400°C. There were wildfires worldwide that gave new meaning to the term 'scorched-earth.' Animals and plants, people of every race, color and creed - except the few that were fortunate enough to have a substantial amount of water vapor in the clouds overhead - were grilled to a crisp in a global barbecue.

The immediate result was catastrophic, but it wasn't over yet. Poisons and toxic waste bombarded the atmosphere. Heavy metals from the asteroid – nickel, chromium and cobalt - saturated the Earth, poisoning the few pathetic plants or animals that survived the heat pulse. Harmful nitrous oxides formed as the gas molecules of the atmosphere ionized in the heat. These combined with water vapor to form nitric acid – acid rain that would inhibit planktonic life. Along with this deadly combination, sulfur dioxide was released from the impacting ground. After the initial heat pulse and global wildfires, there began a sharp cooling trend due to the dust, soot and sulfur aerosols bringing near total darkness to the planet, interrupting photosynthesis and collapsing the food chain. The Earth was essentially a dead rock that would take millions of years to recoup the life it had lost.

Erica traipsed through the cavern of life, still amazed and humbled by the creation of the ancients. The dense foliage and the abundant wildlife in the Rille had everyone awestruck, including the assembly of world leaders that had flooded through the teleporter on news of the impending catastrophe. Although they were sufficiently mournful at the destruction of their planet, Erica still disdained their company. The elite, as always, was spared the final destination.

Not that she deserved to be spared any more than they did. But the choice had been made for her or she would have opted to stay behind and meet her fate in the asteroid bowl of her home.

She looked over at Dmitri, fiddling with the computer beside a fellow astrophysicist, Dr. Bosley. They'd been deeply involved in the mechanisms of the teleporter until they'd managed to understand how to command the computer. The exodus from Earth had stopped moments before the impact. But there were still small banks of DNA to work with to finalize the colonization of the moon.

They had managed to program the computer to reproduce the science teams that had died in the lunar atmosphere only days before David had almost joined them. Cathy was now wreathed in a cluster of geologists and helicopter pilots whereas Vochenkov, the Russian cosmonaut, was chortling with a group of his fellow countrymen. Erica smiled as she saw Cathy break away, her hand entwined with the jovial volcanologist with the salt and pepper hair. He kissed her cheek gently, then pulled her deliberately into the hallway where Erica stood, on the threshold of a green field beyond.

He held out his hand. "Jim Albright."

Erica grasped it firmly. "Delighted. Cathy's told me so much about you. We have a field in common." Her hand spanned the growth at her back. He laughed.

"Yes. A fellow volcanologist. And we have an entire planet to explore, although I doubt we'll find any live volcanoes."

"Never say never." She turned to Cathy whose face was glowing like the ripe fruit in the field. "I'm so glad that you found him back."

She blushed and snuggled closer to him. "Dmitri was right not to lose hope. Even the Atlanteans have a second chance."

Erica frowned. "What do you mean?"

"Oh, didn't you know? Dmitri and Dr. Bosley are going to reconstruct the Atlanteans from the DNA they found in the computer. The ones that made it through, but died up here many years ago. Then we might be able to find out why they died, and prevent it from happening to us."

"That's reasonable," said Erica. "I hope they can get along with the bureaucrats. I don't know if I can."

Cathy smiled. "You don't have to. Just continue being a scientist and ignore them. Our survival will depend more on you than on them."

"As long as there's no prize to win anymore," she said softly.

"We'll make sure there isn't," said a deep, tender voice behind her.

Erica swung around and took in the broad face and cocky grin of the redhead. He was wearing his EMU suit and towing another with him.

"So, are you ready?"

"For what?" she asked, eyeing him severely.

"To see the moon, what else?"

Erica blinked. She'd been closeted in this complex for so long, in constant demand from the scientists and the politicians, she thought she would never escape. But of all people, she'd never thought David would want to take to the field again.

"Are you sure you want to go out there so soon. I mean, you almost died in that atmosphere."

"I didn't have a helmet on then. It's a little different now. Besides, it wasn't all that bad." He winked and arched his eyebrows, smirking comically.

"Really?" She reached up and stroked his pale skin. "I'll remember that if I find an erupting volcano on the dark side."

"You lead, I follow."

She waved goodbye to Cathy and Jimmy, who seemed happy to be rid of them anyway as they drowned in each other's eyes. David took her hand and walked her through the fields and groves. She was startled to see the troop of Navy SEALS pulling out weeds and harvesting fruits and vegetables until she heard a sharp bark from their commanding officer – the slim Chinese astronaut, Jing-Mei Wong. David had been right about her. She was whipping them into shape in no time. There was hardly much need for soldiers in their new colony, or politicians for that matter, but they did need farmers. Erica smiled when she saw the bloodthirsty SEAL, Bruzo, wiping sweat from his brow as he carefully plucked apples from an overladen bow and tucked them in a pouch around his waist.

David didn't pause, though, by the fields and groves. He tugged her onward, toward a huge mat of trees that filled the canyon from one wall to the other. They crossed the threshold from overgrown civilization to wilderness with hardly a gap in between. David took her down a forest path crisp with pine needles, keeping his eye peeled for wolves and skunks. As they passed by a chortling stream, he dipped in his hand and raised it to her lips.

She sipped and swallowed, studying his keen green eyes. Quickly, she broke contact and stepped away when his hand stroked her cheek.

"It seems incredible, doesn't it," said David, "that all this is on the Moon?"

"Um hum," she said distractedly as her eyes came to rest on the airlock at the end of the cavern.

"You don't really care," he pronounced.

"I do, a little. I just care more about what's out there." She pointed passionately at the lock.

"I knew that," he said with a grin. "Here. Put this on first." He handed her the extra suit. "You don't want to pull a David Marsh."

Erica smiled and took the suit from him. "You know, I almost do. Tell me. What was it like to actually feel the very thin atmosphere of the moon?" She thrust into the long underwear and copious layers.

"Suffocating," he said. "Wear the suit. Trust me."

She winced a little at his words, but she looked him straight in the eye before she attached her helmet. "I'll try."

"It's all I can ask." He motioned with a grand sweep of his hand to the airlock door. Stepping to one side, he tapped the keypad lightly with his fingers. The door swung open, revealing the outer wall and another sheet of plastic and duct tape.

"What's with all the duct tape, David?"

"I didn't know there was an airlock, remember? The explosion was depressurization when I tapped the wall with my trusty geologist's hammer and blew a hole in it. But we fixed it real quick. Jing-Mei's a whiz with duct tape."

Erica grinned and shook her head in amazement. "You've had an interesting adventure."

"I'll say."

David keyed open the last seal and they stepped out onto the lunar surface. With flashlight in hand, he drew her down the length of the covered Rille, spearing the darkness until they emerged under the open sky. Erica gazed about her in wonder at the volcanic gully, cloaked in black shadows near the wall, but illuminated like an overexposed photo in the harsh sunlight that penetrated the far side. She stumbled in that direction, hardly keeping her footing until David came and supported her.

"You forgot how to hop," he reprimanded.

She shook his hand from her shoulder and proceeded forward with neat little hops. Soon she was branded in dazzling sunlight and had to pop her visor down. Now she could clearly make out the lunar soil - bright beads of glass flashed in a layer of shatter breccia. She bent down and sifted it through her gloved fingers, mesmerized by the plethora of shocked minerals.

"This is so beautiful," she said.

David nodded. "It is."

Erica lifted her helmeted head and stared at him, perplexed. "You were never interested in the moon as a spectacle in itself. It was always the quest for you – the road to stardom."

"A lot has changed. You might say I've finally taken the blinders off."

She nodded slowly and shoved back her visor, meeting his eyes and trying to fathom how much he had changed. Shaking the dust from her gloved hands, she stood and motioned to the cable still dangling from one of the rovers at the top of the Rille. "Can you take me up the side?"

"Of course. But I warn you, you'll have to hook on with me. You sure you want to get that close to me again?"

"I'm not sure of anything anymore. In many ways, you're still the man I knew, but in others... You finally have confidence in yourself, David. Remember how I always told you that you had great ideas. But you didn't believe me. You had to take mine."

"I should have listened to you." He gazed at her directly. He'd said sorry enough.

She nodded. "I guess I can hook on with you now." She held out her hand. He grasped it and led her to the cable dangling in the deep shadow.

At the base of the cliff David turned and wrapped a belt around her waist, his hands strong and sure as they touched her. She caught her breath and looked away from him, her eyes coming to rest on the series of loops on the cable. He chose the nearest one and clipped her on, then snapped his own link to the same loop. He could have attached her further down. She opted to say nothing and placed a firm hold on the cable.

"I'll be a gentleman," he said as he hit the button for the hydraulic lift. "As much as I can be."

They clunked together a few times as they moved slowly up the rock wall until she clung to his arm and pinned herself against him. The steely armor between them still couldn't keep her mind from drawing the contours underneath. By the time they reached the top she was panting.

"It wasn't that strenuous, was it?" asked David as he clambered over the edge and hauled her with him.

Dammit, he could hear everything through the blasted COMM. "No, it wasn't," she snapped.

He grinned and chuckled ungraciously. Then he grasped her by the shoulders and spun her around.

"So, what do you think?"

Erica blinked. It was as if she'd been stuffed in a closet too long and suddenly released into an open field. The leaden Apennines spread out before her, piercing the black void with their sharp spines and looming over the Rille like sentinels to a strange new world. The ash-shaded rock extended all along the vast plain, coated with jagged rocks and a fluffy layer of dust. But Erica quickly forgot the mountains for the view right in front of her. She stepped into the scalloped rock, so alien yet so familiar. She could see in her mind the asteroid that had carved it millions of years ago. It had shattered the surface, sprayed ejecta all over the plains and left her with this immeasurably beautiful imprint. She couldn't help the rush that exploded through her veins, even though there was an edge of guilt that she should feel this way. The same beast that had made this imprint had just crushed the life out of her home planet. Yet she loved it, through and through. At least she could justify her feelings knowing that there would be renewal on Earth – there inevitably was.

She turned and spun with her arms wide, unable to stop the momentum and not ever caring to.

"David!" she cried. "I'm home."

"Yes, Erica," came his warm and confident reply. "We are."

Author's Note

Despite our present limitations on detecting asteroids and comets, I took some poetic license in the actual time frame of the detection and the devastating conclusion of the asteroid cataclysm in order to keep the fast-paced clip of the story. An asteroid this size would probably be detected within weeks or months, if not years of its approach to earth. However, we would still need a decade to properly prepare a countermeasure. So, in essence, we are still a long way from being comfortable, although we are no longer entirely at the mercy of the heavens.

Acknowledgements

I would like to thank the following people: James Whitehead at the University of New Brunswick for his information about earth impacts, although the theory about impacts under the ice sheet in Antarctica is purely the product of my imagination. The very helpful staff at Kennedy Space Center that guided me around and gave me invaluable insight into space travel as well as the NASA web site and the Apollo mission reports. The librarians at the Ottawa Public Library who are always quick to find good reference material - from string theory to the lost continent of Atlantis.

Special thanks go out to Michael Crawley for his encouragement and support, and Brian, Jessica and Liam for their patience and love. Finally I would like to thank the men and women of the NASA space program, those that gave their lives in order to improve ours, and those that continue to risk everything to make yet another giant leap for mankind.

About the Author

D. J. Jackson lives in Ottawa, Ontario. She grew up in the rural backyard of Toronto, near Stratford. Far from soaking up Shakespeare, she spent most of her time reading science fiction and fantasy. In 1986 she received a Baccalaureate Degree in Science from the University of Ottawa. For many years D. J. worked as a dialysis technician, crafting the odd story on the side until she turned it into a career. She's a member of the Society of Children's Book Writers and Illustrators, writing children's novels as well as adult, but always with a twist of science fiction or mystery.

Printed in the United States
21549LVS00003B/46-162